"Emma Newman is an extraordinary new voice in SF/F."
Paul Cornell, Hugo Award winner, and author of London
Falling *and* Saucer Country

"Emma Newman has built a modern fantasy world with
such élan and authority her ideas of why and how the
seemingly irrational world of Fairy works should be
stolen by every other writer in the field. Her characters
are complex and troubled, courageous at times and
foolhardy. This book of wonders is first rate."
Bill Willingham, Eisner Award winner, and creator of
Fables

"With a feather-light touch, Emma Newman has crafted
a very English fantasy, one brilliantly realised and quite
delightful, weaving magic, mystery and parallel worlds
together with ease. Newman may well be one of our
brightest stars, *The Split Worlds: Between Two Thorns* is just
the beginning of a remarkable journey."
Adam Christopher, author of Empire State *and* Seven
Wonders

"Emma Newman has created a reflection of Bath that
reminds one that charming is not safe. *Between Two
Thorns* shows the darkness beneath the glamour of the
social Season. Learning to be a young lady has never
seemed so dangerous."
Mary Robinette Kowal, author of Shades of Milk and
Honey *and* Glamour in Glass

EMMA NEWMAN

Between Two Thorns

BOOK 1 OF
THE SPLIT WORLDS

**ANGRY
ROBOT**

ANGRY ROBOT
A member of the Osprey Group

Lace Market House,
54-56 High Pavement,
Nottingham,
NG1 1HW, UK

www.angryrobotbooks.com
A Rose by any other name

An Angry Robot paperback original 2013
1

A catalogue record for this book is available
from the British Library.

ISBN: 978 0 85766 319 1
Ebook ISBN: 978 0 85766 321 4

Set in Meridien by Argh! Oxford

Printed and bound by CPI Group (UK) Ltd, Croydon, CR0 4YY

For the one who listened to a crazy idea on a summer afternoon and said yes

1

That night in Bath was the third time Sam's beer bladder had got him into trouble. The first involved a bus, an empty bottle and a terrible underestimation of its volume. The second was at his wedding, when he'd taken an emergency piss behind the marquee, only to discover that with the stately home's floodlights behind him, the silhouette of his relief was in plain view from the top table. Five years later he still hadn't lived that one down.

Clothed in the warm blanket of inebriation, all Sam cared about was finding a secluded spot off the path to ease his discomfort so he could enjoy the walk home without an aching bladder.

The good and sensible residents of Bath were asleep in their beds and the street was far enough away from the centre to be free of drunken locals and lost tourists. The grand Georgian buildings he stumbled past were cast in a soft orange glow by the streetlights, the autumn night mild and still. Despite the crowds and visiting school parties, the endless requests for photo taking and the traffic, he did love the city. It was where he and Leanne had married and built a life together, even though it wasn't the one he'd anticipated. The tourists would never know the city like he did. The old tree in Abbey Green wasn't just a nice place to eat ice-cream near the famous bun shop, it was the place he proposed to her. Milsom Street wasn't just a row of shops, it was the road they had marched down as student protesters back in the days before they somehow forgot how angry they were and got a mortgage.

His wife was out at yet another function with her oily boss and he wasn't drunk enough to forget it. His friend Dave tried his best to get him slaughtered but ended up drinking himself past slurring into belligerence. Sam had poured him into a cab then decided to walk. He couldn't drink like he did on a work night, not with a deadline the next day.

His need to relieve himself had become critically urgent by the time he reached the end of Great Pulteney Street. Heading up Sydney Place, Sam saw a familiar alleyway, one that led to the old gardener's lodge behind the Holburne Museum. It was closed with empty grounds full of trees perfect for his needs so he lurched off the street and into the darkness. He kept a hand on the wall to steady himself, the stone cold under his fingertips. A few steps along he wondered if he'd make it to a tree, when he saw a pair of stout wooden gates open on the right.

A quick glance confirmed there was no one to see him slip into the grounds of the museum. There were trees aplenty, the solid stone wall was behind him and the building was far enough away on the other side of the driveway for him to relieve himself without fear of discovery.

"The perfect crime," he whispered and then sighed with pleasure.

Once it was done and his trousers mostly zipped up, he turned to sneak back out the gates but a thud and hissed curse brought his attention back to the museum.

Light was spilling from a side door and Sam feared an irate security guard was about to run out. He imagined the news headlines: drunken man caught trespassing after relieving himself in museum grounds.

But then he saw a large bundle spilling over the threshold and the light was now hovering above it like a glowing dragonfly. Sam went back to the damp tree and peered out from behind it.

A man stepped over the bundle, out onto the steps. He was thin, very tall, and his limbs looked too long to be normal. His grace was reminiscent of a harvest spider's delicate movement. He was dressed in what looked like a black morning suit, something not unlike what Sam had been wearing that night behind the marquee.

Crouching, the man's long legs folded beneath him as the dragonfly whizzed about over the bundle. He lifted it and Sam realised there must be someone else still inside the museum lifting the other end.

The man took a step backwards, revealing more of the load, and Sam shivered. He'd seen enough films to recognise a body wrapped in cloth, and, from the way the man was moving, it looked heavy enough too. The bundled person wasn't moving; a dead weight.

"Oh, bollocks," Sam muttered, not wanting to witness any more. But he couldn't resist watching as the second person emerged, carrying the feet of the deceased. He was an exact copy of the first, same thin and impossibly long limbs, same clothes, same struggle to carry the body.

"Don't forget the steps, brother."

"Will you keep still!" the first hissed at the dragonfly and it hovered over the steps, casting enough light for them to navigate their way out of the museum, as if it had understood.

There was no car on the drive, and Sam could see the main gates were shut. They were turning towards the trees and he understood all too late why the side gate had been open.

If he ran for the gate now, they'd see him, so he held his breath, stopped peering around the trunk and sucked his belly in, hoping they'd be so busy worrying about the body they'd go past his tree without noticing him.

"This is rather demeaning," one of them moaned. "We hadn't anticipated–"

"Shush. Concentrate on where we're going, the Arbiters are going to realise they've been distracted more quickly than we'd like."

"Couldn't one of the slaves have dealt with this? It's beneath us."

"Of course they couldn't. Stop moaning."

"Oh!" A tiny, high-pitched voice interrupted their bickering. They were only a few metres away; Sam worried they could hear his heart banging. He hadn't seen a third person – had they just come out of the museum?

"What is it?" one of the men asked.

"I can smell a mundane. Very close. Euw! A man and he smells horrid."

The voice was childlike and so quiet. Sam closed his eyes, feeling a rush of self-loathing for putting himself in the path of murderers just because he needed a piss.

The black turned to pink as a light was shone on his face. The sixth beer wanted to make a sudden reappearance. He opened his eyes, squinting, and saw the light coming from what he'd thought was a dragonfly. He'd been so very wrong.

"He's here," the tiny thing said.

Sam wondered if something had been dropped in that last beer. He couldn't remember trying anything at university that could cause flashbacks, even though this felt like it was turning into one hell of a trip.

"What the arse are you?" he slurred. "Tinkerbell?"

It looked like a tiny man, but prettier than any he'd ever seen, wearing a tunic made of dusky pink petals. Its eyes were large, blue, its hair blonde and wispy. It glowed in the darkness and it was pointing at him.

He heard the body being dumped and the two men were there faster than he thought possible. They looked like identical twins, but up close they seemed less human. Their faces were long, in keeping with the rest of them, with sharp features and thin, cruel lips. In the dim light, their eyes looked like blackened almonds.

"What are you doing here?" the one on the left asked.

"Nothing. I didn't see anything!"

The faerie started to laugh, until it was batted away.

"No one will miss a mundane, they kill each other all the time," the one on the right said.

Left's hand shot at Sam's throat, grasping it tight before he could even take a breath to beg for his life. Instinctively, Sam grasped at the wrist and when his hands closed around it the man leaped back as if he'd been electrocuted.

Sam decided to run but, before he had a chance to move, Right had caught hold of his left wrist and was inspecting his hand, his aquiline nose wrinkling in disgust.

"Oh!" the faerie squealed and covered its eyes.

"He's protected."

The brothers were staring at his wedding ring.

"We can't kill him," Left said, clutching his wrist to his chest where Sam had grabbed it. "Lord Iron would know."

Lord Iron? Sam wondered whether he'd passed out halfway through the pee and was just slumped in the autumn leaves having the strangest dream of his life.

"We can't enslave him, and we can't rip his mind out," Right said. "This is almost disastrous."

"Almost, but he doesn't have anything of his own," Left said, peering into Sam's eyes as if he were trying to see the inside back of his skull. "He's defenceless."

Right smiled and blew at the faerie, making it uncover its face. "Bind his memories in chains and put him under the Fool's Charm," he instructed, and it clapped its hands in delight.

"Make the chains strong," Left added, holding Sam's left hand out as far as his arm could be stretched, "and weave the Charm deep into his soul. We will not be compromised by a filthy mundane, not when there's so much at stake."

Right took his other arm and pulled until he was stretched between them, the tree trunk solid against his back. Even though they were thin, they were strong enough to hold him still despite his struggles.

The faerie came closer until Sam couldn't focus on it without crossing his eyes. Its smile made the back of his neck prickle. It hovered near the end of his nose before moving round to his left ear. He couldn't hear the wings, but he felt it brush his earlobe. It felt like a bug and he shook his head until Right pinned it to the tree.

The faerie whispered. Sam couldn't make out the words but somehow his body could. He thrashed in their grip, sweat bursting out on his forehead, tree bark gashing the back of his head.

Spidery men… Dragonflies… Leaves… Gates… taxi… Dave… crisps… beer. Beer, beer, beer.

Black.

2

Cathy's socks were squelching by the time she reached Cloth Fair, a narrow London street tucked beside an ancient church. "Bloody weather," she muttered and then silently took it back. The sky was the colour of a day-old bruise and the wind was bitter but she still loved it just for being there. She never wanted to see a silver sky again.

The street was as empty as she'd hoped it would be. The weather was too foul for people to linger and everyone had gone home from work. She whispered the words of the Charm the Shopkeeper taught her as she knocked the hammer against the metal plate on the door. In moments there was the sound of a lock being turned twice and then the door opened inward, a haze in the air indicating it was leading directly into the Nether property. Cathy took one last glance down the mundane street and stepped through, feeling the gentlest tingle across her face as she crossed the threshold into the Emporium of Things in Between and Besides. She closed the door without turning around, knowing there was only silence and silver mist where there should be thunderheads.

The shop was closed to customers but the Shopkeeper was still in his usual place behind the glass counter, the only clear surface amidst the thousands of bottles, packets and magical curiosities filling the space from floor to ceiling. He wore his usual tweed suit and bowtie and not a single white hair was out of place. He was reading, but the leather-bound book was resting on the counter-top so she couldn't see the title.

He peered at her over the top of his glasses. "You're wet."

"It's raining in Mundanus. Horizontally," Cathy replied. The Shopkeeper pursed his lips at the drops splashing onto the wooden floorboards around her. "Sorry, you know I can't risk travelling in the Nether. The underground was all buggered up and the bus was too full, it always is when it's chucking it down."

"You've been spending far too much time in Mundanus. Your vocabulary is bordering on the nonsensical."

"I do apologise." She made her vowels as plummy as she could as she peeled off her raincoat. "I like the way everyone talks there. It's easy... like wearing a T-shirt after being in a corset."

He cleared his throat. "I wouldn't know." He positioned his bookmark and closed the book carefully before taking off his glasses. "It's your last day."

"Until the next vacation, yes. Here's the key to the flat. I left it the way I found it." She placed it on the counter.

"Mmm." The Shopkeeper secreted it below the counter. "You're determined to continue with your rebellion?"

"Yes."

"And you haven't been approached by anyone... unusual in Manchester?"

"No. Should I have been?"

"Not at all." He retrieved a duster and ran it over the nearest shelf even though there wasn't a speck on it. He had powerful Charms in place to keep it all gleaming; a dusty shop implied a lack of popularity. "But I think it's a risky place to live, Catherine."

She shuddered at the use of her full name. "Do you mean Mundanus in general or just Manchester in particular?"

"Both."

"I disagree. In fact, Manchester is much nicer than London and the people are much friendlier." They both knew it was too risky for her to live in London all the time, so she condensed the time she worked for him into long weekends in her vacation. The mundane flat he provided was nice enough and in a very unfashionable area that was perfect for her needs.

"All of this is unwise, in fact. Recklessness never did anyone any good, you know."

"Are you regretting helping me?" When he didn't reply she hung her coat on the stand, left her bag beside it and came closer. "It's a bit late for that, isn't it? You're in just as deep as I am."

"As I tell all of my customers, I merely supply the Charms, I leave the moral judgement to the buyer."

"It's not that simple and you know it. And anyway, I haven't done anything immoral. What's this about? Has my father been here?"

His dusting was getting more flustered. "Your brother came in yesterday."

She went over to one of the other shelves, trying to distract herself from the surge of anxiety. It didn't work. "Is he well?"

"He wanted a more powerful Seeker Charm." When she froze, he added, "Not powerful enough to break the Shadow Charm I gave you, but..." He shook his head. "You didn't really believe they'd just stop looking for you, did you? Why not seek a reconciliation?"

Cathy frowned at him. He never made suggestions like this before. Even when they made their deal he didn't try to talk her out of her decision. It was a simple transaction:

she would be his bookkeeper in return for the best Shadow Charm he could provide. Why she wanted it and what she was planning to do whilst hidden in Mundanus had never been asked. "There's no reasoning with my family, they won't understand." She rubbed her nose; something had been aggravating it since she came in. "What's that smell?"

He twitched. "I was testing a new product. Do you like it?"

Cathy sniffed. "It's like... cut grass. With almonds." She sniffed again. "I'm not sure it works."

"Evidently," he said, abandoning the duster and tugging his tweed jacket straight as he always did when annoyed.

The Shopkeeper plucked a purple atomiser off a nearby shelf. "I can't sell a Beautifying Mist of Atmospheric Improvement to fine clientele if it makes them behave like a starving puppy."

"The name doesn't work. It's not catchy enough."

He frowned at her. "Catch-ee?"

"Something... memorable and pithy. In Mundanus this would be called an air freshener. And it would smell nicer."

"We are not, thankfully, in Mundanus. I'll send it back to the supplier and tell them to improve the scent." He noticed Cathy leaning closer, sniffing again, and stepped away quickly. "Do you mind?"

"Sorry. Are you wearing aftershave?"

"I have no idea what that is and I have no desire to. Now, would you kindly rest your olfactory talents and instead turn your attention to the purpose of your visit?"

"Are you grumpy because it's my last day?" Cathy asked. Usually the Shopkeeper liked to gossip about the latest ridiculous request from a customer, or to show her new stock. He rarely rushed her. Quite to the contrary, she often felt as if he wanted to keep her there as long as he could. Not that he'd ever admit to it.

"I don't like disruption, you know that."

Cathy smiled, thinking about how resistant he'd been when she first started to work for him, even though the deal had been his suggestion. He knew he needed help but, after hundreds of years of working alone, it took weeks for him to even begin to explain how he ran the shop. There were still parts of the business she didn't understand and suspected she never would. "I'll be back in twelve weeks. Then I'll come back like I did the last time and get the books all straightened up again."

He put the atomiser back and looked at her as if he wanted to say something but couldn't find the best way to begin. "You can't keep me chattering all day, Catherine," he finally said, "there's work to be done."

He headed towards the office at the back of the shop and she followed, leaving the crowded shelves behind. Unlike the majority of the shops she'd become accustomed to in Mundanus, no two items for sale were the same, and there was no obvious order to their arrangement. She'd come to realise that it was far from a lack of organisation on the part of the Shopkeeper, instead it was a way to keep control whilst displaying the abundance of goods. With no labels, price stickers or signs, it meant the customer was forced to consult him before every purchase. It also deterred shoplifting as there was no way to tell what was being stolen; with curse-bearing artefacts placed next to those that gave amazing boons, it wasn't worth the risk.

At first, she'd hated having to work for him every holiday, but over the last year she'd somehow grown fond of him. It was probably something to do with his gruff delight whenever she made sense of the ledger, or his veiled compliments whenever she brought in a new system that made the shop easier to run.

It hadn't taken much to make a difference; he was utterly hopeless at administrative tasks. Thousands of wholesale purchases and sales had been recorded haphazardly in his spidery scrawl. Either he'd never had to refund a customer in all that time or he couldn't bring himself to record them. From what she could tell, he'd been trading for over three hundred years without any system in place and she had no idea how he'd managed to become such a success and maintain his monopoly. The Emporium was unique, the only establishment that catered for the Great Families.

"I remember the important things," he'd said when she commented on the chaos. His memory was remarkable. He could recall where the most obscure stock was secreted and he remembered all of the prices, no matter how obscure. She had suspected he made some of them up, noting inconsistencies across the years, but he'd explained that he charged more if the customer was impolite or poorly dressed.

"This would be much easier if you let me bring my laptop, you know," she said as she followed, the strange smell of grassy almonds tickling her nose. She missed the gentle mustiness.

"How many times have I told you? I will never let one of those machines into my shop."

She liked to suggest it at least once every few months, but he'd never change. He'd never even seen one, she was certain, but, like most of the people caught in the web of the Great Families, he harboured a deep distrust of technology. The Shopkeeper took it to extremes, however, extending it to most things made of metal and not even permitting coins to change hands within his premises. Thankfully the prices he charged rarely had anything to do with money, but it did make the bookkeeping difficult.

He tapped the lamp on the office desk, waking the tiny sprite inside. It was only the size of a ladybird but could still throw out a terrific amount of light. Only the best for the Shopkeeper.

"I've put all of the latest purchases into the *ledger* as you asked," he announced, as if he had done something remarkable. "And I've used my notation system to detail the customers."

She nodded. "It won't take me long, I did most of it yesterday." She'd given up trying to deduce who bought what. If there had been any chance of her finding out, he never would have employed her. She didn't mind though. Unlike most of the people in the life she'd escaped, she had no interest in what everyone else was buying from him. His legendary confidentiality was the only reason she'd been able to approach him for help in the first place.

It had taken a month of her holiday to get things straight, but she knew she'd be leaving everything in good shape before going back to university. She wouldn't miss the uncomfortable wooden stool and the cramped conditions. It was more a glorified nook than a back office, and moving anything on the untidy desk made dust plume and irritate her nose. Why he never used the anti-dust Charms in places customers didn't see she'd never felt cheeky enough to ask.

The Shopkeeper clattered about in the shop. Usually he read as she worked, but he was unsettled today and Cathy felt sorry for him. He didn't seem to have any friends, though of course she only came when the shop was closed, to minimise the risk of discovery. The news that Tom had been back for a stronger Charm was niggling her; perhaps it had upset him too. She'd hoped her family would give up on her, but it seemed they weren't ready to give up the search yet. Poor Tom. They probably had him running all over the place casting Seeker Charms before fleeing from the Arbiters. That it was affecting him was the one thing she felt guilty about. He was the only one she missed.

"Have you finished?" The Shopkeeper lurked in the doorway.

"Nearly."

She'd already assigned a numerical value to the prices of the sold items, making it possible to calculate the profit; all that was left was totalling the column, which she did as quickly as she could. He didn't return to the shop and she looked back up at him. He was staring at her with such sadness that the anxiety bubbled up again.

"You're very good at putting things in order."

It was the first open compliment he'd ever given.

"Thank you."

"I... I will miss you, Catherine."

"It's only a few weeks," she said again, mustering a smile.

The Shopkeeper drifted away from the doorway to potter about in the shop again.

"All done," she said less than five minutes later, tucking the stool back under the desk. "I'll see you in December."

The Shopkeeper fiddled with the hem of his jacket. "Catherine... would you be kind enough to go to the stockroom for me?"

It was certainly a day of firsts. He only ever let her in the stockroom when he was with her, and that was still rare. It only reinforced how out of sorts he was.

"What do you need?"

"Nothing for me... you'll see when you go in there."

He didn't say it like it was a surprise present, more like he'd found a giant spider in there and couldn't bear to get rid of it. Then she remembered she was in the Nether, not Mundanus, and one of the few advantages it had was a lack of insect life.

"Please?" he added.

"All right," she agreed, worried her father might be putting pressure on him. Surely he'd know the only way she could stay hidden for so long would be with the Shopkeeper's help?

She resolved to go and look in the stockroom and then have it out with him over a cup of tea. They needed each other too much now for her father to ruin it all, and she needed to remind him of that fact, especially before leaving for three months. It would be long enough for him to forget how useful she was.

Leaving the Shopkeeper lurking in the dusty nook, Cathy pushed the heavy wooden door open with her backside and went in before its weighted hinges could push her back out again. She reached for the hammer-cord to strike the large globe hanging from the ceiling and wake the sprite within.

But the large room, crowded with shelves and boxes, was already lit. A beat later she smelt a gentle floral fragrance and then she saw Lord Poppy leaning on an elegant black cane and smiling broadly.

Feeling like all of the blood in her body had dropped into her toes, Cathy scrabbled for the door handle, instinctively wanting to bolt out of the room again. She stopped when he shook his head. No act could be more futile than trying to flee a Lord of the Fae Court.

3

A black-haired faerie was perched on Lord Poppy's shoulder, wearing a dress of blousy poppy petals, the red striking against the black of his frock coat. It was scowling at Cathy as if she'd personally offended it. Cathy realised a look of abject horror was not an appropriate nor a polite greeting for the patron of her family.

She dropped into a low curtsy, breathless with panic. She'd never seen Lord Poppy in person, but her father had, and he'd drummed a healthy fear of the Fae into her at an early age. She struggled to remember the etiquette she'd been taught, but using the correct form of address was hardly going to change the fact that she'd run away from the family, disgraced the Rhoeas-Papaver line, and most probably infuriated Lord Poppy to such a degree that he was there to enslave or curse her. Or both.

"Catherine Rhoeas-Papaver," he said slowly, his voice silken. "What an extraordinary delight to find you at last."

She trembled, keeping her head bowed, not sure what to make of the statement.

"Do stand up so I can see you, my dear, one does prefer to speak to a face rather than a crown of hair."

"It's a very dull brown," the faerie commented as Cathy straightened up. "And such a plain face. I'm very disappointed. She isn't worth–"

"Hush, or I shall send you back to Exilium," Lord Poppy said and the faerie pressed its lips together. "Now…"

He walked towards her, the cane striking the floor with every other step. His supernatural grace made her feel clumsy. His skin was flawless, his long black hair beautiful and his lips as red as the poppy petals. His eyes were pools of black, no iris or white discernible, and as quick as she saw them she looked away, chilled.

"I've been looking for you," he said as she shivered. "But you've been hidden away in Mundanus, in the dark city."

She stayed silent, not trusting her voice.

"My sources inform me that three and half years have passed in Mundanus since you first piqued my interest." He stopped barely a metre away, well within her personal space. Not that one of them would appreciate such a human concept. "I simply cannot understand how you've survived so long all by yourself. You have none of your Mother about you, even after all the effort to breed her beauty into the line, no presence, nothing remarkable whatsoever."

Cathy could barely think as her panic reached its crescendo and then an incredible sense of calm washed through her, as if her body had used up all the adrenalin it had. If she didn't remember the hours of training she'd tried to bury along with most of her other childhood memories, this conversation could be the end of her, or of freedom. There was little to distinguish between the two.

"She survived because of the Shadow Charm, my Lord," said the faerie.

Either they could detect it, or they'd got the information out of the Shopkeeper. The former was more likely. If that was the case, Cathy thought, then they would see the curse too, and if there was one thing she had to do, it was convince them she knew nothing about it.

"Ah, perhaps that's the problem, let's get rid of that first."

Thumb and forefinger poised like pincers, he reached towards her shoulder but stopped just above her clothing. He pinched the air and slowly drew his hand back. She could see nothing between his fingers, but noticed the shadow cast by the stockroom's sprite changing. It looked like a blanket was being pulled off her, one invisible to the eye, but visible in shadow. When it broke contact with her body, it faded to nothing.

"Oh. You're still dull. The Shadow Charm hid her from her family," he said to the faerie, "but it didn't help her to navigate Mundanus... it's such an exciting mystery. My dear," he focused back on Cathy, "you are a tight bud with so many hidden petals yet to unfold."

He scooped up her hand with a fluid movement. His was cool and dry, and she was aware of the clamminess of her own, thinking he wanted to kiss it as many of the men in the Great Families still did. But instead he turned her palm towards the ceiling and bent towards it. An inhumanly long tongue flicked out from between his lips and he licked the tender skin of her wrist.

It felt like a feather, leaving no saliva, just a faint tingling and a wave of nausea.

"Mmmm. No trace of interference as I'd feared and no contact with the Arbiters, that's good. She has potential, but far from realised." He was speaking to the faerie again, as if Cathy were simply an exhibit in a petting zoo. "There's little more to her than what we see here. But the curse is interesting."

That drew the faerie close.

Lord Poppy was examining Cathy's face now, searching for a reaction.

"Curse?" she asked, hoping that only innocence would be seen. It was a tiny thread of a lie amongst a tapestry of deception.

He smiled, his thumb now stroking the inside of her wrist. "So you have been good, after all."

"What curse? I want to see it!" the faerie said, but Lord Poppy swatted it away.

"I'll tell you later." It tumbled in the disturbed air before righting itself with a look of indignation. "Now..." Lord Poppy let go of Cathy's hand and she folded her arms. He took a step back, twisting his cane thoughtfully. "There's something I want to know. When a girl as plain, inelegant and quite frankly graceless as you has the chance to ask for beauty, poise or even just good taste in clothes, why in the Split Worlds would she not?"

So this was the reason this nightmare was weaving itself around her. He knew about her coming-of-age ceremony.

She was the middle child of one of the most prominent Papaver families in Fae-touched society, the Rhoeas-Papavers. Her family had many traditions, most of which she'd strained against and resented as much as the next child, but one in particular she'd managed to turn to her advantage. At the age of eighteen, all children had the right to make a request of the head of the Papaver families. When she was brought in front of the Patroon she'd asked to go to university instead of something shallow, as she'd been coached. Of course it had reached the ears of their Fae patron. No women in Fae-touched society ever went to university and few of the young men did either. So many of their parents, born in a different age, regarded further education as a sure means of ruining a young man. Cathy saw it as a sure way to freedom. They couldn't deny her the request and even though they tried their best to make it as difficult as possible she still got to university several months later.

"Is that the reason for your interest, my Lord? An unorthodox request?" Her voice was a little high, but at least she was able to speak.

"It's more than unorthodox, it's positively scandalous. It was sufficient to catch my eye, yes. But it's also the fact you ran away and have hitherto eluded your family with great success. Your tactics even challenged me, and there are not many who have been able to do that, my dear."

"But you did find me." She wondered what boon the Shopkeeper had received for betraying her, and his air-freshener experiment took on new meaning. He'd been trying to mask the scent of the Fae Lord who'd presumably walked through the shop just before she arrived.

"So I did. But, sly one, you didn't answer my question."

"I wanted to go to university because I wanted to learn."

He wrinkled his nose, as if she'd just belched rather than told the truth. It was important to sprinkle some in amongst the lies.

"Learn what?"

"Everything I could."

"But why?"

She had to think about that. "Because I had to know the truth about Mundanus."

He frowned. "Why learn the truth about a place you were never destined to be part of? You must have planned to run away, even when you curtsied in front of your Patroon and accepted his gift."

Her body found a new reserve of adrenalin, but Cathy forced herself to think carefully. She had to gamble. "Not when I made the request to the Patroon, my Lord, but later, yes, I did plan to run away. I had to, otherwise I would have failed."

"So something happened that made you want to stay in Mundanus, even though it would age you? Even though it would disgrace your family and you'd live a cursed life?"

"Yes," she said, throat dry. She couldn't reveal everything, she'd never tell anyone the real reason she'd fled her family. But she had to give him a sliver to be believable. "I fell in love with Mundanus. I didn't want to go back and live in the Nether like everyone in the Great Families. I couldn't bear to leave it. So I ran away and hid from my family so they couldn't stop me living there."

Eyebrows high, he sucked in a breath and the hand that had caught hers fluttered over his chest. "Oh! Oh, darling child, I understand. I know what agony it is to fall in love with something we can never have. And what deserves our love and attention more than Mundanus? Poor, empty world, denied our gifts and beneficence for so long!" He clasped her hand again, this time pressing it over his heart, but she felt no beat through the silk shirt. "Now I understand what a delicious creature of passion you are. It was buried so far beneath an inconsequential face and forgettable body that I almost missed it!"

Cathy wondered if this was what it was like to meet someone who was truly insane. Someone so mad that speaking to them demonstrated how the world they lived in was so very different to everyone else's. She couldn't decide whether delighting the insane was good or bad.

"I'm so glad you understand, Lord Poppy." She managed a smile.

"As am I! I arrived with a heavy heart, convinced that I was going to have to turn your tongue into a tethered wasp and then enslave you for eternity for having been so disloyal to your family." He paused as the colour sank away from her lips. "But now I don't have to, because I understand that it was love that drove you, and how can I deny love? And it really is such a relief, as it would have been so inconvenient – everything has been arranged for so long, I was struggling to imagine how I would recover."

Cathy wanted to take her hand back, wanted to run out of the room and disappear, wanted to huddle in the corner of her student digs wrapped in a blanket and cry over a cup of tea. But he was still pressing her palm against the cool silk and showed no sign of letting go. Then she processed what he'd just said.

"Inconvenient, my Lord?"

"Yes, if you'd been unable to return to Aquae Sulis."

It had been a long time since she'd heard that name, and she hadn't missed it. Hers was one of the most powerful families in Aquae Sulis, the Nether reflection of the city of mundane Bath, both places she never wanted to see again. Whilst the mundane city was beautiful and vibrant, full of greenery and the excitements of modern life in the normal world, such as electricity and films, and technology designed to make life easier and more entertaining, its Nether reflection was not. Only a few roads and buildings had been reflected; she had grown up in Great Pulteney Street, the long avenue of reflected Georgian houses owned by her family, and of course, the anchor properties in Mundanus were protected by their clever network of legal expertise and their stronghold on the mundane Corporation of Bath. Now she'd lived in Mundanus – what she had come to think of as the real world – as an independent woman, she couldn't bear the thought of returning to that suffocating existence. "But... but I don't want to go back there. I can't!"

The smile fell from his face. "My poor love-struck one. Of course you're going to go back. As soon as we are finished here you'll return to your family, you'll obey your father and you'll live in the Nether like all of the privileged, serving your patron."

She forced herself to keep still, though the urge to shake her head and scream was almost unbearable. "But… they'll be angry with me," she croaked.

"Undoubtedly. But it doesn't change the fact that you're needed there. Everything has been planned for such a long time that your wishes are quite irrelevant in the matter."

He sounded like her father. Her yearning to make just one decision for herself was always called irrelevant. She forced herself to focus on questions and answers, rather than emotions. "Why am I needed, Lord Poppy? What use could I possibly be? You said yourself that I'm plain and–"

"Your father didn't tell you? Well, it's for him to do so. You'll find out when you get home. But we haven't concluded our business. Now I know you're genuinely interesting and passionate, and most worthy of further attention, I've decided to bestow upon you three wishes."

The conversation that she thought couldn't get any worse suddenly did. Not the three wishes trap. That was only one step up from the wasp tongue.

"I don't deserve your generosity, Lord Poppy," she said, without thinking.

"You'd rather be punished?"

"No!" she managed to catch the retort before it became a squeal. "I'm sure… your decision is the very best for me."

He pressed her palm against his shirt. She was sure there would be a damp hand-print left behind when he finally let her go. "Good. I will be watching what you choose with great interest, Catherine Rhoeas-Papaver, because I am certain that one who asks for such an outrageous wish at her coming-of-age ceremony could dream up something truly spectacular with three to play with."

The faerie started to giggle. It sounded like a mouse being ripped apart by a cat.

"Now, three wishes are no fun at all if there are no rules. So this is the first." Lord Poppy released her hand so he could accompany his words with an excited flourish. "You must impress me."

She was about to clarify whether he meant with every single wish, but she stopped herself. She might need that as a loophole later on.

"The second rule," Lord Poppy continued, evidently enjoying himself, "is that you cannot use a wish to leave Society. There is no denying who you are, my dear, and you are a Rhoeas-Papaver, one of my most cherished family lines. You have had your love affair with Mundanus, it's time for it to end. But I'll let you into a secret," he whispered. "Love affairs are always at their best when illicit and should always be ended abruptly. It heightens the pleasure and keeps the dreaded boredom at bay."

He was talking about her freedom like it was a holiday fling with a barman but she kept silent, not at all certain that she could speak without getting herself into more trouble or bursting into tears.

"There should be a third rule," he muttered, glancing at the faerie. "It's prettier that way. Three wishes, three rules."

"I have an idea!" It pirouetted in delight. "The wishes have to be made before the grand ball opening the season in Aquae Sulis."

"Exquisite!" Lord Poppy blew a kiss to the faerie, rustling the petals of its dress. The tiny creature's wings fluttered so much they left a trail of faint sparkles. "Then you can begin the season as a fabulous success. Or as a faint shadow of yourself. Oh, I didn't mention the penalty, did I?"

Tears or vomiting, Cathy wasn't sure which now. He'd removed the Shadow Charm but instead of delivering her to the family, Lord Poppy was toying with her. He knew as well as she did that it was inevitable they would find her without magical protection and there was no way the Shopkeeper would dare sell her anything useful now one of the Fae lords had personally intervened. She didn't need a penalty to feel absolutely screwed.

"Should you fail to impress me by the first ball of the season, I shall reach into your soul and pluck out that bright source of your initiative. Then you can spend the rest of your life doing as you are told, perfectly incapable of forming a desire or opinion of your own." He waited a beat, but she remained in horrified silence. "I think that's fitting." He glanced at the faerie who nodded with glee.

4

Max slid the lockpick back into the leather case, tucked that into his inside pocket and pushed the door open. One last check up and down the corridor and there was no one in sight. He stepped inside.

The air inside the studio flat was as stale as he'd anticipated, an unpleasant odour leaking from the fridge in the tiny corner kitchen. The place was very small with huge sash windows letting in light and noise from the London street below. Up here, the traffic was a constant background roar, punctuated by the odd siren and beeping car horn. He could see the roof of the building opposite, and noted no windows or balconies overlooked the flat.

He swept his eyes over the mess as he quietly closed the door behind him. Takeaway cartons were piled on the tiny table in the corner and the sofa bed had been left unfolded with sheets and pillows rumpled on top of it. Clothes were strewn all over the floor and the rickety canvas wardrobe was full of empty wire coat hangers. A couple of drawers were open, but it didn't look as if the place had been turned over. There were too many things still in place that a burglar would have snatched: a jewellery box, a laptop, a small plastic tub of loose change and a few notes.

Even though he was fairly certain what the results would be, Max took the Sniffer out of his pocket, wound it up and set it down on the kitchenette worktop. The squat brass container ticked as its spring slowly wound down, at first looking like an octagonal musical box on stout legs. The eight segments forming its top telescoped open and a tiny horn emerged, not unlike that of a miniature gramophone. The ticking was then masked by a gentle whirring as the device sucked in the air from the room and blew it out of a vent in its underside.

All Charms used by the criminals in the so-called Great Families left a residue in the air, tiny amounts of the fragrance associated with the Fae who originally created the Charm. It was too little to detect with a human nose, and dogs couldn't be trusted, so the Sniffer was used to extract the trace amounts from the air and analyse the strength of the Charm used. Even derived Charms, created by the criminal families themselves, still had the original scents, and thankfully none of them knew the Arbiters had figured out how to trace their handiwork. No perfumes, nor any of the bizarre air-fresheners that seemed to be more popular in Mundanus each time he came in, interfered with the sensitivity of the device, but it was just a question of time before the Fae-touched families found another way to cover their tracks.

As it did its work, Max picked his way across the room, navigating past skirts and dresses, glancing at the stack of well-thumbed fashion magazines by the bed. Not a book in sight. It looked as if she'd been choosing what to wear; most of the garments were in piles around the long mirror hanging on the wall opposite the bed. He didn't bother to look in it himself. He knew what he was wearing and how ugly his face was. He'd been living with it for years.

He glanced inside the corner of the room partitioned off for a tiny bathroom. Every surface was covered with bottles and make-up. Taped to the mirror over the sink was a picture of a brunette with smoky eyes. Perhaps she'd been copying the make-up; speckles of rouge covered the sink and brushes were piled up behind the taps.

He knew the brunette in the picture wasn't Miss Brooks because she was the fourth blonde to disappear from London's St Pancras ward in the last month. He wanted to confirm his theory as soon as he could, so he went over to the coffee table on the other side of the sofa bed, seeing a notepad with something scrawled on it. He hoped that Miss Brooks liked to write things down rather than tapping them straight into those infernal mobile phones.

He nodded as he read the scrawl. *"2 pm!!! Photo shoot – casual and glam – contracts – passport!!!!"* He could picture her taking the call, scribbling notes as she held in the excited scream until she called her best friend to give her the news.

It all led back to the talent agency; the theory was confirmed. A tiny *ping* from the Sniffer drew him back. The horn retreated as the pointer on the side spun to… white. Good, no trace of Fae magic.

Once it was closed again, he dropped the Sniffer into his pocket. He had just enough time to send his findings back to the Chapter and make the rendezvous with Montgomery. If he could help the London Arbiter crack the case he could be back in Bath for dinner.

The windows were large enough to climb out of and he'd seen the narrow walkway outside from the street below. Leaving his trilby on the bed, he forced one of the windows up, admitting the city's roar into the flat. He stepped outside and sent a pair of pigeons up into the sky, cooing in alarm. The walkway was little more than a ledge with an ornate

stone safety rail. Being incapable of fear in that moment
was a boon.

The clear autumn day was a bonus; in the rain the lead
roofing would have been even more treacherous. He edged
his way to the corner where he'd seen the angel. London
architects liked the idea of heavenly figures watching the
streets and he could see why. London was loud, fast and
crowded, even compared to his native Bath on a summer
Saturday. Yet again he questioned the sense of helping
Montgomery with a case outside his own territory.

The angel was twice his size, classical beauty and marble
toga both covered in pigeon droppings. A grand lady with a
bad job, she was holding up an equally filthy cornice. If he
stretched, he'd be able to reach her.

He fumbled under his coat and shirt and brought the
chain up over his head, his neck feeling naked without the
thick, heavy links. It was a suitably ugly thing, engraved with
formulae and carrying the Wessex Sorcerer's seal, still warm
from resting against his chest.

Climbing onto the folds of the angel's dress, he caught
hold of one of her arms and swung round to drop the chain
over her head. After a few pokes and nudges, it dropped
past her nose and fell with a dull chink around her neck. By
the time he'd clambered back down onto the walkway her
stone eyes were blinking, and once his coat was straightened
and buttoned back up again her head twisted round to look
at him.

He took a deep breath, preparing himself for the rush
of connection and then rested a hand on her arm to keep
contact. "Personal diary entry," he said, and the angel nodded.
"I have confirmed my suspicion regarding the talent agency's
involvement after searching the studio flat of a Miss Clare
Brooks, the fourth missing person on the list."

He paused to give the statue a chance to repeat his report back to the Chapter.

"I was right about that damn talent agency." Max's soul's voice was far too low and gravelly to suit the angel's face. "I've found evidence connecting it to the fourth missing person on the list, Miss Clare Brooks, after searching her flat. I'm seriously concerned that something is very wrong in the Kingdom of Essex."

Max blinked at the angel. Was that how he really felt? He cleared his throat. "Montgomery has failed to make contact at the prearranged location. If it happens again I'll have to assume the individual or individuals involved have learnt of his suspicion."

"And I'm worried that the rat Montgomery called me in to find is on to him." The angel's previously serene face was now distorted by a deep frown.

"Maybe he's lying low, or…"

"He might be dead!" the angel interrupted. "This is getting serious and it's not my territory and I don't know what I'll do if this gets any worse."

"All right, all right," he said to the angel, "let's stick to the facts."

"This is a personal entry," it replied peevishly. "It's so rare I get a chance to express myself, I have to make the most of it."

"I'm not going to stand here and argue. I'm going to stake out the agency. It's been a week since Miss Brooks went missing and I know I'm close. I can't trust anyone in London, so I'll stick with it until Montgomery shows up."

The angel's report was closer, though still embellished with "until Montgomery shows up dead or apologetic" tacked onto the end. When it was done, he climbed higher up the sculpture to retrieve the chain, ready for the familiar lurching sensation when contact with his soul was severed.

He'd lost count of the times he'd reported back to the Chapter from Mundanus, but every single time he broke contact it brought back the memory of the day he qualified. That was the last time he'd felt excitement, when he heard he'd passed all the tests and showed enough promise to work in the field as an Arbiter. He was thirteen, and, an hour after they'd told him, they'd dislocated his soul and put the chain around his neck, too tight then to take off.

He knew he'd screamed so much he was hoarse by the time the links were closed, but he knew it only intellectually, like a memory of a scene in a play he'd once watched.

With each successful year in the field under his mentor, a link was added until he was trusted to manage the connection himself and act independently. He had no idea where exactly in the cloister his soul was kept. Nor did he have any idea how it was stored, how the reports he sent back were recorded or how the Chapter Master was informed. But he didn't need to know. He just got on with the job and did his best to ignore how his soul leaked emotion into his reports.

The dislocation was ninety years ago. If he'd spent all that time in Mundanus he'd be a frail old man now, if not dead. He'd have got married, had children, grandchildren, maybe even great-grandchildren. Sometimes he looked at the people, the ones the Fae-touched so disparagingly called "mundanes", and wondered what it was like to be them, if only to try and understand and predict what the criminals would be interested in next. But he had no regrets when he observed them. That was impossible.

Chain back around his neck, window closed, flat swept for any trace of his break-in, and he was on his way to Judd Street. He kept an eye out for statues that could make valid connection points in case of emergency. In Bath he knew every single statue, gargoyle and grotesque in a five-mile radius of the city centre. His knowledge of London was insufficient for this case.

Case? That made it sound official, and it was far from that. He wondered where Montgomery was. It was rare for an Arbiter to ask for help, but to ask someone from a different Chapter? That was unheard of. For Montgomery to ask meant it was serious. That, and the fact they'd collaborated on a tough case in the Fifties, was what made him agree. That had only been an exchange of information, however, not trips to each other's territories without official permission. It had prevented some of Lady Rose's puppets from getting a foothold in Bath and he had found Montgomery to be reliable and thorough. Max wondered why Montgomery had missed the latest rendezvous.

Speculation was futile. Max had no means of contacting him outside the prearranged meetings. They didn't use mobile phones, the Chapter couldn't guarantee their security yet, and being in different Chapters meant they couldn't coordinate as easily as he would with a fellow Wessex Arbiter.

Instead, he turned his mind to the evidence. One innocent could be lost to Exilium owing to poor luck, but to lose four in as many weeks? Montgomery was right; there had to be a crooked Arbiter in the pay of the parasites for something so blatant to happen in such a small geographical area. If Max's suspicions were correct the talent agency operating out of 191 Judd Street was a front organisation for the London Fae-touched. They were probably using it as a means of drawing blonde men and women who fit a profile to a location where they could be kidnapped. Why hadn't the local Arbiters spotted the pattern? Perhaps the more pertinent question was: why were they ignoring it?

Max couldn't understand how corruption of that magnitude could even be possible. A dislocated soul protected them not just from Fae magic but also from temptation, and the greed that fuelled corruption. As far as he knew, no Arbiter had ever been compromised; that was one of the many reasons why the Fae and their puppets were so terrified of them.

He found a café a few doors down. It took him a moment to adjust to the new prices, then he ordered a coffee and settled down at one of the outside tables with a newspaper. He wanted to watch the comings and goings at number 191 whilst waiting for Montgomery. London was becoming more continental every year; he couldn't remember this street café culture from the last time he'd been there. But a lot had changed since the Fifties.

The disappearances were on a seven-day cycle, and Miss Brooks had disappeared exactly one week before. It was quarter to two in the afternoon, a good time to watch as all of the previous appointments had been for 2pm.

He didn't have to wait long. A woman with honey-blonde hair and extraordinarily long legs was tottering towards the agency's door. He quickly fished out his glasses. He'd almost forgotten about them; it was the first time they'd been tested in the field, and they were not part of his usual repertoire.

Through the glasses, she faded to the same grey as everything around her. She hadn't been charmed, and, interestingly, the agency frontage and threshold hadn't been glamoured either. It looked as if it was still a normal mundane office with no anchor for a Nether property. That was good. If they wanted to kidnap her, they'd have to take her somewhere else. He put the glasses away. Wearing them too long made him feel sick, and if anyone inspected them closely they'd see the modifications.

There was a bounce to her step and a smile that suggested she'd had the same phone call as the previous victims. All he had to do was wait.

It was unlikely they'd take her in broad daylight. They'd wait until dusk, first taking her to another location, probably a bar, before posting her through to Exilium. By then he should have passed on his findings to Montgomery. If Montgomery didn't show, Max was on dodgy ground by not having a local contact, but he hadn't had time to resolve that. He would follow them to the temporary location then call in to his Chapter Master if Montgomery didn't show up in the next half hour.

He was onto his second coffee when footsteps approaching his chair made him twist round. It wasn't Montgomery, but he suspected the man was another Arbiter; there was a total lack of emotion on his face and a slight bulge beneath his clothing where the soul chain would rest. Max didn't recognise him and the stranger didn't fit the description he'd been given of the suspected rat. He was dressed in a light jacket and jeans, much less formal than the suit and raincoat Max wore in Mundanus.

"Maximilian, of the Bath Chapter, Kingdom of Wessex?"

"Yes?"

"Good afternoon. I'm Faulkner, London Camden Chapter, Kingdom of Essex."

He pulled the top of his jacket down just enough to reveal the chain and the Essex seal. Max nodded. "Thank you."

"You're a long way from home," Faulkner said, sitting opposite him. "Waiting for Montgomery?"

Max nodded, uncertain how to play this. Faulkner had every right to tell him to leave, and to report his trespass to his Chapter if he felt Max was overstepping the mark. Which he had been, for the last seventy-two hours.

"He's late," he said.

"He's in custody," Faulkner replied, raising a hand to call the waiter. "Something's gone horribly wrong with him;

he's been causing all kinds of problems lately and now we think he's been kidnapping people and trying to pin it on a colleague."

It was a pathetic attempt at a lie. Montgomery was as solid as Portland Stone. Max had heard that the really old Arbiters could get a little frayed around the edges but then they retired to the cloister to train the new recruits. Being closer to their soul again usually cleared up any problems. Montgomery was too young for it to be an issue anyway.

"Did he tell you I'd be here?"

Faulkner ordered tea and then nodded after the waiter left. "After he admitted he'd been struggling. It's been tough in London lately; the Rosas are feuding again. He got caught in the crossfire one too many times. Smoke?"

Max shook his head. "Is my being here a problem?"

Faulkner drew in a lungful of smoke and let it drift from his nostrils. "Not if you leave on the next train and keep this under your hat."

Max fingered the brim of his trilby, flicked a look down the street at the agency. The blonde was still in there. "Is this your beat?"

"Yes. Did Montgomery tell you there was a problem with the St Pancras Ward?" Max didn't reply, choosing to wait to hear what Faulkner had to say. "There isn't a problem any more. I've been assigned to clean up his mess. My ward borders St Pancras. There's no need for you to stay."

Max weighed up his choices. It didn't take long; there were only two: stay and make a fuss, or pretend to leave and watch. The former would cross a line and push Faulkner into reporting him. He'd be forcibly ejected from the city and achieve nothing. The latter would risk the blonde; he'd be too far away to intervene, but his being thrown out of London wasn't going to help her either.

He stood, resolving to gather more information. The paperwork involved in a dispute with another Chapter, especially one in a different Kingdom, wasn't going to do anyone any good. He put on his hat and offered his hand to Faulkner who shook it.

"I hope everything gets sorted out with Montgomery," Max said, for the sake of good manners.

"Have a safe journey home, Maximilian." Faulkner attempted a smile but it always looked ugly on an Arbiter's face.

5

Max headed towards the nearest tube station to make Faulkner believe he really was leaving. Whilst Max didn't buy the brush-off, he did appreciate its delicacy. Faulkner had every right to throw the book at him and frogmarch him onto the first train out of Paddington. Even corrupted, the London Arbiters were still polite.

There was an outside chance Montgomery had lost his way as Faulkner had described, but if that were the case it made no sense to call a Wessex Arbiter from the Bath Chapter to investigate; Montgomery would try to hide it rather than invite attention. That blonde was still in danger. Max needed to find somewhere to watch the agency, and now Faulkner, but also a place where he could report back quickly, should something kick off. If he was to expose corruption in an institution flawless in its loyalty and integrity for almost a thousand years, he'd need damn good evidence.

He looked up and down the Euston Road, uncertain where to go and mindful that Faulkner might have another watching him. If some London Arbiter had been sniffing around in Bath Max would have done the same. So he headed towards a nearby local map attached to a lamppost, playing the part of a Wessex man in a foreign land, as he considered his options.

He needed two things: somewhere high with a clear view of Judd Street, and a contact host to report back to the Cloister. Even a grotesque would work, if a sculptured angel or gargoyle couldn't be found. He looked across the road at the St Pancras Renaissance, the refurbished gothic hotel outside King's Cross, letting his eyes roam over the building. It played into the disoriented tourist act, being an impressive landmark. The move paid off; up high on the clock tower he could see four gargoyles, and he'd be high enough to watch the Judd Street agency.

He made for King's Cross St Pancras station, played a standard double-back trick at the underground station and crept out of one of the quieter exits to approach the hotel. He went towards the doors, keeping his hands in his pockets and mouth shut until he was inside. Removing his hat and moving with the purpose and confidence of a guest past the reception desk, he was up the stairs in less than a minute and hunting a way up into the clock tower.

Ten minutes later he was climbing out of a roof maintenance hatch over a hundred feet above St Pancras station. He'd stuffed his hat into his coat pocket, knowing the wind would take it, so high, and hoped the innocents of London would continue their usual behaviour of never looking up.

He climbed steadily, fearlessly, until he reached a ledge from which he could reach one of the gargoyles. When he got back to the cloister after this, he planned to raise the issue of contact in hostile territory. He'd never appreciated how inconvenient it was to find a contact host until he'd found himself in an unfamiliar city. But he knew what the response would be. Why would you need another way to make contact when you shouldn't be in another Chapter's city anyway?

The gargoyle was solid, ugly and recently sandblasted. It stretched out at least two metres from the wall, as if it had been turned to stone leaping from the building. It took a couple of minutes to climb on and straddle its back near where it jutted out of the clock tower. Max inched himself towards its head, carefully slid his chain onto the stone creature's neck and braced himself.

"Oh, bloody hell, this is high up." The gargoyle's expression twisted into one of terror. "You better hold on tight."

"I am," Max muttered, getting his bearings and identifying Judd Street. He had a direct line of sight to the agency door, and hoped the blonde was still in there. "This is a report to the Chapter Master, his ears only."

"Understood," the gargoyle replied.

As he made his report, Max fiddled with one of the attachments he'd been given by the Sorcerer to improve the magnification of the experimental glasses. By the time he'd given the details and the gargoyle had added its own emotional commentary, his backside was numb and his ears were hurting from the cold wind.

As he waited for feedback and further instructions, the blonde emerged from the agency. She walked a few steps away, then burst into tears. He could see she was still clean. Perhaps she hadn't been what they were looking for, and she was one lucky girl.

Faulkner was still at the café, drinking tea and watching the blonde too. So was the waiter; she was exactly the kind of person the Fae parasites would want. The glasses were giving him a headache and he didn't want to stay up there much longer, but he had to see if she was safe. He lifted the frame to rub his eyes before resuming his vigil.

The discomfort was forgotten when he saw a man come down the street and notice the distressed woman. As he headed towards her, Max leaned forwards, studying the line of the man's nose. He resembled someone he'd dealt with before... someone from the Rosa family line.

He was one of them, one of the Fae-touched, and he was homing in on the blonde.

Max checked on Faulkner who was watching them too. He sat still as the parasite spoke to her, making her look up in surprise, mascara dragged down her cheeks by the tears. Then, without even checking who was in the street, without looking the least bit nervous, the Fae-touched began to weave a Charm.

Through the glasses the Rosa looked brighter and more colourful. It looked as if the colours were bleeding out where his hand touched her shoulder, her dress becoming green again, the honey returning to her hair.

"Why isn't he doing anything?" the gargoyle yelled with Max's fury.

Flicking a glance at Faulkner, Max watched him sip tea as the Rosa worked a Fae Charm – in broad daylight on a public street in Mundanus! – less than ten metres away.

Even though he didn't have the glasses, Faulkner's training would be enough for him to know a crime was in progress. The way the Rosa would be murmuring, keeping physical contact, the way the innocent's pupils would be dilating far too much and her body language changing, it would be obvious!

But that wasn't all of it. The fact that the Rosa didn't even check, didn't care if he was seen, was proof enough that something was rotten in London. In fact, he was close enough to spot Faulkner was an Arbiter; they had just as much of an instinct for identifying their enemy as the Arbiters had for identifying them. Dislocation from one's soul took its toll on them over the years; they were renowned for their ugliness and lack of expression. Usually a Fae-touched would leave the area as soon as they spotted one, finding Arbiters unpleasant to be around. The Fae fled them, terrified by humans without strings to pull.

The blonde was calm and pliant, allowing the stranger to slip an arm around her waist and steer her down the street, past the Arbiter who was pouring himself a second cup from the small teapot.

"That slimy, rotten piece of filth, I'd like to shove that teapot up Faulkner's–"

"Shush," Max hissed at the gargoyle.

He was at the top of a clock tower, unable to intervene, as he knew he would be. But now he was uncertain they'd take her to an intermediate location. Brazenly charming an innocent in the street didn't suggest he'd feel the need for caution in slipping her away to Exilium.

The blonde was already lost, he realised. Charmed into compliance and with no Arbiter intervention, she'd be in the clutches of Lady Rose before the day was out. She was condemned to being a plaything until the foul creature became bored, and then she'd be a slave for eternity, trapped on the wrong side of the split worlds.

If there was any good to come out of this, it was getting the evidence to prevent any more being taken. "Tell the Chapter Master there's an emergency," he said, shuffling himself further along the back of the gargoyle towards its head.

He'd only made a deep connection once before, when his mentor had been there and protected him from outside interference. For the second time that day, the absence of fear was advantageous.

Max reached down, leaning forwards until his belly was resting on the gargoyle's back, stretching his arms around its head until he could cup his hands over its stone eyes. "See what I see," he said, consciously opening himself more to the connection with his soul.

He felt cold and his feet were going numb as his mind struggled to distinguish between him and the stone.

Simultaneously, he had the feeling of witnessing the crime unfold as the blonde was steered towards the Euston Road, and also looking through his eyes as if they were binoculars, another presence watching from a step removed. Even though Max had no idea how he could feel it, he knew the Chapter Master was seeing the same as he did. Max focused on getting as much detail as he could.

He looked back at Faulkner, taking tea as if it were a Sunday afternoon in a world without the Fae-touched. He then focused back on the blonde, wondering where she'd be sent through.

The Fae's puppets could access Exilium from the Nether, pockets of reality created between Mundanus and the Fae's prison. For a moment he wondered if she was going to be taken into the Nether property anchored to the very hotel he was perched upon, but they crossed Euston Road and carried on, passing the station on their right, heading away from the busiest roads.

He craned his neck, waiting for a response from the Chapter Master. Even now he would be consulting the Sorcerer; there'd never been an incident like this in the history of the Bath Chapter.

It was getting harder to see them. Max struggled to make his legs cooperate as he tried to shift his position and keep them in sight.

Then the gargoyle moved.

He grabbed hold of it with his arms and legs as its body swung in the direction he wanted to go. He'd only seen eyes, mouths and, at a push, the head move on statues he'd used for a connection, never this much.

He quickly relocated the blonde and her kidnapper, heading towards an old church. But then a movement at the edge of his vision pulled his attention from the crime in progress.

Another Arbiter was balanced on the hotel roof, slightly below, about ten metres away. He fit the description Montgomery had given him: black hair, large nose, sallow skin and predictably unpleasant to look at.

The gun he was pointing at Max was even uglier.

"Have things got so bad here?" Max asked, knowing that the Chapter Master would be acting now if he wasn't already. He'd be contacting the Essex Sorcerer and demanding aid or entry to the city directly, using the Nether. Whether it would be in time to help him was another matter.

"Only for you," the man replied, and fired.

It was dark by the time Cathy got back to her flat in Manchester, hungry and exhausted by a train journey dominated by paranoia. After Lord Poppy's dismissal she left the shop without even looking at the Shopkeeper and went straight into Mundanus, seeking anonymity in its crowds and reassurance in its normality. The storm had passed and the pavements glistened as she trudged to the underground station, still shivering in her damp clothes. There was no protection from her family now, it was just a matter of time before they hunted her down. She couldn't bear the thought of dealing with that unhappy reunion at the same time as Lord Poppy's challenge.

He'd called Manchester the "dark city" and implied her being there had made it harder for him to find her. It made it worth the risk to go home first. She needed to be somewhere that would make it hard for him to interfere; it was notoriously difficult to navigate through a challenge set by a Fae Lord without screwing up horribly at some point. She didn't want that to happen within a ten-mile radius of polite society. She held onto the tissue-paper hope that going back to Manchester would also make it harder for her family to locate her with the Seeker Charm recently purchased at the Emporium.

She locked and bolted the door, feeling unsafe for the first time since she'd moved in, dumped her bag and allowed herself a moment of self-pity before shuffling into the kitchen to put the kettle on. Noodles and tea first, plans and panicking second. Breaking up with Josh… last.

Her bottom lip wobbled. "Stop it," she whispered to herself. If she started to cry, she'd never stop and there wasn't time for falling apart. If growing up in the Rhoeas-Papaver Family had taught her anything, it was that letting emotion get the better of one was the swiftest path to failure.

She was due to have lunch with Josh the next day but would her family find her before then? She pulled her mobile from her pocket but realised she didn't know what to say to him. She abandoned the phone and filled the kettle instead. Dealing with the shakes from being too hungry and stressed and tea-deprived would be more constructive. She raised an eyebrow at the wartime poster on her fridge: Keep Calm and Carry On.

Teabag in the cup and she already felt marginally better. Just the ritual of tea-making was starting to tell a deep part of her brain that somehow it would be all right. She poured in the water, started swirling the bag, when a rattling at her door made her drop the spoon and hurry into the hallway.

The entire door was shaking, making old paint fly from the hinges. The chain jangled, the handle twitched and Cathy backed away nervously.

There was a loud pop, sounding like a giant soap bubble had just met its end on the other side of the door, and then a gilded letterbox appeared in the centre of the wood. The door finally became still.

"A bloody Letterboxer!" Cathy said, trembling. She'd imagined her wrath-filled father on the other side of the door, when it had been just a simple Charm. As she watched, the little flap in its centre flipped open and a letter shot through, followed by another and then one every second until a small pile rested on the doormat. The letterbox shimmered out of existence with a more gentle pop.

Those letters had probably been sent over a year ago when her family realised she'd run away. Now that Lord Poppy had removed the Shadow Charm, the Letterboxer could complete its task of delivering the letters when the addressee was at home. It was a bold move to use the Charm for someone known to be in Mundanus; if the Letterboxer had been witnessed by an Arbiter there would have been serious repercussions. Her mother had been desperate, and desperate mothers never wrote nice letters.

6

Sam picked at the scab on the back of his head whilst Dave aimed his dart at the board.

"Fiver I get a bullseye," he said, pausing to scratch under his beer gut before repositioning his stance.

"You're on," Sam replied as he pulled a crumb of dried blood through his hair to inspect it. "That policeman made me feel like a complete dick."

"What do you expect?" Dave threw the dart and hit the treble twenty. He could swear as well as he could drink beer.

"I expected him to tell me if my wallet had been found, not take the piss out of me."

He inspected another scabby chunk as Dave pulled the darts out of the board. The office was quiet; the rest of his colleagues, including his boss, were away at a conference. He'd spent all morning trying to get a script to run on the Linux box as Dave had practised the art of doing nothing productive in the most disruptive way possible.

"I just can't believe you thought you'd been mugged."

"I've got bruises as well as this cut on the back of my head, you know."

Dave snorted. "You'd be amazed at what you can forget. Once I woke up one morning with a burned hand and a half-eaten bacon sandwich next to me and not a scooby about how either happened. You're just hoping that you were mugged. Then you don't have to admit to Leanne that you lost your wallet under the influence. Now double or quits I get a bullseye in two darts."

Two darts later and Sam was a tenner better off. Dave swore, unhooked the dartboard from the wall and put the whiteboard back in its place. Darts removed and board slid down the side of his desk, he flopped into his chair and insulted Sam over Twitter.

There was a knock on the door as Sam was chuckling and thinking up a retort. "You expecting a visitor?" Sam asked as he went over and opened it, but Dave shook his head.

"Does a Mr Samuel Westonville work here?"

Dave's chair creaked as he swivelled to see who it was.

Sam didn't recognise him. The man was in his early fifties and his face was reminiscent of a bulldog; too much skin and not enough places for it to cling to. It hung in bags under his eyes and folds around his jawline, like it had been slowly sliding off over the years. He was dressed in a cheap suit that looked about thirty years old and his tie was Eighties-thin. "Is this about my wallet?"

"Yes," he replied. "I'd like to speak to you in private."

Sam was disturbed by the immediate dislike he'd taken to the man. It was usually Leanne who decided what she thought about someone before they opened their mouth.

The only private space was the corner of the room partitioned off for his boss's office, and that was locked. "There's a kitchen at the end of the corridor," Sam suggested, and when the man nodded Sam closed the door behind him and led the way.

The company he worked for had an office in a cheap converted warehouse subsidised by the council. The kitchen was shared by all the offices on their floor, but thanks to its grotty state it was rarely used for anything more than hurried kettle-filling and reluctant washing up.

"Are you from the police?" Sam asked as they walked.

"I understand you lost your wallet two nights ago," the man replied. "At first you thought you'd been mugged?"

"Well," Sam pushed the kitchen door open, "my wife thought that. I've got a cut on the back of my head and a few bruises, but as the copper at the station pointed out, they're probably just from making my way home 'under the influence' if you know what I mean."

The man followed him in, glanced at the stained formica worktop and ageing microwave and stood next to the cheap table and chairs in the centre of the room. "Have you retraced your steps?"

Sam shrugged. "I went back to the pub I think we were at earlier in the evening."

"You think? You sound uncertain."

The man's voice was flat. At first Sam had thought he was bored, then depressed, but now he was facing him as he spoke there wasn't any emotional expression at all. "Sorry, I didn't get your name."

"You can call me Jim."

"And you're with the p–"

Jim collapsed. For a moment, Sam just stood there. There hadn't been any sign he was going to faint, no comment about feeling ill or even a loss of colour. The way he fell was like someone had simply switched him off; he was in an untidy heap with his legs crumpled beneath him, and his head had struck the carpet tiles with a loud thud.

"Shit." Sam crouched next to him, shook his shoulder. "Jim?"

He was far too still. Sam thought of all the times he'd seen people collapse in films, how the ones finding the body checked their pulse. He fumbled with the man's wrist and couldn't find one. With growing desperation he pressed the side of his neck but still couldn't find a pulse.

He ran back to the office and picked up the phone.

"What's wrong?" Dave asked.

"That bloke," Sam panted, dialling 999. "He just dropped dead in the kitchen."

Max dreamt that a woman was looking down at him as he lay on a cloud. Sometimes she turned into a man. Both wore blue and he wondered if they had something to do with the sky.

The man changed back into a woman with blonde hair but not the one he was looking for. This one was older and plumper and writing something down on a clipboard.

"Oh, you're awake. How are you feeling?"

He was slowly becoming aware of an intense pain in his right leg and hip, his shoulder, then it flooded his entire body.

"In pain," he said.

"You're in hospital," she said. "And you're a very lucky man."

"Do lucky men get shot?"

She chuckled and came to his bedside, pressing something into his hand. "This controls your morphine. When the pain is too much just press the button. You can't overdose, don't worry."

"I'm not worried," he replied, trying to lift his head to look down at his body. The blanket didn't look right.

"I'll tell the doctor you've woken up. And the police want to speak to you when you're up to it."

He nodded and she left. The room was small, the walls yellow, strange equipment was positioned near his bed and a black box he suspected was a television was bolted high up in a corner on the opposite side of the room. He stared up at the grey tiles on the ceiling.

Something felt distinctly wrong with his body and he was struggling to just hold onto the button she'd given him.

There was a window to his left that was open a crack. He could hear the city, birds, aircraft roaring overheard. There was also a scraping noise he couldn't explain, but no matter how much he wanted to get up and investigate, his body wouldn't cooperate.

He pressed the button, the pain eased and it felt as if he was floating. He dozed.

The door clicking shut woke him and another woman was looking at the clipboard. She wore a white coat, had long black hair tied back and her skin was a deep brown. She looked tired.

"How are you feeling?" she asked, glancing up at him.

"Something's wrong," he said. "This button is helping with the pain."

"Good." She moved nearer to his head, looking at monitors. "You've been badly hurt, Mr…"

He frowned. This wasn't right. He was in Mundanus! Why wasn't he at the cloister? Why hadn't the clean-up team dealt with all this? All he could remember was the gun's mouth and the wind nipping at his ears as he realised he was about to be shot by another Arbiter. He wasn't even sure what there was to clean up apart from himself.

"Do you remember your name?"

He had to be careful, so he shook his head.

She made a note on the clipboard. "You didn't have any identification on you, no missing persons have been reported who fit your description. I'm afraid we don't know your name either."

"How about John for now?"

"All right. The police want to speak to you for obvious reasons. I don't need to know why you were shot on a roof, I just get to put you back together again."

He nodded. "I understand."

"Well, I get the impression you'd like me to just tell it to you straight, is that right?"

He nodded again, pressed the button.

"The bullet grazed your left shoulder. You're very lucky they were a poor shot."

Arbiters were never poor shots. He filed that away.

"Unsurprisingly you fell. The trees below helped a little but you still fell a very long way. You came in yesterday afternoon and we've had to operate. Your right tibia and fibula were broken in two places. The bones have been aligned and set with plates and screws." She paused, clearly looking for some sort of reaction. There was none. He could hear that scraping sound outside again. She glanced at one of the monitors and carried on. "Your hip was dislocated too, that's been corrected. There's lots of bruising and you had a bad knock on the head, but considering the fall I think you were incredibly lucky."

"What are the plates and screws made of?"

"Titanium. It's very strong and doesn't–"

"Will the titanium be taken out again when the leg is healed?"

"We'll discuss that with the orthopaedic surgeon when he does his follow-up, but I imagine the plates will stay in place for at least eighteen months. Sometimes it's more risky to take out than leave in, but the options will be discussed with you thoroughly."

Mundanus seemed to be advancing more quickly as the years went by. Did the Sorcerers know about titanium being used like this? Had they come to an agreement with the Elemental Court? He was finding it hard to keep focused. "How long will I be in here?"

"At least another two weeks. The surgery went well, the gunshot wound has been stitched up and shouldn't be problematic, but we need to make sure your recovery stays on track and that there's no infection."

"How long until I can walk?"

"You mustn't put any weight on your leg for at least six weeks, but you'll be taught how to use crutches. You may be able to walk with a cane in about two months, if there are no complications and if you follow the advice and physiotherapist's instructions."

He was making her uneasy. He was used to that. Normally he wouldn't have such a long conversation with an innocent, as it always unnerved them to speak to someone like him.

"I'm just taking it all in," he said to alleviate her discomfort, but it didn't work. It didn't bother him, but the more unnerved she was, the less likely she was to be helpful in any way outside her normal role. He might need her help if the police were going to be a problem.

"I'll check on you during my round tomorrow. The police will be in later. There's a button on the wall if you need anything. I'm sure the nurse will check on you soon too."

She left without a smile or further words of reassurance. He was used to that as well; they tended to be cold when there was nothing back from him.

So the Arbiter with the gun missed. He felt his neck although he already knew the chain wasn't there. Was it still on that gargoyle at the clock tower? Or was it in the hands of the London Chapter as evidence of interference? For all he knew, the fallout from that afternoon could still be playing out. Something was wrong; he shouldn't have been brought to a hospital in Mundanus, and presumably he was still in London. Why hadn't the London Arbiters come for him here?

He couldn't believe how tired he felt. Just lying there, pressing a little button and trying to fathom out what had happened, was exhausting. He lay his head on the pillow, simply unable to find any answers in his current state.

As he drifted off, the scraping outside the window got louder. A clunk from the window as it was opened brought him back from the edge of sleep.

An ugly stone face peered inside. It was the gargoyle from the clock tower, and Max's soul chain was still around its neck. For a moment, he considered that a good thing. Then he realised he wasn't in contact with the stone, and it seemed to be moving independently. He wondered if the morphine was making him hallucinate. As far as he knew, movement only occurred in deep connection when physical contact was maintained.

He remained silent as the gargoyle, seeing a room empty of medical staff, pushed the window further open and climbed inside. The legs, which had been fused together to form its attachment to the clock tower, had split and become functional. It looked like a long, lean stone panther with prominent ribs and a demonic face. A very worried demonic face.

It clunked over to the bed, jumped up on the metal frame and settled into a natural perching position, looming over Max's legs. Its weight made the bed shudder. "Well, this is a bloody disaster!"

"It's definitely unusual," Max replied.

"I'm not talking about me, I'm talking about that!" It had the voice of a man who smoked fifty a day and gargled with gravel. A clawed finger pointed at the broken leg beneath the domed blanket. "We're corrupted now. It's a sodding catastrophe!"

"One thing at a time." Max recognised his soul's taste for drama. "What happened to the Arbiter? Why did he miss?"

"Because of me." The gargoyle grinned. Max was certain that most innocents would find its face even more frightening when he did that. "I wasn't going to let that rotten Arbiter finish us off. I whipped us round out of his line of fire, still caught your shoulder though."

"What happened to him?"

"Ahh, well, I played it cool at first; I wanted to see what he did. I think getting hurt when we were linked was too much for you. You passed out on my back and he must've thought you were dead. I knew the Chapter Master was on the case, I could feel it, so I watched. I was worried he'd come over and throw you off, but when you didn't move the rat that shot you connected using one of the other gargoyles on the tower. Swift as you like, he told his Chapter Master you'd sprung them and it was bad."

Max scratched his new beard. "So it's as high as the London Chapter Master? You sure it was him?"

"Who else would he connect with?"

"I don't know. Then what happened?"

"That's where it got a bit hairy." Its huge stone brow furrowed. "He came to knock you off and get our chain. So I had to knock him off first."

"He's dead?"

"I reckon. He landed on the hard bit at the bottom. And you fell, when I was dealing with him. Sorry about that. I couldn't catch you. It took a while to realise I could still move after we broke contact. He didn't land on the trees like you did. There was a *splut*." Its muzzle wrinkled at the memory. "Not nice. Then there was screaming and blue lights and I expected the Chapter Master to send someone through pretty sharpish, but then…" Its stone shoulders heaved a shrug. "Then it all went… wrong."

"Wrong?"

"It felt very bad… the bit of us that could still feel the cloister… something bad happened there, and then we were fully here. Not there at all."

"Has the Chapter Master been in contact at all? In Mundanus or via a messenger?"

"No, that's not it." The gargoyle shook its head. "I don't think the Chapter is there any more. I think someone... broke it."

Max looked back up at the grey tiles as he struggled to think despite the morphine haze. "How does someone break a Chapter? Maybe..."

"Look, we reported a serious breach, we showed the Chapter Master a kidnap in progress with the support of the London Arbiters and nothing happens? The Chapter is either cut off or just not there any more. Either way, we're on our own."

"Have the London Arbiters followed up?"

"The mundane police got there faster than they did. They were distracted by something, maybe cutting off the Bath Chapter. I don't know. Anyway, you were brought here and so was the one who shot you. But the London Arbiters busted him out of the morgue."

"How do you know?"

"I've been listening to the police talking. They want to know what you were doing at the top of the hotel."

"I'm not worried about that," Max muttered.

"Of course you're not, I'm worried for both of us." The gargoyle jabbed its clawed thumb at its chest. "In fact, I passed worried several hours ago and I'm well into the land of seriously frightened. This is bad enough without us being corrupted." It sniffed at the blanket. "We can't walk around with titanium in us for eighteen months."

"I don't have much of a choice. At least not until I get back to the cloister."

"If it's still there." The gargoyle's voice matched its grim expression. "And I'm not sure it is, otherwise how could we be having this conversation?"

"Then I'll go straight to the Sorcerer and tell him and see if he'll take it out."

"Are you mad?" The gargoyle's twitch made the bed shake.

"He'll kill us!"

"I have to report it."

"These are unusual circumstances, and look, if the Bath Chapter has been cut off – or worse, we're the only ones who know what's going on here..." The gargoyle lowered its head and extended its stone body to lean over him as it had out of the clock tower. Its stone teeth were only inches from Max's nose. "If you tell the Sorcerer about the titanium, he won't listen and more innocents will be taken. You know what he's like."

"It's a good argument," Max said, and the gargoyle withdrew. "We have to leave before the London Chapter knows where I am; they won't be distracted for long."

Mustering all the effort he could, he sat up and pulled the blanket, and the frame designed to keep it off his bandaged leg, off the bed. He frowned at the hospital gown, wondered where his clothes were. His coat and hat were hung on the back of the door. They'd suffice in the short term. He started to get out of bed.

The gargoyle howled. "Stop! Stop! Oh! The pain, stop!" It was gripping the sides of its head, its stone eyes rolling like marbles in cups.

Max was aware of the pain too. It was rather extreme. He lay back down, scrabbled for the button and pressed it.

"We're not going anywhere yet," he said, breathless, as the gargoyle whimpered. "You'd better go back outside; you made enough noise to bring every goddamn nurse in this hospital here."

He watched the gargoyle leap across to the window ledge as little blue pinpricks of light peppered the outer edges of his vision. "Keep a lookout," he added, his words slurring.

"Just keep pressing that button," the gargoyle muttered as it climbed back outside. "And hope that Lord Titanium doesn't take an interest."

7

It took two cups of tea and half a bowl of noodles to fortify Cathy enough to pick up the letters and take them through to the front room. She flicked on the light, comforted briefly by the shelves of DVDs, books and the life-size cardboard cut-out of Han Solo standing in the corner.

She dumped the letters on the sofa, closed the curtains and put on the TV. Somehow checking that all of the things she'd set to record whilst she was working at the Emporium seemed so much more important than reading her mother's words. After another sideways glance at the letters, rearranging her entire book and DVD collection alphabetically took on a sudden urgency. She scanned the shelves, dithered over the *Battlestar Galactica* box set for a few moments before plucking out *Aliens* instead. Survival horror seemed more appropriate.

Finally she mustered the courage to read the letters. She had considered burning them, but she'd only wonder what had been said, and besides, if her mother realised she hadn't read a single word when she got back, it would only make things worse.

Cathy turned the pile upside down so the top one would be the first sent. If she was going to do this properly, she needed to see the progression.

She noted the wax seal and quality of the paper. A dull throb was building behind her eyes as she picked it up. She turned it over and read the elegant calligraphy.

Miss Catherine Rhoeas-Papaver,
Where-so-ever-you-are
Mundanus

She shuddered at the sight of her mother's handwriting. Something about the slant of the upward strokes in "Where-so-ever-you-are" conveyed her mother's irritation at her being so difficult to contact and the sight of her full name brought back her old life with a monstrous clarity.

She broke the seal and opened it out. The red poppy of her family's crest was emblazoned at the top of the paper. The date was one week after she'd cast the Shadow Charm and fled Cambridge.

Dear Catherine,

I have no idea what you think you are doing, but I've received a letter from your former chaperone informing me of her resignation and giving profuse apologies that she was unable to improve your wilful nature. She had more courage than your minder who has singularly failed in his duty to keep you safe and seems to have absconded.

I do hope the two of you are not together, lost in the foolish romantic notion of running away to elope. I will be able to keep this from your father for less than a week, so I suggest you return immediately and explain to me why you have abandoned the university course you demanded so brazenly. It embarrassed us immensely to have to acquiesce to such a selfish and unreasonable request. The Patroon was not impressed as you well know.

Do not make this worse. Come back before your father realises what you have done, otherwise I am sure you can predict his response.

Your Mother

Cathy folded the letter and slipped it back into the envelope. It was too easy to predict her father's reaction when he saw her again and she didn't want to think about it. She sucked in a deep breath and made herself eat the rest of the noodles. As she twisted them around her fork she remembered when Josh had introduced them to her as a good thing to keep in the cupboard. They only needed boiling water and were quick to make, as he demonstrated. That was the first afternoon they'd spent together after he came across her in the laundry room of the first-year halls of residence. She was standing in front of the machine with a palm full of coins trying to read the instructions without looking like she had no idea what she was doing.

"Are you OK?" he'd asked and made her jump, sending the coins rolling in all directions. She hadn't got used to men just being able to come and talk to her when she was unchaperoned and her inherent shyness wasn't making it easy to get used to.

They picked up the coins together. She liked his smile and his soft brown eyes. He was skinny and tall and when they stood up again after collecting the errant coins she only came up to his shoulder even though she wasn't exactly short herself.

"Want me to show you how they work?" he offered and she nodded. "You put two fifty-pence pieces in here. Is the powder in?"

She blinked at him. Only two powders sprung to mind: face powder and the powder used in pistols for duelling and she was certain it couldn't be either of them. She regretted not having her laptop and wished she'd Googled it all before leaving her room.

"Washing powder?" he said slowly.

"Oh, is that what goes in that tray bit?"

"So your mum did all your washing then? I've got some you can use, give me the fifty pences."

She searched through the coins in her palm, still getting used to handling change. He gawped at her. "Have you been living abroad or something?"

"...Sort of," she replied and managed an awkward smile. When he returned it the constant terror she'd felt for the past two weeks subsided. Even though she'd spent an academic year at Cambridge, the maid her family insisted on sending with her dealt with all the practical matters, including all the things involving small change. She researched as much as she could before running away, but it was impossible to learn about every aspect of life in Mundanus, and the more time she spent there the more she realised how ill-prepared she was.

He helped her with the washing machines and chatted as they waited. That was the first time she lied about where she'd come from to someone she wanted to spend time with, and it made her guts knot as she lied again and again, weaving threads of lies to make an unusual but plausible story.

The noodles finished, Cathy turned her attention back to the letters. The next one was similar to the first, only more angry, so she chucked it aside. In the third her mother detailed how the minder had finally turned up, cap in hand, and had been interrogated by her father.

He assures us that there were no signs of your plans to leave, and only the brief note you left apologising for the inconvenience is

stopping us from assuming you've been kidnapped. Your father has
not ruled out that possibility, so for goodness sake, Catherine, return
home immediately and explain yourself before we're forced to report
this to the Patroon.

Cathy shook her head at the empty threat. There was no
way in the split worlds they'd go to the Patroon and tell him
their wayward daughter had run away. She wondered what
they'd been telling him. They were lucky he was such a relic
and had no real understanding of life in Mundanus anymore.
He was hundreds of years old and had no concept of how
much the world had changed as he spent all of his time in the
Nether. They'd be able to string him along perfectly well until
he suspected something and asked for verification from one
of the other Papaver lines. If that happened, her family would
be in serious trouble.

That made her pause. Was that guilt she felt?

She ripped open the next letter, dated a month after
she'd left.

Dear Catherine,

We are beside ourselves with worry and missing you terribly.

Rubbish, Cathy thought, but carried on reading.

I know you must be afraid to come back, but I want you to know
I understand this isn't your fault. You were corrupted at a tender
age by Miss Rainer. Ultimately, the blame lies with me for letting
that evil woman into our household, and I will never forgive myself.
*   Her wicked scheme to put the most ridiculous ideas into your*
head and expose you to entirely unsuitable literature is what
brought about this terrible situation we find ourselves in.

The words blurred. Miss Rainer. Every single day she wondered what had happened to her old governess. "Ridiculous ideas, Mother?" she muttered under her breath. "I suppose you would call human rights and women's suffrage ridiculous." Cathy looked up at the bookshelves, filled with "unsuitable literature": science fiction, fantasy, volumes of political discourse and social history, feminist masterpieces and graphic novels. Pride of place, with a shelf all of their own, were the works of HG Wells, Jules Verne, the *Dune* novels, Asimov and all the others Miss Rainer had smuggled in and hidden under her pillow. Not the originals. They'd been ripped apart and burnt by her father. She could still feel his hand on her throat and smell the burning paper as he'd forced her to watch.

Everything had changed that day. It was hard to believe it had been over four years ago; the memory of it was so fresh. She remembered the beating that had taken weeks to recover from fully, the hours alone, locked in her room, sobbing until the turn of the key in the lock made her wipe her eyes and sit up straight and be polite to whoever came in, be it her mother or the maid. She recalled the hours her mother had spent coaching her in the lead-up to her coming of age, the sleepless nights spent weighing up whether to play by the rules or risk everything on asking for the wrong boon.

It had taken months to get to university. They'd had to say yes, it was the family tradition, but most good little Papaver children diligently requested whatever their parents had told them to.

Cambridge was a stepping stone to freedom; it gave her the chance to get out of the family home, which was her first objective, and saved her from the stress of being launched onto the social scene in Aquae Sulis. Whilst she didn't have the same freedom as all of the other students there, she had enough exposure to others in lectures and her tutorial partners to learn enough about Mundanus to know where to look for more information. Everyone had computers and it didn't take much persuasion to convince her minder she needed one for the course. A fellow student bought a dongle for her and helped her get online in return for lunch, and that was the breakthrough she needed. It took a year in Cambridge to plan and execute her escape to Manchester and it had worked perfectly, until that bastard Shopkeeper had ruined it all by tipping off Lord Poppy.

Cathy still had no idea what happened to Miss Rainer. After the night her father found the books hidden in her room all of her lessons stopped, but she'd learnt enough to know that she could never live the same life as her mother.

She went back to the letter.

Your absence has cast a shadow over our household and I am worried about how this is affecting Elizabeth.

Cathy snorted. Her younger sister was probably still gloating about her victory and was glad that her plain older sister wasn't there to jeopardise her chances of a good marriage. Cathy would never forgive Elizabeth for what she did.

Thomas hasn't been the same since he learned of your disappearance and asks whether there has been any news every evening. He's lost weight with worry. I beg you to consider your brother and his feelings, Catherine. I know how close you are.

It was a low blow and the guilt brought tears with it. She wept at the thought of what Tom must think of her, how he must hate her now for being such a coward and fleeing instead of sticking it out like him. But then he was a son and the eldest child; it was different for him. He wasn't seen as a piece of property but as the heir apparent.

She shoved the rest of the letters onto the floor and let herself curl into a ball. She imagined calling Josh, asking him to come over and telling him everything and somehow coming up with a new solution, but that was a stupid fantasy. Even if he did believe her tale of secret families with Fae patrons living just outside of everyday reality, she would only endanger him. She wanted to be held, to smell his aftershave and talk about Xbox games and music and do all the stuff that any other student at the same university could do. A week from now she'd be back in Aquae Sulis in her family's grip once more and she would never see Josh again.

She needed a big cup of tea. She wiped her face and blew her nose on the way back to the kitchen. She needed to think, not cry like some helpless woman. Did Ripley fall apart when they were trapped on an alien-infested base with no rescue for days and limited supplies? "No, she did not," she said out loud.

Dealing with her family wasn't as bad as facing aliens with acid for blood, but they were still an unavoidable horror. And failure to impress Lord Poppy would lead to a worse fate than having to face her father again.

As the kettle boiled for the next round of tea, she leaned against the worktop and turned her mind to what she could possibly wish for. The Fae lords and ladies were fickle and fundamentally inhuman. How the Patroons managed to keep them happy she had no idea. She'd spent as little time as possible thinking about politics and the struggles of the Great Families when she was growing up in their world, and for the first time in her life she regretted it. The problem wasn't a lack of ideas; like all Fae-touched children she'd diligently spent days of her early years dreaming up clever wish combinations just in case. She'd never prepared any to impress a Fae, however.

She made the tea, stirred in the milk. There was no one to ask for help, no books to consult, no website designed for fellow escapees of the bizarre Fae-touched life. If only she knew what would–

"That's it!" she said with a laugh. "It's so obvious!" She took a sip of tea and then a deep breath. "I wish–"

With a tiny pop and a shower of poppy petals, the faerie appeared, just above the pedal bin, making Cathy squeak in surprise and drop her mug. It smashed on the lino, the brown liquid landing in the shape of a faerie's silhouette.

"That's not funny," she said to the tiny creature. "How did you get into my flat?" As far as Cathy knew, the Fae and their minions could only get into Mundanus from the Nether, and her flat had no reflection there.

The faerie ignored her question. "You were about to make your first wish," it said in its melodic voice. "I want to know what it is."

"Because you're the one who grants it on Lord Poppy's behalf?"

"I want to watch you make your first mistake." She glanced around the kitchen, wrinkling her tiny nose. "Mundanus smells horrid. Why would anyone ever want to live here? There must be something very wrong with you."

"Do you want me to make this wish or not?"

The faerie clapped its hands. "Yes, I do!"

"I wish I knew how to impress Lord Poppy," Cathy said boldly, pleased with her choice.

A pulse of magic swept out from the faerie as she cast the wish into the world. It looked like a ripple of sparkling water rushing out from her, making Cathy's skin tingle as it passed through her. She held her breath for the answer.

"See you soon," the faerie chirruped.

"What?" Cathy gasped. "My wish first! Tell me how to impress him!"

"Oh, that." The faerie shrugged. "The wish is cast. My work is done."

"But!" Cathy fought not to stammer. "But you haven't told me."

"You never wished for *that*." The faerie stuck out its tiny tongue. "You mortals never learn. You only wished to *know*. You didn't specify *when*."

8

Max slept for over an hour after the police officers left and when he woke his mouth tasted as if something had crawled in there and died.

The police were frustrated but he'd argued that whilst he might have been trespassing on the roof of the hotel, he was still a victim of a gunshot wound rather than a perpetrator. There wasn't much else to go on until various reports arrived, and he suspected they'd want to bury it rather than have to admit the perpetrator's body had gone missing. He noted they neglected to mention that when they interviewed him.

He waited for a nurse and asked if there was a telephone he could use nearby. When she offered to wheel one in he accepted, adding a request for a local telephone directory and a pair of crutches.

"It's a little soon to be using those," she said.

"I've used them before," he lied. "I want to see if I can remember how to do it."

She eventually relented, probably so she didn't have to keep talking to him.

He had to leave before the other Arbiters came for him, and, without support from the Chapter, the only choice was to go directly to Mr Ekstrand, the Sorcerer of Wessex. Max was fortunate that he'd been picked to run the field tests on the glasses (now missing and potentially in an evidence bag somewhere); he was the only Arbiter apart from the Chapter Master who knew where to enter the Nether to find the Sorcerer's house.

Two hours later he was sitting in a white van listening to an innocent talk about the last removals job he'd had. The gargoyle, masquerading as an eccentric garden ornament, was safely loaded in the back and they were heading down the M4 motorway towards Bath.

The conversation was one-sided and that suited Max perfectly. All he'd had to do was explain how he'd had an accident trying to move the gargoyle for a friend, pay the man all the money he had and they were on the road, no more questions asked.

Sweating from the pain, he drifted in and out, his thumb twitching for the morphine button left behind. He had a sense of his coat being too light and patted his pockets. They were empty. Occasionally he thought he could hear scuffs and knocks in the back of the van as the gargoyle fidgeted, but nothing made the driver break his monologue.

The city of Bath was mercifully quiet by the time they arrived. He directed the driver to a street as close as he dared, explaining that a friend would pick him and the statue up. Gargoyle unloaded onto the pavement, hands shaken, wishes of the best offered and Max found himself on a dark road at the edge of Bath.

He looked at the gargoyle. There were two of them briefly. "I can't bear this pain much longer," it said. "Let's find Ekstrand's house. Wait a second." It reached into one of Max's coat pockets and its muzzle wrinkled as it pulled its paw back out again. "Our stuff, what happened to our stuff?" It was rubbing its claws together. "And where did all this powder come from?"

"Ekstrand's first," Max said and limped along on his crutches, heading towards the end of the street. Expecting trouble, he sent the gargoyle off into the shadows when he heard a car pull up where the van had been but moments before.

The click of his crutches on the pavement was much slower than the brisk clip of shoes behind him. He focused on making it to the anchor property as quickly as he could without passing out. There was a scrape of stone on tarmac, a loud thud and then the gargoyle was at his side, taking a crutch and half holding him up.

"Was it an Arbiter?"

"Yeah," it replied. "Ex Arbiter."

"You killed him?"

"I dunno. I think so. He was crooked anyway. He was pulling a silenced gun on you, would've shot you in the back."

"We could have questioned him."

"Oh. Sorry about that. Distracted." It pointed at the leg in the velcro support. "I'll clean up after you're somewhere safe. Get painkillers. Lots of them, OK? Any flavour."

Max nodded. He saw familiar gates up ahead and the gargoyle didn't need to be told what to do. It went ahead, bounding down the street and sounding like a stonemason's hammer.

The gargoyle held up the soul chain, brandishing the Sorcerer's seal and speaking the words to open the Way. There was a faint shimmer; the gates looked as if they were reflected in water. Max doggedly made the final metres, his shirt soaking wet beneath his suit, his hands blistering on the wooden crutch handles.

The gargoyle helped him step through into the Nether. Max was in so much pain he barely noticed the change in air.

The Sorcerer's house looked exactly the same as the anchor property; a large Georgian mansion in extensive grounds. But the stars were gone, as was the moon, the sky above them the pale misty silver of the Nether.

The door to the house opened and Max expected the butler to step out but the librarian hurried out onto the drive instead.

She was blonde too. What's with all the blondes? he thought, now aware of a ringing in his ears.

"It's Max, isn't it?" she said. "From the Bath Chapter?"

He managed a nod.

"Oh, you look terrible. Let me help you." She came closer.

Her hair was the colour of sunlight. He wanted to touch it. That didn't seem right. He'd never wanted to touch a woman's hair. She was slender as cigar smoke in a still room, her curves in the right places and very pleasant to the eye. She wore kitten heels and a suit straight out of the best of the Forties' movies. He wanted popcorn and to stand there watching her all day.

"What are you doing with that statue?"

The gargoyle moved and she yelped.

"Hello, beautiful." Its grin made her shudder.

"Slight problem," Max said as she gawped at it. "Need to see the Sorcerer."

"I... I see. It's not one of his better days," she said, keeping an eye on the leering gargoyle. "Come in so Axon can give you some help. You look very ill."

"It's urgent," he added as one of the crutches clattered to the ground and the gargoyle shifted to take most of his weight.

"Come inside," she said and ran ahead calling for the butler.

The gargoyle helped him towards the house. "She's hot."

"She's the librarian," Max replied, struggling to manage the worry about his injuries and the first waves of lust he'd experienced since his soul's dislocation. Both seemed to be seeping into him through his physical contact with the gargoyle.

"A librarian? Even better. She could improve my mind at the same time."

He recognised the butler, Axon, as he came out and supported his other arm.

"Good evening sir," he said, as if a man on crutches being half carried by an animated statue were a normal arrival.

"Sorry about the gargoyle, Axon." Max remembered he was a nice guy, for a butler.

"It's no trouble sir," Axon replied and Max believed him. This was probably quite dull for a Sorcerer's butler.

"If you two can manage, I need to clean that..." The gargoyle's stone eyebrows twitched back in the direction of the gates.

Max nodded. "Bring the body here."

"A body too, sir?" Axon enquired. Max nodded. "Very good, sir."

Max made it into the house and was steered towards a large, familiar sitting room. It was cluttered with several lifetimes' worth of objects. On his previous visit, a collection of tiny ivory figurines had caught his eye. This time it was a clock lying partially dismantled on the writing desk in the corner of the room. The room smelt of camphor, a hint of engine oil and wood smoke from the fire.

Two overstuffed sofas dominated the centre and he was eased onto one of them. Axon excused himself, promising to return swiftly, then the librarian reappeared, carrying a bowl and some muslin cloths.

"It's Petra, isn't it?" he asked as she rearranged cushions and then helped him to take off his coat and jacket, and eased him down to lie flat.

"That's right." She smiled. "What happened to you?"

"Got shot and fell off a clock tower."

"Oh dear."

She rinsed out the cloth and wiped his forehead. The cloth was cool, and for the first time since waking up in that hospital Max felt unlikely to die any time soon. With the gargoyle elsewhere he was free of emotional distractions once more.

Axon returned with a large leather doctor's bag and Petra left the damp cloth on his forehead, promising to look for the Sorcerer. Something happened involving a syringe and the blissfully fuzzy feeling returned as he floated away from the pain.

"Is the gargoyle back?" he asked.

"It's in the parlour," Axon replied. "I thought it better to warn Mr Ekstrand first, rather than an animated statue be happened upon unprepared in the receiving room."

"And the body?"

"All taken care of, sir. May I suggest a restorative cup of tea and some light refreshments?"

Max nodded.

"I will prepare a room for you too, sir. I imagine you will be staying here tonight."

"No, I'll go back to the cloister when I'm done."

Axon conveyed concern, impending bad news and slight embarrassment at having to contradict a guest, all with just a minor adjustment of his eyebrows, in that way only butlers can. "I will leave that discussion to Mr Ekstrand." He turned to go and then paused. "I assume the gargoyle does not require refreshments?"

"I don't think so. Should it?"

"I imagine not, sir, being of a stone constitution, but I find it best to never assume anything when it comes to matters of unnatural animation."

Max watched him go, feeling exhaustion lapping at his edges in little waves. He almost drifted off to sleep, but the arrival of the promised tea perked him up.

"I really do think you should speak to him, Mr Ekstrand. He may have important information." Petra's voice drifted in from the hall as he stuffed a sandwich into his mouth.

There was a low mumble, then Axon's voice adding to the mix. Max struggled into a seated position, breaking into a sweat again. He wondered if he'd ever be able to do anything without soaking his shirt.

"He needs rest, sir. I think it advisable to have a brief conversation with him now so that he may be taken to his room to recuperate."

"Very well." Mr Ekstrand came to the doorway. He looked very different compared to the last time Max had visited. Instead of an elegantly cut Edwardian suit, the Sorcerer was wearing loose cotton trousers made from un-dyed linen and a loose smock-style shirt. Both looked handmade, the design favouring comfort over style. He was barefoot, and around his neck hung close to three dozen pendants of different shapes and colours, each of them a magical artefact.

Ekstrand's long face was in keeping with his tall and thin frame, his black hair was in disarray and he hadn't shaved that day. This was not the image that Sorcerers tended to offer of themselves. Max had the distinct impression he'd arrived at a bad time.

"I recognise you." The Sorcerer pointed a long index finger at him from the doorway. "You're the one I gave the glasses to."

"Yes, sir," Max replied. "Please excuse me for not getting up, I–"

"Did they work?"

"What?"

"The glasses, fool!"

"Yes, they did. But I need to tell you–"

"Where are they?" Ekstrand came into the room, but stayed some distance away from Max's sofa. "Are they in your pocket?"

"No, sir, I was shot and fell from a clock tower and when I woke in the hospital they were gone."

"Gone!" Ekstrand shrieked. "They were with you yesterday, in Mundanus?"

Max nodded.

Ekstrand groaned. "They were unique!"

"Tea, sir?" Axon picked up the teapot. Ekstrand peered at it suspiciously.

"It is Assam, isn't it, Axon?"

"Indeed, sir."

"All right," he muttered and started to pace. "It's all happening at the same time. I never did trust Sundays and this only adds weight to my theory."

Petra followed him in and sat down with a notepad and pen. "Mr Ekstrand, I understand how troublesome Sundays can be, but I really do think you ought to sit down, have a cup of tea and listen to what Max has to say. It's very important."

Ekstrand scowled at Petra for a moment and then relented, sitting down stiffly on the opposite sofa. Axon poured the tea as the Sorcerer peered over the tray at Max.

"Are you here to apologise for losing my glasses?"

"No, sir. I'm here because I think something has happened to the Chapter."

Ekstrand's eyes narrowed. "You do, eh?" He accepted the cup and saucer presented to him by the butler and sipped at the tea. He visibly relaxed. "I'll listen to you. It goes against all my rules, but when Petra and Axon agree on something being an emergency on a Sunday evening I'd be foolish not to listen. Battenberg?"

Max nodded. He started at the beginning, explaining how Montgomery had got in touch, how he'd got permission from the Chapter Master to go and investigate purely off the record. He described the connections he'd made with the Judd Street agency, how the Arbiter had sat back as the kidnapping took place, the gunshot on the roof of the hotel.

Ekstrand listened attentively as he chewed on the pink and yellow cake, Petra taking notes all the while. As he'd agreed with the gargoyle, Max didn't mention the titanium pins in his leg. Seeing the Sorcerer dressed so strangely made him suspect he'd made the right decision. Then he told him about the gargoyle.

"And that's why I came straight to you," he said as Axon took his plate and refilled his teacup. "I think the gargoyle... situation is an indication of something happening to the Chapter, as well as the lack of support and clean-up in London."

Ekstrand handed his cake plate to Axon, rubbing his chin thoughtfully. "Where is this gargoyle, Axon?"

"In the parlour, sir."

"Bring it in here. And be careful."

Ekstrand stared at Max as they waited for the gargoyle to be brought in. Max stared back, wondering why the Sorcerer seemed so different from the capable and brilliant man who'd given him the glasses just days before. Had something happened to him too?

"Do you know if something has happened to the Chapter, sir?" he asked.

"I'm not going to talk to you about it. How do I know you're not responsible?" Ekstrand replied.

"Mr Ekstrand," Petra said, her voice as smooth as a fine single malt. "Max needs our help."

The Sorcerer pursed his lips and said nothing more until Axon returned with the gargoyle. Ekstrand leapt to his feet, eyes wide as the gargoyle gave a small, awkward wave.

"Evening," it gravelled.

"In all the worlds," Ekstrand whispered. "I have never seen its like."

The gargoyle winked at Petra who looked down at her notepad.

"Do you… feel anything?" Ekstrand asked.

"Glad to be here," the gargoyle replied. "It was getting a bit hairy at the hospital. I kept seeing Arbiters in all the shadows. One tried to kill us on the way here, you know. A London Arbiter. In Bath. It's not right, I tell you."

"And how do you explain your state?" the Sorcerer asked, getting closer.

"We were connected," it said, jerking a claw towards Max. "Up on the clock tower."

"As I said, I was using a deep connection to gather evidence for the Chapter Master," Max said, watching the Sorcerer just as carefully as the gargoyle was.

Ekstrand nodded. "That's the only reason you're still alive. The soul vessels in the Cloister were destroyed, as far as I can tell, but you were in such close contact, the connection pulled your soul into Mundanus, into this gargoyle."

The gargoyle's mouth dropped open. "Destroyed?" It clutched the sides of its head. "What about the others?"

"All the Arbiters in the field dropped dead. I have no idea what happened to the rest; there's been no contact."

"That's… oh, shit… that's terrible!"

"It's most certainly inconvenient. Luckily for you," he said to Max, "I added an extra function to my formula, detailing that the soul chains should only be destroyed if the Arbiter were dead. Otherwise you'd have died too. Now you're the only Arbiter left from the Bath Chapter."

Max recalled the powder in his pockets. "You worked a formula to destroy our field equipment?"

"Of course. Arbiters were dropping dead in Mundanus, I couldn't have mundane authorities finding a Peeper and working out what it was for. I should have added an exclusion clause for my glasses though."

The gargoyle sank down onto its haunches and looked as if it was trying to cry. Without tears it just looked miserable and made an awful rasping sound deep in its throat.

"Absolutely fascinating," commented Ekstrand, observing its distress. "And a terrible liability. If any of the Fae or their puppets were to get hold of him, we'd be in a lot of trouble. And you," he pointed at Max, "would be susceptible to their magic. The gargoyle has to stay here. We can't have your soul chain running around independently of you."

"Can't we take it off it?" Max asked.

"Too much of a risk for now. It's probably the only thing keeping your soul inside it. You wouldn't want to lose your connection."

"And what about me?"

"I suppose you'll have to stay as well," Ekstrand said, clearly not happy about it. "You're practically useless in your current state, and you have no cloister to be healed in."

Max nodded. "I'm the only eyewitness. When you approach the Essex Sorcerer you'll need me to give evidence."

Ekstrand shook his head. "Not for that, for something in Bath, or rather Aquae Sulis. One of the most important people in Fae-touched society has disappeared, and with all this nonsense going on I haven't had anyone to investigate it."

"But there are innocents being taken in London," Max said. "There are corrupt Arbiters and now they've destroyed the Bath Chapter to cover it up."

"Don't you care?" the gargoyle asked. "Arbiters are supposed to be incorruptible, how has this even happened?

What else are they up to in London? Why are they working with the Rosa family?"

"I'll deal with that another time," Ekstrand said, irritated.

"Another time?" the gargoyle straightened up. "It has to be dealt with now, before more innocents are taken!"

"You," Ekstrand pointed at the gargoyle's chest, "are nothing more than a dislocated soul trapped in an ugly statue and have no right to question my judgement. Besides, any sane individual knows it's utter madness to deal with any serious problems on a Sunday." He scratched his head and shivered. "Which reminds me, I need to check the wards, especially with the two of you in the house. Axon, find suitable arrangements for these two, would you?"

"Yes, sir."

"I haven't finished with you," he said, giving Max one last suspicious look, and then hurried out of the room.

Max dropped his head back on the sofa cushions. Ekstrand was more concerned about a Fae puppet than his Chapter, Arbiters had tried to kill him – twice – and he was corrupted with Titanium. It hadn't been the best weekend. The gargoyle's head settled on the arm of the sofa with a suitably grim expression.

"The Sorcerer of Wessex is mad as a nail," the gargoyle whispered. "We're buggered."

9

Cathy watched the sun come up over the city. Everything she did was punctuated by a sense of finality. This might be the last time she saw in the dawn in Manchester. This might be the last morning she woke as a free woman. This was the last day she would ever see Josh.

She had to end it. Her family could turn up any moment, and she wanted to make sure Josh didn't worry about her after she'd gone. She didn't want to do to him what she'd done to her family a year before. Again, the guilt. She banged her forehead against the window gently, hating herself.

Perhaps this is what it's like when you only have a week left to live, she caught herself thinking, and then immediately pulled herself up. She couldn't think like that. It wasn't over. Besides, millions of people suffered much worse every day.

It didn't make her feel any better.

The appalling night's sleep had been a mess of regrets and fears but she had managed to make one decision: she was going to make arrangements to keep the flat as long as she could and for all of her stuff to go into storage. She had to believe there was a way to escape again and when she did she'd want somewhere to go in Mundanus. If it took longer than the length of the lease at least her stuff wouldn't be thrown out in her absence. There was enough money in her account to keep it going for the rest of the agreed lease and to pay for storage. Then she realised her mother might ask for the jewels she'd sold to fund her escape. The forehead was banged against the window again.

As she dressed in jeans and a top (for the last time?) and dragged a brush through her hair, her thoughts returned to the botched wish. It was the price of being outside Society for so long. She'd got slack and forgotten the first rule of wish-making: be specific.

Then she was thinking about Josh again, as if there were only two topics her head could contain. She felt like a ping-pong ball being batted between them.

She had to think like a member of the Great Families, not a freakish runaway. What could she wish for to help her survive once they'd dragged her back? Would it impress Lord Poppy to go back to Aquae Sulis and dance, sing and play the piano even better than her odiously perfect younger sister? Or would it be better to wish she could speak every language in the world? That had always been a secret wish and one that would be useful if she did find a way to freedom in Mundanus. *When* she found a way; she had to stay positive.

It was tempting, but Lord Poppy probably didn't even realise people in Mundanus spoke different languages. She had a vague memory of a lesson in her youth in which she was told the Fae could understand and converse with anyone, universally understood. She couldn't remember why. Perhaps this is what it's like to go mad, she thought as she pulled on her boots and grabbed her jacket. To think the most stupid, irrelevant things instead of a way to avoid a terrible fate.

She had to get out and walk.

Manchester sparkled in the dawn's gentle sunshine, a delicious assortment of deep-red brick and glass and steel.

The shops were still closed, the streets relatively empty. She found a greasy-spoon café and ordered a coffee and breakfast, only to push most of it around the plate. She headed further into the city as it woke, finding herself in crowds of people hurrying to work.

The sense of finality lingered. Cathy took in deep lungfuls of the air, appreciating its freshness and the gentle blue of the morning sky. Like all Fae-touched children she had been raised in the mundane nursery wing of the family home. The rest of the house, on the other side of the door she was never allowed to go through without a nanny, was in Aquae Sulis. As she got older she was brought through into the Nether reflection of the house more often and every time she got back to her room she'd open the window as if she'd been forced to hold her breath. In the Nether there was no breeze, no weather as there was in Mundanus, nothing but a silver sky. There wasn't even day and night.

She passed the red plaque she'd sought out the first day she arrived in the city, before she'd even arranged a place to stay or used the Persuasion Charm on the university admissions tutor. She didn't need to read the words to know what it said.

"On August 16 1819 a peaceful rally of 60,000 pro-democracy reformers, men, women and children, was attacked by armed cavalry resulting in 15 deaths and over 600 injuries."

Peterloo. The last lesson Miss Rainer gave to her before her radical education was discovered and punished. The beginning of Cathy's true rebellion.

As she walked down Peter Street, Cathy thought of the women who had been in that crowd, in their beautifully white Regency dresses, cut down by Hussars who targeted them for being so outrageous as to participate in a political rally. Their world wasn't much different from the one she was being sucked back into, and yet they were brave enough to take a stand when the majority of society decried them.

What if she were to wish for–

"Cathy!"

Josh bounded up to her in his Labradorish way and scooped her up into a hug, lifting her off the ground. She tried not to breathe in the gorgeous smell of him, studiously looking away from his large brown eyes and messy dark hair. The last thing she wanted to see was his lips and how kissable they were, so she tucked her face into his shoulder and let him squeeze her.

"Hi," she managed to say, returning the hug and worrying about the lump in her throat. He set her down on the pavement.

"I missed you. How was your aunt?"

"Not so good," she said, remembering the lie.

"Sorry to hear that. You OK?"

She didn't let him go, not wanting him to see her face as she struggled to get a grip of herself. "Yeah," she croaked, and he pulled her back into his embrace.

"You free this morning? Let's do stuff and then have lunch afterwards," he suggested. "Forbidden Planet's got some new stock I want to show you."

This wasn't how she'd planned it. Not how she'd expected it to be, anyway. She'd got as far as imagining seeing him at the restaurant and at least saying they had to talk, then there was just a mess of emotion. Uncertain how to handle the inevitable break-up, she nodded, deciding that she couldn't just split up with him in the middle of the street.

He took her hand, then let go and threw his arm about her shoulders, pulling her against him so they walked with their sides touching. He was wearing a military-style jacket and skinny jeans. The top of her head came to his shoulder.

His height usually made her feel safe and was one of the first things that had attracted her to him. That, and the kindness he'd shown her when she'd been struggling to get to grips with real student life.

She remembered his amazement when she'd been confused by a comment he'd made about *The Time Machine* by HG Wells. Even though the nursery wing had been in Mundanus they were still cut off from everyone else so she'd never watched television and didn't even know about a cinema until she arrived at Cambridge. Her minder wouldn't allow her to go or do anything beyond studying for her degree, so she never actually saw a film there.

"You've never seen a film? Where the hell did you grow up?"

That was when she told him the biggest lie; that her family was part of a cult that lived separately from society. It was as close to the truth as she could get; they had their own rules and morality, shunned contact with outsiders and considered their way of life superior to those outside.

"I ran away," she told him and immediately regretted it. Would he think badly of her?

"Why?"

"Because they don't believe girls or women have the same rights as men. They'd marry me off and make me do what they want. I just don't... I just didn't fit in there."

"That sucks," he finally said. And that was it.

He made it his personal mission to educate her about sci-fi's transition from paper to film. Somewhere between *This Island Earth* and *Forbidden Planet* they'd started to hold hands. They kissed halfway through *Journey to the Centre of the Earth* and by *Fantastic Voyage* they were almost inseparable. He'd lovingly introduced her to *Star Wars* in the original film release order, and she realised she loved him at the end of *Raiders of the*

Lost Ark. By *Back to the Future III* he'd confessed he felt the same, inspired by the scene between Clara and Doc Brown stargazing together.

It would have been perfect if it hadn't been for the curse, but in a way that only deepened her trust. He didn't mind waiting, thinking that her reluctance to do more than kiss was a wound from a childhood with religious extremists.

As they walked, he told her about what he'd been doing while she'd been away, but all she could think about was how and where to tell him. Did she spend one last morning with him and tell him over lunch? Did she do it now, before it got too difficult?

Then they were in the shop, greeted warmly by the bloke behind the counter, and Josh was bouncing about the latest reboot.

"I need a cup of tea," she said and he put the comic down.

"Are you feeling poorly?"

"I didn't sleep well."

"How come?"

"I really need some tea," she said, and hurried out of the shop.

"What's wrong?" he asked, following her out and catching hold of her hand. "Is it your aunt? Is she really sick?"

"No." Her voice wobbled and she looked up at the bright shop sign, avoiding his eyes.

"You can tell me, Cathy, come on."

"I'm leaving Manchester."

There was a long pause. "When?"

She shrugged. "In the next couple of days… by next week I think."

"But what about your course?"

"I can't do it any more."

"Have you talked to your tutor?"

"No, I mean, I... it's not too hard, I mean... I can't."

He frowned, standing directly in front of her, drawing her eyes, and she immediately regretted it. She hadn't realised how much she'd planned ahead until it was all over. She'd finish her degree, they'd get a place together and see if it worked out. She'd find a way to unravel the curse, they'd–

"Has this got something to do with your weird family?"

"I can't talk to you about it."

"Shit. Are they putting pressure on you?"

"I said–"

"Because they can't make you leave, you know. They don't pay for your course, you're in control."

She frowned at his chest, trying to work out how to end it cleanly, with respect and love. This was heading in the wrong direction.

"It's not that simple," she said, pulling away from him, feeling sick. "We have to split up."

She felt like she'd just kicked a puppy. His eyes widened and for a few moments he just looked confused.

"Why?"

"Because they won't let me see anyone."

"What, they're going to lock you away and tell you who you see and who you don't?"

Hearing the truth, she started to walk away, fearing she'd make it worse if she said any more.

"Cathy! Are you really dumping me?"

She stopped and turned around slowly. "Yeah."

"What the fuck?"

"It isn't anything to do with you, it's my family! You just have to accept it. OK?"

"No, it's not fucking OK! We've been going out with each other for over a year. I've tried to understand all that baggage you've got from them. I've been patient, I never pushed it with you, and you're just–"

"What, you waited all that time to get into bed with me and now you're pissed off because you didn't get what you wanted?"

"No, I'm just saying that–"

"Because I thought you were with me because you wanted to be with me, not just waiting around until we could have sex."

"Jesus, Cathy, what is wrong with you? You're sounding like some mad woman. What the hell happened in London? Did they put the fear of God in you again?"

She closed her eyes, put her hands over her face as she tried to string her tiny beaded thoughts into something useful. "I'm so sorry. I love you, but it's best for both of us if we just split up now and be done with it."

"How can that be the best thing?" He reached towards her, but she stepped away. "Why let them carry on ruining your life?"

"They're not just weirdoes, they're dangerous!" she blurted, and then swore under her breath. He just looked even more confused. "I just need you to let me go. And to forget we were together."

"Bollocks. Not when you say something like that. We're going to the police."

"No, we're not!"

"You know they have people who specialise in this kind of stuff? Just because your family are religious weirdoes it doesn't mean they have to ruin your life too. You got away from them once, don't let them suck you back in."

This was getting out of hand. The gentle approach wasn't working, and she could see him escalating it into something horrific. If her family found out about him, they'd...

"Cathy?"

She remembered Elizabeth. How many times had her spiteful sister broken hearts and laughed at the consequences? "I just don't want to be with you anymore. OK? It's nothing to do with my family." She thought back to her mother, how cold she could be. "I just made that stuff up, I just can't face the thought of... being with you like that."

He was turning a horrible grey colour. "So you weren't screwed up at all. You just wanted to string me along?"

"Yes." She wanted to chew out her own heart.

"Why?"

"Because I thought it was funny."

His mouth was hanging open. With horror she realised his eyes were glistening. "How could I have been so wrong about you?"

"Probably because you were only thinking about one thing." She smothered her own thoughts and feelings as she took on the necessary role. "That's what men are like, isn't it? Any hole's a goal?"

"Not me!" he yelled. "Fuck. I wasted a year on you?"

"See? I told you! If it wasn't what you wanted, it wouldn't have been a waste!"

"That's not what I meant!" He ran his hands through his hair. "Why are you being like this? This isn't you."

"This is what I'm really like. I... I wanted to see what it was like to go out with a total loser. I'm not going back to a cult." The words gushed, her brain didn't engage. "I'm going back to a bloody rich family and they don't want me to waste my time on sad bastards like you."

"I'm not a... I could've gone out with anyone I wanted!" he yelled.

"Yeah, right! Mr Geek thinks he's God's gift to women, now that's funny!"

"Why are you being such a bitch?"

"Why aren't you getting it, Josh? You're not the one who wasted a year, *I* was. So go on, find all those women desperate to go out with you instead!"

"I bloody well will!"

He didn't move. He was making this so much harder. Cathy felt a rush of pure fury at the way he just wouldn't let go. "Well, go on then! I wish you would find them, then I wouldn't have to look at your sorry face any more!"

Her skin tingled, the sparkling ripple she'd seen in the flat the night before raced out from a spot behind a nearby waste-paper bin, snapped her out of the brutal desire to push him out of her life for his own good.

"Josh—"

"Just… fuck off, Cathy."

He staggered into the road. She could hear the faerie laughing, tuned into its high pitch. Cathy burst into tears at the sight of his distress, hating herself more than she thought possible, fear and guilt rushing in to replace the anger. But she couldn't take back what she'd said, and even though she wanted to gouge her own eyes out for hurting him so, it was still better than her family getting hold of him.

She headed for the faerie, hoping to grab it and throttle it until it took back the magic. The evil thing must have been spying on her and there was no way anything the spiteful creature had cast would be good for Josh. A screeching of tyres and a nauseating thud made her spin around to see Josh rolling along the ground in front of a black Lamborghini. She wanted to scream and run to him, but the air around her felt soupy, her body frozen in shock.

The driver's door opened and a redhead who was seventy per cent legs, thirty per cent Gucci, jumped out and ran to her victim. Josh rolled over and stared at the redhead but Cathy still couldn't move. It was like a film playing out in front of her, one in which she'd once been the lead.

The redhead gushed an apology and then an introduction; Josh mumbled his name back, still groggy. Cathy watched in disbelief as she helped him to his feet, white with shock, a gash on his forehead bleeding impressively, and got him into the passenger seat. The woman gave her the briefest glance, said "I'm taking him to the hospital, all right?" and got back in.

The car sped off, leaving Cathy in a momentary stupor before she remembered the faerie. It was hovering behind the litter bin, clutching its sides as it squeaked with laughter.

She glanced up and down the street, fearful of being spotted by an Arbiter. She'd never seen one before, but if there was ever going to be an occasion that precipitated the first time, this was it.

"You stupid, evil little–" Cathy swiped at it, hoping to grab hold of the tiny creature and crush it.

"Do you mean me or you?" it said, dodging her effortlessly. "If only complete idiocy would impress Lord Poppy, you'd be his favourite by far."

"I didn't mean to wish that! It wasn't one of my three wishes!"

The faerie made a pretence of yawning. "Oh, how many times have we heard a mortal say that? Too late, Miss Plain, your favourite mundane is now as irresistible to women as you wished."

"I never wished that!" she yelled.

"You wished he would find all the women who were desperate to be his girlfriend. Well, what better way than to bring one straight to him? My Lord's magic is too powerful for you to cope with."

"What about the answer to my first wish?" Cathy wasn't certain she could handle this much longer.

It waved a tiny finger at her. "I told you, you didn't express an exact time."

"And Josh, what about him? Will the wish last forever?"

"He's only a smelly mundane. Lord Poppy didn't place any limits on the wishes. He'll never be short of female company until the day he dies."

"You're telling me that his life is going to be changed forever because I didn't specify an absolute?" Cathy kicked the bin. "God, you sound like a bloody lawyer!"

The faerie flew back in disgust. "How dare you! I'll tell my master!"

"Come back here, you little elf-dropping, tell me how to fix it."

The faerie floated back slowly. "You could use your third wish…" It pretended to look shocked. "Oh, but then you'd have run out of chances to impress my Lord. What. A. Shame."

How could she have messed it up so catastrophically *twice*? Once was bad enough. She could still see Josh's face and the hurt she'd caused. Cathy wiped the tears from her cheeks, feeling a pressure in her sinuses that distracted her from wanting to smear the faerie across the pavement.

A can clattered down the street towards her as if it had been kicked, but there was no one else there. The faerie started to snigger again as cigarette butts, sweet wrappers, leaves and other bits of street debris began rolling towards Cathy from all directions. The pressure in her skull increased and with horror she realised what was happening.

"They're coming!" the faerie cheered and disappeared with a tiny pop.

It was a Seeker Charm. Disastrous wishes or not, it was all over.

10

William Reticulata-Iris looked out on Aquae Sulis, the glorious Bath stone and pristine Georgian buildings a welcome sight. It was quiet; those in Society rarely strolled before eleven in the morning and had no need to walk to and from shops as the mundanes did, so the streets of Aquae Sulis were usually quiet anyway.

"Another beautiful day in the Nether," he said to Roberts, looking up at the silver sky. "I shall miss the blue though."

"It's a common problem at the end of a Grand Tour," the artist replied as he sketched. "Perhaps you could look back up, sir."

Will did so, glad to be able to look out of windows without having to pose. "Like this?"

"Excellent."

"I suppose you'll be glad of the rest," Will said.

"I only have a month, and then I'm off again with the Wisterias' youngest."

"He's come of age already?" Will tried to remember the boy, but he'd been too bland to make an impression. "Is he travelling alone?" When the artist nodded, Will gave him a sympathetic glance. "Less fun for you, old chap. Thank goodness Oliver could travel with me, otherwise you'd have been forced to entertain me as well as record the journey."

"I'm sure you would've been able to find your own entertainment without any help from me, sir," Roberts said with a smirk. "Never have I had so many evenings off on an assignment."

"That doesn't leave this carriage, Roberts."

"I am the epitome of discretion," Roberts said. "I'm not the most sought-after Tour artist just because I can sketch in a moving carriage."

The carriage turned a corner and began to climb another hill. They were on the last stretch. Will checked his cravat and put on his gloves. "It's been a pleasure travelling with you, Roberts. I'll write a letter of commendation for your portfolio and I'm sure Mother will give you a generous gift once she sees the painting of the Alpinums."

"It has been a mutual pleasure, sir," Roberts replied as the carriage stopped.

The footman opened the door and unfolded the step. Will jumped out of the carriage, eager to stretch his legs. The family home was, as expected, unchanged, nestled between two other splendid townhouses of the Royal Crescent.

The butler opened the door as he approached, a broad smile on his face. Pleasantries were exchanged as his luggage was unloaded from the carriage, and his gloves and cane were taken. He was ushered towards the drawing room where his family were waiting.

"William!" His mother was the first to rush over and embrace him. She didn't look a day over twenty, her chestnut-brown hair arranged to frame her face beautifully. "Look at you!"

His father greeted him with a firm shake of the hand as his mother kissed him on the cheek.

"You left a boy and returned such a handsome young man!" she said, smiling proudly.

"You're as brown as a filthy stableboy," Nathaniel said, stepping forward to shake hands as Father withdrew. "Mother, stop making such a fuss, he's barely inside the room."

She allowed William to enter. His elder brother's handshake was just as painful as he remembered; Nathaniel was still unable to greet him without trying to prove who was the more important. Will did his best to return the gesture, earning a twitch of Nathaniel's left eyebrow.

"Seems that life amongst the savages suits you, brother," Nathaniel remarked, and moved away to allow his elder sister to have her turn at putting Will in his place.

"William," she said, with a cold smile. "How delightful to see you again." She came over and planted a kiss on his other cheek. He liked how she had to stand on tiptoes to do so. She looked more like Mother than he remembered.

"You are a picture, Imogen," he said as his hand luggage was brought in. *And little more*, he thought, but didn't voice it.

As he accepted her kiss, he saw his uncle waiting his turn. "Uncle Vincent!" He was glad to see his favourite had been invited. Uncle Vincent was the only one in the room who looked older since the last time Will saw him, older even than his father, despite the fact that he was Father's younger brother. He'd clearly been having too much fun in Mundanus. Will made a mental note to arrange lunch with him to hear the juicy details.

"And me!" The little voice heralded an awkward silence.

He searched for its source and saw a small girl with one hand clutched around one of the silken folds of his mother's gown, the other waving to him. Her hair was lighter than his siblings, but she had his mother's eyes, like they all did.

"This is Sophia," his mother said.

"You're no longer the baby of the family," Nathaniel chipped in.

"I'd like to think I haven't been the baby for some time," Will replied, covering his shock. A fourth child? He glanced at Father but he was cutting the end off a cigar and handing it to Uncle Vincent. He looked back at the small girl who had taken a tentative step towards him. He opened his arms and a delighted smile made her face angelic as she bounced over to be picked up.

She wrapped her arms around his neck and kissed him as the others had. "Hello, Will-yum."

"Hello, Sophia," he replied, and earned another kiss.

"She has a tendency to do that," Nathaniel muttered, but Will simply kissed her back, earning a roll of the eyes from his brother but a sparkling grin from Sophia, which seemed much better value.

"Are you home forever now?"

"Yes."

"Will you come and play in the Mundanus garden with me? Imogen won't." She pouted at her elder sister whose nose tilted upwards.

"Catching a ball is simply not incentive enough for losing one's youth," she said.

Will had a sudden craving for the mundane woman he'd chased through the surf on the coast of Sicily. Her skin was bronzed, she'd exuded life, and hadn't given a moment's care to whether the sun and sand would age her. His sister looked like a pale feather of a girl in comparison. All of them would now.

"I'll come and play catch with you," he said to Sophia. "It's all right for big brothers to age a little."

"Only enough to lose their boyish faces," his mother said. "And, at the right time, to edge carefully towards distinguished." She nodded towards Father. "But one must take care never to overdo it."

"Would you like a sherry, Uncle Vincent?" Imogen asked, and Nathaniel smirked at her timing.

Will had almost forgotten what it was like to constantly be on guard. Oliver, his best friend and middle son of the Peonia family, was delightfully straightforward in comparison to his barbed siblings, and had been a fine companion for the Grand Tour. Will hoped all his time with Oliver and Roberts hadn't rusted his social armour.

"Time for your gifts, I believe," he said, setting Sophia down. She lurked near his leg before being coaxed away by their mother.

Sherry was handed out as he opened the smallest of his leather cases. The bag had been with him for the entirety of the trip, either held in his own hand or in sight as it was carried by porters or bellboys. It had been up mountains and down into dingy nightclubs all over Mundanus, in the finest guest bedrooms of the grandest Nether houses all over the world. He was pleased by the way it also had aged just enough.

He lifted out the first box, one of the largest in the bag, and held it towards his father. "For the man who wants for nothing."

His father set his glass down, rested the cigar on the edge of an ashtray and crossed the room as the family watched. Will could still remember all of the gifts Nathaniel had brought back after his tour and he wanted to outdo every single one.

Father set the box down on a nearby table, unwrapped the plain brown paper and uncovered a humidor made of the most beautiful walnut. An unimpressed snort came from his brother's direction.

"The gift is inside," Will said. The box was opened and a row of cigars revealed. "There are three dozen Cohiba cigars that I personally commissioned from the owner of the company, using a blend hand-picked by their best tobacco expert."

He lowered his voice and leaned closer to his father. "They were hand-rolled on the thighs of a virgin Cuban girl with a face like an angel. I took the liberty of using a discreet Charm to put a little of her innocence into each one. It will make for an interesting smoke."

His father actually looked intrigued, lifting one out to run it under his nose. Will noted how Nathaniel picked that moment to refill his glass and felt the warm glow of personal satisfaction. "I'll save my first for after dinner. It's a most thoughtful gift, thank you."

"Your gift next, Mother, I'll just have it brought in."

He waved the footman in who'd been waiting in the hallway. He was carrying a painting wrapped in layers of fabric and canvas to protect it, and once it had been balanced on the arm of a chair it was unwrapped for her.

The painting was of her sister's family, with Will seated next to his cousins. "I had Roberts paint it when we visited Austria," he said, delighted by his mother's astonished gasp.

"Clara doesn't look a day older! And her sons aren't nearly as handsome as you, Will." She radiated delight. "What a beautiful gift, thank you, darling."

He earned another kiss from his mother and a slight frown from Nathaniel. "And now you, dear brother," he said, returning to his bag. "I searched the world for something more dangerous than you and your sword."

Nathaniel laughed. "That's an impressive challenge to set for yourself. Did you succeed?"

"Oh, yes." Will gave his most devilish smile, and when he was sure everyone's anticipation had been built to perfection, he pulled out the tiny package. There was a titter from Imogen and Uncle Vincent. "But first, you need to put these on." He produced a pair of leather gloves with a flourish that drew the family closer.

Nathaniel put them on, looking Will in the eye as he did so. Then he ripped off the paper and plucked out one of the chilli peppers from their wrapping. "Is that it?" he asked.

"That, dear brother, is the hottest chilli pepper in the world. It's called the 'Trinidad Scorpion Butch T'."

"What a vulgar name," Nathaniel said with a sniff.

"It was grown in Australia, I watched this batch being picked. Try it, if you dare."

"After I've seen what you've brought for everyone else," Nathaniel said.

"Coward," Imogen prodded him. "Go on. I want to see if it makes you cry."

"I will if you will," Nathaniel said, holding it out to his brother.

Will had prepared for this moment. "As you wish," he smiled, and bit a tiny piece off. A beat later Nathaniel did the same. He flushed the same red as Will, but dashed out of the room, coughing.

Will grinned as Imogen applauded him.

"That was a little cruel, William," Mother said.

"It was nothing worse than what he gave me," he replied, blinking away the tears that had sprung as he swallowed the sliver of pepper. The weeks of desensitisation had been just enough, though he did fear that he'd never be able to taste anything properly ever again. It was still worth it.

"I hope that's the last of this childish one-upmanship between you," his father said, looking unimpressed.

"I doubt there is anything that could follow it, Father," Will replied.

"It's just a bit of fun, George," Uncle Vincent said. "A little healthy rivalry is only natural."

They exchanged a look that made Will uncomfortable. Again, he was reminded of this life of unspoken things. He sipped the water that the butler had brought in after seeing Nathaniel dash out, and straightened his waistcoat.

"Whilst Nathaniel tidies himself up, I think it's time for Imogen's present," he said, seeing a flicker of excitement cross his sister's face.

He produced the next package from his bag, a slender box wrapped in oriental paper. "I procured this from a most interesting individual in China," he said as he handed it to her. "This is the first part."

She unwrapped it eagerly and pulled the fan out of the box. Spreading it open, she smiled at the blue irises hand-painted in the oriental style. "It's beautiful," she said, but he could see she was disappointed.

"The second part is the secret that only the owner of the fan may hear, one that I must pass to you in private."

Her demeanour shifted into one of delight. "I look forward to it."

"Uncle Vincent, this is for you," he said, passing him the gift.

His uncle smiled broadly at the deck of cards.

"Hand-painted and unique," Will told him. "I'll tell you about the artist over a game of poker."

"I'll hold you to that," his uncle said with a wink.

"But what about my present?" Sophia asked.

"Darling, William didn't–"

"I have it in here somewhere," Will cut in, mouthing an apology to his mother as Sophia rushed over to peep into the bag. "Ah, here it is!"

He produced an ornate key carved out of ivory.

"Oooooh!" Sophia took it. "What does it open?"

"Ah," Will said, thinking quickly. "That key opens a very special box that can only be opened when you come of age."

Sophia pouted. "But that's days and days away!"

Will laughed and pulled out a bag of caramels left over from the journey. "Perhaps these will keep you happy until then."

Duty discharged, he accepted his glass of sherry as they inspected each other's presents. Nathaniel eventually reappeared, giving William a glare as he entered.

"I'd take it as a compliment," Uncle Vincent said to him. "If it had been anything less fiery, it would have insulted your prowess as a swordsman."

Nathaniel chose to agree, accepting his uncle's implicit efforts to calm things between them. "That's a good point, Uncle." He came over and shook Will's hand. "Touché, dear brother."

Their father nodded in satisfaction. "Well, now that William has duly impressed us all, it's time to let him rest and settle back in." He came over and put a hand on his shoulder. "A word with you in my study first, William."

He followed his father out, enjoying the smell of home once again. Beeswax polish mixed with the scent of fresh irises arranged in vases throughout the house. The study was also unchanged.

"You seem to have had a successful trip," his father said as he sat at his desk and gestured for Will to seat himself opposite.

"It was both enlightening and educational," Will replied. The Grand Tour had gone out of fashion in Mundanus but still thrived in Nether society and he was glad of it. Four years of travelling from country to country, visiting incredible places in both Mundanus and the Nether, really had broadened his mind, but not in the way his parents hoped. He'd had fun, met many people and forged contacts in the Nether courts abroad that would help him in the future, but he didn't return full of disdain for the mundane life.

"I appreciate the painting you commissioned for your mother. I know she misses her sister."

Will gave a gentle nod to acknowledge the compliment.

"Now, to business." His father leaned forward, resting his elbows on the blotter. His sideburns were peppered with grey, but he still didn't look anywhere near his age. Not that Will was certain what that was, but he knew his father was over ninety. "But before I begin, I want to know if there's anything you need to tell me about your trip."

"I have a veritable smorgasbord of anecdotes that I'll dine out on for weeks," Will replied.

"I meant anything that needs to be dealt with discreetly."

"Don't worry, Father, I was very careful."

His father held his gaze for a moment, then nodded. "Good. I didn't want to hear about illegitimate children or reports of duelling without knowing first."

Will bit back a comment about knowing how to have fun without it staining one's shirt. He wondered if Oliver was having the same conversation with his father on the other side of the city.

"Now that you've had your Tour it's time for you to settle down and establish yourself in your own right."

Will nodded. He'd expected this, just not so soon. He hadn't even had a chance to unpack. "I understand, although I'm surprised Nathaniel hasn't married yet. Father, is there some kind of problem?"

"Negotiations for Nathaniel are in progress," his father replied curtly.

As the heir to the most powerful family in Aquae Sulis, Nathaniel was one of the most eligible bachelors of his generation. As the spare, Will knew that his parents would agonise less over the match they made for him.

"And how are negotiations for my marriage progressing?"

"It's been decided. We want to announce it at the ball on Friday, if the Censor permits."

Will breathed slow and steady. He'd known all his life that this time would come. He and Oliver had discussed it at length, speculating about who they'd be promised to whilst they were away. He was glad he'd made the most of the trip – It sounded like his father didn't want to waste any time. "And who is it to be, Father?"

"Catherine Rhocas-Papaver."

Will ensured his face was a mask. Later, in the privacy of his own room, he would swear, but, scrutinised by his father, he simply nodded. "I see."

"I know she isn't a beauty, but she secures our alliance with the Papavers, and with that we can control the Council of Aquae Sulis and the city of Bath in totality. The Bath Preservation Trust is well established now and, thanks to our hard work, it's practically impossible for the mundanes to disrupt the city's architecture."

Will struggled to suppress any sign of his disappointment. He'd hoped for Oliver's sister, who was docile enough to forget about when with a mistress, and a good excuse to spend time on the town with Oliver; or, at a push, Elizabeth Papaver, who made up for her vapid nature with her beauty and musical talent. But Catherine Papaver? She'd been so far down the list he and Oliver had debated on the Rialto in Venice that they'd forgotten about her.

Why her? He wanted to stand up and bang his fist on the table and demand the answer. He'd always been good, he'd worked hard to learn the rules of the game and play his part with perfection. To be matched with the dud of the Papavers' latest generation was hardly the reward he expected and deserved, but he had to say something polite. "It sounds like a very strategically important match, Father."

"It's critical to secure our local interests," his father replied. "I understand that she's been in Switzerland for the past three years at a finishing school. Seems the Papavers realised she needed polishing up."

"Has it worked?"

"I haven't seen her. Her father has reassured me she'll be back in time for the Ball. I'm sure they'll have whipped her into shape."

Will didn't raise his hopes. Finishing schools improved posture and table manners but they didn't give a girl a better face to look at over breakfast every morning. He had to think of the family though, and besides, once she'd given him a son or two he could pack her off to a country house.

"I'm honoured to play such a key role in our family's fortunes," he said, making his father smile a little. "I'm sure she'll have blossomed."

She couldn't have got much worse, he told himself. He remembered how bruised his toes had been after she'd trampled on them the night they'd danced years before when they were in their early teens. She had as much grace as a drunken duckling and he had little hope she'd turn out to be a swan.

"Good," his father said, relieved. "I'm waiting to hear back from the Censor about the announcement, but she's been rather distracted."

"Miss Lavandula distracted? Is there a new fashion in town?"

"Her brother is missing."

Will didn't hide his surprise. The Master of Ceremonies was the most important person in Aquae Sulis society and his sister, the Censor, was the second. "For how long?"

"Only a couple of days, but the Censor is worried, I can tell you that. Keep an ear open, will you? No one seems to know a thing about where he's gone. He didn't leave a note or even mention he'd be leaving."

"To go missing this close to the start of the season speaks of foul play."

"It hasn't been ruled out. But that's for me and the other members of the Council to worry about. It's good to have you back in Aquae Sulis, Will."

"Thank you, Father," he said and took his leave.

He was unsurprised to find Imogen lurking at the top of the stairs as he went up to change. "William dear, I have a few minutes spare before I leave, would it be a trouble to you to give me the second part of my gift?"

"No trouble," he said, forgetting that he'd planned to draw it out as long as he could. "Where are you going?"

"Oh, just to the park to promenade with Cecilia. There's a rumour that some controversial individuals have been petitioning the Censor for entrance to the first Ball of the season and Cecilia always knows the latest gossip. It quite makes up for the fact that she insists upon drinking *coffee* at Lunn's."

"Only the most bland adopt such embarrassing affectations," he said, acclimatising to the tittle-tattle of city life again. "Come to my room, I'll tell you the secret there."

The maid was carrying some of his washing out as they arrived. She blushed at him and bobbed a curtsy before hurrying away. He shut the door.

"And how are you, Imogen?"

"Well enough, now tell me this secret!"

He smirked. She hadn't changed. "The fan had a powerful Charm woven into it at the point of making," he said in an appropriately conspiratorial whisper. "Should you find yourself at a soirée or ball and wish to look at someone for a length of time beyond that which would be considered decent, simply fan yourself twice and ensure only your eyes are exposed."

"What will it do?"

"The fan will give you the appearance of looking in the other direction," Will said, seeing its potential dawn on his sister.

"So no one may deduce the object of my affection. What a delightful gift, Will." She pecked him on the cheek again. He'd never received so many kisses in one day. In the Nether at least. "I'm pleased to say that I underestimated you. I thought you'd bring back a dull trinket, not something secret and useful!"

He bowed slightly, enjoying her admiration. "As soon as I heard of the craftsman, I knew I had to get one for you. I understand it's unique in Albion."

She glowed with delight. "Cecilia will positively die of jealousy. Now, Will dear, seeing as you have given me such a deliciously perfect gift, permit me to give you a secret in return."

It was a day of surprises. He allowed her to draw him closer.

"I know they're planning to marry you to Catherine Rhoeas-Papaver," she began.

"Alas, sister, the secret is already out. Father has just broken the news to me."

"Ah, but that's not the secret I had in mind," she said and patted his hand. "You have my sympathy, by the way. No, I wanted to tell you that Elizabeth, the younger and frankly superior sister, has had her eye on Nathaniel for a long time now. The silly thing has been so desperate to impress him it's loosened her tongue on more than one occasion."

"And what has the younger tongue revealed?"

"That Catherine Papaver has a rebellious nature which has been causing her family a great deal of distress. Apparently it was fostered by a governess they sacked shortly before she left for finishing school. If that is indeed where she was sent…" She looked pleased by his frown. "I'd be careful, Will, there's nothing more dangerous to a man's social standing than a wife who refuses to play by the rules. And I do know how fond you are of how others think of you."

11

Cathy sat on the floor of the living room looking at the boxes stacked around her. She'd been up all night packing and was waiting for the removals company to come and put them in storage.

The Seeker Charm had targeted her and then faded without further incident, leading her to conclude that her brother Tom (assuming it was he who had cast it) must have been outside the city and was travelling there now. The Charm would be cast again when he arrived, and would give him an updated location.

She could run. But where? Why? It would be a waste of time and energy now the Shadow Charm had been removed by Lord Poppy. Without the Shadow Charm there was no way to hide from a blood relative casting a Seeker Charm and they would find her wherever she went in Mundanus or the Nether, not that she'd try to hide in the latter. Aside from family estates dotted around the country most of Fae-touched society lived in Aquae Sulis, Londinium or Oxenford, reflections of Bath, London and Oxford. It made it very hard to hide there without help, and with her only ally now compromised there was no one else to turn to.

Her friend in the flat above had keys and detailed instructions in case Tom didn't let her settle her affairs properly. She'd paid for five years' storage and memorised the contact numbers of all the key parties involved, knowing that she would be unlikely to be able to smuggle anything into Aquae Sulis once her family got hold of her. They'd search her, she knew it. Her father would be looking for books.

If her family was desperate enough to use Charms that powerful in Mundanus, she had to assume Tom would be travelling there as fast as possible. Thankfully her parents distrusted diesel trains and modern jet aircraft, so he'd be restricted to travelling by car. But England wasn't that big; even if he was hunting for her on the other side of the country he'd be in Manchester before the day was out.

It was the first time she'd stopped since she'd got back after the mad dash across the city. Whenever she paused, she shook and cried, so she just focused on practical things, things that could be solved by telephone calls and forward planning. If only surviving the social hell of Aquae Sulis was as easy as mundane planning and logistics.

She'd checked her phone several times but there was nothing from Josh. What was she expecting after what she'd done to him? Snippets of their last conversation were replayed again and again in her memory, flooding her with regret and a gnawing grief. Every hour or so she debated whether to call, but then decided it was best to cut herself off. Better for him. But she worried about his head, and whether that woman had really taken him to hospital.

She picked up the phone, thumb poised to text him, but one arrived before she started to type. Throat tight, she opened it only to find it was from one of her friends.

"Have you seen Hot magazine's homepage? Josh isn't in London, is he? LOL!"

She rummaged in one of the boxes for her iPad and Googled the magazine. The homepage featured an exclusive story about an actress she'd never heard of, but the picture made her want to throw up. It was the woman from the Lamborghini. The picture had been captured by some paparazzo lowlife by the look of it; she could see the entrance to a restaurant in the background.

Josh, a dressing on his right temple, was looking wide-eyed at the media frenzy around him, the redhead wrapped around one of his arms, smiling for the cameras. The headline made her head pound. "Who is Ella's new lover?"

She tossed it onto the sofa, unable to do anything save bury her face in her hands. She hadn't run out of tears after all.

The tea was cold by the time she stopped, and she'd run out of tissues. As she hunted for more, a lone pen rolled out from under the sofa, along with a couple of pennies and more than a few balls of dusty fluff.

Cathy just sat there, watching them, the pressure in her sinuses mingling with the headache she already had. She picked up her phone and texted Josh.

"I'm sorry I hurt you. I didn't mean what I said. It was the best year of my life. Take care of yourself. I love you. I really do. Cathy x"

Then she deleted it.

There was a second casting of the Charm. He was getting closer and running a terrible risk using it in a city; there were bound to be Arbiters picking up on the activity.

She put the kettle on and looked at the poster. Keep calm and–

There was a screech of tyres outside. She got a second mug out.

The communal door banged open after another flagrant use of a Charm. She heard heavy footsteps taking the stairs two at a time. The steam plumed from the spout and the kettle clicked off.

There was a hammering on the door, so loud it boomed through the flat. She poured the water onto the teabags as the Charm was used again and it flew open.

"Cat?" her brother shouted.

"I'm in the kitchen," she replied, relieved he was alone. She squeezed out the teabags as he bombed down the hallway and appeared at the kitchen door. "Tea?"

"Cat." He rushed over, threw his arms around her. He was bigger than she remembered, a military historian trapped in the body of an international rugby player. After almost crushing her to death he held her at arm's length. "Is there anyone else here?" he asked and she shook her head. He looked so much older. His bright-blue eyes had dark circles beneath them and his wavy brown hair and sideburns worn longer than she recalled. "I've been looking everywhere for you..." He stopped, tears welling. "I've been so worried."

She had no words. He searched her eyes, looking her over as if he couldn't quite believe it was her.

"Did someone take you? Did someone put you up to it?"

"No."

"Who helped you? Is there another family behind this?"

"No one. I did it by myself."

"Of your own free will?"

She nodded, and got the milk out of the fridge to busy herself and mask her trembling.

"But why? God, Cathy, you've made our lives hell."

"Whose lives?"

"All of us, blast it! Your family! What do you have to say for yourself?"

As she struggled to find something to say she looked at him properly. Tom had broadened in the shoulder and was quite handsome. His face had lost its boyish shape and he'd become a man since she last saw him. He was wearing a three-piece suit in a style very modern for the Nether. It looked vintage in Mundanus but not as out of place as the sheathed sword hanging from his waist.

"It's illegal to carry those here, you know that?"

"Bloody hell, Cat. Don't you understand? I've been running all over the country looking for you. Mother has been in a state and Father... well."

"I know," she said. She'd intended to apologise, but the words just didn't form. She went and closed the front door and came back to pour in the milk and stir the tea.

He took the mug she offered to him, barely even glancing at it. "How did you do it?"

"A Shadow Charm and lots of planning." She was amazed at how calm she felt, almost like she was watching someone else's life end. Perhaps it was the bliss of not anticipating the worst anymore; it was already happening.

"You look older."

"Of course I do," she replied. No doubt her mother would add that to the list of crimes she'd committed; no one aged in the Nether. Once a girl reached adulthood she was moved out of the nursery and into the Nether, rarely being allowed back into the real world, to protect her youth.

"It suits you."

"Perhaps I'll set a trend," she muttered. "Your tea is getting cold."

He shook his head. "You've no idea. Don't you care?"

"You ask me that? You're the only one I thought would understand."

"I know it was hard for you."

"Hard?" she laughed bitterly. "There's an understatement."

He looked down at the tea for the first time. She knew

he was remembering all the times she'd hoped he would intervene, all the times she hoped he would stop her father. He never did, but then neither did she. How could they have?

"You had it the worst, it's true, but running away? Do you realise the amount of pressure we've been under? The lies we've had to tell to explain your absence?"

"I bet Father was more worried about the scandal than what could have happened to me."

"You selfish, spoilt little bitch."

Her mouth fell open. He'd never said anything harsh to her in his life.

"You didn't stop and think for one minute what it would do to anyone else, did you?" He shook his head. "I thought you'd been kidnapped. I thought you were in Exilium at one point. I even thought you were dead. I couldn't believe that you'd just disappear without telling me."

She bit her lip. "I'm sorry, Tom." Unable to look into his eyes, her attention drifted down to his hands. She blinked.

He looked down at the wedding ring. "That's one of the things that happened whilst you were missing."

"Who…"

"Lucy Californica-Papaver."

"A Californica? I don't understand."

"It was to end the feud."

"And to bring their money into the family, no doubt," she added, but he remained silent. "An American. Do you like her?"

He waved the question away. "We haven't been married for very long."

"Were you given a choice?"

He gave her a long, hard stare. "Father had to tell everyone you were away in Switzerland at a finishing school. You had influenza and regrettably were unable to travel back for the wedding. Understand?"

She shut her eyes as the most awful thought crept in. With Tom now married she was next on the block. Elizabeth was the jewel of their generation. Her parents would be keen to make a good marriage for her, meaning they would dispose of the plain, troublesome middle child as quickly as possible.

"What?" Tom asked. She could feel her lips tingling as the blood rushed out of them.

"Lord Poppy said I was needed in Aquae Sulis," she whispered, leaning against the worktop as her legs shook.

"You spoke to Lord Poppy?" Tom slammed the mug down. "When?"

"Two days ago. He lifted the Shadow Charm. That's why you could find me."

"Bloody hell, Cat! He said you were needed and you're still here?"

She chewed a thumbnail. "I had things to do."

His disgust was evident. "I don't know whether to admire your bravery or be concerned for your sanity."

"When's the first ball of the season?"

"The day after tomorrow."

"Not next week?"

"No. And stop stalling, Cathy, it's time to go."

"Lord Poppy said I needed to be back by then. Why? What's going to happen?" He didn't reply, instead gulping down the tea, so she took a guess. "Are they going to marry me off?"

"Father will talk to you when–"

"Shit!" He blanched at her outburst. "That's it, isn't it? Who is it?"

He groaned, rubbed his eyes like a man trying to wake up from his own nightmare. "Catherine. Stop thinking about yourself for just one moment and get your coat."

"Who is it?"

Looking up at the ceiling in frustration, he dumped the mug and adjusted the scabbard. "William Reticulata-Iris. He got back from his Grand Tour yesterday. The engagement is to be announced at the ball."

Cathy shook her head, backing away towards the door. She remembered the last time she saw William Iris. He was fourteen and too confident; she'd been an awkward twelve year-old forced into dancing with him at his request. He'd only done it to humiliate her. He was cocky, egotistical and as shallow as the rest of them. "No. No way! I'm not going to marry him. I'm not going to marry anyone!"

Tom held up his palms. "Cat, calm down. We can talk about it on the way home. You knew this would happen one day, it happens to all of us. I had to get married, we all have to do what's best for the family, and the alliance with the Irises is critical."

"Fuck the Irises!" she shrieked and his pale cheeks flushed crimson.

"You've been in Mundanus for too long," he said with a grimace. "Now pull yourself together and stop this nonsense. You've had your fun, now you have to face your–"

"You sound like our bloody father!" she yelled. "This wasn't just having some fun, I made a life of my own!" Just three days before her life had been an open vista of possibilities. She had choices, from what to do with her life down to when she made a cup of tea and what she ate for lunch. All of them, large and small, were telescoping into a dark tunnel leading to a life she couldn't bear, a life of quiet servitude and fitting in, of performing for society's expectations in public and behind closed doors much worse, accepted as part of wifely duty. "I can't live like they do."

"I've had enough of this." Tom reached for her hand, which she snapped out of his range.

She darted into the hallway. "I'm not going to be married off like some–"

"You are a Rhoeas-Papaver, one of the Great Families, and you will come back to Aquae Sulis with me now." Tom was looking angry. She'd never seen that before.

"No, I–"

Before she realised what was happening, he'd lunged at her, banging his shoulder into her stomach and flipping her over into a fireman's lift. His arms wrapped around her legs and he headed for the door.

"My stuff!" she yelled.

"You don't need any of it at home," he replied.

"You can't do this!" she said, pummelling his back with her fists, furious at being handled like a troublesome child. Why did he have to be so big? "This is kidnapping."

"This is the way it's going to be, Catherine," he said, opening the door and checking no one else was coming out of their flat at the same time. "And don't even think about screaming," he added, as she sucked in a deep breath to do so. "I have other Charms at my disposal that you do not want me to use."

That kept her quiet as he descended the stairs. It was too humiliating for words. Her fury made it hard for her to think about anything but clobbering him over the head at the first opportunity and making a run for it.

"Now," he said, hand on the handle of the communal front door. "Do I need to lock you in the boot of the car?"

"No," she said quietly, thinking that if he put her down by the car, she could sprint away and call for help.

"And Catherine," he added, turning the handle. "If you do anything except get in the car and put your seatbelt on without saying a word, I will use a Doll Charm on you."

She thought she was going to be sick. She'd heard rumours of that Charm, one of the least acceptable in Society;

it rendered the victim powerless over their body but still aware. The victim could be frozen rigid or kept pliable like a rag doll. Either way it would make escape impossible and he'd have to carry her into the family house utterly helpless. It would be obvious that she'd resisted him.

"I understand," she whispered, cowed.

He dumped her by the side of a black VW Golf, too modern to belong to the family. She saw the hire-car information on the passenger seat as he unlocked the door for her. It took several goes; he was briefly befuddled by the buttons on the keychain remote, and he held her arm with his other hand as he muttered in frustration.

He opened the door for her and pushed her inside. She sat on top of the bits of paper, realising that this was it, she was leaving Manchester, kidnapped by her own brother.

"Seatbelt," he ordered and she clicked it into place. The thought of seeing her parents by the end of that very day made her throat tight. Cathy tugged down her sleeves, twisting the cuffs as the panic surged through her, unravelling her ability to do anything except shake violently.

The door was slammed shut and he marched around to the driver's side, looking up and down the street nervously. She was amazed no Arbiters had appeared. Perhaps they weren't as scary as she'd been led to believe.

"Can't I just get my bag?" she asked as he got in and put on his seatbelt.

"No."

Just one minute would be enough time to grab her phone and hide it somewhere useful later on. "But I have things I need in–"

"Don't you understand, Cat?" He twisted in his seat to face her. "It doesn't matter any more. It's over."

He stalled the car as he tried to pull away and she sank in the seat. Could she bolt at a service station? She sighed at herself. Lord Poppy wasn't going to forget about her, even if she did manage to get away from Tom.

"I'll never forgive you for this," she said, watching her street disappear in the wing mirror.

"As you'll soon discover, sometimes we have to do things we don't want to," he replied, tapping the sat nav. She noticed his hands were shaking. This had been hard for him too. He was just as trapped as she was.

"We could make a plan, Tom, if we worked together–"

"Stop it!" he shouted and hit the steering wheel with the palm of his hand. "Just… just accept it and start working out what you're going to say to Father, not how you can get out of this. Whether you like it or not, whether you hate us or not, you will be engaged to William, you will do your duty, you will marry him, and you will live in the Nether and that is that."

She turned away, curling up her legs and looking out at the city and its traffic. She felt her heartbeat pounding in her temples, her stomach knotted. She still had a wish to make and the only thing she wanted she wasn't permitted.

It was hard not to think about giving up.

Soon they were leaving the redbrick urban sprawl behind and the view opened out onto green fields and occasional farmhouses.

"When will we be there?" she asked.

"After dark."

"Why don't you take the motorway if it's such a rush?"

"I don't like driving on them. Everyone drives too fast."

She faced forwards and noticed how slow he was driving. "You know we can go up to sixty on this road?"

"I'll go at the speed I want to," he replied, arms held rigidly straight at the wheel.

"What's Lucy like?" she asked, hating the atmosphere, bored with the questions and worries battering her skull.

"Clever. Funny. She has good taste."

"You like her then?"

He shifted uncomfortably. "I was relieved she wasn't like her parents."

Cathy smiled. Poor Tom, utterly incapable of talking about how he felt. "I'm sorry," she said, the guilt welling again. "I missed you. I thought about you all the time."

"I just can't believe you did it by yourself. I thought I was going to have to fight off kidnappers and rescue you."

"But you turned out to be the kidnapper," she said and then clamped her mouth shut. "Sorry, that came out wrong."

"It just came out," he corrected. "It was exactly what you were thinking. I see you've lost your good manners and the ability to keep your thoughts to yourself."

She kept her mouth shut, trying to disprove him.

"What did you think you'd find in Mundanus?"

"I already found it," she said. "Freedom." And love, she thought, but didn't dare mention anything to do with Josh.

"But what did you want to actually do there?"

She fiddled with a cuff again, uncertain whether to tell the truth. It wasn't that she didn't trust Tom. She was worried he'd laugh at her. Her mouth twitched into a smile at the memory of when Josh had coaxed it out of her. He'd asked a few times at the end of a film and she'd brushed the question off, finding it hard to undo a lifetime of hiding her ambition from everyone around her. Then he tickled her until she'd fallen off the sofa but she still refused to tell him. He sat back and with a terrible sadness in his eyes said, "If you don't feel safe to tell me, that's OK."

That was the first moment she wondered if she was falling in love with him. She sat back on the sofa, tucked her toes under his leg and took a deep breath. "For the first few months away from my family I thought about opening a bookshop with an open fire and comfy chairs and free tea."

"Sounds good. Only sci-fi books?"

"Maybe. Lately I've had another idea… but I don't know if I could do it."

He smiled, rested a hand on her knee. "What did Doc Brown say?"

She grinned. "'If you put your mind to it, you can accomplish anything.' OK. Promise not to laugh?"

"I promise."

"I want to do something in human rights. I want to protect people who don't have a voice."

He nodded. "Cool."

She searched for any hint of scorn, any impending jibes, but there was nothing except a gentle smile. "Josh," she said, leaning closer. "I… I think I l–."

"Did you hear me, Cat?" Tom called. "What did you want to do in Mundanus?"

She blinked. "I wasn't sure yet." She swallowed the lump in her throat and looked out over the fields.

"Did you really want to stay in Mundanus forever?" he asked after a few minutes.

"Yeah," she said wistfully.

"Even though you'd get old?"

"Oh, for God's sake, there's more to life than worrying about bloody wrinkles, you know."

He winced. "Don't speak like that once you get back to Aquae Sulis. They'll pick you up on every little thing."

"Didn't they always?"

He nodded. "You'll just have to make the best of it. William's family are very wealthy and very powerful. It's a very good match. You'll want for nothing."

"Except freedom, some basic human rights, the ability to own my own property – because that's all I'll be: property."

"Cat."

She closed her eyes, overwhelmed. If she'd had an off button, she'd press it now. She was too tired to think straight and too wired to sleep.

The car's brakes squealed and she was thrown against her seatbelt. When she opened her eyes, she saw a car blocking the road ahead, a black vintage Bentley with a driver in goggles and leather driving gloves still behind the wheel. A young man in his early twenties was leaning against it, slapping his paired kid gloves against the palm of one hand.

He was dressed as if he'd stepped out of a shooting weekend in the Twenties. He too was wearing a very out-of-place sword.

"A Rosa," Tom said. "Fool, what does he think he's playing at?"

The buttonhole was the main clue: a gorgeous deep-red rose. He had a handsome face but an unfortunately large nose, dark hair scraped back and an arrogant tilt of the chin.

Tom brought the car to a stop in a narrow layby. "Stay in the car," he said and got out. Cathy pulled up the handbrake before it could roll backwards and got out to join Tom, who clicked his tongue in irritation but carried on.

"I say, what on earth do you think you're doing?" he said, striding up to the man. "You could have caused an accident."

"Thomas Rhoeas-Papaver?"

"I am," Tom replied, a foot taller than the source of his irritation. "And who might you be?"

"Horatio Gallica-Rosa," he said with a slight bow. "And you must be the elusive Catherine Rhoeas-Papaver, so famously being schooled in Switzerland." His eyes ran up and down her jeans and hooded top. "Is that the fashion over there?"

Catherine took Tom's advice to not speak her thoughts; there were far too many expletives. Something about the way Horatio looked at her got her hackles up. She decided to clean the rust off her old skills.

"Mr Gallica-Rosa," she said, with a small curtsy that felt ridiculous in jeans and trainers. "Good day to you. Has your car broken down? Do you require assistance?" The words felt so wrong, like someone else was speaking them.

"All manners now, I see," he replied petulantly, resting his left hand on the pommel of his sheathed sword. "Pity they weren't in evidence yesterday."

She frowned. "I'm sorry, I don't understand."

"Don't play the coquette with me, Miss Papaver." He sighed at her blank stare. "The wish magic you cast, you foolish girl. Your meddling prevented the delivery of a mundane that was promised to me by Lady Rose."

"How dare you speak to my sister in this manner," Tom said as Cathy tried her best to link either of the wishes to Lady Rose. Between the sleep-deprivation, background dread and rising anger at having been called a "foolish girl" there was little left for deduction.

"Which mundane?" she asked, resting a hand on Tom's arm.

"Ella Jacobs, the film star. The woman currently cavorting around Londinium with a veritable brown-paper bag of a mundane who was never destined to meet her."

The Guccified redhead, Cathy realised. "Lady Rose promised *her* to you? A mundane? Wouldn't the Arbiters have something to say about something that dodgy?"

She heard a tiny groan from Tom and realised she'd stopped thinking about how to speak.

The Rosa tutted. "That is irrelevant. What is of the utmost relevance, however, is how your trickery, and quite frankly disgusting thoughtlessness, has resulted in depriving me of one of the most alluring beauties of this mundane generation." As he spoke, he took a step towards Tom. "In accordance with the rights of my birth, and with the approval of Lady Rose, I demand satisfaction." He looked up at Tom, who was turning that awful shade of scarlet again. "And I assume, that as Miss Papaver's only brother – and may I offer my deepest condolences to you for such a difficult burden – you will be the one to give it."

12

Max had no idea he'd slept late until he looked at his watch. It was mid-afternoon and the room was dark; all houses in the Nether had heavy curtains to compensate for a lack of discernible night time. He ached. It was too dark to see the gargoyle but he knew it was in the corner nearest the door, just like he knew his fingers were cold and his leg hurt like hell. He pulled the cord by the side of the bed to summon help.

Axon was proving to be an excellent nurse and helped him get into a presentable and mobile state. He gave Max leather gloves to protect his hands whilst using the crutches and another shot of morphine. Axon didn't ask stupid questions or make accusations either. All the while, the gargoyle watched, its scowl demonic.

"I'll serve a luncheon of cold meats in the dining room, when you're ready to eat," Axon said and left.

"We need to talk," the gargoyle said, clunking over to sit between the bed and the door.

"I'm hungry." Max hoped that a full belly would help with the lightheaded fuzziness the morphine had caused.

"We can't just ignore what's happened in London," said the gargoyle, coming closer. "Our first duty is to protect innocents, and they're not being protected there. It's up to us to step in."

"The Chapter is gone. Without the Chapter Master, Mr Ekstrand is my direct boss now. What he says, we do."

"My stone arse!" The gargoyle sat back on its haunches, its face level with Max. "He's obviously a few sandwiches short of a picnic and he doesn't know what it's like out in the field. We do."

Max shook his head. "Disobeying a Sorcerer is not the most sensible course of action."

"I'm not saying we go and stick our fingers up at him and catch the first train back to London, I'm saying we can't just shrug and forget about it."

"I don't plan to do that. I'm going to ask him more about the Chapter, now I'm feeling better. I wasn't at my best last night either. And we can't rush into anything with the London problem; we don't know how high the corruption goes, or how widespread it is. Montgomery and Faulkner now are connected to the Camden Chapter. Are only Faulkner and the one who shot me corrupt? Is it all of that Chapter's Arbiters except for Montgomery? Is it the Chapter Master?"

"I was thinking about this whilst you were asleep," the gargoyle said. "We need to find out if that kind of corruption is in other places."

"But how? Even if we ignored the fact that we'd be breaking territorial rules, we have no support staff or liaison teams to flag up anything for us to look into. In London we're blind."

"True," the gargoyle said. "What I don't understand is why he isn't hopping up and down spitting for blood after all his Arbiters, bar us, were murdered. Why isn't he banging on the door of the Camden Chapter, or the Sorcerer of Essex?"

There was a knock on the door before Max could reply and Axon came back in. "Mr Ekstrand has asked for the gargoyle."

"What does he want with me?" The gargoyle sounded nervous.

"I have no idea," Axon replied and stood aside, gesturing for the gargoyle to leave. "Would you like to have lunch now?" he asked Max, who nodded.

He ate alone in a dining room with walls covered in landscape paintings whilst considering his options. It didn't take long. The food was simple and tasted good. Cold cuts with salad seemed to be just what he could manage. Axon had arranged a chair and cushion for his leg and the woolly feeling in his head slowly improved until he felt ready to talk to Ekstrand.

He made his slow and tiring way into the hall and heard the Sorcerer's voice.

"Good afternoon. How are you?"

"I'm very well, thank you, how are you?" That was Petra.

There was a long pause. "I'm not sure what to say," the Sorcerer eventually replied.

"Generally, 'I'm fine, thank you' will suffice."

"Even if I don't feel fine?"

"It depends on who the person is; whether you're addressing an acquaintance or someone you know well."

Max went to the door and saw Petra stand up as Mr Ekstrand hurried to the other side of the room. He was dressed in a casual lounge suit and woollen waistcoat. She was wearing another curve-hugging suit. Unlike the night before, Max felt indifferent about it.

"Good afternoon," Mr Ekstrand said to Petra, taking hesitant strides towards her with an outstretched hand. "How are you?"

Max cleared his throat.

"Ah!" Ekstrand beamed at him, none of the suspicion from the day before in evidence. "Maximilian, how are you? Do come in."

"You look better than yesterday," Petra said, helping him onto the sofa and placing cushions behind his back.

"I slept well." Max watched Ekstrand sit opposite him with a fixed smile on his face. "Is everything all right?"

"Yes, I am fine, thank you." Ekstrand spoke like a poor actor in a play. "I imagine you're wondering about the gargoyle. I've prepared it for fieldwork and we had a very interesting conversation about hospitals. It's in my laboratory whilst the modifications settle."

"Good," Max said, deciding not to concern himself with the change in the Sorcerer's behaviour; it seemed to have made him more useful.

"Now that you're up and about, I need you to get this investigation underway."

"Mr Ekstrand, Max can't even walk yet!" Petra said, sitting down nearby with her notebook and pen.

"He can with those," Ekstrand flapped a hand at the crutches. "Besides, we don't have time to waste; the season is about to start and I need to know what's going on with the Master of Ceremonies."

"Lavandula?" Max said. "He's the one who's gone missing?"

"Indeed," Ekstrand said, his focus interrupted by a flash of delight at seeing tea being carried in. "Axon, you read my mind. Earl Grey?"

"Of course, sir," Axon replied and served the tea discreetly as Ekstrand continued.

"Lavandula is arguably one of the most cooperative Fae-touched within the boundaries of the Heptarchy." Ekstrand took his cup and breathed in the ribbon of steam. "Earl Grey is the most superior of all teas, I find, don't you?"

He glanced at Petra as he said it, as if looking for approval. She rewarded him with a nod and he turned back to Max. "Mr Lavandula always informed me of any new Nether properties in Aquae Sulis, and the families involved. It's far more civilised than the way things are in Londinium and Oxenford. And now he's disappeared. I need him back." He frowned into the bottom of his teacup. "I don't like change."

"Do you suspect foul play?"

"Absolutely. Why would the Master of Ceremonies leave two days before the start of the season without telling me?"

"Perhaps he had a personal emergency," Max said.

"If he did, then I should know about it." Ekstrand sipped the tea. "Personal or not, any emergency that calls him away without so much as a polite letter is my business too. Besides, he understands the importance of doing things properly so he would have sent a messenger. Something is wrong, and I don't want to be forced to get used to a new Master of Ceremonies when I've just become accustomed to this one."

"And there's the data from the other night," Petra said, and Ekstrand set his cup down.

"Indeed!" He looked up at the ceiling, and then that odd fixed smile was back on his face again. "Would you like to see the monitoring chamber?"

"All right," Max said, noticing the way Ekstrand looked to Petra for approval again. She gave him a little smile, which pleased the Sorcerer immensely.

Once Max was up and the crutches in position, he followed the Sorcerer out of the sitting room and down the corridor, along a wing of the house he hadn't yet visited. The first few doors were painted white and were the same as any period house in the Nether or Mundanus. But the further down the corridor they went, the less conventional they were. One was covered in writing that had been painted on with something sparkling like starlight. Another was made of a smoky crystal slab, replete with the occasional flaw. The one Ekstrand stopped in front of looked more like a pressurised door from a submarine, made of riveted metal and with a small wheel instead of a handle.

"This is one of my favourite rooms," he said. "It's also top secret."

"I understand, sir," Max said, wondering why he was being brought into the Sorcerer's confidence when, only the day before, Ekstrand had been reluctant to even talk to him.

Ekstrand twirled the wheel, the door hissed and opened inwards. Max took care with the crutches to get over the lip of metal, not seeing all of the machinery until he was inside. The room was large, comparable to the generously sized living room, but felt cramped, filled with pipes, wires, dials and all manner of machinery that made no sense to Max.

At the centre of the far wall was a large drum of paper and several mechanical arms tipped with miniature brass model hands holding quills connected to individual ink reserves. They were moving independently, leaving ink trails on the paper as it turned on the drum.

"This took me years to build and refine," Ekstrand said as he patted his pockets. "I read about something called a seismograph and it inspired me to adapt the idea for my own purposes. None of the other Sorcerers have one." He turned back to Max. "That's because their understanding of the sorcerous arts is inferior."

"What does it measure?" Max asked, hobbling closer to the drum as Ekstrand located his spectacles.

"Nether entrance and egress in the city of Bath. Isn't it beautiful?"

Max was indifferent. "You know when the Fae-touched go in and out of Aquae Sulis?"

Ekstrand nodded, grinning. "And their staff. Whenever they open a Way, the sensors I have all over the city detect the activity and convey the information here. The only drawback is having to have extra coal brought in to feed the boiler. Petra tried to make me read a book about something called electronics that she believes would be more efficient, but I don't like that idea. For one thing, it would need electricity, which is vulgar. For another, I simply cannot put my trust in a machine without visible cogs, gears and levers. Who knows what 'electronics' might really be doing?"

Max, assuming the question was rhetorical, moved closer to the drum. "I always wondered how the Chapter Master knew so quickly when there was increased activity in certain areas."

Ekstrand nodded. "Axon keeps an eye on it, and sometimes the others too, but only on Saturdays. Obviously."

"Others?" Max asked, but Ekstrand had moved on and was rummaging in a box of paper by the side of the drum.

"Here it is," he said, holding up a section of paper. "See here, this is what it looks like when a Fae-touched or one of their servants opens a Way in the normal fashion."

He pointed at one of the lines that wobbled no more than half an inch away from its normal trajectory. Max looked back up at the drum and saw a similar wobble being produced by one of the quills and then another. "It's busy today."

"Yes, the season begins tomorrow, so they're all running around like idiots. Now look at this." He unfurled the paper a little more, revealing a huge block of black ink. "Know what that is?"

Max shook his head.

"That is someone opening a Way that is locked, using incredible force to do so."

"A break-in?"

"Exactly."

"At Lavandula's house?"

"Yes. Petra did some calculations. But look at how long it was being held open."

Max inspected the paper, realising that the lines marked time as well as location. "It seems much longer than all the others."

"Someone broke into his Nether house from Mundanus, held the Way open and then left again."

"I can't imagine another one of the puppets being strong enough to break his lock," Max said.

"They're not. He had the best protection Charms in the city."

"Not one of the Fae?" Max said.

"I think it's very possible, which is why you're going there now to see what you can find. If the Fae Court is meddling with key people in Aquae Sulis, nothing good is going to come of it."

"I agree, sir. May I ask a question?" At Ekstrand's nod he said, "Regarding the loss of the Chapter, sir... it must be connected to the corruption in London."

"I'm making preparations to look inside the Cloister. I don't want to rush into anything reckless."

"That's excellent news, sir. May I have permission to go and see what happened there, and to ask Axon to monitor the London press for any signs of–"

Ekstrand held up his hand. "London? Are you still determined to go back there?"

"Not physically, sir, I'm not very useful, and it's clear that's a hostile territory now, but I do think it has to be followed up."

"If there's corruption within one or possibly more north London Chapters, it becomes a matter for the Heptarchy. All of Albion's Sorcerers need to be contacted and a Moot called. It takes a dreadfully long time to do that."

"But if you told them why, surely they'd meet quickly?"

"I can't disclose the reason for the meeting unless all are present."

"In case the Sorcerer of Essex is the source of the corruption?"

Ekstrand laughed as if Max had told a brilliant joke, then stopped when he realised that an Arbiter would never do such a thing. "Nonsense. Because Dante is likely to take terrible offence if I so much as hint that there's a problem in his Kingdom, and that would cause another war. Much better to embarrass him in front of all the other Sorcerers, then they'll back me up when I demand an explanation."

"How long will it take?"

"Not long. A few weeks maybe."

"The innocents are being taken now, sir. We don't have a few weeks."

"I can't help the fact it will take time to open a proper dialogue; there are protocols to be followed, it's a sensitive business getting in touch with a Sorcerer, let alone to make everyone aware something's gone rotten in his territory. If we progress an investigation without informing him, it would be a terrible breach of sovereignty, not to mention appalling manners. We can use the time to determine what exactly happened to the Chapter; it may well give us more to take to the Moot about what the Camden Chapter has been up to. Besides, there's no guarantee the loss of the Chapter and the corruption in London are connected. Just because they appear to be doesn't mean they are. It could be that an experiment went catastrophically wrong and killed everyone in the cloister."

"I'll go now and see what happened," Max offered, all too aware they didn't have enough information.

"No, you don't understand. I can't just send you in there and I can't scry because the equipment in the cloister has been damaged. The anchor property is still intact, so there are no structural concerns, but whatever destroyed the soul vessels may still be active. It may be that the individuals responsible are waiting for you, especially if this was an effort to cover up your reports of corruption."

Max nodded, now seeing the problem. Ekstrand was being sensible. The buildings the Fae-touched lived in and Ekstrand's house depended on the existence of physical buildings in Mundanus. The properties in the Nether, like the one he stood in now, were reflections of the real buildings, bound by magical anchors that only Sorcerers and the Fae themselves knew how to create.

Nether buildings were stable and structurally safe as long as the Mundane anchor building remained so, and it meant maintaining the Nether property was effortless – all bound magically within the anchors. The fact the cloister was still intact gave hope for restoring a functional Chapter in the future, but there had still been a breach in security that couldn't be forgotten.

"How could an attacker have got inside?" he wondered aloud.

"They may have already been there," Ekstrand replied. "There are too many questions and not enough facts. I'll establish a new way to scry. It simply takes time to reduce risk, that's all."

Max nodded slowly, knowing he had to be patient. "May I be there when you first look?"

"Indeed, I'll summon you."

"I'll look into the disappearance of the Master of Ceremonies in the meantime," Max said, satisfied that something was being done, even if none of it seemed fast enough.

"Excellent." Ekstrand tossed the evidence back into the box. "And may I say, it's been a pleasure talking with you today," he added, in that poor actor tone. "I do hope you have a...

pleasant journey." He took off his spectacles, looking dissatisfied. "Do come again!" He shook his head as he tucked the glasses back into his jacket pocket. "It's so difficult," he muttered and ushered Max out.

Cathy stepped in front of Tom before he could reply. "He will not give you this satisfaction!"

"Catherine," Tom growled, his hand on her shoulder.

The Rosa's eyes widened in genuine shock. "How dare you behave in such a reprehensible manner! Have you no respect for the way things should be done? I have taken the trouble to find your brother to answer for your misdemeanour, pray do me the courtesy of stepping back and allowing your honour to be defended appropriately."

"But it's not even necessary!" she said as Tom succeeded in shoving her aside.

"What evidence do you have for this accusation, sir?" he asked the Rosa.

"Only confirmation from Lady Rose herself." His smug expression made his nose appear even larger. "When I saw what happened last night in Londinium I appealed to the Rosa Patroon, who intervened on my behalf. I'm given to understand that Lord Poppy himself approached Lady Rose to explain this bizarre turn of events, and confirmed your sister made the offending wish."

Tom turned to her, his mouth opening and closing and eyes wide like a goldfish tipped from his bowl. "What on earth?"

"It seems your family has very little awareness of your sister's actions," the Rosa added, now building himself up to a full-blown gloat.

"This is ridiculous," Cathy said. "Not only is it offensive–"

Tom yanked her away from the Rosa, who was starting to chuckle. "Don't make this any worse," he hissed, turning his back on the accuser and blocking his view of Cathy. "Is what he said true?"

Cathy wanted to push past Tom and argue for herself, but he saw her intent and held onto her arms. "Catherine, I swear, if you don't explain yourself right now–"

"I made the wish," she said, trying to wriggle out of his grip. She had planned to keep all that to herself, not wanting Tom, and eventually the rest of the family, to know about her failures to date. "Lord Poppy forced them on me, I was trying to sort it all out when you came and–"

"So his accusation stands?" Tom's cheeks blazed but his lips were white.

"Sort of. I didn't do it intentionally."

"When this mess is sorted out, you and I are going to have a frank and honest conversation."

"Fine, but Tom, you don't need to fight. It's absurd."

"He has called me out," Tom whispered. "Now I cannot do anything but accept, or risk damaging our family's reputation even further. Now stay here, and for goodness' sake don't speak a word."

He turned back to the Rosa, who had lit a cigarette and was leaning against the car again, smiling as if he were watching a comedy play out on a stage. "Straightened it all out?" he asked.

Tom cleared his throat as Cathy forced herself to think like one of them again. Something about this seemed wrong, but she couldn't work out why.

"Have you a second sir?" Tom asked, implicitly accepting the challenge.

"I have indeed. Name yours, sir, and they will set about making the arrangements."

"I counter your accusation with one of my own!" The words had flown out of Cathy's mouth before she had fully decided what she was going to say. As fast as she could recall the case, the words tumbled from her mouth in the formal style she hadn't spoken for years, before either of the men could silence her. "I hold that I did not directly cause the offence, and I do not benefit from the offence, therefore I place responsibility for your grievance onto the soul of the party who directly benefits: Mr Joshua Collins, mundane, unaffiliated to any of the Great Families."

The Rosa tossed his cigarette away. "Is there precedent?"

"Oh, yes," she said, fearing that Tom was about to suffer an aneurysm. "Lady Rose would know of it, as would my patron. In fact any of the Fae Court would know of the dispute between Lady Wisteria's favourite and the head of the Lavandula family in 1657. The latter argued that as he did not directly benefit from the effects of a miscast spell, responsibility for the grievance fell upon the actual benefactor, a mundane by the name of Wokingham, who bedded the milkmaid who'd been accidentally hit by the Beautifying Charm."

The Rosa considered this as Tom stared at her. "So be it." He bowed. "I'm not so boorish as to maintain a dispute with the wrong party. Consider my challenge withdrawn, Mr Papaver."

Tom breathed out in relief and shook the Rosa's hand. "I shall consider this conversation between us forgotten," he said.

"I think this meeting will be difficult to forget," Horatio replied, glancing pointedly at Cathy. "I will seek out this bland benefactor 'Collins' and call him out in a manner he will understand. Good day to you."

Cathy's heart fell into her trainers. "You're not going to challenge him, are you?"

"I have not received satisfaction," Horatio replied, pulling his gloves back on and walking round to the passenger seat as the driver adjusted his goggles. "Therefore I will obtain it from him."

"But he's a mundane!"

Horatio laughed. "It makes no difference to me. Makes it easier in fact, less political fallout." He glanced at Tom. "Wouldn't you agree? One less mundane in the world is hardly something worth our concern. Good day."

Tom returned his bow and they watched him climb into the car. When it was out of sight, Cathy pulled Tom towards the VW. "Come on! We have to get to London before he does, that's where Josh is!"

"Just wait one damn minute, Cat," Tom said, twisting himself free. "You owe me an explanation. What are these wishes that Lord Poppy gave you? Why didn't you mention them before?"

"There's no time for that now, you heard him, he's going to kill Josh! We can't let that happen."

"Why would I drive to London when we're required in Aquae Sulis post haste? I've never heard of this Collins, I have no idea who he is and frankly do not care to discover."

"But it's my fault he got mixed up in this!"

"And how did that happen?"

Cathy looked up at the sky. "He was my boyfriend."

She didn't look back at him for a few beats, but when the silence persisted, she finally did. His face was covered by both hands.

"I don't know where to start," he said, dragging his hands down slowly, stretching his face into a horrible expression. "Before we get any further, are there any other horrendous secrets you're keeping from me?"

"No. Can you shout at me in the car please?"

"I take it a 'boyfriend' is the mundane equivalent of courting a young man without parental permission?" he asked, arms folded, resolutely still.

"Yes. And I know what you're worried about so why don't you just come out with it?"

Tom looked away, deeply embarrassed. "This is an absolute nightmare."

Cathy rolled her eyes. "You're only upset because you think Josh and I slept together, right?"

"How could you have become so crass so soon?"

"We didn't."

His eyebrows shot up. "A mundane with traditional values? I find that hard to believe."

"No, it was the bloody curse." This time it was she who hid her face with her hands. She rubbed her skin, wanting to wake up out of the same nightmare as her brother. "Look, when I went up to Cambridge, you didn't think Father trusted the chaperone and the minder, did you? He put a curse on me, to make sure I didn't lose my market value."

"Catherine! What a way to speak of your own purity."

"Oh, please. I'm not stupid, that's what it comes down to, isn't it? Have to guarantee the goods are pure and unsullied when selling them off to the highest bidder."

Tom didn't have an argument to put forward against the truth, no matter how crass it sounded. "Father told you he'd cursed you?"

"No. I managed to get away from the minder and hide in Manchester but I didn't find a way to break the curse."

"How did you find out about it?"

She blushed. "You really want to know?"

"Not really, but I feel I must."

"Every time I... whenever I... if I had those kinds of intentions near a man... Oh, God. Can't you just take my word for it?"

"I have to know whether our family has an even worse problem than I thought."

"If I tried to take my clothes off near a man, with the intention of... being close to him, they would put themselves back on again. I couldn't even unbutton my shirt or take off my shoe if that was what I was planning to do."

He looked appalled. "So you only discovered this curse because you tried to..." he cleared his throat, "sleep with this Collins man?"

She nodded, her blush competing with his.

"I don't know what to say. Of all the things I've thought of you, Catherine, I never thought you'd have such low moral standards and loose virtue."

"Oh, give me a break, it's different in Mundanus. If anyone should be offended it's me! I have every right to do what I like with my body!"

"I refer you to my earlier comments regarding your selfishness," he said stiffly. "I'm relieved Father had the foresight to take these measures. It's been proven that you didn't deserve his trust at all."

She forced herself to breathe out slowly. "It's a different world, and anyway, this doesn't change the fact that we need to go to London and save Josh."

"You want me to go against Father's express wishes so we can save a mundane man who sought to deflower you?"

She was about to argue more, but realised it wasn't the time. "I want you to help me save an innocent man who doesn't deserve to be murdered because I am such a bloody idiot, OK? I want you to be the kind of brother who wouldn't want that either. If he dies, I won't be able to live with the guilt."

He glanced at the car. "I don't know how fast we can get there."

"Let me drive," she said, holding out her hand. "I passed my test, don't worry."

He dropped the key onto her palm. "I can't believe I'm doing this. We need to leave London as soon as we can when this is done."

"I know," she said, running over to the car.

"And if I think, for one moment you're planning some kind of elaborate escape–"

"I know, Barbie time," she said, adjusting the seat and mirror as he clicked his seatbelt in place with a confused expression. "Now don't freak out. I'm going to give it some wellie."

"I don't even understand what you mean," he muttered as she revved the engine, working out the clutch point.

Then she floored it, and he didn't say a word for the rest of the trip.

13

Cathy cautiously pushed open the door of the Emporium of Things in Between and Besides and peeped in to check for other customers. There were none.

The bell tinkled above her and the Shopkeeper looked up from his book.

"Catherine!"

She went in, defensive. "Hello."

"I'm so glad you're back."

"I'm not here to work for you."

He gave her a sad look, tucked his bookmark into place and closed the book. "Not for that reason. I wanted to explain before; I didn't tell Lord Poppy you'd be here, but you didn't give me a chance."

"Really?" She always found it so hard to tell whether people were telling the truth.

"Really, Catherine. I'm amazed you think I'd do that. Is your regard for my discretion so poor?"

She bit her lip. "Not many people would tell a Fae Lord to get lost."

"That's true, and why I could not. But he worked out where you were all by himself. I have no idea how. He told me to make sure you didn't guess he was there. I had to obey."

"OK," she said, coming into the shop. "I'm sorry I was horrible to you. I was upset."

"Understandably."

"And everything is all bug… is falling apart and I need your help. A Rosa is on the way to London to kill a mundane, and it's my fault."

The Shopkeeper came out from behind the counter, too intrigued to remember to take off his glasses. "Are you certain?"

She nodded. "He told us. He was totally chilled out about it."

"Chilled?"

She sighed. "He didn't give the impression he was concerned about murdering a mundane." Speech in the Nether was so long-winded.

"I know the Rosa family is arrogant, and is powerful in Londinium, but even so… there are still Arbiters to consider, even if one is unconcerned by moral issues."

"It's Horatio Gallica-Rosa. Is he good with a sword?"

"Only the best in Londinium, arguably Albion. The only other young blood I'd consider his equal is Nathaniel Reticulata-Iris. It's just as well they live so far apart."

"Bollocks," Cathy muttered. "Look, I reckon I've got an hour at the most to make sure he fails. What've you got that could help?"

"You want to use a Charm on a member of the Rosa family? They'd find out, you know, it would make things worse."

"What about one I could cast on Josh, the mundane, to protect him?"

The shopkeeper rubbed his chin thoughtfully. "I don't need to counsel you against using a Charm in Mundanus, do I?"

"I know the risks. I don't have much time. Tom is waiting outside."

"He found you then?"

She nodded, not wanting to go there. "Please, anything. I'll owe you."

"It would have to be strong, but subtle," he murmured, his grey eyes scanning the shelves. "Fast-acting and short-lived, to ensure it couldn't be identified and traced back to you..."

Cathy bounced on her heels, aware of time slipping away. If she stepped out of the Nether outside the shop, they'd be in Smithfields. She had no idea where Josh was, but Tom said he had a couple of Seeker Charms left that she could use when the time came.

"I have it!" the Shopkeeper said, dragging over the wheeled stepladder. "A Luck Charm, one that's very potent with a tight localised effect. It's very easy to cast, just a matter of ensuring contact with the individual who needs the luck." He climbed up to one of the higher shelves, rummaged amongst the boxes and came back down to her holding a plain wooden tube.

He unscrewed the top. She expected a telescope to slide out of it, but instead something more like a small egg dropped into his palm. He showed it to her. "It is as it looks," he said. "The shell is very fragile, it breaks easily on contact, so you don't have to hit him too hard with it. Speak his name on contact, so all the luck goes to him."

"Will it leave a mark though?"

"It's white for a few moments, then disappears, so you'd better time it well. Apply just before the Rosa attacks; the mundane will have anywhere between five to ten minutes of extraordinary good luck, then he's on his own. It's impossible to trace to you."

"But they could trace it here," she said, watching him carefully wrap the egg in tissue paper.

"As I have had occasion to explain many times in the past, I simply sell the goods, I do not choose what to do with them. And I never disclose what I sell to whom."

She took the wrapped egg and kissed him on the cheek. "Thank you. I'll come back when I can, OK?"

He didn't reply, just brushed his cheek with his fingertips as she dashed out of the door.

Half an hour later, Cathy and Tom were chasing a lone mint imperial down a street in Notting Hill. They'd parked the car, the traffic too heavy to make progress, and cast the last Seeker Charm Tom had to narrow down Joshua's exact location.

It wobbled briefly outside a tall wooden gate that was already open, before changing direction to go through and head up the path, then toppling onto its side at the bottom of a doorstep.

They stopped at the gate. The front door was already open; they'd got there in time to see Horatio's back as he stepped into the house and slammed the door behind him.

"Shit!" Cathy said, diving behind the wall and out of sight should the Rosa turn around. "How did he get here so fast?"

"He might have used the Nether, I think the Rosa family has properties in the midlands," Tom replied. "Perhaps one of them is connected to a Londinium house, then he'd just have to step through into London. It's what I would have done, if we'd had property outside of Aquae Sulis."

"We just have to hit Josh with the egg..." Cathy said, looking up at the upper storeys of the town house.

"I could throw it, if I had a line of sight, but we can't go in there, Cat, I can't risk upsetting the Rosas in their city."

There was no apparent access to the rear of the house from the front gate. "Maybe we can go round the back." She set off down the outside of the wall. The house was on a corner and she hoped there would be access, not that she knew what she'd do if there was.

There was a garden, but no back gate, only another property backing onto the house Josh was in.

There was a sound of a door opening and footsteps on flagstones. "If you don't get out now I'm going to call the police!"

It was Josh. Cathy heard a beep of a mobile phone button, then a thwack and the sound of it smashing on the floor.

"You bastard!"

"Answer my question!" the Rosa yelled.

"Can you climb the wall?" she asked Tom but he shook his head. He pointed to the house that backed onto the garden. "We could try there."

They sprinted round the corner, vaulted the gate and Cathy rang the doorbell, imagining Horatio cutting Josh down as they tried to avoid a scandal. She rang a second time but no one answered. Tom put his hand on the handle and used the same Charm he'd used to break into her flat. The door swung open.

"Upstairs, at the back," Cathy said, and they took the stairs two at a time.

There was a door ahead of them, a bedroom, sumptuously decorated with a mercifully large view onto the garden. Tom lifted the lower half of the sashed window. They could see Horatio drawing his sword as Josh backed away across the grass.

"Give me the egg," Tom said and Cathy unwrapped it with trembling hands. Holding it gently between thumb and forefinger, he leant out of the window and, after a moment that seemed like a day to Cathy, he tossed it high into the air.

"What are you doing!" she squealed as it flew upwards, not straight at Josh.

"Watch," he said and she saw the egg hit the peak of its trajectory and then begin a downward plummet.

"Joshua Collins," she whispered as the egg splattered the top of Josh's head.

He cried out and looked up for the offending bird.

"It's done," Tom said. "Let's go."

"I have to make sure he's OK," Cathy said, but Tom shut the window and pulled her away.

"There's nothing we can do now anyway," he said, dragging her out of the room. "We've wasted enough time."

"I have to know!" she said and kicked him in the shin. Leaving him clutching his leg, she raced down the stairs, through the house to the back door, grateful to see the key left in its lock. Tom was catching her up as she bolted into the back garden and raced to the bench she'd seen against the dividing garden wall.

"Cat!" he hissed as she jumped up onto it and looked over the top. There was no one in the garden, but she could see movement inside the house.

Cathy scrabbled over the top, kicking Tom in the process as he tried to grab her feet. She fell into the bushes on the other side, scraping her elbow on the way down. She hurried towards the house, keeping behind the shrubs on the right hand side, as sounds of smashing and chaos rang from the open back door.

She reached the back wall of the house, dropped to a crouch and crept below the nearest open window, where she dared to peep inside.

She saw Horatio staring at the broken blade of his sword in disbelief, a battered lampshade perched on his head at a jaunty angle like a boater hat. Josh staggered into view, holding a large copper saucepan, hair wild and clothes rumpled. She could make out a stylish room in the background, with a TV that cost more than a term's fees.

"I'm not familiar with your fighting style, sir." Horatio was stalling for time as he struggled to regain his poise. "It's beyond chaotic."

"I told you, if you don't leave, I'm calling the police," Josh shouted.

"But our business is unfinished," Horatio continued, rounding the sofa. He glanced at a point behind Josh's shoulder with a shocked expression and Josh fell for it, turning to look as the Rosa took the opportunity to step and thrust with what was left of the blade.

The dirty tactic would have worked, if a large white bird hadn't flown into the room through the very window Cathy was using to spy, making Josh duck instinctively. The bird caught the blade's swipe instead and the decapitated gull landed with a thud at his feet.

Horatio stared at the dead bird, aghast. "This is ridiculous. I have no idea which of the families are protecting you but–" He was cut off as Josh exploited the opportunity to swing the saucepan at the Rosa's head. It connected with a terrible clang. The swordsman crumpled like a broken marionette leaving Josh white-lipped as the bloodied feathers settled at his feet.

"Holy crapola," he said, dropping the saucepan.

Cathy was about to stand up and knock on the window, desperate to make sure he was OK and to speak to him one last time. She just wanted one kiss, one minute to say sorry, but then she heard the slam of the front door.

"I'm home!"

Josh rubbed the top of his head, feeling for what he thought was bird droppings, frowning when nothing was there. "I'm in here, Ca–" He shook his head. "Ella. I'm in the den, don't freak out. Actually, wait there."

He rushed out as Cathy turned away and dropped onto her backside, suddenly exhausted. She saw Tom peering over the wall, beckoning frantically. She didn't want to move, she didn't want to do anything. The only place she was going now was an elegant prison. Why walk towards it?

But then she imagined Josh taking her replacement into the living room and she didn't want to be found in the garden by the rich bitch. She hauled herself up, picked her way back through the shrubs and Tom reached over the wall to pull her over.

"You stupid little–"

Cathy burst into tears and he pulled her into a hug, wrapping his arms around her and holding her tight.

She sobbed into his coat until they heard a police siren. "We have to go, Cat," he said and she nodded.

"I really love him."

"I can see that now." He kissed her forehead. "I'm sorry, Cat, I really am. It's all over. We have to go home."

14

Axon drove Max and the gargoyle to the other side of Bath, and parked the car just up the road from the Holburne Museum. It was a bright autumn day in Mundanus, so the gargoyle was hunkered down in the back seat of the large estate car Axon used to run his mundane errands.

Max looked back at the gargoyle, trying to get used to the formulae carved all over it and the medieval-style bracers it was now wearing. They were decorated with an elaborate design that made Max's head ache.

"These things are itchy." The gargoyle held up its wrists. "But I have to keep 'em on, apparently. Extra protection."

"What from?"

"I dunno. Bad breath? Who cares? Everyone we ever knew is either dead or missing, there's all kinds of dodgy stuff going on in London and the Sorcerer doesn't give a rat's arse, and you're asking about these stupid itchy armbands?"

Max faced front again. "I haven't forgotten about London, or the Chapter. But the Sorcerer is right; we do need to look into this."

The gargoyle muttered something he couldn't hear. Its grumpiness was like a bad smell filling the car and just as hard to ignore.

"Stay here," he told it once the car's engine was switched off.

"How long will you be, sir?" Axon asked.

"Less than half an hour." Max struggled out of the car and onto his crutches.

He wanted to take a look at the mundane perimeter first, knowing that someone had broken into Lavandula's Nether house after going through the museum grounds in Mundanus. The main gates were locked and a notice hung over the handles:

Closed – Apologies for Any Inconvenience.

He made his way round the railings until he reached the large wooden gates he knew were set into the wall. They had a new hasp-and-staple lock, fitted with a shiny padlock that he picked with little effort.

He went through and pushed the gates closed behind him, already tired from the effort of moving with crutches. He crossed the drive up to the anchor property, which was the usual Georgian affair the puppets liked. He went to the side door. The front entrance was too exposed for his liking.

He propped one of the crutches against the wall and slipped his right hand into his pocket. His fingers found the knuckleduster and he wriggled them into place. Quickly checking to make sure no innocents were looking through the railings, he adjusted the metal until it sat comfortably at the base of his fingers. The sorcerous markings glinted in the sunlight. He made a fist and inspected the band of thick metal running across it. Pristine.

He knocked three times, slowly, and listened for the telltale echo reverberating into the Nether house anchored to the mundane property. There was a pause, but there always was. If an Arbiter was expected, there would be careful preparations to ensure that everything was in order. If the knock was an unpleasant surprise, there would be arguments about who would open the door and what would be said.

The door opened, a tell-tale shimmering over the threshold indicating that it was the Nether house he was seeing into rather than the museum. Miss Lavandula had answered the door herself, opening a Way into Aquae Sulis as she did so. He hadn't expected that.

Her dress was the same dark blue as her eyes, high-necked and close-fitting in the Victorian style, hair worn up, jewels at her ears. She had the skin of a woman in her late twenties yet her file at the cloister listed her age as over three hundred years old. She was composed, inclining her head at him. As Censor of Aquae Sulis she'd had a lot of practice receiving unwanted guests and remaining polite.

The Censor was one of the many titles the puppets had picked and twisted from Roman times; she had the power to deny people access to Aquae Sulis, for whatever reason she liked, and, if she permitted them to enter, she effectively determined their social standing within their Society. As Master of Ceremonies, her brother created social events that could make or break a family in one night. Between them they had the residents of the city terrified of what they could do to them with nothing more than a comment, a look or even just a strategic omission from a guest list.

"I've been waiting for you," the Censor said, gesturing for him to come in.

He held his breath as he crossed the threshold, a habit they all had. His ears popped and there was a feathery touch on his face as he left Mundanus and crossed over into the Nether. Through a nearby window he caught a glimpse of the reflected Great Pulteney Street of Aquae Sulis but he didn't linger over it. The Nether had lost its novelty a long time ago.

The door was closed behind him. "Good afternoon, Miss Lavandula. Thank you."

It was so much easier when they invited him in. Forcing entry made everyone less reasonable to deal with.

"I knew it would reach an Arbiter's ears soon enough. Though I would have thought this a matter for Society, rather than your kind."

"Any unusual events in Aquae Sulis are our business, ma'am, especially those that may have long-term consequences. Do you know where your brother is? If so, I won't trouble you."

She took a breath; he knew she was weighing up whether to lie to him or not. It was in their nature, instinctive to one as old and powerful as she. "No," she finally said. "I do not."

"Would you mind if I asked you some questions?" It was a courtesy; he had the right to pursue an investigation and she was obligated to cooperate. It was one of the oldest laws.

"Not at all," she replied with a cold smile.

"When was the last time you saw Mr Lavandula?"

"Monday afternoon."

"Did he seem worried about anything?"

"My brother never worried, Mr…"

"Call me Max."

Her nostrils flared slightly. "My brother never worried about anything, Max."

"Even in the last days before the new season?"

"I assure you those are the most relaxed for him. The events are arranged, invitations sent and everything set into motion. I am the one most in demand the week before the season begins."

"About that," he said, slipping the knuckle-duster off in his pocket and retrieving his notebook. "Have you had any requests from unsavoury individuals to enter Aquae Sulis?"

"One always does at this time of year," she sighed. "But no one that made me concerned for my family's safety."

"So you are concerned for your brother?"

She stiffened. "Of course. I know my brother would not leave Aquae Sulis voluntarily at this time of year, and, if something had called him away, he would have told me immediately."

"That's why you closed the museum."

She nodded. "I didn't want any unscrupulous individuals to send in staff to snoop around once they realised he was gone."

He stared at her as she spoke, examining every movement, every flicker across her features. He believed her, and he could see she was genuinely worried. "Have you been contacted by anyone regarding your brother's disappearance?"

"No. You're the first." She looked at his leg cast. "And it seems you've been delayed."

"Unrelated," he said. "No ransom demands?"

"Nothing."

"When did you first realise he was missing?"

"We were supposed to breakfast together on Tuesday morning and discuss the last-minute entrants to the city. He never arrived."

"And when did you last see him on Monday?"

"He left my residence at about 6pm and I believe he was intending to come home."

"Did he have any guests?"

"No, but the staff would have been here."

"I'll need to speak to them too."

"Of course. They don't seem to know any more than I do though."

"Are they here now?"

"No. I didn't want anyone here except myself when your enquiries were made. One does all one can to avoid gossip at a time like this. You'll be able to interview them at my residence."

That explained why she opened the door. "Did your brother have any engagements on the Monday night?"

"He dined with the Irises. I know he came home, the footman and the maid told me."

Max thought back to the data from the Sorcerer's machine. It placed the break-in at close to midnight. It fitted so far.

"I'd like to take a look around."

Her lips pressed together; it was the last thing she wanted. "If you wish."

He went from room to room, no sound but the click of his crutches on the wooden floor. He couldn't do as thorough a search as he would have if he'd been mobile and free of supervision, but he wanted to see if anything leapt out, to follow up later.

"No signs of a struggle anywhere?" he asked and she shook her head. "Nothing taken?"

"No."

He couldn't manage the stairs; he was starting to sweat and the fatigue was becoming hard to hide. "Thank you for your cooperation," he said, heading for the door.

"I'd appreciate it if you could be discreet," she said, fingertips on the door handle. "I'm sure you can imagine how delicate a situation this is."

"I'm not exactly on speaking terms with your people," Max said. "And we're not known for socialising."

She just nodded and opened the door.

"I'll let you know if I find anything," he said and left.

He emerged into Mundanus. The pain was making him less observant, but it made sense; she'd be worried that people would be watching the house in Aquae Sulis.

He looked through the gates and down the hill. The whole of Great Pulteney Street leading up to the house was mirrored in the Nether, forming one of the main thoroughfares in

Aquae Sulis and watched at all times by their servants. That
was why the mundane property had been broken into.
Whatever the assailant did inside, be it knock him out or kill
him, it was done with the door held open providing a quick
and uncomplicated escape into Mundanus. The body could
have been carried out of the garden gate, put in a car and
driven anywhere.

But why? No ransom, no demands of any kind if the sister
was to be believed. It made no sense.

Then he remembered that it was one of the Fae Court
who'd broken in, not some screwed-up puppet. They didn't
think like people. But they weren't murderers, and certainly
not of one of Lady Lavender's favourites. She'd be kicking up
a storm in Exilium, no doubt.

It was just as possible he'd decided to cut and run, tired of
being the most important man in Aquae Sulis. It was unlikely,
but possible. Did the puppets have nervous breakdowns too?
Then he remembered what the machine had told them. If life
had got too complicated for Mr Lavandula, he wouldn't have
needed to break out of his own house.

He scanned the trees between the drive and the gate,
doing his best to ignore the sweat rolling between his
shoulder blades. The long grass and bushes could have
snagged something. He got a few steps closer and a surge of
pain stopped him.

There was a scratching sound on the other side of the wall
and then two clawed stone paws appeared at the top. The
gargoyle swung itself over and landed in the garden with
a decent thud. Max waited for any shouts, but thankfully
there were none. "I told you to stay hidden."

The gargoyle checked no one else was there and then
scampered over on all four legs. "Will you just rest, for
goodness' sake? You're hurting us."

"I just wanted to check over there." Max nodded towards the trees. "Anywhere between the door and the gate, something might have been dropped, it's been closed to Mun–"

"I know. Wait and don't move," the gargoyle ordered and went searching.

Max swayed, wondering if Axon had a syringe in the car. Was he becoming addicted? Did he care? Was he anything more than sore hands, bruised armpits, a throbbing temple and a leg that was so painful it made him want to pull it off and hop home?

"Hey!" The gargoyle was waving something at him near one of the trees. Max made his way unsteadily, and they met halfway. "I found something."

Max put his weight on his good leg, tucked the crutches tighter under his armpits and took the wallet as the gargoyle headed back to the tree. Its black leather was worn, stuffed with receipts, old tickets and a five-pound note. There were credit cards, a driving licence, a swipe card for one of the local business centres. Jackpot.

He pulled out the licence. "Samuel James Westonville" was printed below a picture with an address in Bath that would come in handy. He sifted through the receipts, the breakthrough distracting him from the pain. Pizza, beer, toiletries, DVDs: this was an innocent's wallet, and the last receipt was dated on the Monday night at 10.55pm.

"Over here," the gargoyle called, and he tucked the wallet inside his jacket. The gargoyle was halfway up a tree trunk, its thick arms and legs wrapped around it like a koala bear. It pointed out a bit of bark with a claw.

Max leaned closer and saw the dark stain and the lone brown hair snagged on a knot, waving in the breeze. He plucked it free and dropped it into an evidence bag he had folded in his back pocket. He broke off the stained piece of bark too and nodded at the gargoyle.

"Good work. We've got a lead."

15

Cathy stared at the Holburne Art Museum as Tom parked the car in Great Pulteney Street. It was dusk and a few tourists were strolling down the road admiring the architecture. It was strange seeing the anchor property as a public building when Cathy knew it better in the Nether as the home of the Aquae Sulis Lavandulas, her uncle and aunt who were the Master of Ceremonies and Censor, respectively. In the Nether version of the same street in Aquae Sulis their house dominated the social structure of the area. Her mother, who was a Lavandula before being married into the Rhoeas-Papavers, gave her father the social boost enabling the family to acquire the terrace closest to the residence of the most powerful people in the city. Tom, as their eldest son, had the privilege of living in the same street, but further away.

She looked at the house she'd grown up in, remembering the nursery wing at the back, safely tucked away from any curious mundane eyes. The servants would be in the anchor property, working hard to maintain the luxurious lifestyle of the Nether house. Her parents were in there, just on the other side of the veil that separated Mundanus from their pocket reality. So close and still, thankfully, so far.

"Come on," he said when she didn't move. "Let's get you sorted out here before you face them."

Cathy unclipped the seatbelt and with leaden legs got out of the car. Her mouth was dry and her neck ached. Somehow she'd fallen asleep on the way back and now everything felt slightly unreal.

The fact that he took her right up to the mundane anchor property of his own house said a great deal. Those in Society rarely went into Mundanus but, when they did, they generally went in and out at the edge of Aquae Sulis, thereby minimising opportunities for the residents of Bath to notice people seeming to walk into a house and never coming out again, or at least approaching a garden gate and appearing to go through but never reaching the front door of the house. Tom evidently didn't want the residents of Aquae Sulis to see her return, and in her dishevelled state it made sense.

Tom muttered the Charm of Openings at the gate, put his arm around her and steered her ahead of him and into the Nether. It had been a long time since she'd seen the silver sky of Aquae Sulis and she hadn't missed it. The air was unnaturally still. She felt her chest tighten and her heart race. Instinctively she stepped back but Tom was in the way. He squeezed her briefly and the panic subsided.

Inside, the house was warm and bright. It smelt of freshly baked bread and cinnamon. She could hear a piano playing.

"Lucy?" Tom called. "I'm back."

The music stopped and his wife called from a room towards the back of the house. Cathy fidgeted. She just couldn't imagine Tom married. She couldn't quite believe this was his house and that he was living apart from their parents. Whenever she'd thought of him he was still gangling and affable, still living under their father's oppressive glare. It was hard to reconcile that with how everything had changed.

A petite woman came into the hallway, dressed in a long green gown that accentuated her tiny waist. She had the straight shining blonde hair that her little sister would have done despicable things to have, large blue eyes and fair skin. She seemed kind as she smiled and hurried over with her hands outstretched towards Cathy.

"You must be Catherine!" she said. Her voice had the tiniest hint of an American accent. "I'm delighted to meet you at last!"

Cathy clasped Lucy's hands even though it felt bizarre to do so. She didn't want to cut her dead in her own home. Lucy's hands were delicate and soft and she looked like a child next to Tom.

"Thanks," Cathy said awkwardly.

"Lucy, do you have a dress Cat could borrow?"

They both looked up at him. "Not any that would reach her ankles," Lucy replied, appraising Cathy's height. "Don't worry about fashion, dear, your parents know you've been on the Continent." She stood back, still holding Cathy's hands, and looked at her clothes. "I'm glad you're sensible enough to dress in the mundane style for travel, it's the only way to do it as far as I'm concerned. I'll ring for the footman, he can bring in your cases and we'll press a dress in no time. Your parents must be dying to see you!"

"Cat's baggage was lost," Tom said. "We're in a bit of a fix, aren't we, Cat?"

Cathy refused to reinforce the lie, not wanting to play Lucy for a fool.

"It's no problem," Lucy said, pulling her towards the stairs. "We'll get Catherine bathed whilst you go home and pick up one of her dresses. You did leave some there, I imagine?"

"I'm not sure I'd fit…"

"I'll be back soon," Tom said. "I want to tell them you're here safe and sound anyway." He gave her one last worried look. "You won't…"

"Go!" Lucy laughed. "She'll be fine and we'll have a chance to get to know each other."

Tom left and initially Cathy wondered whether to make a bid for freedom. But then Lucy would be left to take the blame and, whilst Cathy didn't know her, Lucy seemed so harmless she couldn't bring herself to get her into trouble. And there was still nowhere to run where they couldn't find her.

"You must be exhausted," Lucy said, leading her up the stairs after calling for the lady's maid. "You'll feel so much better after a soak and a light supper. By the time you're done Tom will be back and you can dress and go to see your parents."

Lucy's voice was soft and warm, but the accent bizarre. Cathy wondered if she was trying to hide her American roots. Perhaps Tom had asked her to try and fit in. That was the main expectation placed upon young brides: to blend into Society just enough to avoid malicious gossip, but stand out just enough to receive admiration, all of which would be directed at the husband, of course, for having impressed the families enough to secure a prize calf. Both Tom and their sister Elizabeth had been born with an innate sense of how much to stand out and how to blend in at the right time but Cathy never had a clue. She couldn't understand how they could be related.

"I have a robe you can borrow," Lucy said. "You can change in the guest bedroom and bathe in my bedchamber. The fire is lit already. Had I known you were coming here first I'd have made other arrangements."

Cathy had forgotten about how they lived. How would she forget the convenience of hot running water? Showers?

Flushing toilets? The Great Families called the mundanes "savages" but there was better sanitation in Mundanus.

Before they'd even reached the bedroom a small army of servants had been put to work and Cathy realised that she'd tuned out of the conversation.

"Perhaps they'll find them," Lucy was saying as she opened a door.

"Find what?"

"Your bags. Were they misplaced at the port? I remember the delays I had when I moved here. It seemed to take just as long to get out of the port as it did to cross the Atlantic."

"Umm…" Cathy couldn't settle on a reply. She'd got used to big lies, ones that explained away her entire childhood, not stupid things like turning up waif-like in the most inappropriate clothes ever seen in Aquae Sulis.

"I'll send for tea," Lucy said, letting go of Cathy's hand at last to go over to the bell-pull.

"I don't want tea," Cathy blurted. She wanted a Leffe blonde beer in a tall, sweating pint glass. She wanted a kebab. And a cuddle with Josh.

"Look, something is obviously wrong here." Lucy moved away from the bell-pull. "You don't seem like a girl coming home. You seem like someone dragged off the street and wondering where the hell she is." Lucy was sounding very American all of a sudden.

"It's that obvious?"

"Honey, you're no actress."

Her new sister-in-law sounded more like a mundane than a daughter of a wealthy Society family but Cathy didn't have the mental space to fathom that puzzle. She sat on the bed and put her head in her hands. It was as heavy as a bowling ball and felt just as thick. "What has Tom told you?"

"That you've been away in Switzerland and that your travel arrangements were disrupted." Lucy sat next to her, strangely close. Perhaps it was an American thing. "He's been so tense. All he said was that he was waiting for a message to come and pick you up. He raced out of the house first thing this morning before we'd even had breakfast."

"Oh."

"He lied to me, didn't he?"

Cathy reddened. "Well..."

"It's OK, I knew something was up."

Cathy twisted to face her. "I didn't mean to dump him in it."

"I know he doesn't trust me yet. It's OK, really."

"How long have you been married?"

Lucy frowned. "Where have you been?"

"Oh, bollocks to all of this," Cathy said, throwing her hands up in the air. "I wasn't in Switzerland, I was in Mundanus. I was at Cambridge for a year and then I ran away about eighteen months ago. I look like I've been dragged off the street because I practically was. I didn't want to come back."

Lucy's eyes were as round as chocolate buttons. "You ran away and hid in Mundanus?"

"Yeah."

"And lived there, all that time, without any help?"

Cathy regretted her honesty. "Yeah."

"Awesome!"

She twitched. "You don't think I'm some horrible, selfish cow?"

"No," Lucy said with a laugh. "I figure you've got guts to live in Mundanus. It's not an easy place to go if you're brought up in Nether Society. And I've met your parents. I'm impressed you stood up for what you wanted, they're pretty intimidating. So I think you're awesome."

Cathy scratched her head. "I didn't stand up for myself, I ran away like a bloody coward. I avoided all of the messy stuff back then, so it's even worse now. I don't know what I'm going to say to them. It's all got a bit complicated."

Lucy grinned. "You Brits, you worry too much about what other people think." She cleared her throat. "Sorry," she said, the vowel sounding closer to the Queen's English. "Listen, I can't imagine what you've been through with Tom but I can see you're upset and I can see you're exhausted. Take a bath, have something to eat – when Tom gets back I'll ask him how things are at your place and, if your parents are angry, well, maybe it'd be better for you to stay here and see them in the morning after you've rested."

Cathy felt herself welling up. "Sorry," she said, sniffing, horribly embarrassed. "My eyes are scratchy, you know, because I'm tired."

"I know." Lucy smiled. "I'll get you that robe."

Cathy looked down at her battered trainers and grubby jeans. This was potentially the last time she'd wear trousers and comfortable footwear. "What is wrong with you?" she muttered to herself as the sniffing threatened to become snivelling. "You're thinking about that now? Focus!"

But she couldn't. Somewhere deep down, beneath the extraordinary fatigue, the hollow hunger, the anxiety, impotent rage and hatred of her return to the Nether, there was the knowledge that she'd have to think up a fantastic third wish and faster than she could bleat "But it's all so unfair."

The room was decorated like an Edwardian hotel; impersonally luxurious, floral and full of chintz. She lay back on the bed and looked up at the glass bowl of the light fitting, thinking about the tiny sprite trapped inside. Her whole life before she'd ran away she'd never even thought of them, now she found herself relating. Apart from the shining part. She'd never do that, literally or figuratively.

The robe was brought in by a silent maid who curtsied without making eye-contact. It was thick cotton, dark blue and long enough to make Cathy suspect it belonged to Tom rather than Lucy. She could hear the patter of feet up and down the stairs as the servants carried buckets of hot water to the neighbouring room to fill the bath.

Reluctantly, she took off her clothes and shrugged on the robe, waiting for the invitation to bathe. She caught a glimpse of herself in the cheval mirror and saw how wrecked she looked. Her hair was just a tangled lump held in place by an elastic band she'd found when packing. It looked like someone had stapled a dead hamster to the back of her head. Stray wisps and her reddened eyes made her look slightly crazy. She was so pale and the skin around her eyes was so black she looked unwell. She certainly felt it.

She flopped back onto the bed, feet dangling over the edge and closed her eyes, knowing the maid would collect her when the bath was ready, and drifted towards a restless sleep.

"Miss Plain? Miss Mundane? Wake up!"

Waking was like climbing out of a well. A sharp pinprick on the tip of her nose made her eyes half open but, when she saw the faerie hovering just a few centimetres above her face, she was wide awake and scrabbling up the bed away from it.

"Time's up!" the faerie chimed with delight.

"It's not – there's still nearly twenty-four hours till the ball!"

The faerie sighed. "Lord Poppy has been so patient, considering how dreadfully boring you've been." It flew over to the mirror. "He doesn't want to wait a moment longer." It tapped the glass and it rippled like the surface of a lake. When it settled again, the room was no longer reflected. Instead Cathy could see a beautiful meadow under a blue sky.

Exilium.

"He's waiting," the faerie said with a clap of her hands. "Come on!"

"But I'm not even dressed, I can't go there in a bath robe!"

The faerie blew a raspberry. "Wearing clothes won't make any difference to how ugly you are or make you more interesting. Stop wasting time."

Cathy got off the bed, tightened and double-knotted the robe's belt and approached the mirror. Of course he wanted the final wish to be made in Exilium, it would make it so much easier to enslave her, or reduce her to an automaton as he'd threatened. She'd never been in the other world, but she'd had countless lessons about how dangerous it was. On the other side of the mirror a careless word or even just a simple lapse in etiquette could lead a mortal into slavery as quickly as an insect dropped in a specimen jar.

Her family's patron was waiting, and there was nothing to be done. Cathy held her breath and stepped through.

16

"If Elizabeth Papaver is wearing blue I swear I shall die."

Will raised an eyebrow at Imogen, wondering if there would ever be a year when his sister wouldn't make such a fuss on the way to the opening ball. It always peaked when they were in the carriage, and always focused on what everyone else would be wearing.

"I thought you bribed someone to look at the delivery before it left the tailors," Nathaniel said, not bothering to hide his boredom.

"Elizabeth might have paid them more to tell me the wrong colour," Imogen said. "It does happen. And ladies have seamstresses, not tailors."

"Oh, for goodness' sake, Imogen," Will said. "Even if she does wear the same colour as you, it won't exactly be the scandal of the season."

It silenced her long enough for them to leave the Crescent. Will knew why their parents always rode in a separate carriage ahead of them; so they didn't have to listen to her nervous prattling.

"I wonder what *Catherine* Papaver will be wearing," she said. "I do hope it isn't yellow. That would make her look positively horrendous."

"It doesn't take much," Nathaniel said and they sniggered.

Will decided to remain aloof from it all. He wasn't looking forward to seeing Catherine either, but he'd made his plans and all was prepared. Being sucked into cruel speculation wasn't going to achieve anything.

"You have to accept it, William," his mother had said to him that morning. He'd sought her out after a sleepless night of endless imaginary arguments with his father. "Marriage happens to us all."

"But why her? Why not Elizabeth?"

"Do you really want to marry that empty-headed child?"

"No," he'd admitted. "But at least she wouldn't embarrass us. What did I do to insult Father so? I've never given him cause for anger or disappointment. Why punish me like this?"

"Oh, Will." His mother sat next to him. "It isn't like that at all. Don't you see how this proves how much trust he has in you? He knows he can depend upon you to make this a success."

Will struggled to bring his thoughts back to the carriage when his brother cleared his throat.

"Father says the Master of Ceremonies wasn't back this afternoon," Nathaniel said, having realised Will wasn't going to be baited.

"How strange," Imogen said. "Cecilia hasn't heard a thing either."

"Cecilia Peonia is an empty-headed fool," Nathaniel said. "Of course she hasn't."

"She happens to have one of the best ears in town for the latest news."

"Only one?" Will asked.

"And an excellent nose for gossip," Imogen continued, ignoring him. "For her not to know a thing about all of this is most unusual. I feel sorry for the Censor, it must have been a terrible week."

Will tried to imagine what it would be like to have an elder brother disappear without a trace.

"What?" Nathaniel asked as the broad smile bloomed across Will's lips.

"Nothing. Ah, we're here."

Nathaniel was first out of the carriage after the footman had lowered the steps, then Will, who helped Imogen. His parents were straightening their attire nearby, closer to the entrance of the Assembly Rooms, and the streets of Aquae Sulis were filled with the clatter of horses' hooves and carriages delivering attendees.

Imogen was keen to get inside as quickly as possible. She'd made that clear as they'd left the house; the silver embroidery of her bodice against the indigo of her dress was designed to look its best beneath sprite light inside the ballroom, not the diffuse grey light of the Nether. Nathaniel in contrast was happy to pose on the pavement, watching the other guests arriving, making sure he cut the finest silhouette with his formal attire and rapier.

Will scanned the carriages. None were emblazoned with the Papaver coat of arms, so he extended his arm to Imogen, thinking that, if he could keep her sweet for even just the first hour of the ball, it would be to his advantage as well as a first.

They made their way into a long, wide corridor filled with people meandering towards the ballroom. They were a little early; his father didn't believe in being fashionably late, which always irritated Imogen as it deprived her of a large audience for her entrance. Will was indifferent, used to being the one overlooked. He wasn't as famed as his brother, nor in line to inherit the family's power, and Imogen was good at stealing away any other surplus attention.

"I've heard a rumour," she said, in her best conspiratorial whisper, "there's to be a surprise special guest this evening."

"Perhaps it will be the Master of Ceremonies," Will replied, uninterested. Normally he would have been happy to be entertained by such intrigues – they passed the time, after all – but tonight he had an agenda that took the shine off it all.

As they walked between the marble columns, he was greeted by people he hadn't seen for years and certainly hadn't missed. He made promises to play cards, to delight them with tales of adventure and to pass on the gossip from the colonies. He could hear murmurings about the absence of Mr Lavandula and wondered if the Papavers would want to delay the announcement because of the absence of Catherine's uncle.

They entered the ballroom and it was as Will expected: unchanged, lavishly lit, beautifully decorated with its plain blue walls and elegant white stucco borders. The musicians were already in place up on the first-floor gallery overlooking the expansive space. Will could see the parents and chaperones of young ladies being approached by his peers, all eager to make arrangements for the minuet dancing that would begin the ball.

"And who, pray tell, is that?" Imogen whispered to him, skilfully indicating the direction with her new fan. It was still folded and now strung on a silver chain attached to her bracelet to hang free as she danced.

Will noticed the young man talking to Oliver Peonia. His friend usually had a constant half-smile on his face and cheeks like apples, round, red and shiny, but as he spoke in close conference with the stranger, Oliver was stern and rather pale.

He noticed Will and the spontaneous flash of his eyebrows in silent greeting was enough to make the stranger turn and look in their direction. Will spotted the deep red rose before any other feature, and from Imogen's surprised gasp he assumed she had also.

"That can't be the surprise guest!" she said behind her fan. "Not a Rose! Cecilia would have told me."

"Looks as if he's already making an impression," Will remarked, studying his best friend's demeanour.

"They're coming over," Imogen said. Will felt her grip on his arm tighten. "He's rather handsome. I've never met a Rose before, but I've heard they're ruthless. How exciting."

"Good evening," Oliver said with a bow. "Imogen, what a pleasure to see you again."

He kissed her hand and Imogen waited patiently until it was over.

"Good evening," Will replied, adding his own bow.

"Will you permit me to introduce my guest?" Oliver was trying his best, but Will could see that he was distinctly uncomfortable. "Imogen and William Reticulata-Iris, this is Horatio Gallica-Rosa of the city of Londinium."

Horatio bowed and Imogen extended a gloved hand as he reached for it. He kissed it lightly. "A pleasure. You are indeed as lovely as I have been told."

Imogen blushed the appropriate amount. "Are you in Aquae Sulis for the season?"

"Indeed. I've heard so much about it. Would you do me the honour of partnering you for the first minuet?"

"I would be delighted. William, I believe Father wants to speak with you." She was using their code to indicate she wanted to be left alone to speak with the Rosa.

"Do you play cards, Mr Rosa?" William asked.

"I have been known to play a hand of poker now and then," Horatio replied with a dangerous look in his eye.

"Then perhaps I will see you in the card room later," Will concluded and took his leave of them.

Oliver also made an excuse once he realised what Imogen wanted and fell into step with Will. "You may need to warn your brother about him, my friend," he whispered.

"Oh?"

"Horatio is the finest duellist in Albion, or so he is wont to believe." Oliver leaned in closer. "And he's heard of Nathaniel's reputation as a fine swordsman. A cautionary word in your brother's ear may be wise."

"Regardless of wisdom, my brother has never taken any of my advice, and does not respond well to warnings," said Will dismissively. "If he insists on getting into a duel, that's his affair. Now, tell me, why are you sponsoring a Rosa for the season?"

"Father insisted." Oliver's glance at his parents as they passed was rather cool. "And don't ask me why, I have no idea. That Rosa is an oily wretch and I fear he will do nothing but cause trouble, as they always do. Have you heard the rumours about his family?"

"I've heard enough to infer they take the most direct path to their goals, even if it takes them through unsavoury places."

"I've heard their wealth is drawn from a network of criminal activity in Mundanus." Oliver glanced back at Horatio. "He's greasing up your sister, Will, shouldn't you go back?"

"What a vulgar turn of phrase," Will said with a smirk. "An excellent souvenir of the Grand Tour, I shall do my best to make it popular this season. Imogen can take care of herself. If there's anyone who should be worried it's Cecilia for not informing her that a dashing swordsman is in town."

"Cecilia was just as shocked as I was," Oliver said, briefly distracted by a young beauty sweeping past. "It was sprung on both of us this afternoon. Something's rotten about it, I just don't know what. How did the gifts go down?"

"Well. Yours?"

"Jolly good actually. Father has promised me the estate in Derbyshire."

"Congratulations. Mine has secured me a bride."

Oliver stopped. "Gosh. Who is it to be?"

"You'll see," said Will with a wink.

"Oh, a disappointment then," Oliver said. "If you were pleased you'd be falling over yourself to tell me."

Will laughed. "Now I see the danger of travelling the world with one's best chum; you know me too well now."

The ballroom was filling up; he could no longer see Imogen and Horatio. He caught a glimpse of the Censor talking to his father, a statement in and of itself, as dozens of people had been desperately trying to catch her eye. When they parted, his father surreptitiously beckoned him over.

"I'll see you in the card room later, old boy," Will said to Oliver. "The pater wants a word."

He navigated through the greetings and "welcome back"s and smiled at his father.

"The Censor is agreeable to announcing the engagement before the country dances," he said, sotto voce. "I had hoped for one before the ball begins, but she has something else to announce, apparently."

"I've heard there is a surprise guest, and it isn't the Gallica-Rosa over there trying to woo Imogen."

"I'll see to that in a minute. A Rosa?" He shook his head in disapproval. "The Censor has been distracted this week, but that is hardly an excuse for allowing the riff-raff into Aquae Sulis. Perhaps it's just as well to announce it later; the Papavers haven't yet arrived."

"Perhaps they want to be fashionably late," Will suggested, now appreciating the crowd filling the ballroom. "Though any later than this would be approaching the embarrassing end of fashionable."

A light knocking reduced the crowd's low roar to a murmur as all faces turned to the gallery and the Censor rapping her closed fan against the rail. "Ladies and gentlemen, it is my pleasure to welcome you to the Assembly Rooms this evening, and to the opening ball of the Aquae Sulis season." Miss Lavandula's voice projected magnificently. She was dressed in a lavender-blue ball gown, and a dazzling diamond brooch drew Will's eye to her décolletage. "My brother sends his profound apologies for not being here this evening. He's abroad dealing with a matter for our patron."

Will noticed the ripple of commentary that spread through the room. He wasn't sure if anyone believed her, but saying her brother's absence was due to a demand from their patron made it impossible for anyone to speculate openly without being seen as crass. If he had disappeared, she had bought herself a few weeks at the most.

"But I can assure you that he arranged everything for a most spectacular season before he left," she continued, drawing the crowd's attention fully back to her address. "With the blessing of the Council of Aquae Sulis, I will be acting as Censor and Master of Ceremonies until his return." Another ripple; her announcements were like pebbles being tossed into the social pond. "Whilst we will of course miss him, we shall not let him down. In a moment, the first minuet will begin, but first, I'd like to present to you our guest of honour for this evening."

She looked to her left and beckoned someone onto the balcony with a smile. A young Indian woman, with hair like a river of black silk and flawless mahogany skin, walked out to take her hand, eliciting an excited rush of whispers from the assembly. She was dressed in a richly decorated sari that couldn't have been more different from the corseted fashions on display.

"Ladies and gentlemen, it is my deepest pleasure to introduce you to Maharaj Kumari Rani Nucifera-Nelumbo, daughter of the Maharaja of the princely state of Rajkot in India."

There was a spontaneous burst of applause and the princess smiled down upon them. Will looked for Oliver, wanting to share his anger. He'd spent two months trying to secure an audience with the princess with the express purpose of sponsoring her into Aquae Sulis on behalf of the family. She'd refused polite requests and gifts; now he knew why. Someone had beaten him to it.

"Princess Rani has been sponsored into the city by the Alba-Rosa family, represented this evening by Cornelius Alba-Rosa and his sister Amelia from Londinium." They were beckoned onto the gallery too, where they were met with applause and no little speculation. Amelia was strikingly beautiful, the white of her dress making her skin creamy and the dark brown of her hair richer. So that was who had pipped him to the post. Oliver was lost in the crowd and would no doubt bait him about it later. He did spot Horatio though, whose lips were pressed tight together with barely disguised fury.

"It seems the Gallica isn't very happy about this," Will said to his father, the applause protecting him.

"The Albas and Gallicas are feuding again," his father replied. "Horatio Gallica-Rosa probably thought he'd have the admiration of Londinium for getting into the city for the season."

"And now he's nothing special," Will said, looking back up at the Albas, considering how furious Horatio must feel to be so spectacularly upstaged. Amelia's gaze fell on him and lingered for a few moments. Will smiled and she returned it, openly and without a coy glance away. His smile broadened at her boldness, but then she was ushered away by the Censor as the musicians began the opening bars of the first minuet.

"Are you going to dance?" his father asked.

"No, I was waiting for Catherine. I thought it would be politic."

The floor cleared as those planning to converse rather than dance gravitated to the edges of the room. Imogen was taking her place with Horatio, who was putting on a good show of not caring about the Albas as they entered.

William saw his mother. She made straight for them. "The Papavers have arrived."

"They're rather late," Father muttered.

"But something's wrong," Mother continued. "Catherine isn't with them."

Max knocked on the door covered with sparkling words and entered at the sound of Ekstrand's voice. Inside was a modest ballroom with a large mirror filling most of one wall. A small amount of light cast by an oil lantern resting at the Sorcerer's feet revealed formulae chalked, painted and scratched onto the floorboards. The symbols arced out from the mirror, and as he hobbled closer Max realised the mirror was actually at the centre of a series of concentric circles of formulae, unbroken across the wall and floor.

Ekstrand was dressed in the same way as he'd been the very first time Max met him, when he was given the field glasses for testing. He wore a black morning suit with long tails, and his hair was neatly coiffed. He gave a curt nod. He held a thick tray upon which sat an artefact looking like a cross between a cockroach and an owl. It was made of wood and brass, had many spindly legs and a pair of huge eyes with closed brass eyelids. It was currently inert.

"We'll begin once Axon is here. Where is the gargoyle?"

"I told it to wait in the parlour, as you asked, sir," Max replied, leaning on his crutches.

"As you can see, I've prepared substantial wards." Ekstrand pointed at the formulae. "We can't be too careful."

There was a knock on the door and Ekstrand called Axon in. "Any problems, Axon?"

"None, sir. I'm ready." There was the sound of a rifle being closed.

Max glanced back at the butler and watched him pull the butt of a large-calibre elephant gun into his shoulder and take a marksman's stance, the barrel pointed at the mirror.

The ring of a tiny bell sounded from the artefact and each of the mechanical legs lifted and settled again. Max recognised the signs of calibration, even though he'd never seen an artefact of that exact design before.

"The twin has entered the Nether," Ekstrand said. "I'm going to activate the link. Be ready."

Ekstrand pressed a small nubbin on the top of the brass head and there was a gentle mechanical whirring as the eyelids opened, revealing two mirrored disks. At the same time the large mirror on the wall rippled as if it had become liquid yet remained impossibly flat and vertical. The distorted reflection of the three of them in the room with the lantern was replaced by the silver sky of the Nether and the familiar headquarters for the Bath Chapter loomed high.

"Excellent," Ekstrand muttered.

Judging by how huge the building looked, and the angle, Max surmised that a replica of the artefact on the tray was now in the Nether – the "twin" – and that the image reflected in its mirror eyes was being shown in the mirror in front of him, like a huge scrying glass. Max had no idea how it worked. It wasn't his place to understand sorcery.

The cloister, at first glance, looked undamaged. It was a large two-storey building with stout fortified outer walls reminiscent of a Norman fort, although it was much larger than its anchor and the majority of real Norman buildings in Mundanus. The Sorcerers, unlike the Fae, were able to embellish an anchor property's reflection in the Nether, and from the cloister's design Max theorised that they were somehow able to combine reflections to make amalgamated buildings in the Nether. Its windows were small, some only arrow slits, and there was a squat tower at each corner.

"You can read a cloister and learn all about the Sorcerer," Max recalled his mentor saying as they stood outside it years before, not far from where the twin artefact was.

He'd pointed out the Norman influence, the initial vision for the cloister established by the first Sorcerer of Wessex, who'd been inspired by the architecture of the time. Inside, the building was more medieval in style. His mentor told him that it was Ekstrand's predecessor who'd ripped out the heart of the fort and put in the cloister, giving the building a completely different interior once past the outer wall. They didn't talk about what Ekstrand had changed, if anything, and Max wasn't sure how many other Sorcerer Guardians of Wessex there had been. The Chapter Master didn't think Arbiters needed to know such things.

Ekstrand pressed something on the artefact's back and it started to walk forwards; it was then that Max realised the tray had a frictionless surface. The image on the mirror shifted, the twin moving forwards too.

"No damage, no signs of forced entry," Max said as the artefact approached the arched wooden doors.

It went inside, Ekstrand manipulating its direction and speed with the twin, concentrating intently.

Seeing the entrance from only two inches above ground level gave an odd impression of the archway and its thick walls. It also made the sole of the boot the artefact discovered within seem as tall as a tree.

"A body," Ekstrand said.

"And no one has cleared it," Max added.

Ekstrand manoeuvred the device around the boot, the scrying glass revealing the plain, functional clothing of one of the cloister staff. The forward movement seemed to slow down.

"There's something impeding its progress," Ekstrand said as he scrutinised the twin device on the tray.

"Congealed blood," Max said. "In the Nether it would take longer for the moisture to evaporate so it wouldn't have dried out yet."

After a few moments the view changed and a dark patch on the man's shirt filled the glass. "You're right," Ekstrand said. "I'm going to press on."

A second body soon came into view, another member of staff, close to the body of the first. "It's hard to tell what inflicted the injuries," Max said, seeing another bloodstain on the clothing. "I'm guessing they're stab wounds, but I can't be certain without going there myself."

"Not yet," Ekstrand replied, directing the artefact out of the other side of the entrance archway and into the first cloister.

There were more bodies. The device was turned in a circle and, almost everywhere the scrying glass could show, there were slaughtered men and women. Ekstrand turned the device right and picked a path between two of the deceased. There were no red patches on the clothes in sight.

"Can you move it to look at the neck, sir?" The view changed as the artefact turned slightly and headed towards a shirt collar. Max recognised one of the researchers. "He's been strangled. What's that?"

He pointed at something green in the background, the colour out of place amongst the sandstone. The device was steered around the body, and Max looked again at the man's face, recalling his attention to detail and reliability. He looked like he was asleep.

The device made its way past the hand of another victim, in gigantic proportions that filled the screen for a moment, the wrinkles in the skin looking like crevasses, the pale knuckles like a mountain range. Another face came into view, this time a woman with her eyes open and glistening like wet marbles. A green stem replete with jagged-edged leaves emerged from her open mouth. A thorn had pierced her lower lip.

"Rose," Ekstrand said and Max nodded.

"I've never seen a Rosa do anything like this," Max said.

"I doubt they'd have a Charm powerful enough to do that. This is the work of Rose herself, or the brothers Thorn." He adjusted a dial on the artefact's back, part of the casing opened and the small horn of an in-built Sniffer emerged. After a few seconds, remarkably quickly, another little *ping* indicated enough air had been processed to identify a residue. Ekstrand nodded. "It's Rose. Without a doubt."

Max looked down at the floor, turning his attention inwards. As far as he knew, no Fae had ever openly attacked the Sorcerers since they'd been imprisoned in Exilium. Whilst they could enter the Nether and, under particular circumstances, certain places in Mundanus, most never dared, too fearful of retribution for breaching the laws agreed by Fae royalty. They still tried to meddle with innocents, but always through their puppets. Nothing like this.

"Something must have changed," Ekstrand said. "And it has to be related to the London problem. It's too much of a coincidence that the Arbiter there turned a blind eye to a Rosa's crime. Rose must have known you were reporting it and attacked the Cloister to stop the information getting back to me."

"But why not try to hide that fact?" Max asked. "What would be the point of covering up Rose corruption in London only to make it obvious they'd murdered an entire Chapter?"

"Perhaps that is a statement in and of itself." Ekstrand was scowling at the glass. "Does this not say, 'The Rose did this, and we're not afraid of your reprisal'?"

"I'm not sure." Max adjusted his grip on the crutches, his palms aching. He didn't feel satisfied by that explanation, but he didn't have enough evidence to counter it. He spotted a body that had collapsed over one of the internal window ledges facing into the quad. "There's a body on the left, over there – can you use it to move the artefact to a higher position?"

As Ekstrand worked, Max thought over everything he knew and concluded it was in fact very little. Innocents had disappeared in London with a pattern suggesting Fae involvement, all connected to a modelling agency in Judd Street that was probably a front organisation owned by a Rosa puppet. He had witnessed a kidnapping, and the corruption of two Arbiters from the Camden Chapter, first-hand, and they'd tried to kill him. Twice. As he tried to report the crime, his own Chapter had been destroyed.

Now there was evidence that the Roses were behind the destruction of the Chapter, as well as involved in the London corruption, it seemed that the two had to be connected. But something didn't sit right with it all.

"How could Lady Rose, or the brothers Thorn, find the cloister?" he asked.

"I don't know how anyone outside the Chapter could have found it, Fae or otherwise," Ekstrand replied. "But it's clear the Roses are up to no good in London and prepared to go to extreme lengths to keep anyone else out of it."

"Is there any way the residue could have been left by another, to frame the Roses?"

"None. It's Rose, no doubt about it. None of the Fae can use each other's magic."

Max watched the glass. The twin artefact was now picking its way up the body's legs. At the highest point it could reach, Ekstrand turned it and adjusted where it stood to take in the carnage filling that side of the cloister walk.

"It looks like they killed each other," Max said after a few moments of studying the positioning of the bodies. "That's what I couldn't understand; if assailants entered through the door, the alarm would have been raised and reinforcements sent to defend. But there aren't enough bodies in the entranceway to reflect that, and the bodies here are too spread out. It's like the alarm wasn't raised at all."

"The Roses are particularly adept at stirring passions," Ekstrand said. "It's speculation at this point, but I suspect they cast a Charm that drove the staff to kill each other. It must have been airborne, and incredibly powerful." He paused, looking away from the glass for a moment. "I may have underestimated these Fae."

"But what about the Arbiters not in the field? They would have been immune."

"Murdered by staff on the rampage?" Ekstrand suggested. "We'll know more once I've secured it and sent you in. But there's no possibility of that until I've cleared the air and checked for any traps they may have left behind." He turned to face Max. "No one must know about this."

"Until the Moot," Max nodded.

"No!" Ekstrand shook his head as he set the tray down. "The other Sorcerers are the last people in the worlds I'd want to know about this."

"But the Fae have destroyed a Chapter, and it's got to be rooted in London's corruption. Surely the Sorcerers need to know how serious this is?"

"No one must know that we've been so seriously compromised. If anyone outside this room discovers what has happened we will have two more major problems on our hands," He held up a finger. "One: the other Sorcerers will know that we are vulnerable. The Sorcerer of Mercia has always had an eye on my territory, he could use this as an opportunity to take my domain. Two: if word gets out to the Fae-touched in Aquae Sulis and surrounds they'll be stealing innocents and acquiring properties faster than one crippled Arbiter can deal with. We need to understand how the Roses found the cloister, how they've corrupted the Camden Chapter and how far up that corruption goes. If we drag the Roses in front of either the Sorcerers or the Fae royalty, we may lose our chance to find these things out as well as reveal our weakened state."

Max looked from him to the glass. "I understand, sir. I have a lead on the disappearance of the Master of Ceremonies. I'm planning to follow it up tonight."

"Good," Ekstrand said. "Leave this to me, I'll let you know when the cloister is secure. And Maximilian?"

"Yes sir?"

"Be careful. A crippled Arbiter is better than none at all."

17

When Cathy stepped through the mirror into Exilium the colours were even brighter and for a moment all she could do was take in its beauty. The green of the meadow was the purest one could possibly imagine, as if someone had distilled the essence of green and fashioned individual blades of grass from it. The sky was the deep blue of the most perfect summer's day in Mundanus.

The space behind her rippled once and then she saw nothing but meadow and sky. She didn't know a Charm of Openings to get out of Exilium; if Lord Poppy or the faerie didn't open a Way for her, she'd be trapped there, forever.

She could still remember the day her mother told her about Exilium. She described it as the most beautiful prison that could ever be, reminding Cathy of her mother's life. Even back then the seeds of rebellion were growing in her gut. The details were vague; the evil Sorcerers split the worlds to keep the wonderful, kind and beautiful Fae away from people, depriving Mundanus of magic and the joy of the Fae. When she'd asked if their family lived in Exilium her mother had laughed and said she was one of the privileged who lived between the Split Worlds, in something they called the Nether. Her mother said they were lucky but the reasons why didn't stick in Cathy's memory. After her experience with Lord Poppy she felt more sympathy for the Sorcerers. Mundanus was better off without the Fae.

The faerie was flying ahead, too fast for her to keep up without sprinting. There was no way she was going to arrive in a bath robe *and* be sweaty and out of breath so she walked, calling to mind the rules of Exilium. All she could remember with certainty was that she shouldn't eat or drink anything. Less than a second after she recalled the rule, her stomach grumbled and her tongue was sticking to the roof of her mouth. She did her best to ignore them and kept going. The grass was soft and springy beneath her bare feet, the sun gentle. If she hadn't been walking towards her doom, it would have been quite pleasant.

The faerie was leading her up a gentle hill, and when she reached its crest Cathy could see a small wood straight ahead. The faerie had brought her through mercifully close to Lord Poppy's domain. She didn't waste any time. Like a dentist appointment, it was better to get it out of the way as swiftly as possible.

When she reached the trees, a path through them came into sight, made of thousands of poppy petals, which felt blissfully soft underfoot. Soon she was at the edge of a clearing where a cluster of red blooms crowded around Lord Poppy like adoring children. The faerie hovered at his shoulder, conveying a startling amount of hatred with such tiny eyes.

"Ah, my little sunlit one." He smiled and held out a hand towards her. "Time for your third wish, Catherine Rhoeas-Papaver. I wanted to hear it in person. I like to watch condemning words fall from mortal lips, it amuses me so."

She went to him, trying not to display her reluctance. "I must confess my Lord, I thought I had a little more time; the ball isn't until tomorrow."

"Oh, but my dear, time is a fickle thing, especially when one is here in our beautiful prison. Why, a moment in Exilium can be a year in Mundanus, and a week in the Nether. Sometimes it is but a moment. However, I'm certain the ball has already begun."

His long fingers clasped around her hand and a pulse of magic passed through her.

I've already impressed him.

She looked at him as the thought landed in her mind like a letter on a mat, feeling the effects of her first wish coursing through her, slowing her racing pulse. What better way to impress one's patron than to defeat the best swordsman of the Great Families without lifting a finger? More than that, she'd humiliated the Rosa. Lord Poppy told Lady Rose that her wish was responsible, leading Horatio to seek her out. Now she understood he'd done that simply to land her in a predicament. He wanted to see how she'd navigate her way out of trouble.

Cathy reined in her elation. It wasn't over yet, and she was an entire world away from any Arbiter's protection. It was also possible that if she made a mess of the third wish Lord Poppy would conveniently forget about the Rosa and enslave her anyway.

"I hope my third wish will impress you, Lord Poppy," she said as steadily as she could, "if I haven't already." When he said nothing, she closed her eyes, feeling his grip tighten around her hand. Free of purely trying to impress him, she turned her mind towards what she really wanted, and how to translate that into a wish. It came to her, fully formed, as if it had always been deep down and released to float up to the surface. "I wish I could achieve my full potential," she said, opening her eyes, "in such a way as to not draw the attention of the Arbiters, nor endanger my life, nor those of

the individuals I love and care for – be they Fae, a member of
the Great Families or a mundane." As she spoke the words,
she remembered writing it out as a child, learning it by heart
when her father had given a gruff nod instead of ripping it
apart. The last words were a later addition.

Lord Poppy remained motionless, scrutinising her intensely
for a moment before his cold inspection melted into a smile.
"How delightful, and how clever of you. For is that not what
we all wish for our favourites?"

"I aim to please, Lord Poppy," she said, trembling as his
grip tightened even more.

"I grant you your wish, Catherine Rhoeas-Papaver, though
I warn you, the path to one's fulfilment is never easy for
someone such as you."

"Such as me?"

He licked his lips. "Mortal," he finally said. "You have
surprised me, I'm not ashamed to admit it. It's been such a
long time since a mortal was able to do that. Oh, some of
your family and distant relations have amused me, some
have pleased me, some have disappointed me. But none have
ever done anything *unexpected*." He pulled her hand closer,
pushing the loose sleeve of the robe down to her elbow and
leaned forwards. He ran his nose along her arm, sniffing her
skin gently, making her rigid with fear. "I'm tempted to keep
you here."

"But… you said if I impressed you I'd–"

"Oh, yes," he said, dropping her hand. "We made a
contract, I recall. How positively tedious. Very well, you shall
return to Aquae Sulis." He took a step back, looking her up
and down as the faerie scowled at her. "Do you know the
story of Cinderella?"

She nodded, unable to speak, the dread clogging her throat.

"It must have been one of your favourites?"

"It couldn't have been," the faerie said before she could reply. "In Cinderella it was her sisters who were ugly."

Lord Poppy swatted it away. It flew up into one of the trees and stamped its foot on a branch.

"Doesn't every girl dream of being Cinderella?"

"I didn't," Cathy admitted, truth being the best policy in Exilium.

His face fell. "Really? Another surprise. You seem to be woven out of them. I want to keep you. I don't care about contracts made in the Nether anyway, only those made in Exilium really count for anything."

"But... but you said I was needed in Aquae Sulis!"

"Oh, yes, that's true," he sighed. "Well, that settles it. You will be my Cinderella–"

"I could just miss the ball," she offered, not liking where he was going.

"No! I won't hear of it! It's the first ball of the season, and I want my new favourite to be there, and be the centre of attention."

"But–"

"Enough!" he said and she shut her mouth. "I have never met a mortal with so many words ready to interrupt! Why are you making such a fuss? Any young woman in the Great Families would give many years of their life to have what I'm about to give you."

She had to accept that whatever he was going to do, it was going to be awful and inevitable.

"But before you go," he said, lifting her chin, "let me give you some advice, to help with your third wish. Send a servant into Mundanus to purchase canvases and paints. The rest will become clear."

"I can't paint!"

"You should try," he replied. "I want you to fulfil your potential. You wouldn't want to disappoint me, would you?"

"No, my Lord," she said, focusing on the grass and poppy flowers instead of his black eyes.

"Excellent. Now…" He stooped to pick one of the poppies at his feet and then blew gently across its petals. "Close your eyes. Good. Now breathe in deeply."

She felt a petal tickle her chin as she breathed in the scent. In Mundanus the red poppy was scentless, but in Exilium it smelt divine. She felt dizzy, then a tingling on her skin and her shoulders felt bare. Something was tickling her legs and she felt a slight pressure around her waist. With horror she realised the robe had gone, replaced by something much lighter.

"Don't open your eyes until I tell you," he whispered in her ear. "Now, as much as I want to stay and play with you, I understand Lady Rose will be at Court today and I wouldn't want to miss the look on her face when I mention your name." He sighed like a sated lover. "I will watch your progress with interest, Catherine Rhoeas-Papaver." She felt his hand on her back, a tingling across her face and chest as something changed in front of her. "Open your eyes!" he said and pushed her forwards.

She felt the gentle brush of the threshold between Exilium and the Nether across her face as she stumbled through. She was at one of the side entrances of the ballroom in the Aquae Sulis Assembly Rooms, usually kept closed during the minuets so that people didn't stray onto the dance floor and interrupt the dance.

As she just had.

The music stopped and the dancers moved back, startled by the sudden appearance of a young woman staggering into their midst. A dreadful silence filled the room as she stood shivering, every eye upon her.

The faces blurred into a tableau of expressions ranging from shock to amusement. She looked down, seeing a gown made of poppy petals floating out from her waist to mimic the shape of a ball gown. The petals were clinging to her upper body like they were held by a static charge but she was decent at least, and wearing shoes so soft they felt like they'd been stitched out of petals too. Her hair felt strange.

She couldn't lift her face as she felt the attention upon her, a thousand memories resurfacing: of saying the wrong thing, tripping over skirts, sneezing at exactly the wrong time and all the agonising moments in between. She was eight again, standing next to the piano, her family, the Irises, the Censor and Master of Ceremonies all watching and waiting for her to sing and nothing but the dying croak of a sick bullfrog emerging. Over the years she'd soaked up the disappointed expressions as people saw her plain features after admiring her beautiful sister, the kindest in Society offering a maddening pity instead, none of them wondering whether there was a sharp mind beneath. And, all the while, the awful urge to laugh in the tight, nervous staccato the fear always brought with it.

A steady click of shoes made her look up, fearing it was her father, who must have been somewhere in the crowd, but it was a young man striding confidently across the ballroom, the dancers parting to let him reach her. He wasn't as tall as Tom but broad in the shoulders, his brown hair streaked in places with sun-kissed strands and long enough to brush his collar. He was tanned, not the usual pale-skinned face of one of the Great Families. His eyes were dark brown and focused very much on her. Something about them was familiar but she couldn't place him. A blue flower was tucked into his buttonhole, but she was so panicked, she couldn't remember what it was.

He stopped a couple of paces away and gave a deep bow with a slight click of his heels. He straightened and held out a hand, which she stared at, dumbly. He took a step forward and scooped her hand up to his lips, sending a murmur through the crowd. Still holding it, he looked into her eyes and said, "Catherine Rhoeas Papaver, may I welcome you back to Aquae Sulis."

She just blinked, her voice lying dead somewhere in her stomach.

Unfazed, he looked up at the gallery. "If the Censor permits, I feel a waltz would be the only dance that could follow Miss Papaver's spectacular entrance."

All of the musicians, and all of the spectators, turned as one to look at the Censor, who gave a slight nod.

The music began and the man pulled her closer. "No greeting for me, Miss Papaver?"

"I can't dance," she said, trying to slip her hand out of his, but he didn't let go and now his other arm was about her waist.

"Don't worry about that."

As they started to waltz, Cathy felt light, her steps confident, as if her feet knew where to go even though she didn't. He guided her around the room as the crowd drew further back, preferring to watch the spectacle rather than join them.

"Don't watch your feet, look at me." He looked amused. "Don't you remember me?"

She could feel the flush rising up her throat. "No."

"I'm William Reticulata-Iris."

Somehow she didn't crush his toes, and his arm tightened around her waist as she gawped at him.

"Smile," he said through his teeth.

"I didn't recognise you," she said. "Sorry."

"I barely recognised you," he said, his whisper tickling her ear. "You look divine. You've blossomed."

She pulled a face. "Yeah right."

His eyebrows shot up. How he kept guiding her around the floor and looking as poised as he did so, she had no idea. "Are you branding me a liar?" When she kept quiet he smirked. "Or do you consider me a fool with poor taste? Either way, surely you should smile for the crowd whilst you insult me."

"I'm not falling for this," she whispered back. "I know you don't want to marry me, as much as I don't want to marry you, there's no need to pretend."

"Careful," he said, squeezing her hand. "You don't even know me yet."

"Exactly," she replied. "It's absurd. And if you think that dancing with me and whispering some bobbins into my ear is going to work, think again."

"What if I was telling the truth?"

She tried to look at him properly, but he held her close. "Shut up," she said.

"This isn't the nicest thank-you I've ever had for saving someone from social death."

"Oh, so you think that because you've rescued me I should just melt at your feet?"

He laughed. She didn't like it. "I think you could at least be gracious. Don't waste this opportunity, Catherine – our families are watching."

"I don't care," she lied.

"Well, I do," he said, the lightness gone. "And you will not embarrass us. Smile, dance, say the right things in the right places. If you genuinely have a problem with the arrangements made by your parents, then we will discuss that at the appropriate time. But you will not behave like a spoilt brat on the most important night of the season."

"You speak as though we're already married," she said, now wanting to step on his toes but not managing to find them.

"As far as our social fortunes are concerned we are already

tied," he said. "We have to accept it and do our best."

"I don't—"

"You take yourself too seriously," he cut in. "Treat this evening like a game and you'll enjoy it so much more. I'll even help you to play it. You don't want to forfeit. Hell hath no fury like a father disappointed."

His words chilled her into silence. They swept in circles about the floor as she concentrated on avoiding eye contact with the spectators. It was only as they were coming to the end of the dance that she realised he'd cast a Grace Charm on her. She didn't know whether to be furious or grateful.

There was a spontaneous burst of applause as William brought them to an elegant finish. He bowed, she curtsied, he kissed her hand once more. Then the crowd closed in around them.

18

"There's no hope for you, Catherine," Elizabeth said in the carriage. "Lord Poppy's gift was wasted on you. I can't believe you were dressed in a magical ball gown, put in the middle of the ballroom and just stood there like a… like a… dying fish. Why, in the time it took William Iris to get to you I'd thought of a thousand witty or charming remarks that would have made that entrance perfect."

"Well, I just happened to think of one intelligent remark when I was with Lord Poppy, and that counted for more," Cathy snapped.

Her mother climbed into the carriage with the help of the footman, and then her father. It felt like the interior chilled by several degrees as he settled into place. The steps were folded up, the door shut and they were on their way.

"And everyone was looking at you, all evening," Elizabeth continued. "Did you make any new friends? Did you secure any interesting invitations? No. Nothing. It's so unfair! Mother, don't you think so?"

"I think you could have at least pretended to be pleased," Mother said, and Elizabeth nodded.

"You either looked sour or shell-shocked the whole evening. It was so embarrassing."

"Yes, I found it very embarrassing," Cathy said, doing her best to look out of the window so she didn't have to look at her father. "Though I have no idea why *you* would find it so. I think the adjective you're looking for is 'jealous'."

"Will you both be quiet," Father rumbled and Elizabeth sank into a sulk.

"No one noticed my new gown, even though it was more fashionable than Imogen's," she whispered to Mother and then was silent for the rest of the journey.

Cathy's feet were throbbing in time with her head. She couldn't remember the last time she'd actually had a good night's sleep. Losing a night and a day inflicted the same fuzzy-headed detachment as working through the night to get an essay in on time. Her body felt out of step with the social activity around her. Whilst there was a huge sense of relief now that the ordeal of the wishes and the ball was over, she wasn't looking forward to getting home. Lucy had offered a room at their house, but her father had declined on her behalf. She was going to have to get used to people doing that.

It didn't take long to get back to Great Pulteney Street and just the sight of it made her feel nauseous. She'd had nightmares about returning to the family home for weeks after she'd run away. Her only hope was that being a clear favourite of their patron would be enough to placate her father. They'd spent hours at the ball pretending that everything was normal, none of the family wanting anyone to guess it was the first time they'd seen her in almost three years.

Once they were in the house Elizabeth stamped up the stairs and disappeared behind a slammed bedroom door before her mother had even taken off her shoulder cape. Cathy looked down at the dress, still there, wondering how she was to take it off.

"Once you have changed, Catherine, come to my study," her father said.

Her teeth started to chatter so she clamped her jaw tightly shut and went up the stairs, a maid she didn't recognise following her silently.

Her room hadn't been touched since the day she left, aside from being dusted. She glanced at the dolls on the shelves, the jewellery boxes, the attempts to give her a pretty girl's bedroom, perhaps in the hope that the twee delicacy of it all would somehow rub off onto her.

It felt like it belonged to someone else.

The maid began to lay out the underwear and Cathy gazed at it in dismay. It looked like fancy-dress costume now, something for a re-enactors' fair rather than everyday life. She'd got used to the ease of modern clothing and its practicality. She liked the fact that women could dress like men in Mundanus and no one batted an eyelid.

"It's a marvellous dress, Miss Papaver," the maid said once she was done. "However did you get into it?"

"Dresses like this are conjured up," Cathy said, looking at the mirror. It was beautiful and really didn't suit her. It made her look like a paper doll dressed incorrectly, as her head didn't match the rest of her. She could see now why her hair felt strange; it was swept up and arranged in an elegant chignon held in place by tiny sprites. "I have no idea how to take it off," she said, tugging experimentally at one of the petals and then all of them fell off, as if they'd never been a dress at all. The sprites disappeared and her hair tumbled about her shoulders as she covered herself as best she could.

The maid simply dropped the chemise over her head. Cathy remembered she needed to get used to being dressed instead of just chucking on the first thing she saw in the drawer. She resisted the urge to send the girl away, not wanting to make a fuss so soon after getting back home.

By the time they got to the corset she already felt fully dressed. She steeled herself for the constriction, knowing her waist had thickened thanks to the fast food she'd discovered in Mundanus. The maid was very polite about the fact that she broke into a sweat getting the back to close. Cathy's ribs were already starting to ache.

"I'll speak to Mother about it," she said, wanting to spare the girl the embarrassment. She was helped into the simple gown that she used to wear before she went up to Cambridge and stared at herself as the maid did up the hooks and eyes at the back. Looking at herself neck downwards it was like nothing had changed, and if she wasn't careful she'd think her time in Mundanus with Josh was just a fantasy. But when she looked herself in the eye, she could hold on to the fact that she'd escaped once. Everything had changed, regardless of whether they laced her up into clothes that barely fit any more.

Her back was aching too by the time she reached the door of her father's study. She felt lightheaded; whether it was the adrenalin or the fact she was trying to remember how to breathe differently she wasn't sure, but she took a moment to ready herself before she knocked.

"Come in."

She went inside, and that one step over the threshold reduced her to the terrified thing she'd been in her adolescence. He was standing instead of sitting at his desk, never a good sign, and still dressed in his black tie from the ball. There was just as much grey at his temples as before and his black moustache still dominated his face. She couldn't look him in the eye so she glanced at the glass cabinets in the corners of the room, still full of military regalia from the First

World War. Then her gaze fell on the silver-topped swagger stick held in its own display rack in pride of place on top of the desk. Within his reach.

"That was an impressive entrance this evening, Catherine," he finally said. "But it seems you still have a yen for putting your family through unnecessary anxiety, even after Thomas managed to bring you back to Aquae Sulis."

"I had no idea that was going to happen. I was waiting for the bath to be filled at Tom's house and then Lord Poppy summoned me into Exilium. I swear it, Father."

"That was yesterday evening."

"Lord Poppy made it so I missed a night and a day and I don't know how. He said time works differently there; it only seemed like half an hour to me."

His pale-blue eyes scrutinised her closely and she looked down at the rug, knowing its pattern all too well. The room still smelt of wood panelling and the dusty books on the shelves filling three walls of the room. "It seems you have won his favour."

"Yes, Father."

"How?"

"It was the way I handled three wishes he gave me."

"Why did he do that?"

"Because he'd heard about my coming-of-age request and was curious."

"You have a lot of explaining to do. How did he find you?"

In a wavering voice, she told him about being found at the Emporium, doing her best to cover for the Shopkeeper by not explaining the arrangement with him. But once she'd started, he wanted to know what she'd wished for and her heart was banging so loud she feared he would hear it.

He tutted in disappointment when he heard how the first wish had fared, then she faltered as she came to the second, opting to say only that she'd lost her temper and a mundane had been caught in the wish magic by accident.

"Why were you making wishes on a street in Mundanus?" he asked, his right index finger tapping the corner of the desk.

"It got... complicated," she managed to say. Then she had to explain what happened with the Rosa – neglecting to name him, having seen him in the ballroom earlier that evening – and how arguing her way out of responsibility had resulted in going to Londinium to save the mundane.

Then she realised she never should have started.

"Who was this mundane? Why did you care what happened to him when you knew you were required here?"

"He was my friend."

"More than that, I fear," he growled and went to one of the drawers of his desk. She gripped her dress, clenching the fabric in sweating fists as he took out a small velvet pouch. "Thomas has vouched personally for your virtue but I need to be certain." He tipped an oval stone onto his palm; it looked like a milky opal. "This is what you have reduced me to, Catherine. I never thought I would have need of this. Now stand still."

It took all of her self-control not to flinch from him as he pressed the stone against her breastbone. She had nothing to fear from any test of her virginity; his curse had done its job well enough. He watched the stone, which felt icy cold, and then removed it with obvious relief. It looked no different.

"What happened to the Rosa?" he asked, dropping it back into the pouch and returning it to the desk drawer.

"He was humiliated. That's what impressed Lord Poppy and why I'm his favourite now." She wanted to remind him; it was her only defence.

"And the third wish?"

She told him and he nodded. "I remember that one. Then he dressed you and pushed you through into the ballroom?"

"Yes, Father, that's why I was so shocked. One minute I was in a bathrobe in Tom's house, the next I was in a dress at the ball."

His grim scrutiny continued. "I have no idea why you ran away, and I do not care to know. Needless to say, I am disgusted with your behaviour and will never trust you again. This is how it will be from now until your wedding day: you will not leave this house without my explicit permission and only then with a chaperone I have personally approved. You will not go into Mundanus. You will attend the social functions we deem necessary and you will behave impeccably. You will not discuss your time in Mundanus. As far as anyone is concerned you have been in Switzerland as was established to cover your time in Cambridge."

As he spoke, she realised how little she cared about what he thought of her. Living in Mundanus and seeing the way their society had evolved without being under the control of the Fae had opened her eyes. He was a monstrous man, living in a monstrous society. She was determined not to forget that.

"Do you understand?"

"Yes, Father."

"Thankfully your engagement has not been damaged by your frightful behaviour and I want to keep it that way. I will not discuss your history with the Irises and I expect you to follow my example. I'm pressing for the wedding to take place at the end of the season."

"But that's only six months!" she cried, horrified. How could she find a way out in such a short time?

"It would be six days if I had my way," he said. "And you, ungrateful wretch, should be thankful that I have secured such a prestigious match considering how poorly you conducted yourself before you ran away, let alone in light of it."

She choked back angry words, instead digging her fingernails into her palms. "I'm so sorry I have never lived up to your expectations." She struggled to rein in the sarcasm. "At least I made our patron happy."

"That is the only reason we are having this conversation," he said through his teeth. "It was the only excuse that could have satisfied me. But it doesn't undo the dreadful disregard you have demonstrated for your family, and it most certainly does not change my opinion of your character. Were this marriage to the Iris boy not critical, I would be tempted to disown you." He let that hang between them for a moment. "Now, we must move forward." He breathed out slowly, and she could see him trying to manage his temper as he paced back towards his desk. "In light of your success with Lord Poppy, I am willing to put your disgusting behaviour behind us, but only if you apologise."

"Apologise?" She could feel him trying to push her back into an old role, one she was determined not to be trapped in again. "Hasn't it occurred to you that *your* disgusting behaviour might have had something to do with why I ran away?"

"What did you say?" he roared.

"You know it isn't right to beat your child just because she can't sing a bloody song! I should have stuck up for myself a long time ago, then maybe–"

He swiped the stick off the desk so swiftly that its display rack was swept off, too. She brought her hands up instinctively. The first blow knocked her to the floor; the second, across her shoulder, made her screech and scrabble away from him, the full skirts of her dress tangling around her ankles. Her back hit a bookcase and he leant into the next blow, hitting her shoulders as she tried to curl into a ball.

There were two more blows to her arms that made her cry out and then the door banged open.

"Charles! You fool, stop that at once!"

Cathy still had her arms wrapped around her head, but through the gap between her elbows she could see the hem of her mother's dress.

"This wilful brat needs discipline," he shouted.

"This 'wilful brat' needs to be presentable in Society, not black and blue, you idiot. What would the Irises say if they saw a mark on her?"

She watched his feet move back, heard the clatter of the stick as it hit the desk. "Get her out of my sight," he said, and she felt her mother's arms working their way under hers, trying to get her onto her feet.

"Get up!" she hissed in her ear and Cathy struggled to comply, the pain making her whimper despite her efforts to hold it in.

She was steered out of the study and up the stairs. It was the first time her mother had intervened, and, whilst she was still reeling from the violence, a part of her was elated that not only had she stood up to her father at last, but her mother had too. Perhaps she had changed also, perhaps she'd thought about why her daughter had resorted to fleeing the family home and wished she'd protected her when she'd had the chance.

Her mother was silent all the way up to her room. She helped Cathy to the bed and turned to leave. "Thank you," Cathy said, and her mother paused in the doorway.

"I didn't do that for you," she said, not turning around. "You deserve every one of those bruises for what you did to us. Just don't let anyone else see them, or next time I won't stop him."

The door was slammed shut and then locked. Just like after he'd beaten her for reading the wrong kinds of books and admiring the wrong kinds of ideas. Then she realised that nothing had changed and there was no escape and, just like before, she sobbed into the pillow as the welts burned their way to bruises.

19

Sam slapped his hand against his forehead.

"You forgot, didn't you?"

Leanne's hands were on her hips, her head tilted. It was her favourite position when she was about to launch into a prize rant.

"Sorry, love, I ran out of cash and the new cards haven't arrived yet."

"Did you chase the bank?"

"...No."

"Why didn't you ask me for some more?"

He shrugged and didn't feel like he could say it was because he'd been trying to keep out of her way. She'd been prickly since she came home on the Friday night and he wasn't certain he could do or say anything that wouldn't make it worse.

"Oh, bloody hell, Sam! I ask you to get one thing – and it was alcoholic – and you still forgot!"

"It was this bump on the head!" he said, following his wife out of the dining room and into the kitchen. "I've been all over the place this week."

"Give it a rest. You've only got that bump because you were off your face with Dave."

"I was only at the pub because you were out. Again."

"So it's my fault you had so much you can't even remember where you left your wallet?"

He backed off, not wanting the special night in to be ruined by another row. "We've got beer in the fridge," he said, trying to slip his hands around her waist as she stirred something on the stove.

She shoved his hands away and went to the sink. "Oh, we're saved. I'm sure some cheap pilsner will really bring out the subtle flavours."

He winced. She was getting sarcastic and that was a step up the danger scale from just being annoyed. After sarcastic was shouting, then it was tearful, then it was sleeping-on-the-sofa time.

"I'll go to the shop now. I'll be back before it's ready, OK?" When she nodded he approached her cautiously and kissed the back of her neck. "Can I have a tenner?"

"Oh, for Christ's sake." She dried her hands and got out her handbag.

Sam looked up at the ceiling as she rummaged, feeling like a boy waiting for his pocket money. He hated it when they were like this.

He took the note silently, a twenty, and she went back to the cooker. "Get red, and not some cheap crap, OK?"

He saluted her. Bad move. He left the kitchen.

In the hallway, as he slipped his shoes on, he looked at the framed picture that used to be his favourite. It was a photograph of them together at university, when her hair was long and her clothes loose and floaty. His hair was tied back in a ponytail that was long gone. Now he had the short hair of a grown-up with the mortgage and nine-to-five job they both swore they'd never have. Leanne's job was more than nine-to-five though, and since she'd swapped the bohemian look for the crisp suits and high heels of the corporate life, she'd tightened up, got thinner, less fun. He'd done his best to keep up by getting a challenging coding job at a start-up with prospects but he just couldn't bring himself to go the whole hog and sell out completely like she had.

It was hard to believe the photo had been taken nine years ago and the friend who took it was now dead. That day had been perfect; they were slightly pissed and laughing their arses off about Pete not knowing what a douchebag was. It was puerile but it still made him smile all these years later. The picture captured them holding onto each other, laughing so hard they could barely stand up. It reminded him that there was a time when they didn't fight constantly, a time when they seemed to be walking in step with each other, instead of in different directions.

He grabbed his keys and the phone rang. Please don't be Dave, he thought as he picked up. "Hello?"

"Oh. Is that Samuel?"

Sam banged his forehead against the door. "Yeah, is that Mr Neugent?"

"Yes." There was a long pause. "Is Leanne there?"

She came out of the kitchen. "Who is it?"

He slapped a hand over the mouthpiece. "Dave."

"It's Marcus, isn't it?"

"It's Saturday evening, for Christ's sake," Sam said as she took the phone.

"Hi, Marcus," she said in her phone voice. "Oh, it's charging, sorry. No, it's no problem, go ahead."

"Bollocks," Sam muttered and chucked his keys back in the pot on the hallway table. He went to the fridge, grabbed a beer and opened it.

"I need to go out." Leanne said from the door a minute later. "There's a big function on tonight and Marcus had someone else lined up to go but they've called in sick–"

"So he wants some other bird to hang off his arm?"

"I happen to be the assistant director of the EMEA region," Leanne said, storming over to the oven to switch off the hob. "Not just some bit of skirt to wheel out for the clients. Bloody hell, you just can't accept that I have a career, can you?"

"Bollocks! What I can't accept is how that arsehole runs your life. It's Saturday night! This was supposed to be a special night in and now you're just going to drop everything to go and laugh at his jokes and look pretty for the fat businessmen there who don't give a shit about how clever you are."

"'Special night in'? Says the man who couldn't even be bothered to buy a bottle of wine?"

"I forgot!"

She pushed past him, heading for the stairs. "That says it all, doesn't it? And now when I have to go to work, you get on the high horse. You can't have it both ways."

"Go to work? You're off to some swanky hotel aren't you? You're gonna be drinking wine and eating canapés and making Marcus feel like he's got a bigger dick than everyone else, when, let's face it, he *is* the biggest dick in the room."

"It all comes down to dicks for you, doesn't it?" she was marching into the bedroom now. "You just can't handle the fact that I have some direction in my life. It isn't my fault you don't know what you're doing with yours!"

"I thought I was being married to you," he said and she stopped.

"We just want different things," she said. "If you don't want to be a high flyer, can't you at least support me?"

"Not if being a high flyer means you spend more time with that cock than with your own husband."

She groaned and went to the wardrobe. "Has it ever occurred to you that I might like to spend time with ambitious, dynamic people?"

"What's that supposed to mean?"

"Nothing." She pulled a dress off a hanger and started to take her jeans off.

"So you're saying you prefer to see him than me? Is that what this is really about?"

"No, for God's sake, Sam, just... just let me get ready will you?"

"Are you sleeping with him?"

She froze, one foot in the jeans, one foot out. "What did you just say?"

"I was just wondering how ambitious you are. Are you shagging your boss?"

He saw the tears well and felt awful. The balloon of anger inside him popped.

"You know what? I'm going to stay at the hotel tonight. I don't want to come back here."

"Lee, I'm sorry, I'm a twat."

"Then you can lie there," she pointed at the bed, "thinking about whether I'm shagging Marcus and why on earth I may well want to do that! Now sod off and let me get ready!"

She pushed him out of the bedroom and slammed the door in his face. "Lee," he called through it but she didn't reply. "Leanne, I'm sorry."

"Piss off, Sam."

"I didn't mean–"

"Piss off!"

He banged the door with his palm. "Fine!"

He went back downstairs, took another forty out of her purse and threw on his jacket. Keys grabbed, he banged the door as loud as he could as he left.

By the time he got to the pub he'd worked himself into the perfect amount of self-righteousness to get completely slaughtered. It wasn't his fault, it was Marcus.

"Pint, please," he said to the landlord.

"Argument with the missus again?"

"It's her prick of a boss," Sam said, passing over the first of the notes, wondering whether he could get drunk on sixty quid. "Honestly, I'm royally fucked off with it all, you know?"

"Yup."

"We were supposed to be having a night in, then he calls and it's all out the window."

"Yup." The pint was set down, Sam took a long drink and pulled out his mobile to text Dave.

The reply was quick enough. "Sorry m8 at wedding free wine free beer nuff said."

"Bollocks," Sam muttered and took the pint over to a table to nurse it by himself.

The place was starting to fill up. Halfway through the second beer a hen party came in, all feather boas and raucous laughter. Sam sank lower in his chair, worried that a miserable bloke on his own would just be impossible for them not to ridicule.

"Excuse me."

A damn ugly man holding a trilby and wearing a dodgy raincoat was standing in front of him. He looked like a noir fan who took it too far.

"Samuel James Westonville?"

"...Yeah."

The man sat down, dropped the hat onto the table. "I have your wallet." He pushed it across the table.

"Blimey!" Sam opened it. The cards were still there and more money than he remembered too. "You're an honest bloke, thanks. Let me buy you a drink!"

"Orange juice, please," the man said, pointing at a bust leg. "The painkillers don't agree with whisky."

Sam got the drink and went back to the table. "Where did you find my wallet?"

"I wanted to talk to you about that," the man said.

Something about this guy wasn't quite right. "Who did you say you are again?"

"I didn't. My name is Max. I'm a private investigator."

Sam nearly choked on his beer. "You're shitting me."

"I beg your pardon?"

"A private investigator, eh?" Sam hurried on, seeing that the guy had no sense of humour. With a face like that it was no surprise. "Is that how you found me?"

"I saw you leave your house and followed you here."

That spooked him. "OK. How did you know where I live?"

"It's printed on your driving licence."

"Oh. Yeah. OK."

"So, Mr Westonville, I found your wallet in the grounds of the Holburne Museum, which is currently at the centre of my investigation."

"You did? How the arse did it get there?"

Max stared at him. "You don't remember being there?"

Sam shook his head.

"When did you realise your wallet was missing?"

"Tuesday morning, on the way to work. I thought I'd lost it at the pub round the corner. That's near the museum actually. I was a bit worse for wear, woke up with a sore head. But it wasn't at the pub when I checked. I don't remember going into the museum though. It would have been closed by then."

"It was in the grounds."

Sam shrugged. "Sorry, mate, no idea how it got there."

"Could it have been stolen?"

"Maybe."

"So you were at the pub on Monday evening?"

"I... yes, I must have been."

The detective leaned forwards. "You don't remember? Think carefully. It's very important, Mr Westonville. What was the last thing you recall about Monday night?"

"I was at work... I met up with Dave, he's my best mate and we were planning to have a couple of jars."

"Jars?"

"Beers. I wouldn't normally on a Monday night but my wife called and said she was going to be home late and then up, up and away, Mary had a little lamb its fleece was white as goosey goosey gander, where shall I–"

Max held his hand up as Sam blinked at the beer. "Let's go over that last part again, Mr Westonville."

"Call me Sam, please," he said after another drink. He placed his palms flat on the table. "OK. So... Leanne called and I was a bit pissed off with her so I twinkle, twinkle little star, how I sing a song of sixpence, a pocket full of rye!"

He clamped a hand over his mouth, sucking in deep breaths through his nose. "What the fuck is in this beer?" he said once he'd stopped, pushing it away from him.

"Mr – Sam, I need to ask you a few more questions, but we need to talk in private. Would you come with me, please?"

Sam looked at him with a raised eyebrow. "I want to see some ID first." Nothing about the way the man acted made Sam want to be anywhere private with him.

"I'm afraid I don't have any you'd recognise."

"Well then, sorry, but no. No offence, but you could be anyone. Thanks for bringing my wallet back. I'll buy you another drink if you like, but if it's all the same to you, I'm going to stay here, in a public place." He glanced at the beer. "And I'm going to move off the beer and onto spirits."

"I understand," Max said, standing up. He didn't seem offended. "Have a good evening, Mr Westonville."

Sam leant back in the chair watching the PI leave. He wondered whether he should just go home, but the thought of returning to an empty house with a failed romantic dinner half cooked in the oven made him miserable. He flipped through his wallet, double-checking everything was there, then ordered a whisky. Sam smirked at the memory of Max, glad to have the wallet back and well on the way to drunken oblivion, judging by his fuzzy head and the gobbledegook he'd spoken.

The hen party left, the regulars got more drunk, and one of Leanne's favourite songs came on the jukebox. Just as he was sinking into the maudlin phase, berating himself for losing his temper with her, he saw a slender hand rest on the back of the chair opposite.

"Do you mind if I sit here?"

The blonde looked like she had stepped out of a movie. She was too beautiful for his local pub; her blonde hair shone despite the dingy lighting, her lips were deep red and eminently kissable.

"Um… no," he said. "Are you waiting for someone?"

She smiled, and it made him want to rest his chin on the table and drool. "Looking for someone," she said.

She was wearing an old-fashioned suit and it reminded him of the detective for some reason, though through the lust and drunken fog he couldn't work out why.

"Anyone in particular?"

"A man."

"A particular man?"

"Someone to keep me company."

He swallowed. This was the moment he'd dreamt of all his teenage years. Then he thought of Leanne. He looked down at the table, feeling a pang of guilt.

"It's just that I need to walk home, and I don't like walking alone at night."

"I suppose I could do that," he said.

"If it's not too much trouble?"

He shook his head. It was a bit weird, but he wasn't going to do anything contrary to what a married man should. Even so, it felt dangerous.

"Thank you so much," she said, standing as he struggled with his jacket, trying not to sway. "I was hoping a friend would meet me but he didn't show."

He's a pillock, Sam thought, necking the last of the whisky. "Do you live very far away?"

"Not too far. Too close for a taxi and too far to walk it alone at night."

"My name's Sam, by the way."

She smiled again. He had an urge to keep finding ways to make her do that, and he struggled to repress it. "I'm Petra. It's a pleasure to meet you."

20

As his valet tied his cravat, Will prepared himself for the meeting ahead. To everyone else it was a candlelit dinner with his fiancée, but to him it was simply business negotiations with a difficult party.

Catherine Papaver was proving to be tougher to win over than he'd thought. For any other woman in Aquae Sulis – no, the entirety of Nether Society – being the belle of the ball would have been a dream come true. Not for her. They would have been delighted to have been treated like the most beautiful woman in the world by a son of a powerful family, soon to be husband. But for Catherine it simply wasn't enough.

Every time he had complimented her it was thrown back in his face. Every time he danced with her and gave her the opportunity to win the admiration of her peers, she rejected him, and made no effort to engage in small talk. She'd wasted an incredible opportunity to be launched onto the Aquae Sulis social circuit.

He'd been convinced that making a plain woman feel admired would win her over; after all, wouldn't that be what she'd want the most? Especially after all those years in her younger sister's shadow. Elizabeth was one of the beauties of her generation and made her pretty peers look plain.

When he'd got back from the ball, exhausted by his efforts, he'd doubted whether it was worth the trouble. It wasn't as if her dislike of him would jeopardise their marriage; the engagement contracts had already been signed by their fathers. But a woman in love was so much easier to keep in line. With the alliance between the families being so critical, it made sense to try to make the marriage as successful as possible. Her being a surprise favourite of Lord Poppy meant Catherine's favour could have other benefits. He decided to persevere. Besides, he'd never shied away from a challenge.

"Is there anything else I can do for you, sir?"

"No, thank you, Jones," Will replied, inspecting himself in the mirror. "I think a cape and cane for this evening if–"

The door opened without a warning knock and Will took a breath to berate the intruder for such poor manners. But then he saw Sophia standing in the doorway, sniffing.

"What is it?" he asked, bending down onto one knee and opening his arms to her.

She ran into them. "Imogen said I'll be sent away into Mundanus forever!"

He chuckled. "No, just until you're all grown up. That's what happened to all of us. When you're a nice young lady, you'll move out of the nursery wing in Mundanus and into the main house in the Nether with us all the time, that's all. If you stayed in the Nether, you'd never grow up."

She pulled back, her bottom lip wobbling. "No, Will-yum," she said, tears rolling down her cheeks. "Imogen said I'll be left in a wood and wolves will eat me up because there's only allowed to be three children."

"Take no notice of her," he said, kissing her forehead. Even though he'd only been home for three days, he was already quite fond of the strange little thing. He'd never known such an affectionate child. "I know a secret, would you like me to share it with you?"

She forgot about her misery in a moment, nodding eagerly as the tears dried on her cheeks.

"Cook has made me some custard tarts as a special treat, but she hasn't told anyone else. Would you like to have one?"

She nodded, making the gentle ringlets bounce on her shoulders. "Yes, please."

"Jones will show you the way. Go on now, I have to go out for dinner with the young lady I'm going to marry."

"Can I be a bridesmaid?"

"If Mother says so, yes. Go on now."

She squeezed him tight and kissed his cheek, then extended her hand to Jones, who looked at it awkwardly for a moment before taking hold and walking out of the room with her.

When she was downstairs, he went to Imogen's room and rapped on the door.

"Come in."

Imogen was seated at her dressing table, holding a necklace up against her dress.

"Is it true you told Sophia she'd be eaten by wolves?"

"I may have said something along those lines."

"You really are a heartless specimen, aren't you?"

"She broke my favourite bracelet."

"She's only three!"

"She's almost four and should know better. Besides, there should only be three of us, everyone knows that."

"Everyone?"

"Everyone important. Why do you think we're not allowed to talk about her outside the house? Why do you think the housemaid is looking after her in Mundanus and not a nanny from the Agency? Father is embarrassed and if the Patroon finds out, that's it." She twisted around to face him. "Don't get attached to her, Will. She shouldn't be here."

"How can you speak like that about a little girl?"

She rolled her eyes. "I'm just pragmatic."

"Pathetic more like, upsetting a child because she broke a bracelet when you have dozens of the things. Besides, I don't know of any such rule. Father only has one brother."

"Don't you know anything? They had a sister but she died of a fever when she was small." She spoke as if it were common knowledge. "Where are you going dressed up like that?"

"I'm meeting Catherine for dinner," he replied, adjusting his collar, wondering what else he didn't know about his family.

"Why on earth would you want to do that? You'll be seeing her every day soon enough."

"Call me a fool, as you doubtless will, but I thought it would be wise to at least try to get to know the woman I'll be married to by the end of the season."

"You are a fool. I'd make the most of your freedom whilst you can and have dinner with someone pleasant to look at instead." She dropped the necklace into her lap, frowning. "By the end of the season? That's rather quick, isn't it?"

He shrugged. "Is it?"

"They want to palm her off onto you as soon as they can. Don't forget what I told you, William. She's trouble."

"Have a good evening playing with your baubles," he said. "Do try not to traumatise any other small children."

He closed her door and headed for the stairs, hearing voices in the lobby below. He recognised his Uncle Vincent's low rumble instantly.

"How is she?"

"Fine, Vincent, absolutely fine."

His mother was talking to him, but something about her voice made him slow down and peep over the handrail. Uncle Vincent was in his coat and hat and Mother was looking up at him, standing closer than Will imagined she would be. The way they looked at each other made him uncomfortable, but then he pulled himself up. They'd known each other for decades, of course they were close.

"Uncle Vincent!" he called as he descended the stairs. "How are you?"

"Fine, Will m'boy."

"Join me for a drink at the club later?"

"I'll do my best."

"Have a nice evening, dear," Mother said, coming over to peck him on the cheek.

He smiled at her, but was still unnerved when he climbed into the carriage. She never used to do that. He adjusted his gloves and tried to think ahead to the dinner and what he would talk to Catherine about, but his mind kept returning to the way his mother had been standing so close to his uncle. He shook his head and looked out of the window, forgetting momentarily that there was no scenery to take him out of his thoughts. He felt a longing for greenery and for a changing sky, for women who laughed in the tumbling foam of Sicilian waves, and for salt on his lips that tasted like freedom.

Catherine looked very different at the restaurant. Will realised how much of a difference Lord Poppy's gift had made. She was pale, appeared more tired than she should and was wearing a most austere outfit, something he'd expect from his grandmother's generation. She was helped out of the carriage by her brother. There seemed to be some tension between them but Thomas Papaver was much better at hiding his feelings than she.

"Good evening," Will said, shaking him by the hand.

"Good evening, William," Thomas replied as Cathy lurked nearby.

She was doing her best to distance herself, even to the extent that she stood apart from them and was looking away as they shook hands. Her manners were abominable and her lack of social grace was second only to her lack of physical grace. Imogen was right; they were trying to palm her off and he could see why.

"Good evening," he said and she jumped slightly, as if she'd been daydreaming.

"Hi," she said as Thomas cleared his throat loudly. "Good evening," she added hurriedly and extended a gloved hand towards him which he kissed dutifully.

"Shall we?" He gestured to the restaurant and offered her his arm.

"I will be at the table in the corner," Thomas said and took his leave.

The restaurant was quite full, it being the season, catering for guests in Aquae Sulis as well as residents before they went on to whichever social event they had slated for the evening. They were seated at a reserved table in one of the most private nooks, drawing attention as they walked past the diners and leaving a wash of whispers in their wake.

Will inspected the wine list as the waiter brought the menus. It gave them both something to do for a minute, for which he was grateful. "What will you have?"

"The steak."

"Medium or well-done?"

"Bloody," she said, looking him right in the eye.

"Really?" He laid his menu down and the waiter took the cue. It was one of the minor advantages of being an Iris in Aquae Sulis; they always had the best service.

"Rare steak for my fiancée," he began as she was taking a breath. He gave the rest of the order with the distinct impression he'd offended her. The waiter collected the menus and hurried off. "That was what you wanted?"

"I could have spoken for myself," she replied.

He sat back and looked at her, puzzled. Her eyes were a pleasant pale blue, quite attractive with brown hair usually, but hers was too mousy and noncommittal in colour to be as striking as her sister. Her lips were a little thin, her nose inoffensive enough; it was more the sour expression that never seemed to leave her face that gave the impression of ugliness. "Is that what they're teaching in Swiss finishing schools now?"

The flush in her cheeks helped her complexion. She shut her eyes, as if readying herself for an exam rather than dinner.

"Sorry," she said finally, opening her eyes but not looking at him. Instead she started to fiddle with her napkin in a most irritating manner.

"So," he said, leaning forward again, determined to make the best of it. "I thought it would be beneficial to discuss the future in a setting more conducive to conversation."

"What's to discuss? It's a fait accompli, isn't it?"

She said it with such heaviness he didn't know how to respond. "The contracts are settled, yes; it doesn't mean there isn't anything to talk about." When she just stared down at the napkin he sighed. "Catherine, I'm not an ogre. I really do want this to be a success."

"That's a contradiction in terms," she muttered. "Look, I know you mean well, but really, there's no point. We don't want to marry each other. It doesn't matter how much you decorate a dog turd, it still smells of–"

She put a gloved hand over her mouth. He didn't know whether to laugh or be shocked. "What an interesting turn of phrase," he commented as the wine was brought over. He tasted and approved it as she blazed scarlet. Once the wine was poured he picked up his glass, briefly considered a toast, but decided against it and took a long draught instead. "I know how you feel and I'm aware of your poor regard. You do little to hide it."

A flash of guilt crossed her face. She was as easy to read as Sophia. "Oh, I'm sorry," she said, genuinely. "It's nothing personal, really, I swear it. You're very handsome and rich and all of that stuff. Anyone else would be delighted."

"Well, I feel so much better," he said with a wry raise of an eyebrow, which seemed to soften her a little. "Why aren't you?"

"I don't think that's a conversation we should have."

"I have the distinct impression that there is a lot you want to say but feel you can't."

She looked at him then, maintaining eye contact longer than ever before. "You don't know the half of it."

"That's what I'm trying to say. Talk to me, Catherine. Tell me how we can make this more bearable. Is there anything specific about being married to me that upsets you?"

"Apart from—" She cut herself off again, dropping her head as she appeared to struggle with herself. She glanced over towards where her brother was sitting and her shoulders sagged.

It was a risk, but he decided to take it. He reached across the table and took her hand gently. "I won't report anything you say to another soul."

She was shaking, seeming more like a prisoner on the scaffold facing a noose rather than a woman of privilege facing her fiancé. "I don't like life in the Nether," she eventually said.

"I see," he said, keeping hold of her hand, feeling its slight dampness at the palm of the glove. "Have you been back to Mundanus since you came of age?"

She laughed, not a gentle, ladylike titter, but a guffaw that made the diners closest to them look over. She bit her lip and nodded.

"I must confess, I miss the sunshine," he said, and was rewarded with the first genuine smile he'd ever seen on her face.

"And the blue sky. And the breeze, don't you? And those crisp autumn days."

He nodded, heartened by the breakthrough. "I even miss the rain. In the Amazon, the rain was thunderous on our tents."

"You went to the Amazon?"

"Yes. We trekked for a couple of months. Oliver wanted to catch a moth or a butterfly. Something small and winged at least. I forget what exactly."

The flurry of conversation stalled and she withdrew her hand awkwardly. In fact, almost everything she did was riddled with awkwardness. He was determined to keep some of the momentum. "If you could visit Mundanus, would it make the marriage more bearable?"

She shrugged. "I suppose. Visiting isn't the same as..." Another abrupt stop. He had the feeling he was only hearing ten per cent of what was on her mind.

"But it's better than nothing. Perhaps you just need to get it out of your system. How about a weekend there as part of the honeymoon?"

"A whole weekend," she replied sarcastically.

"Most husbands would not be so generous," he snapped, irritated by her unladylike retort.

"There you are with the gratitude thing again." She shook her head. "You throw me a bone and hope I'll sit up and do nice tricks for you."

The waiter arrived with the food before he could reply. There were a few minutes of silent eating and he used them to consider his approach.

"I'm starting to think there isn't anything I can say to you that will make you feel better about this," he said.

She was pushing a potato around her plate. "I think you're right."

"This is how I see it." He laid his knife and fork down, sipped the wine. "I have done everything I can to open a dialogue with you. I used a powerful Charm to help you at the ball, I did everything I could to make you look good."

"Only so you would look good," she muttered, but he ignored it.

"I've given you the opportunity to discuss any grievances or concerns you may have and I've attempted to offer a solution. Every single time you've either ridiculed, scorned or even been offended by my efforts and I have no idea why. It seems to me you're determined to be miserable about this marriage and if that's the case, there's nothing I can say or do about it. So, you have a choice."

"Oh, really?"

"Sarcasm is not becoming in a lady."

"Spare me."

He clenched his jaw, aware of the diners around them. "Your choice is to continue to be rude and obstructive and marry a stranger with little regard for your feelings, or to meet me halfway and be gracious enough to see that an improvement in your behaviour will make the rest of our lives much more pleasant."

Cathy blanched, but remained silent, simply staring down at the meal she'd barely touched.

"You have a lot to think about. In the meantime I'll tell you about the Amazon so that the people watching us will think we are actually having a conversation. I strongly suggest that by the soirée at the Peonias' house tomorrow evening you will have something more positive to say to me."

"Is there no way to avoid this marriage?"

"No," he replied firmly and picked up his cutlery again.

She sat in silence as he trotted out a tale from his Grand Tour and she barely responded to his jokes. Occasionally he asked her a direct question so she would be forced to interact with him for the sake of appearances. He decided against dessert.

"I know I'm upsetting you," she said as he dabbed his mouth with the napkin. "I can't tell you why I'm like this and you were right – there is nothing you can do or say. I'm sorry."

"Don't be sorry, Catherine," he said, standing up to pull her chair out as she stood too. "Just be civil. It's not too much to ask."

He escorted her out of the restaurant, Thomas joining them outside. She looked close to tears as she was helped into a hansom cab and her brother made an embarrassed goodbye for the both of them.

He pulled on his gloves, cane tucked under his arm as he waited for another cab.

"Good evening, Mr Reticulata-Iris."

He turned at the voice, not placing it immediately. Horatio Gallica-Rosa had emerged from the restaurant and was making his way towards him.

"Good evening."

"I'm planning to go to the club. Is that where you're heading?"

Will paused. It was members only. "Yes."

"Oliver has sponsored me in," Horatio replied, seeing the momentary confusion. "Would you like to share a cab?"

"Thank you, yes," Will replied, even though it was the last thing he wanted.

Soon enough one came round the corner and they both climbed in after Horatio instructed the driver.

"How was dinner with Miss Papaver?"

"Very pleasant," Will lied.

"I was most interested to see the announcement of your engagement last night," Horatio said. "I take it you don't know about Miss Papaver."

"Know what, exactly?" Will said, hackles up. He didn't like his tone.

"Ah." Horatio inspected a stitch on his glove. "Well, it's fortunate we ran into each other like this. Permit me to give you a word of advice, Mr Iris. If I were you, I would call off the engagement as soon as possible."

"And why would I do that?"

"Because Miss Papaver, as the more astute of us may have noticed last night, has not spent the last three years at a Swiss finishing school. She's been living in Mundanus, in the dark city of Manchester, I believe."

"Whatever gives you that idea?" Will asked, playing it calm, nonchalant.

"Only the fact that I intercepted her and her brother on a mundane road out of the city a few days ago. She was dressed as a mundane, her brother clearly had little idea of what she'd been up to in recent times and her behaviour was reprehensible. Of course, that isn't the main reason I wouldn't marry her for all the tea in China."

He was drawing it out, hoping to make him squirm. Will remained glacial, not wanting to give him the pleasure. "It can't be because of her taste in clothes."

Horatio chuckled. "Indeed, no, it's because she was obviously having an affair with a mundane, someone she went out of her way to protect from my wrath. Which is the reason our paths crossed. Of course, you are entirely free to ignore my advice."

"Are you certain about the mundane?"

"Oh, yes." His wolfish smile made Will want to hit him. "I know what a woman in love looks like. And I didn't see that this evening. Oh, and there is, of course, the evidence from my patron that linked her directly with the misdemeanour that brought about these revelations." He flicked a speck of dust from his trouser leg. "Evidence enough, I fear."

"Indeed," Will said, grateful that the carriage was stopping outside the club so he didn't have to share it a moment longer with the odious man. "I will consider your advice carefully."

"Not much to consider, old chap," Horatio said, stepping out first. "I'm just pleased I had the opportunity to save you from the embarrassment. A secret like this always comes out, one way or another. Wouldn't you agree?"

21

"It's just at the end of this street," Petra said, and slipped her hand into the crook of Sam's arm. "So what do you do for a living?"

"I'm a computer programmer. You?"

"I'm a librarian. I don't know a thing about computers."

"Really? Don't all libraries have them now?"

"Not the one I work in. The owner is very traditional. It's a private library."

Sam nodded and smiled at Petra. She was so much warmer than his wife. Then his smile faded. Don't think about Leanne, he urged himself, she's off having the time of her life with that evil dick of a boss.

"Is something wrong?"

"No, no."

She stopped outside a set of gates leading up to a huge house. "This is it."

Amazed, he scanned the frontage with its stone pillars, impressive triangular pediment and the elegant fountain at the centre of the circular drive. It was Georgian and worth millions. He'd never been into a house that grand without having to pay for a ticket beforehand. "You live here?"

She nodded. "Would you like to come in for a nightcap?"

He hesitated, not sure what to say. "No" would be impolite but "yes" seemed like the first step towards infidelity.

"I hate going into the house by myself. I know it's silly, but it's the dark."

"Um, OK, I'll see you in, then I need to go home."

"Of course."

He followed her up the drive as she got her keys out of her bag. "I'm really grateful for this," she said, putting the key in the lock and turning it. She opened the door, but bent down to straighten the seam of her stocking before she stepped into the house. Eyes glued to her shapely legs, he stumbled in after her, trying not to imagine the tops of the stockings. She closed the door behind him, smiling in a way that almost made him forget he was married.

She guided him into a spacious living room, lit several large candles on the mantelpiece and pointed to one of a couple of sofas in the middle. "Take a seat, I'll get us a drink."

"But I should really…" He began, but she left. "…get home."

He looked around the room. It was cluttered and old-fashioned and there was a hearty fire burning in the grate. He frowned at it. She couldn't have been out that long. Or maybe there was someone else in the house, but if that were the case, why had she asked him in? He decided it was time to leave, impolite or not.

Before he reached the door Petra returned with two glasses of whisky, followed in by a tall, thin man dressed in an old-fashioned tweed suit and the private detective from the pub.

"What's going on?" he asked as she handed him a glass.

"Sorry," she said. "We really need to talk to you."

"Bollocks," he muttered. "I knew something was wrong with all this."

He put the whisky down, not trusting it. The tall man was staring at him in a way that made him edgy.

"This is the one?" he asked Max.

"Yes, sir."

"I see," said the tall man and walked out again.

"Who's that bloke?"

"He owns this house," Petra replied as Max hobbled to a sofa and eased himself down.

"I suppose you're not a librarian either."

"That was true." She looked offended. "I wouldn't lie about something as important as that."

"So is the tweedy guy your husband?"

"No, my boss."

He came back in, but about a dozen other men followed him into the room, each one of them stranger than the last. Not one wore anything resembling modern clothing; their suits looked like costume from a range of historical films. All carried notebooks and pencils.

"Is there some sort of weirdo convention in town?" No one answered him. "Look, I was happy to answer your questions in the pub but this is taking the piss."

"Good evening," the tall man said before turning to Petra. "I haven't the faintest idea what he was just talking about. I take it he's comfortable?"

"He's just a little annoyed at being brought here under false pretences," she explained.

"Hello, I'm right here," Sam said.

"Hello, yes, I understand you lost your wallet," the tall man said, speaking slowly as if he were talking to a child. "And when Max asked you about the night you lost it, you spoke rather strangely."

"Yeah," Sam said, glaring at Max. "Is he your boss too?"

"Yes," Max replied. "We think you might be a witness, but you can't tell us what you saw because something has been done to you."

"Maximilian!" The boss held up his finger. "No more, I want my students to work this out for themselves. But first…"

He reached into his jacket pocket and pulled out a magnifying glass unlike any Sam had ever seen before. The large circular lens was held in an ornate brass frame, engraved and decorated elaborately. He moved closer, holding it up towards Sam.

"I'm not going to stay here and be treated like a bloody lab rat! You lot are mental, I'm off!"

He headed for the hall but something stepped in the doorway that looked disturbingly like a big gargoyle. "Sorry, mate, can't let you go anywhere."

He yelled and jumped back. "What fuckery is this?"

"Hardly subtle," the boss said to Max, as if he had something to do with it.

The detective just shrugged. "I didn't tell it to do that."

"Just stand still, there's a good chap," the boss said.

"Bugger off!" Sam said, tripping over the edge of the rug in his fluster.

"Sam," Petra said, setting her drink down and coming over to him. "We're so sorry to upset you like this, we don't often have guests like you."

"What, normal?"

She smiled. "In a manner of speaking." She touched his arm and he thought of her stockings again. Sometimes he hated his brain. "If you could just bear with us for a few minutes. Mr Ekstrand is going to see if something has been done to you, to stop you talking about what happened the other night."

"I don't give a rat's arse about what happened."

"But a man is missing, Sam. He might have been murdered and you're the only one who might've seen something." Her voice was so soft, so soothing he almost forgot about the boss and the other crazies. "It won't take long, we need you to be brave. Can you do that for us? For me?"

Somewhere at the back of his mind he knew she was playing him, but he found himself capitulating all the same.

She nodded to her boss who came closer and inspected him with the magnifying glass, slowly and methodically looking at every square inch of his head and shoulders and then down his arms. He paused over the wedding ring. "Very interesting," he muttered, and then carried on. When he was finished, he stood back and peered at Sam in the same way a man might peer at an exotic insect kept in a glass tank. "Tell me about the night you lost your wallet."

Sam looked over at the detective, expecting him to chip in, but the ugly man just nodded to him.

"I went to the pub on the way home from work and half a pound of tuppenny rice, half a pound of treacle." He squeezed his eyes shut, certain that wasn't what he meant to say. "No, hang on, he had ten thousand men. He marched them up to the top of the – oh, sod it!"

The boss turned and looked at the group that had followed the detective in, all of whom had pencils poised and were shuffling closer. "What could cause that sort of behaviour?"

"A Charm, sir!" a young and gangling lad said eagerly.

"Of course, which one?"

"A Fool's Charm sir!"

"Good, good. What else?"

"But that's the most likely, sir," said another, who was sweating profusely.

"A good sorcer–"

Petra coughed loudly, distracting him. He glanced at Sam and frowned, nodding to himself.

"Err, it's always better to be thorough. Other lines of enquiry could be…?"

The first shoved his hand in the air. "May I ask the subject a question, sir?"

"Subject?" Sam said, offended, but none of them seemed to notice.

"By all means, yes, you may ask," the boss replied.

"Did you sustain any injuries on the night in question?"

"I had a bump on my head when I woke up the next morning."

"Ooh!" The eager one bounced on his toes. "It could just be a head injury, sir!"

"Interesting point, good. How do we rule that out?"

They stood chewing the ends of their pencils for a few moments. "Ask him how many fingers you're holding up?" one at the back said hopefully, earning an irritated groan from their teacher.

"Perhaps I can offer a suggestion?" Petra said, and they all looked at her. "We need to know where the bump is."

"It's here," Sam said, brushing the back of his head. He wondered whether to make a dash for the window.

"That disproves the head injury theory," she said. "The visual cortex is at the back of the brain so none of the language centres would be affected, and besides, his symptom only presents when he tries to recall the event. It's not Tourette's either," she added as the sweaty one took another breath. "That's completely different."

"You are just a librarian, right?" Sam asked.

"I do actually read some of the books too."

"Any other possibilities?" the boss said. "I can think of one and whoever names it may read a book in my library. As long as you don't remove it. And you can't touch any on the shelves down the lefthand wall. And not any books that begin with P, S or W." When no one said anything he sighed. "Are we certain he is actually speaking gibberish?"

"Oh!" Eagerboy, as Sam now thought of him, leapt in the air. "It could be a variant of an Apollo's Curse sir! He might be speaking the truth in his mind, but the curse may be acting on everyone around him so he can't be believed."

The suggestion was met with a nod from his teacher and then a variety of congratulatory grunts and pats on the back from his bizarre peers.

"Yes, that's the only other possibility. But there is an obvious way to disprove this. What is it?" He didn't give them as long that time. "Because the Arbiter heard the gobbledegook too, and as you all know, Arbiters are immune to–"

Petra coughed again.

"…immune to coughs and colds," the man said, eliciting a number of confused expressions.

"Is this some kind of school?" Sam asked. "Will someone just please tell me what the arse is going on here?"

"You were in the wrong place at the wrong time, I think," Petra said, rubbing his arm gently. "Weren't you at all worried that you couldn't remember that night?"

"Well, I was, but then my mate had just about convinced me it was cause I'd been on a bender."

"Do they all talk like him in Mundanus?" the boss asked the detective, who nodded. "Well, I'm confident it's a Fool's Charm, though with the way he talks it's hard to tell when he's talking about that night or just spouting rubbish."

"Oi!"

"So, putting this hypothesis together with the fact that he was in the vicinity of a serious incident involving foul play, I'm happy to press on with treating him as a victim of the Fool's Charm. Now, we also have reason to believe that the individuals involved are actually…" He glanced at Petra who was shaking her head at him. "Ah. Yes, that they are of the highest status amongst the criminal fraternity who live on the other side of the... divide, so to speak." He winked at his students theatrically.

"Do you mean one of the Fae lords, sir?" Eagerboy asked and Petra tutted.

"Did he just say–"

"Shush," Petra said to Sam, patting his arm again.

"That being said, I think there's only one option. We need to dislocate his soul and then interrogate him whilst we can. As you all know, their Charms only work on the soul and–"

"Now wait just a cocking moment!" Sam interjected. "Look, Mr... Ekhart?"

"Ekstrand. Mr Ekstrand."

"Look, Mr Ekstrand, I haven't got a scooby what you lot are on about, but when people start talking about dislocating souls, it puts the shits up me. That just doesn't sound natural."

Ekstrand took a moment to reply, as if he was still working out what he'd said. "Some very naughty people," he began, in his talking-to-a-child voice, "have done something very bad to your head. They are very powerful naughty people, so we have to do something very serious to you to get the information we need."

"Don't talk to me like I'm some sort of chimp, what exactly do you want to do?"

"It would kill him," Max said. "He's too old, the body would die after dislocation."

"What the–"

Petra put a finger to his lips. "Sir, there's also the wedding ring. You made a remark when you saw it through your glass."

"Oh, fiddlesticks and flapdoodles!" Ekstrand pounded his temples with the palms of his hands. "He's protected by Lord Iron. Damnation."

"Lord who?"

"Just be quiet," Ekstrand snapped, now pacing. "This is disastrous. Options."

"We... we could try hypnosis," one of the students called out.

"Rubbish. Next!"

"We could brainwash him into thinking it's a different day of the week," Eagerboy said, "so that when he tries to remember, the Charm is tricked into disguising the wrong day."

Ekstrand paused with one foot still in the air. "Interesting, but no, it assumes the Charm is only tied to time, and not context. Rubbish, you can't go in my library now, you're clearly not intelligent enough."

"There's only one option sir," Max said. "One of *them* has to unravel the Charm."

"And how on earth could we make that happen?"

"I think it's possible," Max said, as the gargoyle nodded in the doorway.

"Oh, now wait a minute, I'm dreaming, aren't I?" Sam said, reaching the only conclusion that made sense. "How do I wake myself up?"

"You're not dreaming, Sam," Petra whispered.

"Lady Lavender will be very motivated to have the Master of Ceremonies found, otherwise she'll lose a huge amount of influence in Aquae Sulis," Max said. "We could approach the Censor, ask her to help."

"He would have to be taken into Exilium," Ekstrand muttered, looking at Sam out of the corner of his eye. "This is an appalling breach."

"If we want that information, and Lavandula agrees to help, we have to bring him in or kill him afterwards." Max was so matter-of-fact that Sam believed he would kill him then and there if it served their purpose.

"We bring him in," Petra said, her hand tightening on his arm. "It isn't his fault he was there. Look at him. He's harmless."

Sam tried his best to look as harmless as possible, disturbed by what he'd heard. He hoped their attention would shift and he'd be able to make a run for it.

"He's clearly an idiot," Ekstrand said.

"Hey! Stop talking about me like I'm not even here!"

"He knows about computers," Petra said and Ekstrand narrowed his eyes at him.

"Really?"

"He speaks their language," Petra added.

"Is this true?"

"Yeah."

"And he's protected, as you said," Petra said. "We can't kill him."

"We can if there's a breach involved, Lord Iron would understand," Max said.

"Would he?" Petra raised an eyebrow. "Do we want to take the risk?"

"No," Ekstrand concluded. "I have enough to worry about. Max, go to the Censor first thing in the morning and make it clear to her that if she doesn't secure help from her patron, we may never find her brother. All of you," he looked at the students, "need to write up this evening's investigation and make a list of the questions you may want to ask the subject about life in Mundanus. Dismissed."

They all bowed and left, once the gargoyle stepped aside.

"And Petra—" Mr Ekstrand stroked his chin, looking at Sam. "Ask Axon to find our subject a secure room for the night."

"I want to go home," Sam protested.

"That's out of the question, I'm afraid," Ekstrand said. "You're too valuable to send back into Mundanus. You didn't have anything important to do tonight, did you?"

Sam was too tired and drunk to think of anything quickly enough. "Not exactly." At least with Leanne being away for the night she wouldn't freak out. Then he wondered if that was actually a bad thing. "What's Mundanus anyway?"

Petra steered him towards the door. "We'll talk about that another time. You need to sleep. Tomorrow is going to be a long day."

22

Will knocked on the door of his father's study, not looking forward to the conversation he was about to have. At the call he entered to find his father studying what looked like a property contract. A frown had taken residence and looked like it was settled in for the evening.

"I thought you would have left by now," he said, setting the paper down, directing the frown at his son instead. "It is the soirée at the Peonias' tonight, isn't it?"

"I need to speak to you about something before I go." Will closed the door behind him. "I'll pass on your apologies."

"I've already sent a note. Sit down, Will, something is clearly troubling you."

Will did as he was invited. "Father... I need to borrow your purity opal."

The frown was swept away by a look of surprise. "How in the worlds did you know about that?"

Will smirked. "A girl in the French Court told me about it. She said all the heads of families have one."

Father pursed his lips. "You know what my next question is."

Will nodded. "It is for Catherine Papaver. I've heard a rumour and whilst I don't trust the source, I felt it prudent to have all the facts."

"A rumour that precipitates such a request is serious indeed, considering the contracts have already been signed."

"That's why I want to be thorough, Father."

"Who's the source of this rumour?"

"The Gallica-Rosa."

"Not trustworthy."

"Even unreliable sources can cause trouble."

Father nodded and unlocked the top drawer of his desk. "I'm sure I don't need to emphasise how discreet you must be. Don't let another soul see you use this."

Will nodded and took the small velvet pouch. "How do I use it?"

"Press it directly against her skin and hold it there for a few seconds. If it turns black... the rumour is true."

Will tucked it into the inside pocket of his jacket. "Thank you, Father, I assure you I will be careful."

The Peonias lived in a large house but not in one of the fashionable streets of Aquae Sulis. Nevertheless, their soirée was the place to be that evening; Will and Imogen's carriage had to wait for a space to clear before they could pull up.

"We wouldn't have had to wait if you hadn't taken so long," she muttered at him.

"But now we can be fashionably late," he said, and helped her out.

He spotted the Papavers as soon as they entered one of the reception rooms. Thomas and his wife Lucy were chatting with Oliver's parents whilst Catherine stood near the punch bowl in a world of her own. Will suppressed a surge of irritation. She should have been engaged in the conversation too, but instead she clearly thought herself above it all. When they married – if they married – that would have to change.

She was dressed very conservatively again, the dress far higher in the neckline than everyone else's. He wondered what her mother was thinking, instructing the maid to dress her so. Did they not care about whether she was fashionably attired now that she'd been promised to him and no longer needed to impress anyone?

Once he had shaken hands with Oliver and kissed his sister's hand, form dictated that he greet his fiancée before anyone else. Will kept it brief, bowing and kissing her hand, noting her stilted movements even in such a simple interaction. He hoped the opal would turn black and provide a decent reason to break the engagement. Then he remembered what his father had said about needing the alliance to be a success and suppressed his selfish desires.

Free of his initial obligation he headed for the card room, planning to while away some of the evening over hazard and poker, knowing that would remove the pressure to stay near Catherine. He planned to draw her away later on, once people had filled their bellies with punch and stopped watching out for who was there and who was not.

On the way he had brief conversations, maintaining a couple of running jokes with his peers and generally doing his best to make a good impression. The air in the hallway was thick with perfume and the heat of the social throng. He wondered whether the attendance was high because of the sponsorship of the Rosa. Everyone wanted to know the story behind it.

"Good evening, Mr Reticulata-Iris."

He turned at the woman's voice. It was a Rosa from the other line, the Alba who'd managed to snare the Indian princess. He bowed and kissed her hand as he tried to remember her name. Her gloves smelt of rose petals. "Miss Alba-Rosa," he said, smiling. "What a pleasure to see you."

"And you, Mr Iris. I was commenting to my brother yesterday that it was such a shame I didn't get a chance to dance with you at the opening ball."

"I'm sure I can correct that oversight at the next one."

"I would like that very much. You dance a fine waltz. Your fiancée is very lucky."

He smiled. "I was on my way to play cards."

"Oh." She looked disappointed and pulled him across the hallway to stand next to her against the wall, so they could speak without blocking the way. He was astounded by the gesture, but took care not to show it. She leant closer, the scent of roses floating up from the décolletage at which he was studiously not staring. "I understand it would be a faux pas for me to join you."

"At cards?"

"Yes. I've heard it's not the done thing for ladies to play at the same tables as the gentlemen, is that right?"

It had never occurred to him for it to be otherwise. "Absolutely," he replied. "It would not be proper for a gentleman to win a hand and take a lady's money."

"Such a shame," she sighed. "I wanted to see if you were as good at poker as you are at the waltz. One can tell only so much from the way a man dances."

He enjoyed the thrill her flirtation sent through him. "Am I to understand that it's different in Londinium?"

"Oh yes, at certain soirées the ladies and gentlemen play at the same tables. It makes it so much more interesting." The way she said it made the thrill pulse into excitement. He wanted to touch her cheek, to stroke the back of her neck. He hadn't felt this way since Sicily, and never before in Society. "You'll have to come up for the season. I'm sure Cornelius would sponsor you if I introduced you to him."

"I would very much like to meet your brother," he replied.

The way she spoke and held eye contact was quite intoxicating. There was none of the shyness nor the coy games played by the young ladies of Aquae Sulis about her. She was a delight for the eyes too. Again, Will hoped the opal would turn black. "Is Princess Rani here?"

"She's having her own Grand Tour. Aquae Sulis was just one place on a very long list."

"Not tempted to accompany her?"

"Not when there's so much to hold me here. I hope you will dance with me at the next ball, Mr Iris." She waved to someone behind him, leaving him with a smile to remember her by.

He deliberately settled at a table on the other side of the room to the Gallica-Rosa, forcing himself not to think of Amelia. He feared if he played a hand with Horatio, the Rosa would make a comment committing him to a path he didn't want to take without knowing if his fiancée had any honour to defend.

When he was almost two hundred of the Queen's pounds up and in need of a drink he left the table and returned to the main reception room. Imogen slipped her arm into his on the way, fanning herself excitedly.

"I've heard the most fascinating rumour, dear brother," she said, and Will steeled himself for disaster. "Apparently, the Gallica-Rosa has told Cecilia he has a surprise that will make the princess seem dull in comparison."

Will hid his tension behind a bored expression. "Oh? What does he have up his sleeve? A Prince from Atlantis?"

"A house in Aquae Sulis apparently, but that is to go no further. Cecilia told me in the strictest confidence."

"Are you certain?"

"Cecilia is. And she's trying very hard to make it up to me for not telling me he was coming for the season. He's dripping with money, too. I think she's hoping to catch his eye but I'm certain I can–"

"Keep away from him, Imogen," he said, too sternly.

"He's been sponsored in by your best friend."

"Under duress. Father has a very low opinion of his family. It won't go anywhere."

"He may change his mind if he becomes a resident," Imogen said with a smile. "Oh, and by the way, what in the world is Catherine Papaver wearing? I'd give her my seamstress's details, but I fear she would wear her creations so poorly I'd be forced to find another."

"I believe Cecilia is trying to catch your eye," he said, glad to have a reason to get rid of her. He didn't need her prattling to distract him.

He scanned the room for his fiancée, spotting her brother still talking to Oliver's father, probably about cricket or rugby; they were both sports bores. He caught sight of Lucy's red dress and saw her leading Catherine out of the room and onto one of the balconies. Intrigued, he got a glass of punch and went to the french doors in an effort to listen in.

"I had no idea it was going to happen," Catherine was saying. "I'm so sorry."

"It's fine, really," Lucy replied. "Tom nearly burst a blood vessel but that's not your fault. I'm just glad you were able to come back to us."

"I just wish he could have let me come back to your house, not right into the ball. That was so awful."

"Well, it's all done now and you're the toast of the Papavers."

"Hardly."

"Well, I've heard nothing but good things. It's been a long time since one of us has been a favourite."

"Do you mean the Rhoeas or Californicas?"

"Either."

There was a pause. Will sipped the punch and tried to look like he was watching people go by, rather than being tuned into the conversation outside.

"So how are things? Was it as bad as you feared?"

"Worse."

That piqued his interest.

"Oh, Jeez. I wish they would let you stay with us. I'd like the company."

"I wish they would too, but that's never going to happen."

"At least William seems like a nice young man."

There was a longer pause.

"I don't want to talk about him," Catherine finally said. "I don't want to talk about any of that."

"You're gonna have face up to it sometime, honey," Lucy said, sounding far more American than he'd realised. "We all have to."

"Not tonight," Catherine said, and the finality of her tone made him worry she was coming back in. He had to take the opportunity to get her alone. He went out onto the balcony.

"Good evening," he said, ignoring the dread on Catherine's face as they both curtsied.

"Mr Iris," Lucy smiled. "I was just singing your praises."

"How kind of you, madam, I hope my fiancée didn't contradict you." He earned the blush he was hoping for on Catherine's cheeks, then berated himself for playing such games with someone so inept. "I would very much appreciate the opportunity of a moment with my fiancée, if I may be so bold?"

Lucy raised an eyebrow, gave Catherine an encouraging smile. "I'll be just inside."

Catherine looked as if she were going to be sick.

The balcony overlooked a modest garden but, having spent so much time in Mundanus, he realised how pathetically fake it all appeared without proper sunlight. The Charms required to keep the plants alive were more a demonstration of wealth than anything else. He'd never appreciated before how hollow a gesture it was. Although he found it distasteful he was grateful they both had something else to look at.

Catherine moved to the stone rail, avoiding his eyes. It gave him the opportunity to palm the opal; it felt cold and the heat of his hand failed to warm it. The neckline of her dress was far higher at the back than he'd hoped it would be and barely any of her flesh was exposed; even her gloves came up to where the short sleeves of her dress ended. He wondered how he was going to test her without her knowledge. Perhaps he'd need to come up with a story to explain it away instead.

"Did you want to talk about something?" she said nervously.

"I wanted the opportunity to see how you are."

"And whether I'm going to be civil?"

He went to stand next to her and she shuffled away a step. "Perhaps we can start again?"

She still couldn't bring herself to look at him. "I know you're trying really hard. And I know I'm not very good at all this."

"I just want you to relax," he said. "That's why I came out here, I thought it would be easier without an audience."

She nodded. "I don't like everyone watching. I don't know why they're so interested."

"You're Lord Poppy's favourite."

"And your fiancée."

"That too." He moved closer and she twitched. "Why do you insist on keeping me at arm's length? It's almost as if you don't want to get to know me."

"I just—"

"I wonder if you're scared that if you do get to know me, you may actually want to get married."

"There's nothing worse than an amateur psychologist," she muttered.

"Perhaps, if you gave me a chance, you'd change your mind."

"What if I were to suggest your ego simply can't handle the fact that I'm not falling over myself to marry you?"

That made him pause. "Has anyone told you that you may be too clever for your own good?"

"Frequently," she said bitterly and looked back out over the garden. "I know I'm supposed to smile and go along with all this, but I just can't. You know, the last couple of days I've actually wished I could? It would be so much easier."

"Then why not just let all this tension go? Why not let me win you over?"

She pulled a face. "Did you read some schlock romance novel whilst you were on the Grand Tour or something?"

"Catherine," he sighed.

"Perhaps this works on silly girls who think the only thing to aspire to is marriage, but it won't work with me."

"I don't think you're a silly girl."

"Then stop treating me like one," she snapped.

He almost turned on his heels, but decided on a different course of action. She was trying to keep him away with words; no matter what he said, she had a way to shoot him down. The only way he was going to get close enough to test her was to stop talking.

The plan was to gather her into his arms and kiss her passionately, pressing the opal to the back of her neck as he did so, in the hope that she'd be so caught up in the clinch that she wouldn't notice. He gently put a hand on the back of her waist, and she jumped and looked at him in surprise.

"What are you doing?" she asked as he slid his hand up her back, slowly, gently.

"I want to show you that it's not all bad," he said, slightly concerned by how she winced as he moved his hand upwards. Did she find it so unpleasant? "I want to stop treating you like a silly girl and as the woman I'm going to marry."

He slipped his hand upwards to brush the back of her neck, leaning closer as he gently angled her towards him, pressing the opal against her skin as he did so. He hoped she would accept the kiss, but instead she started to move away. He caught hold of her arm with the intention of pulling her into an embrace that all of the young women he'd kissed on the Grand Tour would have melted into.

He wasn't expecting the yelp of pain. Keeping the opal in place and her as close to him as he could with his hand on the back of her neck, he looked down at the arm she was trying to pull away from him. Without saying a word, he rolled the top of the glove down to expose her skin, revealing a deep purple bruise and then another only inches away.

Speechless, he let go of her neck, dropped the opal into his pocket without taking his eyes off the injuries and pulled down the other glove. Two horrendous bruises covered that arm too, and he wondered if the reason she'd flinched when he ran his arm up her back wasn't because she'd resented his touch but because there were other bruises.

She looked terrified, but not of him. "Your brother?" he asked, but the immediate shocked expression told him it wasn't Thomas. "Your father?"

She looked away and he let her go. "Don't tell anyone," she said in a timid voice, not the one he was used to.

He was too furious to speak so he left her on the balcony hurriedly pulling her gloves back up to cover the evidence. He no longer cared about what the opal could tell him.

23

Cathy sat hunched over her dressing table, head propped up on her hands. She ached all over. Where she wasn't hurting from the beating she was stiff from the seemingly endless dancing.

She felt sick with worry. William looked furious when he saw the bruises but she had no idea what was going to come of it. If anything did, she knew it wasn't going to be good.

She got up and paced. It was all she did these days; she lay on the bed, she sat at the dressing table, she walked back and forth. This was the ultimate punishment: being locked in a room with only herself for company. No books, not even innocuous ones, and, of course, no television or internet. She was driving herself mad. All of the things she was missing out on, all of the worlds she was being denied, and the endless speculation about Josh and whether he was still staying with that coat hanger of a woman haunted her.

Surely Josh would be bored of the redhead by now. Perhaps she was doing the woman a disservice but Cathy knew Josh valued a woman's mind more than her looks; she herself was the proof! She had to get back to Josh, explain it all and apologise. If she could find a way to escape and stay hidden, she could protect him too, surely? She pushed to one side the fear that he wouldn't want her back.

She had to get out of the Nether and hide again, but her current plan was as flimsy as a mille-feuille pastry: to escape when William took her to Mundanus.

That's as far as the plan had got and it had two major flaws. One was that she would be married by then, the second was that Lord Poppy would be able to find her, even if she did manage to wheedle another Shadow Charm out of the Shopkeeper. If she could find out how the Fae lord tracked her down, there was a chance she could stay hidden, but without that knowledge the risk was too high. Being an Iris would add another layer of complication to the pudding; rich and powerful families weren't generally known for their sympathy when it came to any potential disgrace in Society.

She fantasised about climbing out of the window and somehow making it down to the gravel three storeys down without breaking her neck and out of the grounds without being seen. She made constant mental lists of what she'd do next; speaking to the Shopkeeper was always first, and there was a Way to the Emporium from Aquae Sulis. Getting there without being seen would be difficult. Next a mad dash to Manchester, going to one of her friends, getting the keys to the storage place... then it all unravelled, unable to keep its own integrity so far from anything realistic.

When she ran away the first time she was in Cambridge and had only a minder who liked his whisky too much and a chaperone who never wanted to leave the house as the modern life of Mundanus terrified her. She had the time and the means to research her options and carefully formulate a plan. Now she was locked in her room, high in a house in the Nether, full of staff briefed to keep a close eye on her, with hourly checks that she was still there and not up to mischief. Her father was never going to underestimate her again.

His comment about disowning her kept coming back. That's what she really needed: to be completely abandoned by the family and kicked out of the Nether. For anyone else in Society it was a terrifying threat, being denied a life of privilege and condemned to aging and scrabbling for survival. For her, it would be bliss.

But being disowned would earn the wrath of Lord Poppy, against not only her but the rest of her family, and as much as she hated her parents and her sister, she didn't want to cause them that amount of distress. They simply wouldn't be able to cope. Elizabeth would probably be taken in by another family as she was too beautiful and talented musically to lose to Mundanus, but her parents would be broken. Tom, with his own household now, would escape the worst, but still be devastated.

She leaned forwards until her forehead was on the polished wood, wishing she could climb out of her skin and fly away. The memory of Will's kiss made her groan with embarrassment. She just couldn't handle his attention. He was obviously trying so hard and he was right; she did keep throwing it back at him. Her stomach twisted with guilt. It wasn't his fault he'd been betrothed to such a freak. He must think so little of her, not able to even be polite, but every time he tried to be civil it made her want to scream with rage at his efforts to weave her back into being a little doll, existing only for male attention and care. Having seen what life could be, she couldn't pretend to play the game he'd urged her to.

"There has to be a way out of this," she muttered. "Don't give up. Don't–"

She heard the doorbell clang in the hallway below and the sound of the butler's shoes clipping across the tiled floor. Hurrying to press her ear against the bedroom door, she chewed her lip, wondering if it was William, and what disaster his discovery was going to bring.

It was impossible to tell who had come; she couldn't make out the voices, but she deduced it was a woman from the sound of the shoes on the tiles. Lucy?

The sound of the drawing room door closing relaxed her; it must've been a guest for her parents. She sat heavily on the bed, tired of this life already. She wanted to play Mass Effect and eat chocolate and forget about it all, just for a few hours.

Then she heard footsteps running up the stairs and towards her door. Her stomach tightened as the key turned in the lock and the maid came in.

"The mistress says you're to be dressed for a visitor," she said breathlessly, rushing to the wardrobe, which had been filled with new dresses.

"Who is it?" Cathy asked, glancing at the door, which had been left open. She felt so tempted.

"The Censor herself!" the maid said, pulling out a cream day dress matched with a jacket to cover the evidence of her father's beating.

"She wants to see me?" Cathy said, now in a full-blown panic. "Why?"

"She wants to take you out for tea," the maid said, closing the door and beginning to unhook the back of the simple day dress Cathy had been put into that morning.

"Me?" Cathy mumbled, trying to puzzle it out. Had William said something to her? Was the Censor going to ask her about the bruises?

Should she tell the truth? The Censor was her aunt, after all, but there was no love lost between them, and the Censor would be keen to avoid any embarrassment seeing as the beater's wife was her only sister.

By the time she'd been laced into the new dress and the jacket buttoned high, she'd decided to let the Censor speak first and bring it up if it was on the agenda. That was probably what form would dictate anyway.

The Censor was waiting in the hallway as she descended the stairs. Cathy's sweating hand gripped the handrail so she didn't trip over the frills of her petticoat.

"Good morning, Catherine," her aunt said with a smile as her mother lingered nearby, watching.

"Good morning, Lady Censor," Cathy replied, curtsying at the bottom of the stairs.

"Your mother tells me your diary is free today. I trust you have no objection to spending the day with me?"

Cathy shook her head, surprised. "No," she said as her mother glared at her. "Not at all. On the contrary, I would be delighted."

"Good. Off we go then. It was lovely to see you, Isabella," she said to her sister, who smiled and withdrew as Cathy was escorted out of the house.

The Censor's carriage was waiting. Just the fact of it being outside their house would be remarked upon as others passed. Everyone wanted to have the Censor pay a personal call, especially now the Master of Ceremonies was out of the country.

Once they were inside and skirts arranged comfortably the door was shut and the carriage moved off.

"How was the soirée at the Peonias' last night?" the Censor enquired and Cathy wondered if it was the first test.

"Very popular," she said, not wanting to commit herself to saying anything about William.

She readied herself for the next question, but when they rounded the corner the Censor drew the curtain over the door's small window and her false smile faded.

"You and I are not going to Lunn's and we will not be having lunch. I had to say that to get you out of the house."

"Where are we going?"

"That will become clear soon enough. Now you need to listen to me carefully. The people I'm taking you to will tell you what you need to do. I want you to do exactly as you're told."

"What people?"

"Be quiet and listen. This is very important. If you do not obey their instructions perfectly, I'll know and I will personally see you destroyed. And I'm not talking about being shunned by Society, I'm talking about ensuring you're sold into slavery and made to suffer for the rest of eternity."

Cathy blinked at her. "I'm your niece."

"An accident of birth will not protect you if this is not a success."

Cathy gritted her teeth, forcing the abuse she wanted to spout at the woman back down her throat. "I'm also Lord Poppy's favourite," she finally said. "I'm sure he wouldn't be too happy if you were to–"

"Listen to me, you stupid little girl. Your brief flirtation with success is utterly inconsequential. You may be Poppy's favourite today, but I am the Censor of Aquae Sulis and if I tell my patron you failed to cooperate, she'll have no difficulty in correcting Lord Poppy's opinion of you."

"I'd be more likely to succeed if you tell me what I'm supposed to be doing."

"As I said, the people involved will tell you everything you need to know. When this is over, if you're successful, I'll take you home and you will not tell a soul of what has transpired. If I hear even a hint of gossip about anything other than you and me having lunch today, I will make good on my previous warning."

"Is there no reward if I'm successful?"

The Censor's lips curved into a smile that made Cathy shiver. "Only the satisfaction that you've been a good citizen of Aquae Sulis."

Cathy didn't ask any more questions. It was clear no answers would be forthcoming, so she sat there, bouncing up and down uncomfortably on the seat, daydreaming about leaping from the carriage and making a dramatic escape. She also imagined punching the Censor in the face. Neither came to pass.

They rode in silence, going steadily uphill. Cathy suspected they were heading out of Aquae Sulis. After a few minutes the carriage lurched to the left as they turned a corner sharply and the ground beneath them seemed far less even. It came to a stop and the driver knocked three times on the roof of the carriage.

"Remember what I told you," the Censor said. She whispered a Charm of Openings as she touched the handle of the carriage door and then it was opened, revealing the blue sky of Mundanus.

Cathy was ushered out of the carriage. She almost fell down the steps when she saw the green field and felt the cool breeze. She glanced behind her, seeing the interior of the carriage appearing to float in mid-air, then it was gone as the Censor closed the Way back into the Nether. She realised she'd left her bag in there, not that it contained anything useful.

This was her chance. Cathy gathered up the absurd amount of fabric that made up the skirts of her dress, but just as she was breaking into a run her arm was grabbed from behind. She cried out at the pressure on one of the bruises as she was twisted around, not gently either.

The man wore a butler's suit and was clean-shaven. Another man, wearing a trilby and raincoat, was leaning on crutches just behind him. He was too ugly and she had a horrible feeling he was an Arbiter.

"Are you Catherine Rhoeas-Papaver?" the butler said, not letting go.

"Maybe," she replied, wincing at the pain. "Do you mind?"

He ignored her. She noticed a large car parked just inside the open gate to the field, and the city of Bath was visible over the downward slope of the hill.

"Blindfold her," the Arbiter said.

"Now just wait a minute," Cathy objected as the butler pulled the strip of black fabric from his pocket. "Is this really necessary? Will you please tell me what the hell is going on?"

The Arbiter stared at her. It was the closest she'd ever been to one and it was just as unpleasant as she'd been told it would be. "It is necessary. We'll tie your hands if you don't cooperate. And don't think about bolting; this guy used to play rugby before he became a butler."

She'd already given up on the idea. Running in a corset and fussy dress was not easy at the best of times; they'd easily catch her.

"I do apologise," the butler whispered as he tied the blindfold.

"I'm going to check her for artefacts," the Arbiter said, and then she felt hands patting her sleeves and fingers feeling round the inside of her jacket collar. He even prodded at her hair, making her twist her head away as best she could. "Anything you want to declare now?"

She shook her head and then was steered across the field, stumbling over the little hillocks of tufty grass, the bruise complaining all the way.

"Put her in the boot," the Arbiter said and she heard it being opened.

"But–"

She was scooped up, dumped in and the boot slammed shut before she could present her argument. It was locked and she struggled into a more comfortable position, finding it hard to breathe when corseted and crumpled up against a jerry can. It smelt of oil and was horribly uncomfortable. She tried to rein in her panic at being locked into such a small space.

The car rumbled into life, the entire boot vibrating, then it set off and she was thrown about inside as it drove across the field. It improved slightly once they were on the road. By the way she slid into what felt like a toolbox she deduced they were going downhill and presumably back into the city.

She shoved the blindfold up onto her forehead, but it was pitch-black and disappointingly unlike the car-boot interiors she'd seen in films, which always seemed to have just enough light to see the action. She fumbled for the lock, but it was useless, she couldn't feel any way to unlock it from the inside.

Struggling to keep her nerves under control, she forced herself to think about her situation logically. The last thing she'd expected was being dumped into the hands of an Arbiter by the Censor of Aquae Sulis. What the hell was going on? She thought of her parents at home, probably delighted at their wayward daughter being invited out for the day by the most important person in Society, when in fact she was locked in the boot of an Arbiter's car in Mundanus. She started to laugh, her nerves making her predicament seem very funny all of a sudden. Her dress would probably be ruined. How was the Censor going to explain that away?

Once she stopped giggling nervously, she could think more clearly and it occurred to her that, whilst she was clearly being used as the proverbial pawn in a game much bigger than she could comprehend, it could work in her favour. She hadn't considered it before, but the Arbiters and perhaps even the Sorcerers could help her get away from Aquae Sulis. By the time the car stopped, she had a new plan, and she readied herself by putting the blindfold back on, not wanting to give them a reason to be irritated with her.

The boot was unlocked and opened, her blindfold checked. She was helped out by the butler, who apologised surreptitiously again, and she found herself standing on gravel. A driveway?

"Mr Arbiter?" she said to the blackness.

"Yes?" He was close by.

"I need to speak to you. It's not what you'll expect."

"We need to speak to you too, and I am certain you won't be expecting what we have to say either." She could hear him moving off on his crutches. The butler's hand was around her arm again, but she noted it was in a different place from before.

"Listen, I need your protection."

The sound of the hobbling stopped. "From what?"

"Not what, who. My family. You could do that, right? I mean, you stop the Great Families doing stuff all the time to protect people."

"We protect the innocents," he said. "Not the parasites."

"But I'm not like them!" She heard him moving away and was steered in the same direction. "Really! I don't want to live in Aquae Sulis any more, I need your help!"

"I wasn't born yesterday, lady," he replied. "I've heard every trick in the book. Save your breath."

"It's not a trick!"

"Steps ahead," the butler said as she tripped on the first.

She heard a door opening and felt the flutter of returning panic. Where was she being taken?

There was the tell-tale sensation of entering the Nether. Her feet had been on gravel, then they'd climbed three stone steps and now their footfalls sounded as if they were walking on a wooden floor. The door was closed behind them; it sounded large and heavy. They were inside a house in Aquae Sulis, but which one?

"This way, please," the butler said, as if she had a choice.

"What's this about? Where are we?"

They didn't answer and when her hand twitched towards the blindfold, the butler said, "Please don't touch that, Miss, I would hate to have to be unpleasant."

As much as she was trying not to admit it to herself, she was scared. She was marched down what felt like a very long corridor, this time on carpet. Occasionally she could hear the ticking of clocks and creaking floorboards upstairs. Eventually a door was opened ahead and she was steered to the right, their footsteps clicking on wooden floorboards again.

Somehow she knew there was someone else in the room. The butler pulled her further in and then pressed down on her shoulders. "Please sit down," he said, and she felt a hard chair beneath her.

"This is the one the Censor delivered?" It was a new voice, male, deep.

"Yes, sir," the Arbiter replied.

Sir? His boss? That meant–

"Are you a Sorcerer?" she asked, gripping the edges of the chair so they couldn't see her shaking.

"Be quiet." The man's shoes clipped across the floor towards her. She had the intense feeling of being scrutinised. "There's a curse upon her."

"Has the Censor tricked us?" the Arbiter asked.

There was the rustle of fabric, like pockets being checked. "Hold still," the man said and she heard the snip of a pair of scissors not an inch from her right ear.

"Hey! Did you just cut my hair?"

"Keep her here. If she tries to leave, use this."

She had no idea what "this" was, but she didn't want to find out. She heard the man leave, but the butler and the Arbiter were still in the room as far as she could tell.

"Listen, I was serious about what I said before," she said.

"If you speak another word I'll stuff a sock in your mouth," the Arbiter said. "I'm not taking any risks with you."

She sighed and slumped in the uncomfortable chair. It wasn't too long before the door opened again and there was a second set of footsteps.

"What the hell?" Another man's voice.

"Be quiet," said the man she suspected was the Sorcerer.

"Is it a problem?" the Arbiter asked.

"Not for our purposes," the Sorcerer replied.

"Are you OK?" said the new one. She could hear him coming closer.

"Stay back," the Sorcerer said. "She's not as harmless as she may appear to be."

"What do you think I'm going to do?" she asked. "This is a bit over the top, isn't it?"

"One should never underestimate one of your kind," the Sorcerer mumbled. "Now, we don't have a great deal of time. Did the Censor tell you why we've brought you here?"

"No. Can I please take this blindfold off?"

"No, you may not. I understand you're the favourite of Lord Poppy."

"Is that why I'm here?" There was a pause. "Yes, I am, even though I don't want to be."

"She's been trying to make us think she isn't like the rest," the Arbiter said.

"The rest of what?" the new guy said and was shushed into silence.

"Will someone please tell me why I'm here?"

"You are required to take a gentleman into Exilium to meet Lord Poppy. There is–"

"Now just wait a bloody minute," Cathy said, now angry. "You convince the Censor to drive me out of Aquae Sulis, chuck me out into a mundane field, then your mook comes and throws me into the boot of a car, blindfolded, no explanation. I'm brought God knows where and you want me to go into Exilium to speak to Lord Poppy? No fucking way!"

There was an uncomfortable silence.

"This sounds a bit like kidnapping," the new one said. "I don't want to be involved in anything like this."

"Neither do I," Cathy said, liking him more than the others.

"Were you or were you not told to cooperate by the Censor?" the Sorcerer asked.

"She didn't tell me you wanted me to go into Exilium! Don't you know how dangerous that is?"

"Of course I do, but this is a necessity. We have a man here who's been put under a Fool's Charm and we need the memory that it's hiding to be revealed."

"Do it yourself," she said, folding her arms. "There's no way I'm going to see Poppy."

"I can't without killing him," came the reply.

"I'm not discussing this a moment longer with this bloody blindfold on," Cathy said but her hand was pushed back down as she reached up to take it off. That hand then rested on her shoulder, ready to act if she moved again. She hoped it was the butler and not the Arbiter, not that it made much difference.

"That won't be removed until you are in Exilium," the Sorcerer said.

She sucked in a breath, steadying her nerves and frustration. "Listen. If I'm going to risk more than my life for this, there has to be something in it for me. If I get this Fool's Charm lifted, I want you to–"

"There's no negotiation to be had, puppet," the Sorcerer butted in. "You have no bargaining power. If you won't cooperate, I will not hesitate to inform the Censor and I'm certain she could make your life very difficult indeed."

She let her head drop. He was right, she had as much leverage as a lettuce leaf. One day, she promised herself silently, I'll be free of each and every one of you heartless bastards.

"I don't have anything to offer Poppy."

"You'll think of something, I'm sure. Being his favourite sets you in good stead."

"Who put the Charm on the man?"

"One of the Fae lords."

"Oh dear," she said, not holding back on the sarcasm. "I'm guessing you don't know which one?"

"No." Unsurprisingly, he was reluctant to admit it.

"Let's hope it isn't Poppy."

"You don't seem to have much respect for your patron."

"I'm not like the rest of them. But you don't believe me and you don't care, so if I have to do this, then let's get it over with, even though it's the worst plan in the world. You do know that, don't you?"

"It's the only option we have," the Sorcerer replied. "Get the Fool's Charm lifted and come back here, then you'll be returned to the Censor with a glowing report."

"Whoopydo."

"I'm going to open the Way. You will be guided through, then you may remove the blindfold."

"What about getting back?"

"Your companion has a key. It can only be used when you are both in contact, and it will only bring you back to this room."

"So don't bludgeon him over the head and try to run away, is that what you're saying?"

"I simply wanted to make it clear. Any questions?"

"None that you'll answer. Oh, wait! Do I look like I've been thrown in a grotty car boot? Because if I do, you need to fix that. The Fae are shallow bastards and it could screw everything up."

"I'll get the clothes brush sir," the butler said and she heard him walking away. The hand didn't lift from her shoulder. She shivered.

"You certainly don't talk like they do," the Sorcerer said thoughtfully.

"Their ruses get more sophisticated all the time, sir," said the Arbiter, from right behind her.

"Oh, for God's sake," she said. "You hardly have the moral high ground here."

"We had to take this action because the law has been broken," the Arbiter replied.

"Not by me," she said, and sank into silence.

The butler returned and she was invited to stand as her clothes were brushed. The activity elicited an astonished gasp from the new guy.

"Bloody hell!" he said, which sent a flash of excitement through her. He must be a mundane; no Fae-touched or any of the Sorcerer's people would have reacted like that. She hoped he would give more away but he was shushed before he could say anything else.

"My apologies for the state of the car boot, Miss," the butler said. "Your dress is as it was when we first met you."

"Remember what I told you," she heard the Sorcerer say quietly, presumably to the man under the Fool's Charm.

There was a sound of a curtain being drawn back, then one similar to a watch being wound, a loud knock of something against the wooden floor and then birdsong filled the room. Cathy was pushed forwards. A hand took hers and then with the next step she felt uneven ground instead of wooden floorboards and smelt the sweet scent of flowers on the breeze. She was in Exilium again. And she was not happy about it.

24

Will's father held out his hand. "Well?"

He dropped the opal into his palm. "She's pure," Will said, with a confidence he didn't feel.

"Thank goodness for that." Father slipped it into its velvet pouch and locked it away. "And you're certain no one saw you?"

"I'm certain, Father," he said, smiling; sat down at the wave of his father's hand. I didn't even see it myself, he thought. "And I've been thinking about all this... I'd like to marry Catherine sooner than we've discussed."

Father leaned back in the chair, tossed his fountain pen onto the desk and laced his fingers. "What's brought this about?"

Will chose his words carefully. "I believe Catherine would be more confident socially once we're married. The scrutiny of being the only engaged couple of note during the season is proving to be unpleasant for her."

"She'll be just as much the focus of attention as a young bride."

"But it will pass quickly enough, and I plan to take her away for a honeymoon."

"And what of the rumour?"

"I haven't heard anything more, but I have the feeling it's not going to go away. Another reason I believe marrying sooner would be prudent."

"I'm glad to see you taking your responsibility so seriously, Will." Father tapped his index fingers together. "I confess I was anticipating far more resistance, considering who you need to marry."

Will was relieved his mother hadn't revealed her son's true feelings. "I've had my Grand Tour and it served its purpose admirably. I'm ready to settle down." He hoped he sounded convincing.

"That being so, I feel I can speak with you frankly. I was summoned by the Patroon this morning to discuss this."

Will frowned. "Is the Patroon actively involved in all Iris marriages? Or is that unusual?"

"The conversation we had was certainly unusual," Father said. "The Patroon has been interested in this match for some time. After all, it was he who suggested it."

That surprised Will. The Iris Patroon was the head of all the Iris families, responsible for hundreds of people across dozens of family lines. Will found it hard to believe the Patroon would make all the matches himself; surely that would be too much trouble? In fact he was certain the head of each line was responsible for the marriages taking place within their family.

"I thought it was you and Mr Rhoeas-Papaver who came to the agreement," he said.

"We discussed the possibility of a union between our families some time ago. I had Nathaniel and Elizabeth in mind for a while but it was the Patroon who insisted it be you and Catherine. Will, Lord Iris himself is pressing for this marriage to go ahead. The Patroon summoned me to confirm everything was progressing as it should, and I had the distinct impression that Lord Iris is putting pressure on him to see this through."

"What did you tell him?"

"That the contracts are signed, the engagement has been announced and the wedding is being planned. I didn't mention the rumour."

Will nodded. "I can see why, Father. You wouldn't want that to get back to Lord Iris."

"Not when it comes from a weasel of a Rosa, who, less than an hour ago, presented the deeds to the reflection of Prior Park."

"Really? The place that's a mundane school?" Will had heard it spoken of at dinner parties. It was one of the great mysteries of Aquae Sulis; a fantastic property with no one resident, even though several families, including his own, would have paid a princely sum for it if anyone had known where the deeds were hidden.

"Yes, *the* Prior Park, and now he claims ownership of a property in Aquae Sulis he's exercised his right to request citizenship of the city from the Council."

"A Rosa in Aquae Sulis permanently?"

"That's what he's pressing for, and seeing as he's the source of this rumour, and given the concern expressed by the Patroon that this marriage go ahead without any problems, I'm tasking you with ensuring he doesn't make it public."

"I'm starting to wonder if it should be treated as a threat, Father," Will said. "Interesting that he gave me the chance to break the engagement first, don't you think?"

"I think you shouldn't underestimate this Rosa. We've been trying to track down the ownership of that property for over a hundred years, I'm amazed and quite frankly horrified that the deeds are in their hands. If we're to keep the Rosas out, as we should, we need to be absolutely certain the rest of the Council will vote correctly, and the marriage to Catherine Papaver binds her father to supporting me when the time comes. Do whatever it takes, Will, but make sure that Rose keeps his foul lies to himself."

"And the marriage date, Father?"

"I'm speaking to Charles Papaver later today, I'll see what I can do."

Cathy pulled off the blindfold and checked where they were before opening her mouth. She couldn't see any trees nearby and the meadow they stood in was free of flowers. She breathed out in relief, then spun around to catch a glimpse of where she'd been taken in the Nether, but the Way had already been closed. It seemed the Sorcerer was very keen to keep his face a mystery.

"Bloody hell."

She looked at the man holding her hand. He was a few years older with dark brown hair and he looked very tired. His jeans and jacket, coupled with the shocked expression, confirmed her suspicion he was a mundane. He noticed her looking at him and let go of her hand.

"Are you all right?" she asked.

"Well… I'm not hurt, at least. Are you OK?" he asked.

She shrugged. "As OK as can be expected. That's not much."

"Sounds like they put you through the mill. That clothesbrush was bloody amazing though."

"I'm Cathy," she said, holding out her hand at an angle to be shook, rather than kissed.

He did the right thing, much to her relief. "I'm–" He cut himself off. "They said I shouldn't tell you."

"Who? The incredibly kind kidnappers we were just with?"

"Good point." He shrugged. "I'm Sam."

"Look, Sam, we're in deep shit here. You do appreciate that, don't you?"

"I've been in it for a while now," he said as he turned in a slow circle, taking the scenery in. "They've treated me a bit better than you, but they won't let me go home. Shit, this place… have they drugged me or something?"

Cathy sat down and patted the grass next to her. "We're not going any further until I know what the hell is going on, and you need a minute too. It looks like you're in just as a bad a situation as I am, and, believe me, I would really like to talk to someone normal right now."

"They said I shouldn't talk to you at all," Sam said, sitting down beside her. "They said you're dangerous and can do all kinds of tricks to make me fall in love with you and do what you say."

"Bollocks," Cathy said and Sam grinned.

"I thought as much. They're so strange. You seem the most normal out of all of them, apart from your clothes. What's with all the period costume?"

"This is not what I would choose to wear, believe me." Cathy tugged at the jacket's high collar. "I'd kill for a pair of jeans and my old trainers again. People in the Nether are about three hundred years behind the times, and weird. They're not part of the real world, what do you expect?"

"Err, can you go back a step? Pretend I don't know anything."

"Do I need to pretend?"

"No."

She smiled. "We're in Exilium. It's a really pretty prison, made for the kinds of things we're here to talk to."

"Are they criminals?"

"This isn't a good place to debate that," Cathy whispered. "And like all this kind of stuff, it depends who you speak to."

He nodded. "This is the weirdest prison I ever saw. But then, it's been the weirdest couple of days of my life. I know something's wrong with me, but the way they're acting... it's creeping me out. They only let me send a note to my wife when I pointed out she'd call the police, and I'm not even sure if Axon really posted it."

"Axon?"

"The butler."

"Oh. He seemed the most decent out of all of them."

"He's all right. Petra's the nicest, she's the librarian, but they said she had to stay away from you."

"Sounds like they made me out to be something really awful. If I was like the rest of the Great Families, they'd have every right to be nervous of me, but I'm not like them, I swear it."

He was looking right into her eyes. "I believe you," Sam said. He rubbed his eyes and shook his head. "So this is Exilium... what's the Nether? I keep hearing that word."

"It comes from 'neither here nor there'," she said. It felt odd explaining it. "It's between the real, normal world – what they call Mundanus – and here. It's where the Great Families live. And Sorcerers too. That was his house, wasn't it?"

"Yeah. It's a really weird place. The sky is all fucked up too."

She chuckled. "That's because there is no sky. I think. I don't really understand the physics of it all. Suffice to say that in the Nether, you're not in the real world, you're not here, you're in between. And you don't age there either."

"That's why I haven't needed to shave!" he exclaimed. He shrugged at her raised eyebrow. "I get hung up on the little questions. Mr Ekstrand really is a Sorcerer, then? Opening the door to this place was the first time I saw him do anything like magic. Oh, crap, what am I talking about?"

"It's all going to be OK," Cathy lied. "How did you end up with a Fool's Charm?"

He rolled his eyes. "Wrong place, wrong time was how Petra put it. I got pissed, I ended up behind the Holburne Museum gardens, apparently. Max found my wallet there. He was the guy with the broken leg."

"My God, my uncle lives there, in the Nether version of that house. Did they say why it's important to lift the Charm?"

"They said some bloke has gone missing and I might be a witness."

"Now it makes sense," Cathy muttered. "No wonder the Censor was laying it on thick; something's happened to my uncle and the Sorcerer must have approached her for help. She didn't want to risk herself, so she packs me off to them. What a cow." Her aunt couldn't even bring herself to tell the truth to her own sister and niece. If she'd told her what it was all about in the carriage she would have helped without hesitation. But then her aunt probably only saw her as an untrustworthy and rebellious carbuncle of a girl who needed to be half scared to death to keep in line. Cathy looked at Sam, not wanting to think about her family. "I'm surprised the Sorcerer couldn't lift it."

"It's too strong or something. And I'm protected by Lord Iron, whatever that means."

Cathy shrugged. "Never heard of him."

"He's in the wedding ring business, I reckon." Sam held up his bare left hand. "They said I had to take it off before I came here. I just hope that when this is all cleared up they'll let me go home – my wife must think I've done a runner."

Cathy wasn't certain the Sorcerer would let him go without any trouble. There were rules about what mundanes should and shouldn't know, and Sam was on the wrong side of them. But she didn't know much about how the Sorcerers dealt with that kind of problem, and she didn't want to worry him more than he already was. "Well, now we know what this is about, we'd better get moving," she said. "Give me a hand up? These corsets are a pain."

He helped her up and she lifted the hem of her dress so she could walk over the uneven ground without tripping.

"So you said this place is dangerous." Sam looked around. "It doesn't seem too bad to me."

"Trust me, this is the most dangerous place you'll ever visit. One tiny mistake and you can be turned into a slug, or enslaved or worse."

"An enslaved slug?"

"Very funny."

"And who is this Poppy guy we need to see?"

"He's the patron of my family."

"And what does that mean?"

"We're all scared of him and have to do what he says."

"Like a mafia Don?"

"I've noticed the similarity, but here's not the place to talk about that. Just don't touch anything, do anything or even say anything unless I tell you, OK? I'm going to do everything I can to make sure we both get out of this in the same state as we came in. What does that key look like, by the way?"

He pulled a door knob out of his jacket pocket. A large emerald was set into it and runes covered every square centimetre of its surface.

"Put it back," she whispered, desperate to look at it more closely, but afraid their arrival had already been noticed. She'd never seen a Sorcerer's artefact before. It certainly looked very different from the ones sold at the Emporium.

"Think it will work?"

"I'm sure they want you back," she said.

"You really don't seem like they said you would be."

"It's because I'm not. But we'll talk about that later, OK? If we don't focus on getting this done, the mess I'm in will be academic."

The club was quiet enough to be relaxing yet full enough to be entertaining. Will sauntered to the bar and ordered a gin and tonic, glancing at the high-backed leather chairs filled with gentlemen lounging with cigars and discussing nothing of interest.

Glass in hand he strolled past the billiards room and ended up in the card room. Its wood panelling gave the large space a sense of age and cosiness. Oliver was sweating over a hand in the corner. No matter how hard he tried he was hopeless at poker. Will waited for the hand to finish before going over to him.

"How about a game of whist, old chap?" he suggested, knowing they'd be hard to beat after the amount of practice they'd put in over the Grand Tour.

"Rather," Oliver said and withdrew from the game.

They sat opposite each other at a new table, sending out a silent signal for another pair of players to join them. Will was in no hurry so he didn't wave anyone over, content to while away the time with his best friend until they were joined by others. He hadn't counted on Horatio Gallica-Rosa walking in with one of the Wisteria twins.

"Ah, a game of whist, just what I was in the mood for!" Horatio said and pulled back one of the free chairs. "You don't mind if we join you, do you, Oliver?"

"Of course not," Oliver said, unconvincingly.

The Rosa sat down, and opposite him the Wisteria, who looked quite pleased with himself. "Good afternoon," he said and both Will and Oliver nodded politely.

The first hand was dealt and the Wisteria gushed about the soirée the night before. It was embarrassing, but Horatio was amused by him and Oliver accepted the praise on behalf of his family graciously.

"Your fiancée was a picture," Horatio said as the next round was dealt.

"Oh, were you there?" Will asked. "I do apologise, I missed you."

"Too busy gazing into someone's eyes, I wager," Horatio said. "I saw you both in the corridor."

Will didn't look at him, instead choosing to study his hand and keep calm. So what if he saw his brief flirtation with the Alba-Rosa girl? It was hardly scandalous. "It was a fine evening. Your parents must be delighted, Oliver." He smiled at his friend.

"Rather," said Oliver with a grin, the red apple cheeks returning.

"This is an excellent club," Horatio remarked. "I was worried I'd miss Black's in Londinium, but not any more."

"You speak as though you're not planning to return," the Wisteria boy said, with just enough inelegance to make Will wonder if he was trying too hard to set Horatio up with an opportunity to gloat.

"Oh, haven't you heard?" he smirked in that sleazy way of his. "The Council is considering my application for citizenship, now that the deed for my house has been presented."

"A house in Aquae Sulis?" Oliver gasped, with all the social grace of a baying donkey. "I thought that was just a rumour."

"Well, so many rumours turn out to have a basis in truth. Wouldn't you agree, Mr Iris?"

"I find it astounding that a deed to an Aquae Sulis property just turns up," Will said, ignoring the comment. "What good fortune your family is enjoying."

"Indeed. Seems it was misplaced and forgotten about for decades. Our family has so many properties in Londinium and elsewhere it didn't occur to us to look for it."

He won the trick and Will knew it was because Oliver had made a stupid mistake. The news had upset him, evidently.

"We're planning a party," Horatio said, dealing the next round. "I'm sure that so many people in the city would be delighted to see inside after all these years. You're all invited, of course."

"Why thank you!" the Wisteria boy chirruped like an excited songbird. Will could imagine him hurrying home that evening to tell his family he played cards with no less than an Iris and the up-and-coming Rosa. What impressive social climbing, his mother would think, and kiss his cheek with pride.

"I'm sure it will be a great success," Will said as Oliver nodded. "There's nothing better than curiosity to draw a fashionable crowd."

"Speaking of which," Horatio said with an oily smile, "I was wondering which finishing school your fiancée attended."

"One in Switzerland."

"Which one exactly?"

"I don't recall."

"Really?"

"Sorry to disappoint you," Will said, moderating his tone carefully. "I'm sure Mrs Rhoeas-Papaver will be able to give you the details if you need them so desperately. Feeling the need to improve upon your manners?"

Oliver snorted as the Wisteria sucked in a breath.

"Simply curious," Horatio replied, lowering the hand of cards so he could focus more on Will. "She has such an unusual manner."

"And what—"

Will was cut off by the arrival of a young man who was only vaguely familiar. He placed himself between Will and Horatio, bending over to speak in Will's ear.

"Excuse me, Mr Reticulata-Iris? I'm dreadfully sorry to interrupt, I was wondering if I could have a word?"

Will, grateful for an excuse to leave the table and let the conversation simmer back down, made his apologies and accompanied the man to the bar.

"I'm Cornelius Alba-Rosa, I believe you spoke to my sister at the soirée last night."

"Oh, yes, a pleasure to meet you at last," Will said, shaking his hand as they sat down.

"Forgive my rudeness in the card room but, between you and me, I had the feeling that Gallica toad was about to cause a scene."

His voice was soft, his manner gentle. Will could see the resemblance to Amelia, and something about Cornelius's smile made him warm to him, despite the fact that he was a Rosa.

"Speaking from experience?"

"You could say that." Cornelius pulled out a slim wooden cigarette case but seemed to have second thoughts. "I'm about to meet Amelia for afternoon tea at Lunn's. Would you care to join us?"

The idea of seeing Amelia again was so much more appealing than staying at the club. "I'd like that very much."

"So how do we find this guy?" Sam asked. They'd only been walking for a few minutes.

"Exilium doesn't work like the normal world, or even like the Nether." Cathy wished she could take the jacket off but didn't want to reveal the bruising. "You find places by wanting to arrive."

"Eh?"

"Don't worry about it," she replied. "I think I've got it covered."

It was hard work willing herself to find Lord Poppy when in reality he was the last person she wanted to see. She was thankful she'd been given a refresher lesson on surviving Exilium by her mother, just in case she was summoned back to their patron. It was the longest interaction she'd had with her since returning home. The lesson wasn't exactly delivered with love. She wondered if her mother was even capable of that.

"It's so nice here," Sam sighed. "Shame we have to do something and not just relax."

"Careful," Cathy said. "Don't let your mind drift. This place can suck you in. I've heard that people have been lost here forever just because they stopped thinking about what they came in for. And that's the people who actively chose to come here. Keep your mind on what we need and getting back home again."

He nodded, but she wasn't convinced he was really taking it in. She must sound like a lunatic. He probably hadn't believed a word she'd said. She felt sorry for him; as much as she hated all this, at least it made sense to her. He was just some poor bloke sucked into the crazy with no point of reference at all.

"We'll get through this," she said, slipping her hand into the crook of his elbow. "In a weird way I'm glad she sent me and didn't do it herself. She would have been horrible to you."

"That Censor you mentioned?"

"Yeah."

"So she stops people from saying bad stuff about you guys?"

Cathy shook her head smiling. "Not censor like those film classification guys, Censor as in the ancient Roman office. They basically say who is allowed into Aquae Sulis Society and what status they have once they get there."

"Sounds powerful. What's Aquae Sulis?"

"Not what, where. It's parts of Bath reflected in the Nether; the Great Families use the Roman name to distinguish between them. And yes, the Censor is very powerful. The only person as powerful as her is the Master of Ceremonies and he's the one who is missing. The Censor said he was abroad; she must have been covering up. He's my uncle, you know. And the Censor is my aunt."

"You must be worried."

She shook her head. "We're not close. They think I'm rubbish."

"Did you hear that?" His head snapped round.

"What?"

"Someone laughing, I think. They sound familiar."

"Shit, that's never good," Cathy muttered and felt him pull away in the direction he was looking. "Sam, let's keep going."

"But I can hear someone. I don't remember seeing those trees before."

She followed his pointed finger and could see a small copse of trees. "That's because they weren't there. We must have drifted."

"Poppy might be there. Let's look anyway, I'm sure I heard someone laughing," he said, breaking into a jog.

"Wait!" she called, but he was off. "Bloody hell," she groaned, trying to catch up but it was hard in the ridiculous outfit.

By the time she reached him he was already past the outer line of trees. She looked for flowers and faeries but saw none. She caught hold of his hand before he went in any further.

"Come on," she said, trying to pull him away, but he resisted.

"Look."

He pointed further into the copse and she glimpsed something glittering, but no poppy petals. Would there be a path if he wasn't expecting her?

Her moment of indecision was too long and he set off towards it. "Sam..."

"I just want to look and then we'll move on. We'll be careful."

She wondered how many slaves had said that in their last moments of freedom. Staying alert, she kept hold of his hand and watched out for any signs of whose domain it was.

"I think there are people up ahead," he said, at least having the sense to drop his voice to a whisper.

"Remember, let me do the talking," she whispered back, trying to get a better look. If there were people ahead, they seemed very still.

The trees thinned and opened out onto a clearing, just like when she'd found Lord Poppy before, but there were no flowers and no Fae lords to be seen. Instead, there were flesh-coloured statues, four women and one man with various shades of blonde hair, wearing sparkling and rather revealing clothes. They were in a variety of poses, like they had been frozen mid-dance.

Beside them was a long table made of a great tree that had been toppled and sliced in half. The other half looked like it had been made into chairs, each one carved with the distinct shape of each of the Great Families' flowers. She saw one with a carved stylised poppy just like the one on her family's coat of arms. She spotted an iris too.

The table was covered in fruit and looked like a dream feast. Perhaps it was a neutral meeting place for the Fae lords and ladies. If that was the case, they needed to leave.

"Let's go," she said, pulling at his hand again.

"Hang on," he said, staring at one of the women. "She's familiar. I think I've seen her on the telly." He pulled her closer. Cathy kept looking around and behind them nervously but he just wouldn't get the hint.

"There could be–"

"Holy crap!" he yelled and jumped back. "Feel!"

He thrust her hand in front of the statue's face, Cathy felt a gentle breath on her skin. Now she was really looking, she could see it was a real person who had been frozen. She wasn't sure which was more disturbing, the fact that someone was trapped in their own body, or that it was so unsurprising.

She stooped to part the grass by the woman's feet, finding the band around the woman's left ankle, glittering like it was made of crushed diamonds. She shook her head sadly, feeling sorry for the trapped dancers, but there was nothing she could do for them.

It wasn't until he sucked in a breath that she realised Sam had gone towards the table. She was terrified he'd eaten something, but then she saw what had shocked him, and it was far worse.

It was a faerie belonging to Lady Rose, one of the most powerful figures in the Fae Court. And it recognised Sam.

25

Amelia was dressed in a jade-green gown and looked divine. Will enjoyed kissing her hand, and held it a moment longer than he should as her scent filled him. Something about the way she looked at him as he pressed his lips to the back of her glove made him bold enough to do so.

"What a lovely surprise," she gasped in a most becoming way, and arranged her skirts as they waited for the waiter.

"Your brother rescued me from the Gallica," Will said. Seeing how fond Amelia was of her brother, Will suspected winning Cornelius's friendship would set him in good stead with her.

"He hasn't been causing problems again, has he?" she asked, and Cornelius nodded as he ordered afternoon tea for the three of them.

"Again?" Will asked.

"He's been horrid to some of the people in Londinium," Amelia began but Cornelius held up a hand.

"Darling, do you think it's right to spread gossip in Aquae Sulis about a Londinium man?"

"I haven't said a word about him to anyone else. If Mr Iris has already seen some of his true colours, then it's hardly gossip." She smiled at him as she tugged at the fingers of her gloves and removed them. "I consider it timely information."

"Call me Will, please," he said to both of them. "And I would be grateful to learn more about him. It seems he's keen to make me lose my temper."

"He does that," Cornelius sighed. "He likes to work out what upsets a chap so he can offend them to the point of being called out."

"He's desperate to show off his swordsmanship," Amelia added, sliding forwards in her seat to pour the tea for the three of them. A tall multi-tiered cake stand arrived as she did so and the waiter put their choices onto little plates. "It really is very tiresome. I think he's excited to find new people to duel. It's only natural he should target you."

"Really?" Will took a cup from her. "I would have thought he'd be eager to bait Nathaniel."

"Oh, but you're more handsome and more popular than your brother."

"Amelia," Cornelius said in a gently cautionary tone. "Please forgive my sister, Will, she's been known to speak her mind on a few too many occasions."

"I just speak the truth," Amelia said, winking at Will as Cornelius stirred his tea. Will nearly choked on his Bath bun.

"There's also the possibility he's hoping your brother would stand in for you," Cornelius said, leaning back and breaking the moment of eye contact. "Either way, it's reprehensible behaviour, and when I saw the way he was looking at you in the card room, I simply had to intervene."

"For which I'm even more grateful now," Will said. "To think I could have played straight into his trap. What an odious wretch."

"It's sad really," Amelia said. "Such a shame he resorts to such measures to bolster his fragile sense of worth."

"It's more than sad," Cornelius said. "It's positively dangerous. The Londinium Court breathed a sigh of relief when he announced he was going to Aquae Sulis for the season. I fear your city is in danger of taking on Londinium's burden permanently."

"You're referring to this fabled property?" Will frowned at his nod. "Yes, that was rather bad news. I'd be very surprised if the Council didn't award him citizenship; having a property already is ninety per cent of the battle."

A look was exchanged between the siblings. They held each other's gaze for a moment and then Cornelius nodded at his sister. He leaned closer to Will as Amelia pulled her chair in a little more.

"Amelia and I have been discussing this very matter. Can we count on your discretion, Will?"

"Indeed," he replied, setting his cake plate on the table.

"We don't want that Gallica toad to get into Aquae Sulis either," Amelia said. Will found her conspiratorial tone quite endearing. "Quite apart from the fact that he's an 'odious wretch', as you said, who would spoil such a haven of civility, it would also upset our parents greatly."

"I'm sure you appreciate how it would impact upon our status as an opposing Rosa family," Cornelius added, "to have one of our enemies achieve such a social triumph in the very same season we finally managed to secure entry."

"You really must tell me how you persuaded Princess Rani to travel back with you," Will said, remembering how irritated he'd been at the first ball. "Another time, of course. And yes, I do appreciate how upsetting that would be. I've heard there's bad blood between your lines."

"That was Horatio's doing," Amelia whispered. "Our families have been at peace since the Tudor alliance, which was so successful for both of us. But that prideful sack of hot air couldn't bear the fact that Cornelius was picked by–"

"Amelia," Cornelius interrupted her gently. "I'm sure Will doesn't need to be bored by the machinations of our families."

She blushed, making the green of her eyes all the more striking. Will cursed himself for being such a fool as to try and save Catherine from her father when he could easily have destroyed the engagement and pressed for a union with the Alba-Rosas.

"Suffice it to say," Cornelius said, "we're motivated to help anyone who wishes to keep the Gallica line out of Aquae Sulis."

"But isn't it rather late?" Will watched Amelia pour another round of tea. Her hands were slender and delicate. "He said he has the deeds to the property. Nothing can be done about that."

"Not necessarily," Cornelius said. "It's our belief that if we could secure sufficient support in Aquae Sulis, we could persuade our Patroon to force the Gallicas to transfer the deeds into our ownership."

"It would make much more sense to have a popular Rosa line in the city than one that has already put important people's noses out of joint," Amelia said, taking the opportunity to look into Will's eyes for a few beats as Cornelius attended to his new cup of tea.

"That makes a great deal of sense," he replied. "Would your parents leave Londinium?"

"I doubt it," Cornelius said. "They're too involved at Court. I should imagine it would be Amelia and I, don't you think so, dear?"

She nodded. "And I would be delighted. It's a beautiful city. To live here would be divine. You and Cornelius could play cards and I could become friends with your sister."

Will imagined Amelia being a larger part of his life and found he liked it. "I think it's an admirable proposition. As you say, it makes so much more sense for your Patroon to have a family capable of establishing friendships here and for

us to keep the likes of Horatio out." He set his teacup down
and offered his hand to Cornelius. "I'll speak to my father.
He's on the Council, perhaps they could drag their heels
whilst you establish yourselves more. I'll speak to my mother
and see about having you both invited to a dinner party so
you can rub shoulders with some of the other councillors."

"That would be greatly appreciated," Cornelius said with a
firm handshake and warm smile.

"I would love to meet your parents," Amelia said, offering
her hand. "You're very kind, Will."

He kissed her hand, his lips touching her skin for the first
time. Soft and warm, she smelt of rose water and he wanted
to turn her hand over and kiss her wrist before moving up her
arm. When he flicked his eyes up at her, he had the distinct
impression she wanted the same.

"I'll see you soon," he promised.

Cathy stayed in her crouch. The faerie was so fixated on Sam
it hadn't noticed her, and she wanted to keep it that way.

"Whoa!" Sam was pointing at it, agog.

"You!" The tiny creature pointed back at Sam with a
mixture of shock and confusion. "What are you doing here?"

"Bloody hell! You can talk! You're like a boy Tinkerbell.
That's so cool!"

As Sam was horrendously mundane at the faerie, Cathy
edged around the frozen slaves and took the opportunity to
scurry behind one of the carved chairs, putting her behind
the faerie as it floated towards him.

"You don't recognise me… do you know where you are?"

"Exilium," Sam replied. "I didn't know little dudes like you
would be here though. You're so tiny! And you talk! That's wild."

Cathy grabbed the rim of one of the wooden platters on
the table.

"And how did you get here, mortal?"

Before he could reply, Cathy leaped up and swung the platter at the faerie, scattering the berries piled on top of it. It connected with a satisfying thwack and the creature tumbled out of the air. She ran after it, slamming the platter upside down over it, giving it enough room so it wouldn't be squashed, but hoping to keep it pinned whilst it was dazed.

"Get me one of those jugs!" she yelled at Sam who was staring with a gawping mouth.

He got one from the table and handed it to her. It was heavy enough, filled with what looked like wine. She put it on top of the platter.

"Come on!" She grabbed his hand and pulled him from the clearing.

"How could you do that?" he said, still shocked enough to be pulled away. "It was a—"

"They are evil little bastards," she said, steering them through the trees as fast as she could. "Honestly, all the stuff you ever heard about faeries, it's not true. Imagine an evil psychopathic version of Tinkerbell who hates all humans and you'll get closer. Now run, for God's sake! If it finds us in here we'll end up like those dancers!"

"What about them? We can't leave them!"

"There's nothing we can do."

When he started to run properly they reached the edge of the trees much faster, and burst out into the sunshine-drenched meadow. Cathy didn't stop until the trees were receding into the distance, then realised she couldn't run much further without passing out.

"Bloody corset," she muttered, desperate to take a deep breath.

"This place is weird," Sam said, slowing to a stop and half holding her up as she heaved for air. "You never said there would be Tinkerbells."

"I hoped we wouldn't run into any. It recognised you."

Sam shrugged. "I've never seen anything like it before."

"If we see any others, remember what I said. They are spiteful little gits, and all they want to do is make our lives hell."

"Hello!"

They both jumped at the tiny voice. Another faerie, this one more feminine and dressed in poppy petals, zipped around in front of them.

"Oh, bugger," Cathy groaned.

"I'm so glad I found you!"

"Go away."

It looked genuinely hurt. "But I'm here to help you."

"Yeah, right."

"I already have, I tricked the Rose faerie into thinking you went another way. He's very angry."

"I don't believe you."

"Why?"

"Duh! I know what you're like."

"How can you? We've never met before. And I was so excited." It sniffed.

"Don't be mean," Sam said, holding out a hand for the faerie to land on.

"Didn't you hear a word I just said?" snapped Cathy, scowling.

The faerie waved at Sam, who grinned and waved back with one finger, then stuffed his hand in his pocket, embarrassed. "You're looking for Lord Poppy, aren't you? I can help you!"

Cathy peered at the creature, confused. How could it behave so differently? It looked the same, but it was probably a trick. "Prove it," she said, folding her arms.

The faerie leapt off Sam's hand and flew towards a gentle hill. "Follow me!"

Sam started off and Cathy looked skywards, wondering what appalling things she must have done in a previous life to deserve this. She decided to go as far as the crest of the hill, and then its trickery would be exposed.

They climbed. Cathy's stomach rumbled and her ribs ached. Sam seemed happy just to watch their pseudo-guide flutter about ahead of them.

Just like the time she was brought in before, a copse of trees could be seen from the crest of the hill. She could even see a red poppy bobbing at the edge of the trees.

"See!" The faerie zinged back to her, looking hopeful.

"Mmm," Cathy said, not feeling any different towards the thing. "That's the place, Sam. Just stay quiet, OK? And he's a little different, so try not to react like a... tourist."

"OK." He offered his arm but she declined, not wanting Lord Poppy to see them arrive that way.

"Just stay close."

"When this is done," Sam said as they trudged down the hill, "we should go out for a beer."

"You don't know how much I would like that," Cathy said, giving him a sad smile. "But I doubt it will happen."

They reached the trees and she breathed as slowly and steadily as she could to get her nerves under control. Lord Poppy was in sight soon enough, looking just as he had before, as if he hadn't moved in the days since she spoke with him.

His smile was predatory, his gaze sweeping over her and then staring at Sam with open curiosity.

"Ah, my favourite returns, what a delight! A surprise visit *and* a gift, how thoughtful!"

She realised he meant Sam. "Oh, um, he's not a gift–" Lord Poppy's smile transmuted into something thunderous "–in the sense that you may think, Lord Poppy. Rather, something trapped in his mind is a gift far more interesting than he is.

He's just a boring mundane, no gifts or talents whatsoever, I wouldn't dream of bringing you anyone less than spectacular."

Her quick words smoothed the scowl into an intrigued smile. "How interesting. But first, my soft little petal, come here so that I may admire you."

She took a few steps closer, glancing nervously at the faerie as it flitted over to sit on his shoulder, smiling happily.

"You look so much better than the last time I saw you. What a delightful sparkle there is in your eye."

"It's difficult to hide my delight at seeing you again, my Lord," she said, amazed at how much easier it was to spout rubbish after being in the Nether for a few days.

"And I see you've met this one." His black eyes glanced at the faerie.

"She doesn't like me," the faerie said quietly.

Lord Poppy frowned. "What's this? Why don't you like her?"

Cathy shuffled. "She was less than helpful when I had the three wishes to think of, my Lord."

"Impossible! That wasn't her. How could you think such a thing? She looks completely different!"

Cathy peered at the faerie. It was identical to the one who'd ruined Josh's life. But Lord Poppy was staring at her, waiting for a reaction. She raised her eyebrows. "I must be mistaken. Please accept my apologies."

The little thing clapped its hands, dived off Poppy's shoulder and pressed a kiss on the end of her nose.

"You mistook her for the one I've locked in a box," Lord Poppy said casually. "That was the one who upset you. Sour little creature that it was, this one is much nicer, wouldn't you agree?"

Cathy just nodded, not really caring, just wanting to navigate the fastest path through the conversational labyrinth.

"Now, what little nugget is trapped in this mundane's mind? Why is it interesting?"

Cathy had been considering what to say since they set off down the hill, and had decided upon a risky strategy. "I believe it's something that could get Lady Rose into a little bit of trouble."

"Only a little bit?" Lord Poppy said, disappointed.

"I've been told I have a gift for understatement, my Lord. Of course, it also isn't my place to decide how much trouble she could be in; it requires your knowledge and brilliance to make such a judgement."

Lord Poppy beckoned Sam over with a long finger, tilting his head as he looked at him. When he was close enough, Lord Poppy curled his hand around the back of Sam's neck and drew his face towards him. Cathy shivered as the Fae lord licked Sam's forehead, remembering when he'd done the same to her wrist at the Emporium.

"Oi!" Sam rubbed his face as he was released. "Did you just lick my forehead?"

Cathy pulled him back to stand next to her. Lord Poppy was looking up at the sky, smacking his lips together like a sommelier trying to identify a vintage.

"A Fool's Charm, definitely a Rose, very strong too. How interesting. What have they locked inside you, little mundane?"

"We'd like to find out," Cathy said. "Would you be so kind as to lift the Charm for us, my Lord?"

"Would I?" he mused, still staring at Sam. "Would I.... yes, I believe I would be so kind."

Cathy breathed out in relief.

"If you give me another memory in return," Lord Poppy added.

"Eh?" Sam looked at her. "Does he mean–"

"Only one?" Cathy asked, frantically trying to think of a way to limit it.

"Only one," Poppy confirmed. "Of my choice. He won't miss it, I'm certain."

"Agreed," Cathy said as Sam took another breath. It was probably the best deal they could get, and the longer they spoke to the Fae lord, the higher the probability of screwing something up.

"Marvellous." Poppy's smile was terrifying. "Come here," he said to Sam. "This will hurt and may drive you mad."

"What? Then I don't want to do it."

"But it's been agreed," Poppy said calmly, unconcerned by the way Sam looked like he was about to bolt. He lifted his cane off the ground and pointed it at him. The poppies near Sam's feet twisted around his ankles.

"Hey!" Sam yelled as Cathy covered her mouth, trapping the objection she'd almost blurted out.

"It's for your own safety," Poppy said gently and thrust his cane into the ground to free both hands.

"Cathy!" Sam said desperately, trying to twist around, but the poppies grew higher, now creeping past his knees and holding him tighter.

"Stay calm," she said, trying her best to look confident, hoping he'd get through it.

As Lord Poppy stooped to pluck a seed pod from amongst the blooms, Sam tried to peel off some of those wrapped around his legs, only to have his hands snared also. The Fae tipped a single seed onto his palm and discarded the pod.

"Open your mouth," he said, amused by Sam's panicked struggling.

"You've got to be joking," Sam said.

"Do it, Sam," Cathy said. "Please, don't make it any worse."

"No bloody way!"

Lord Poppy yawned and flicked a finger at the flowers. Two shoots raced upwards, prising Sam's mouth open as he tried to protest. Cathy tasted blood on her tongue as she bit her lip, gripping the fabric of her skirts tightly, feeling terrible for Sam.

The Fae lord dropped the seed in Sam's mouth; the poppy stems then shut his mouth and held it closed by pressing against his jaw. The poor man sucked frantic lungfuls of air through his nostrils, blinking rapidly, and then squeezed his eyes shut as a terrible screeching sound rose up from his throat.

Cathy reached for him but Lord Poppy caught her hand before she could lay it on Sam's shoulder, shaking his head, a broad smile on his face.

A sheen burst out on Sam's forehead, then Cathy realised it wasn't sweat, but instead something that sparkled in the dappled sunlight. It coalesced into the shape of chain links, growing in intensity as Sam fought his bonds. Then it evaporated, rising as sparkling steam, and Sam collapsed onto his knees, snapping some of the flower stalks twisted around his legs.

The stems holding his mouth shut receded as Poppy returned to him, lifting his chin with a finger. "Still in there, are we?"

"I remember," Sam gasped. "I remember all of it."

"Good," Poppy grasped his hair. "Then I will judge its worth and take my payment."

Without warning, he tipped Sam's head to the side and bent over him, his long, horribly pointed tongue darting into Sam's ear like a hummingbird's beak into a flower. "Hmmm," he said, his tongue withdrawing after a couple of seconds.

"Oh, God, did he just lick the inside of my ear?" Sam rubbed his head frantically, the flowers that had imprisoned him now falling away. He struggled back onto his feet, backing away from the Fae. "That's disgusting!"

"Shush," Cathy said, taking hold of his hands and trying to calm him. "Later, we talk later."

He nodded, shivering. She pushed him behind her.

"Lady Rose has been busy," Lord Poppy said, extracting his cane from its resting place.

"Which memory did you take?" Sam asked and Cathy shushed him again.

"One that is gold and green and tastes of nothing at all. You won't miss it," Poppy said.

"Thank you, my Lord," Cathy said, curtsying deeply. She grabbed Sam's hand and took a step to leave.

"Oh!" Lord Poppy said, in such a tone that Cathy started to shake again. "I almost forgot. We haven't discussed my compensation."

"Compensation, my Lord?" Cathy tried not to squeak.

"Yes, for taking the mundane away with you and not leaving him here for me to use as I see fit."

"But–" Sam shut up when she squeezed his hand as tight as she could.

"I understand," Cathy said, hating him, hating all of them, Fae and Great Families alike. There was no point in arguing; this was Lord Poppy's domain.

"I will be satisfied if you promise to give me a painting that is the best of your generation."

She goggled at him. "I haven't even had a chance to buy the canvases yet!"

"Oh, sweetest child, you're my favourite." Lord Poppy swept towards her and stroked her cheek. "That's why I haven't given you a deadline. I can wait."

"Thank you, my Lord," she forced herself to say.

"Run along now," Poppy said. "I have a party to attend, one I believe may prove more entertaining than I previously thought. I'll be sure to make it last as long as possible. Do come again, Catherine Rhoeas-Papaver, your visits never fail to be surprising. And don't worry about anyone else interfering – I'll send this one," he waved the faerie over, "with you to see you on your way safely."

Cathy curtsied again, trying not to flinch as the faerie came and kissed her on the cheek. "Thank you, my Lord."

"And Catherine," he said. "Don't trust the Rosas."

26

Sam pulled the doorknob out of his pocket once Lord Poppy's domain was out of sight. Cathy had sent the faerie away and he'd never wanted a beer so much in his life. Now he knew what happened that night he could tell Ekstrand, go home and do his best to try to forget it all over again.

"Before we go through, Sam, can I talk to you about something?"

"Shoot."

"I need your help. I ran away from my family and made a life in your world but the one that stuck his tongue in your ear found me and sent me back to them."

"Why did you run away?"

"A zillion reasons," she sighed. "If I tell you, will you promise not to tell anyone else?"

He could see she was trembling. "I promise."

"My father… is violent when people aren't as accomplished as he wants them to be. I've never been very accomplished."

"He hits you?"

She undid the jacket and let it fall from her shoulders, revealing bruises in startling shades of purple and green.

"Shit. Can't you go to the police?"

"There aren't any police in the Nether." She did her jacket back up again. "And they want to marry me off to a man I hardly know, and they don't care that I don't want to."

"Can't you run away again?"

"If I could, I would, but they keep me locked in my room and even if I could get away from them, there's nowhere to hide from the magic they've got."

"Holy crap, that sucks."

"Reckon. Look, I know we don't know each other very well, and I wouldn't normally ask for help, but–"

There was no way he could ignore it. "What can I do?"

She breathed out in relief. "The Sorcerer is the only chance I have. I need his help, but he hates anyone from the Great Families."

"I've got an idea," he said. "This time, leave the talking to me, OK?"

"Deal. Thanks, Sam."

"If you need somewhere to go in Mundanus when you first get away," Sam added, "call me. Are you good at remembering phone numbers? I don't have a pen."

She nodded. "I have a phone too. I'm going to get it back as soon as I can so I'll give you my number in case you need me."

They exchanged mobile numbers and repeated them back to each other until confident they would be remembered.

"I'm sorry it was so horrible when he removed the Charm," Cathy said. "I had no idea what it would be like."

"It wasn't your fault. Now let's get the hell out of here. You need to hold my left hand," he said and she did so.

There was a metal bolt sticking out of the back of the doorknob, like one that would normally go through a door to connect with the handle on the other side. He knelt down, pulling her with him, and thrust the bolt into the ground. He felt the earth beneath their knees vibrate.

"Quick," she said. "I bet everything in Exilium can feel that."

"Open," he said, recalling the Sorcerer's instructions, and turned the doorknob.

The outline of a door burnt into the grass around them and Cathy pulled him up and outside the rectangular shape. Before he could complain, the grassy door swung inwards, revealing the room below. The doorway appeared to have opened in the wall of the room.

"Oh, man, that breaks my brain."

"It's like Portal," Cathy said.

They knelt down at the edge to peep in. It was dark in the empty ballroom they'd left, apart from a single lantern next to the wooden chair Cathy had been sitting in when he'd first been brought into the room. The sunlight in Exilium didn't penetrate the gloom. He could see the Sorcerer was being cautious again, knowing that she wouldn't be blindfolded when they came back.

"You know Portal, the Xbox game?" Cathy said.

"Never played it," he replied. "How do we not break our necks?"

"We slide over this side." She pointed at the edge that met the floor of the room. "When we're through, gravity will sort out the rest. Come on."

"You go first," he said, unconvinced, and worried the Sorcerer would just abandon her in Exilium if he went first.

Cathy did as she'd described, for a moment looking like she was going to fall into the space, but instead landing on the ballroom floor, which, from Sam's viewpoint, looked like a wall. A second after she'd landed Axon stepped out of the darkness with another strip of fabric.

"Sorry, Miss." She must have recognised the butler's voice, for she just sat there as it was tied.

Sam came through inelegantly and he heard a gentle *whump* behind him, which he assumed was the Way closing. Once the nausea had passed, he opened his mouth to ask whether the doorknob would be left in Exilium but decided against it; they wouldn't answer anyway. He was sure the Sorcerer had thought of that.

Cathy was helped to her feet. Axon kept his hands on her upper arms.

"Was it a success?" Ekstrand asked, still dressed in his suit and cloak, reminding Sam of a stage magician.

"We're fine, thanks for asking."

"I can see that. Did the parasite lift the Charm?"

"Yeah."

"Excellent. Send his puppet back to the Censor. Tell her she cooperated."

"Wait, let her stay," Sam said and put his hand on her shoulder. "She's not like you said she would be."

"This is exactly what I feared," the Sorcerer rumbled.

"Check me out with your magnifying glass if you don't believe me. She didn't do anything to make me fall in love or any of that other guff."

Ekstrand did as he suggested. "You do seem to be free of anything obvious. Why do you want her to stay?"

"She can help us, we're going to need someone on the inside," Sam said. "The man who's missing is the most important person in Aquae Sulis, which is like Bath but in the Nether, right?"

Ekstrand nodded. "She told you this?"

"Yeah, she explained it all to me. And she knows what an Xbox is."

"A what-box?"

"Exactly! You said they aren't connected with my world, with Mundanus, but she is, and you know why? Because she was telling the truth when she said she isn't like them. Lady

Rose sent these two weird, *weird* blokes to get the Master of Ceremonies, so if you want to find where he is, I reckon the best chance you've got is getting our friend Cathy here to milk her people for information."

"Lady Rose is behind this?" The Sorcerer stroked his chin.

"And Rosas have come into Aquae Sulis for the season, two different families, for the first time ever," Cathy said. "It can't be a coincidence."

Ekstrand was frowning at her. Sam could feel her shaking beneath his hand. "See? Cathy can help."

"We have the right to make any enquiries we wish," Max said. "If we question the Rosas, they have to cooperate."

"Oh, come on," Sam said. "If their boss is anything like that Lord Poppy bloke they'll never tell the truth; they won't want to land themselves in the shit!"

"We can make them tell the truth," Max said. Sam believed him.

"But if they even get a hint of you coming after them, they'll cover their tracks," Cathy said.

"Yeah!" Sam agreed. "The lady's got a point. And if they know you're onto them, they might kill him, if they haven't already."

"I could spy for you," Cathy said. "I have to go to the same functions as these people; now I know their patron is involved I can look more closely into what they're doing. My father is on the Council of Aquae Sulis. I can find out more than the average person there."

"This is most unorthodox," Ekstrand muttered.

"That's why it'll work," Sam said. "They'll never see it coming. They'll never guess someone in their world is actually working for you. See?"

"He has a point, sir," Max said. "The puppet may well see and hear much more than we ever could."

"Will you please stop calling me that!" Cathy said. "Look, if I'm going to help you bust one of the Fae, I think it's only fair you help me in return."

"Nothing has changed," Ekstrand said. "You must cooperate because of your obligation to the Censor."

"Oh, God," Cathy mumbled, lowering her head. "This is a nightmare."

"Sir, a word?" Max said, hobbling to a corner, where Ekstrand joined him.

"Would you like to sit down, Miss?" Axon asked and Cathy nodded. Sam helped to guide her to the chair.

"Axon, could we have something to drink? I'll make sure she doesn't go anywhere."

Axon looked over to Ekstrand who nodded. Sam was sure that, if he wanted to, Ekstrand could keep her in the room regardless of who was watching.

Once the butler was gone, Sam crouched in front of her and took her hand. "We'll sort something out," he whispered. "Maybe if I told them why–"

"No, I'm not going to play the bloody victim card to every single bloke I come across. I didn't want to show you. It's embarrassing enough."

"Stop whispering," Ekstrand said and Sam stood, glaring at him.

The Sorcerer crossed the room, stood closer to Cathy than he had before and scrutinised her through the magnifying glass again. Cathy shifted uncomfortably, sensing his proximity.

"You will help us to find the Master of Ceremonies, be he alive or dead," he finally said, making her jump. "And you will do this to fulfil your obligation to the Censor. However, if you prove to be capable, and help us to achieve our goal – with the minimum of fuss and with absolute discretion – I will offer you a favour in return for the next time you help me."

"You're more like the Fae than I bet you want to believe." Cathy sounded exhausted.

"Insulting me is hardly going to aid your case," Ekstrand said.

"I just hope we can come to a mutually beneficial arrangement before the end of the season," Cathy said.

"Why?"

"Because after that, your help is a lot less valuable to me."

"We'll see what happens," Ekstrand said. "Now, Samuel, tell me more about these men you saw, every single detail, no matter how insignificant."

"Can't you take her blindfold off at least?" he asked.

"No."

He sighed. "Sorry, Cathy." She shrugged, but perked up at the sound of Axon returning with a clattering trolley of refreshments. Only Cathy accepted the offer of tea as Sam told them everything he remembered.

"So I think he must be dead," Sam said when he'd finished. "That bundle didn't move once." He stuffed a tiny cucumber sandwich in his mouth, duty discharged.

"They could have used a Doll Charm," Cathy said. "He wouldn't have been able to fight back if they cast it on him unawares, and he wouldn't have been able to move or speak."

"Is that what happened to those people we saw in Exilium?" Sam asked but Ekstrand clicked his fingers.

"Focus!" he snapped. "The men you describe sound like the brothers Thorn to me. I'll check once we're done here. Now, pup–" He sighed. "Catherine?"

"Yes, Mr Sorcerer?"

"You said there are two Rosa bloodlines in Aquae Sulis for the season. Have you noticed anything about them so far?"

"The Albas brought an Indian princess to impress the Censor into letting them in. The Gallicas... well, there's a rumour that they've found some deeds to a Nether property. Everyone's going on and on about it."

"A Rosa owning a property in Aquae Sulis?" Ekstrand exclaimed. "Nonsense! The Irises and Papavers have too strong a hold over the Council of Aquae Sulis and the Corporation of Bath to ever let a Rosa in. They don't want their city to be overrun like Londinium was."

"Yeah, that's what people are saying, but the Gallica is smug enough for it to be true. If it is, you can bet your life they'll hold a party there to show it off."

"But it makes no sense," Ekstrand muttered to himself. "Why are the Rosas interested in Aquae Sulis? They've always been content with Londinium."

"It's too much of a coincidence," Max said. "You need to focus your attention on the Gallicas and, if you can get into this house, have a good look around."

"I'll get something for you to contact me should you find anything," Ekstrand said, and left.

"The Gallica bloke is a complete git," Cathy said in Max's direction. "He tried to kill a mundane in London."

Max frowned at that. "Did the London Arbiters intervene?"

"No, I saved the guy – that's not widely known, OK? The Rosa didn't seem to give a toss about the Arbiters showing up. It surprised me at the time actually. I guess you guys aren't as scary in London."

Max was silent then. Sam patted Cathy on the shoulder gently, wanting to reassure her but also wanting some contact with another person who felt just as nervous as him. She seemed to be dealing with it well. He wondered if she was panicking on the inside like he was. They were talking about things that were so outlandish he just wanted to go home and watch the football or have a takeaway, or both, something utterly normal in the world as he understood it. Exilium already seemed unreal in his memory. Had he imagined that place, the fairie, the door in the ground? If not, were they going to let him walk away having seen it all?

Ekstrand returned, holding a large tube and a wooden lozenge. He handed it to Max. "When you take her back, explain how this works to her."

"Are you sure, sir?"

"It's protected, one use only. Even if she gave it to the Fae, they'd be unable to use it; I've keyed it to her with the hair I took earlier."

"Yeah, about that," Cathy began but Ekstrand didn't let her continue.

"It's time for you to leave now," he said. "Once you find out anything that can connect the Gallicas to what happened to the Master of Ceremonies, contact me directly. Don't go through the Censor, I don't trust her."

"What should I be looking for?" she asked as Axon took her sandwich plate.

"Anything that seems out of place," Max said. "Keep an ear out for anything to do with these deeds and, if you get a chance, look around that house. Just don't be obvious about it."

"OK, I'll do my best. Take care, Sam, OK?"

Axon gently took her hand and invited her to stand. "You too," Sam said, wishing he could go with her. Preferably to a pub.

Once they'd left the house, Ekstrand called Petra back downstairs to the living room and, much to Sam's surprise, she embraced him.

"I was so worried about you! What was it like?"

"Awful," he said, and she responded with another longer embrace and back rubbing, like she'd known him for years. He tensed, unused to intimate contact from any woman other than his wife. Petra pulled away without any of the embarrassment he was feeling and retrieved a notepad from one of the chairs.

Ekstrand filled her in and she made detailed notes as Sam paced in front of the fire, thinking about what Cathy had told him. Life in the Nether sounded like Victorian England, and he worried that Cathy was going to be hurt again before anyone helped her. Sam had no idea how to find her again, not that he felt he could really help. If he was completely honest with himself he didn't really want to get any more involved than he already was. He needed to get home and make sure his wife wasn't going crazy with worry. Their marriage had enough pressures upon it without all of this too.

"The Master of Ceremonies told me about every single property in Aquae Sulis and all of the houses there are accounted for, that's what I don't understand," Ekstrand was saying when Sam tuned back in. "None of them belong to the Rosas."

"Perhaps it's one he didn't know about," Petra suggested.

"Impossible."

"Perhaps he was lying to you," Sam said and was about to say his goodbyes when Ekstrand replied.

"Eminently possible, in fact, probable."

"If we can find a link between that property and the Master of Ceremonies, we have a motive for murder," Petra said, tapping her pen against her chin. "The Rosas would kill for a permanent ticket into Aquae Sulis."

"You mean they'd kill a bloke just to nick his house?" Sam asked. "Couldn't they just buy it from him instead?"

"You don't understand," Ekstrand sighed. "Nether properties can only be established by Fae or Sorcerers and the puppets can't do it. It requires ownership of a mundane property too, as the Nether version is simply a… reflection of what exists in Mundanus. It can't be conjured up out of thin air."

"The Fae-touched of Aquae Sulis control ownership of desirable properties in Bath, and ones in the Nether, very strictly," Petra added.

"Really?" Sam stuffed his hands in his pockets. "I've never heard anything about people stopping others buying houses. Surely that would come out in the press?"

"They own the press," Petra said, smiling.

"This is one of those giant conspiracy theories, isn't it?" Sam shook his head. "I don't believe any of that stuff."

"Do you think we would lie about this?" Ekstrand asked with a scowl.

Sam preferred him when he was being a teacher. The stage magician version of Mr Ekstrand was the wrong side of intense. "No, course not," he said hurriedly. "It's just a lot to take in."

"Are you sure he's worth the trouble?" Ekstrand directed the question at Petra.

"Yes, sir, but let's keep focused on the house, shall we? Perhaps there's something from the monitoring data that could give us something useful?"

"It would take months to review it," the Sorcerer sighed. "Even if I set all of the apprentices to work."

"Depends on what kind of data it is," Sam said without thinking. When they both looked at him, he shrugged. "If it's something that can be reduced to numerical values then a pretty basic script could analyse it. Most computers could handle something like that if there wasn't too much d–"

"You mean you can actually do something useful with them?" Ekstrand looked shocked.

Sam smirked, at first thinking he was being sarcastic, but then he realised Ekstrand genuinely didn't have a clue. "Have you ever seen a computer?"

Ekstrand wrinkled his nose, as if Sam had just asked him if he ate puppies for breakfast. "Goodness no, why in the worlds would I want to do that?"

"So you don't know what Mundanus is like these days then?"

"I know enough."

"You realise computers do everything there now, don't you?"

Ekstrand blinked at him, then shot a nervous glance at Petra. "Is he trying to unsettle me?"

"Let's talk about Mundanus another time, Mr Ekstrand. I believe Sam was offering to help with the data problem."

Sam patted the air. "I was just theorising. I need to go home. To my wife, and my job."

"Do you have a computer at home?" Ekstrand asked. After Sam's nod he said; "Excellent, then you can go home and write us this 'basic script', yes?"

"I don't want to be rude, but I don't work for you. I just took a leak behind the wrong tree at the wrong time, none of this is anything I want to be involved in."

"But you are involved now," Ekstrand said. "That can't be undone."

Petra stepped forward after she brushed the Sorcerer's arm. "Sam, we don't want to frighten you, but you've seen things that most people aren't supposed to know about."

"I won't tell anyone," Sam said with a nervous laugh. "No one would believe me."

"There are rules, old rules outlined in a treaty that mean we have to be very careful here. I'd like to think we could make the best of the situation by... finding a way to move forward that doesn't involve compromising your freedom."

Sam's heart raced. "I'd like that too. How about I sign a non-disclosure agreement? I signed one for work, I'm trustworthy."

"Petra, this is wasting time." The Sorcerer glared at Sam.

"If we reimbursed you for your time, and drew up an agreement, would you write a script for your computer to help us?" Petra asked, unfazed by the Sorcerer's menace.

Sam nodded, happy to agree just to make it out of the house. "What kind of data is it?"

"Lines on large rolls of paper," Ekstrand replied.

"Like data from a seismograph," Petra clarified.

"So we'd be looking for anomalies, right? I could write a script for that. If you want the results quickly I'd need someone to input the data for me because that's what will take the time. I'd tell them how to translate the readings. I could get that part set up whilst I work on the script. We could start today if you let me go home." He hoped he didn't sound too desperate. He was ready to promise a lot more if it meant they would let him go.

Ekstrand looked uncomfortable. "Petra, can you deal with this?"

"Of course, sir, but I doubt you want me to accompany Sam back to Mundanus?"

"Absolutely not, I'll send one of the apprentices with him."

"I'll take care of the details, sir," Petra reassured him, and the Sorcerer left with a flourish of his cape. Sam imagined dramatic old-fashioned film score music to accompany it.

"He's certainly eccentric," he said.

"He's a brilliant man," Petra replied. "Now, let me get that data for you and we'll make a plan."

27

Sam was not in the best mood when he finally got home. He'd been dropped off by Axon with several boxes of paper and Eagerboy, who was positively fizzing with excitement at his new assignment.

Axon assured him he'd delivered his note two days before, but there was no doubt that Leanne would be frantically worried by now. His returning home with a strange bloke on top of disappearing without warning wasn't going to help either. He'd spent the journey cooking up an explanation for the apprentice's strange manner and clothing, readying himself for the challenge, only to find the house was empty with a pile of post on the mat. Sitting on top was the note Axon had delivered.

"Lee?" he called up the stairs. Nothing.

He pointed the living room out to Eagerboy, whose name was actually Gordon, but he didn't suit it. "Go and take a seat, I'll be with you in a minute."

"Thank you," he said, eyes wide, darting from one thing to another so quickly he looked like he was about to have some sort of fit.

Sam went up the stairs, peered into the bedroom. The bed was made. He checked the wardrobes, imagining them filled with empty coat hangers, but all of her clothes were there. He breathed out, some of the tension easing. The memory of their last argument was still fresh.

He wanted to shower, eat, drink a beer and catch up on the football, but Eagerboy needed to be put to work before he started asking annoying questions. Sam padded back down the stairs into the kitchen where he could smell something mouldy.

He flicked on the light and saw the saucepan from their aborted meal still on the stove, something green and fuzzy growing a new skin over the remains of the sauce. He opened the oven and saw the large dish, still full, where it had been left.

Leanne hadn't been home either.

Jaw clenching, he went to the hallway and saw the little red light flashing on the answering machine he always forgot to check. The display told him there were ten messages.

She'd left him? He pressed the play button and sat on the bottom stair, chewing a thumbnail.

"Sam, are you there? Look, I have to go to Brussels, something's come up and we need to fly there right now. I should be back late tomorrow, OK? We'll talk when I get home."

The date stamp was late that Saturday night. That was three days ago. The noise in the background suggested she was calling from her mobile somewhere noisy, like the party she was at perhaps.

Something came up? If it was Marcus he would–

The beep announced the next message. "Sam, did you get my message? We're at Heathrow. Are you sulking? Call me."

He fast forwarded to the last message. "It's Monday evening and we're on our way to the airport, I'll be back late tonight."

No "goodbye" or "love you" and no apologies. She would

be home later and pissed off at him for not calling.

He was feeling pretty angry himself. He'd spent the weekend worrying about whether she was going crazy wondering where he was and the whole time she'd been swanning around Brussels with Marcus.

But he needed to think. There was a guy sitting in his living room who'd last seen Bath at the end of the First World War and it looked like Sam wasn't going to be able to extricate himself from it all as easily as he wanted. Petra had hinted that they might want to employ him but what did that actually mean? Would he have to go back to that asylum-like house and learn about stuff that sounded like it should be on kids' TV? As he sat at the bottom of the stairs in his average suburban house, the weekend felt more than unreal; it felt like the beginning of madness. Was that what this all was? He rubbed his scalp as the fear of going mad filled him. He'd been working hard, he was worrying about his marriage, he drank too much one night, banged his head and then maybe he'd just lost the plot. Maybe he'd spent the last few days in some random woman's house having the beginning of a nervous breakdown.

"Fuck," he whispered. He couldn't go to pieces now. Eagerboy wasn't a figment of a crazed imagination. He needed to be trained up and his wife would soon be home with questions.

He noticed his mobile on the shelf next the phone, abandoned after their argument. It had half a pip of power left and the voicemail symbol was flashing. He called her mobile and to his relief it went straight to answerphone.

"Lee, sorry I didn't call. Stuff came up at work for me too, and... well, I'm glad you'll be home soon. Love you."

He ended the call, looking at a photo of the two of them laughing hung on the wall next to him, wondering where that had been taken. Had they ever been like that? He couldn't remember the last time they laughed together. He couldn't remember the last time they did something other than the banal oiling of domestic life.

"You hungry, Gordon?" he called.

"Oh, yes, rather."

"I'll introduce you to pizza and beer," he said. "I've got a couple of things to do first, OK?"

When he and the kitchen were cleaned up, pizza delivered and beers cracked open, Sam felt more ready to tackle Leanne when she arrived. In between bites of pepperoni, he fielded endless questions from Eagerboy, ranging from how they made the wireless send pictures as well as music (that was the television) and what the dipping-sauce tubs were made out of. There was effectively a whole time-travel-esque adventure happening for the guy sitting on his sofa, but Sam's chief worry was what to tell work about being AWOL. He texted Dave to let him know he was still alive, and received a message back that he'd reported him sick to bail him out, thinking he was recovering from another bender. Sam smiled for the first time since he'd got home. At least someone was looking out for him.

Too tired to train Eagerboy in how to use a computer, he changed the channel for him and left him gawping at the latest Attenborough documentary. He was glad he only had an HD television; a 3D one could have given the guy an aneurysm.

As he was clearing the pizza boxes away, he heard Leanne's key in the lock.

"Hello?"

"Lee." He came and took two large bags from her and gave her a hug. She looked exhausted. "I'm sorry about Saturday."

"OK," she said, closing the front door. "I got your message – thanks. I was worried, you know."

"Yeah... about that..."

"I have the most amazing news though," she said, heading for the kitchen. "I've been given a promotion and we're moving to London!"

"Eh?"

"We were at the party on Saturday and Marcus got a call from the Brussels office, all hell was breaking loose, and anyway, he asked if I would go and I said yes–"

"Like you always do," Sam muttered but she didn't hear him.

"–and before I knew it we were at Heathrow and I just haven't stopped since."

Sam tried to drive away the image of Marcus shagging his wife non-stop for two days in a distant hotel room.

She poured herself a glass of orange juice and gulped it down. "Planes always make me thirsty. So anyway, he was so impressed by how I handled it all he gave me the promotion on the spot. He's starting a new department based out of the Canary Wharf HQ and he wants me to be a director! The salary is amazing. I'll have a huge office and minions!"

"So... how long have you got before you need to accept or decline?"

She put the glass down. "What do you mean? I already accepted. I start next month. They'll pay for our relocation and there are company-owned apartments that we can rent really cheaply. And not just any old crappy flats, they're really swish, he showed me some pictures. This is it, Sam! We're finally going to get the life we want!"

"*We* want?"

"Oh, crap, here we go. Can't you just be pleased?"

"You didn't think you should discuss it with me first?"

"We've always talked about moving to London."

"Just talked about it. This is completely different."

"How can I turn that kind of an offer down? We'll live in–"

"Excuse me, but–" Eagerboy was at the doorway. Leanne yelped in fright.

"Leanne, this is Gordon. From work. I was about to tell you, he might be with us for a few days... see, this project has come up and needs extra hours so Gordon will be staying with us, OK?"

"Hello," Leanne said to him uncertainly.

"Good evening," he replied. "May I commend you upon a most impressive home."

Leanne gave him the suspicious look Sam had been expecting.

"Is something wrong?" Sam asked.

"The gentleman speaking out of the televisual device has changed and started urging me to buy 'car insurance' but I have no car... I'm most confused."

"Oh, OK, I'll be there in a minute."

Eagerboy went back to the living room. Leanne looked at Sam. "Where does he come from?"

"It's a sad story actually. He grew up with his grandparents who were a bit weird, and they died and it turns out he's this genius but he doesn't know anything about the modern world."

"And your boss sent this naïve genius home with you?"

Sam shrugged. "We've got a spare room and we'll be pulling all-nighters."

She closed her eyes and held her hands up. "You know what? I'm too tired to care. I need a bath and an early night."

"What about this London business?"

"Can we talk about it tomorrow?" she said and yawned.

"Whatever." She left him in the kitchen. He grabbed his machine and went to find Eagerboy. "Wanna see something cool?" He sat next to him and opened up the laptop. "This, my friend, is a computer. Before we get to work, let me introduce you to the internet, which is mostly funny pictures of cats with captions and every flavour of porn the human mind can invent. Which would you like to see first?" He didn't mind which one Eagerboy chose; both were better than thinking about the state of his marriage.

Elizabeth pushed at the edge of Cathy's ball gown with a groan. "Mama, this is absolutely unbearable! My dress is being crushed by Catherine's monstrosity!"

"It's not my fault," Cathy said, reddening, trying to occupy as little of the carriage seat as possible.

"Elizabeth, stop fussing and be grateful that your sister finally took an interest in what she wears," their mother said.

"Typical that she chose the most inconvenient, most unfashionable shape there is!"

"The Censor wore a crinoline not three days ago," Mother said sharply. "And she made the most excellent point that, as the privileged, we should be able to pick and choose from amongst the best of the fashions. Crinolines may be less convenient, but they do give the impression of a tiny waist, and I think it's wise of Catherine to choose a style that draws one's eyes away from her face."

Cathy shook her head at her mother. She couldn't give a compliment without kicking the legs out from under it. She felt like a fool in the vast amount of burgundy satin, but it was the only way she could smuggle in the device the Sorcerer had given her to send a message. The tube was tied in a stocking and strapped to one leg, the capsule strapped to the other in its own stocking, using bandages she'd managed to trick the maid into giving her for a fake twisted ankle. The stockings gave the smooth surfaces enough grip to be held in place but she'd tied them so tight, for fear they would slide down whilst she was dancing, that she had pins and needles in her legs. She just hoped she could remember how to use them; the Arbiter's hurried instruction had been given almost a week before.

Then she started to giggle. It was the nerves, and the simple absurdity of the situation; she was crammed into a carriage wearing a ridiculous gown with her hateful family, an illegal sorcerous artefact strapped underneath her hooped petticoat less than a metre away from her father.

"Stop that," he said and she chewed the inside of her cheek to drive away the urge.

"Papa, is it true that Lady Rose made the new Nether road to the Gallicas' house?"

"Her patronage was involved," he replied gruffly. Cathy had never seen her father in a good mood; it never coincided with her presence, but he was particularly sour this evening.

"And is it true that Horatio Gallica-Rosa will become a citizen of Aquae Sulis now?"

"That's for the Council to debate, not girls to gossip about."

"But it's important! I have to know whether to worry about Imogen catching his eye."

"The Albas are much more pleasant, if you must seek the attentions of a Rosa," Mother said.

"Oh, yes, William Iris seems very taken with them," Elizabeth said, aiming an acidic smile at Cathy. "Why, I've heard that he's been seen with them every day this week."

Cathy ignored her. She couldn't care less about what William Iris had been doing and who he'd been doing it with. She wondered whether Sam had managed to talk his way out of the Sorcerer's clutches yet. He seemed like a nice guy and he probably had a lovely wife. She imagined them going to the cinema together and sharing the popcorn like she and Josh used to. She forced herself to focus on the conversation in the carriage.

"I wouldn't trust any of the Rosas," she said, thinking about what Sam had seen.

"Have you heard something?" It was the first interest Elizabeth had shown in what Cathy had to say.

Cathy tried her best to give the kind of enigmatic smile that Elizabeth would use in this situation.

"Are you feeling unwell?" her mother asked and Cathy gave up.

"I thought you liked Nathaniel Iris anyway."

"Of course I do, I just need to be strategic," Elizabeth said with all seriousness.

"Do you even know what that means?" Cathy asked, but Elizabeth was no longer paying attention.

"A new road, just to travel to your house, fancy," Elizabeth breathed, looking out of the carriage window like an excited toddler. "Papa, if he becomes a citizen and Imogen marries him, I'll never forgive you." She was ignored for a comment that would have earned Cathy a stern word. "We're there!" Elizabeth clapped, then grasped Cathy's hand. "Don't you dare do anything embarrassing tonight. Especially with that dress on."

"If I do, I'll make sure it's when you're nearby," she replied. "I'd better get out first, don't you think?"

Elizabeth gasped. "Is that why you wanted to wear it?"

Cathy was unable to think of a reply disparaging enough for her needs.

The footman helped her out, her mother wrestling with the crinoline hoops from behind. She took a few tentative steps, trying to ascertain whether the tubing and capsule were still where she'd strapped them. All seemed as well as it could be.

Tom and Lucy came soon after. There was a seemingly endless stream of carriages arriving; it was more like the first ball of the season than the average private ball. But this was far from average, and everyone wanted a glimpse inside the house that was the talk of the city.

Lucy waved at Cathy, who returned it as Tom goggled at her dress and then was prodded gently by his wife to escort her in.

Cathy walked with Elizabeth, following their parents into the grand entrance hall. It was slow going as the people ahead kept stopping to comment on the extravagant rococo décor. Cathy would have been bored senseless if she hadn't had a mission. When she thought about it that way she actually felt quite excited about the evening.

"Mr and Mrs Gallica-Rosa are here!" Elizabeth whispered. "I had no idea his parents were coming. I must get a closer look at his father."

"Why?" Cathy asked, worrying that Elizabeth was going to steer her over to the people she least wanted to meet. It wouldn't have been the first time.

"I want to see whether they age well."

"Oh, look, there's Nathaniel," Cathy pointed him out. "Is that Amelia Alba-Rosa he's talking to?"

"No!" Elizabeth hissed and abandoned her as swiftly as Cathy had predicted. It was time to disappear into the crowds.

Blending in whilst wearing a burgundy crinoline was slightly more difficult than she'd predicted. She was turning heads, without tripping or saying something inappropriate, and she hated it. She avoided eye contact as best she could, hurrying towards one of the darker corners at the foot of the staircase, trying to fathom out the layout of the house.

The majority of the guests were gravitating to a large set of doors on the right, and when she craned her neck she could see a huge ballroom lit by startling numbers of sprites trapped in elaborate crystal chandeliers. That was the room Nathaniel had been heading towards, and most likely where William would be. He was the one she wanted to avoid the most. She was sick of the stilted greetings they had to endure every time they attended the same event, the bowing and hand-kissing and all the other subtle ways of reinforcing their positions in Society.

She imagined running up a few stairs, turning around to address the crowd below and shouting, "This is all bollocks!" as loud as she could. The fantasy made her smile for a moment, but she realised she was trying to avoid the inevitable. Time to be brave.

It was impossible to scuttle in the shadows in a dress the diameter of a small kitchen table, so she decided to brazen it out. Enough people were curious about the rest of the house to collect in little groups, drifting to doorways on the ground floor to peep through and comment on the stylish furniture. She tagged on to one of them, mimicking the behaviour of the nosey guests, realising it was exactly what she was supposed to be doing.

It was hard to determine if anything was out of place when there was such a riot of decorative extravagance everywhere she looked. The group had reached a size that was becoming more shameless about its intent, one lady at the front commenting that there should be a tour of the house as well as the ball. Another questioned whether it was possible for it to be one of the most desirable houses in Aquae Sulis when its anchor property was a school. Cathy knew the anchor property of that lady's house was a hotel and couldn't see why she felt that was any different.

"Good evening, Miss Papaver."

The female voice was pleasant but unfamiliar. Cathy was dismayed to see that it had come from Amelia Alba-Rosa, who had fallen into step alongside her.

"Good evening, Miss Rosa," Cathy replied.

"What do you think of the house?"

It was the question Cathy had been dreading. What should she say? "It's… not to my taste," she said, hoping that was inoffensive enough.

"Oh, I'm so glad you feel that way," Amelia said. The jewels in her hair were the same colour as her eyes and the way she smiled made Cathy feel even less secure than usual. She was truly beautiful in a way she never would be, even more striking than Elizabeth. "I find it all rather over the top, don't you?"

Cathy nodded with an uncertain smile. Why was Amelia talking to her? "I didn't think you'd be here tonight," she said, and immediately regretted it.

"Oh?"

"Well… it being a Gallica-Rosa house."

"The Gallicas will show off to anyone they can, even those they don't like," she said. "In fact, I wouldn't be surprised if Cornelius and I were top of their list. They must have been desperate to rub it in."

"Does it bother you?"

"Not as much as they'd like. May I compliment you on your dress? So many people have commented on it."

"Probably not in the way my mother would wish."

Amelia laughed, making Cathy feel even more awkward, since she wasn't trying to be funny. "Nonsense. And I'm sure it will work."

"What do you mean?"

"Didn't you wear it to impress Will?"

That made Cathy laugh a little too loud. "No! Why–" She cut herself off. Of course that would be a perfectly reasonable assumption for anyone else in Aquae Sulis. Then she realised what she'd called him. Perhaps there was something in what Elizabeth had said. And, more than that, Amelia was making it clear to her; she'd never refer to him in such a familiar way by accident. "It was my dressmaker's idea," she lied.

"Well, I'm sure it will impress. You're very lucky to be engaged to him." Cathy's eyes widened at the intimacy of the comment and Amelia blushed in response. "I'm sorry, that was very rude of me."

"It's all right," Cathy said with a shrug, uncertain what to say and desperate to extricate herself from the conversation.

The group had moved down the hallway, the lady at the front encouraged by her peers to open one of the closed doors they'd come to. The ballroom din was now just a background rumble and the ladies at the front were tittering in excitement behind their fans.

"He's been so kind to my brother and me," Amelia said. "And I would like it very much if you and I could become friends."

Cathy stifled her first response of "why?" and forced herself to smile. "Oh, that's nice," she said, and winced at how it came out. "Look," she said, realising she didn't really care. "I'm not very good at this small-talk stuff."

Amelia's smile was sweet. "That's why we should be friends. It cuts out that bit of the conversation and gets right to the interesting things, don't you think?"

"I'm not very interesting," Cathy said as the group filed into the room with nervous laughter.

"I don't believe that for one moment," Amelia said, and Cathy had an awful feeling that something lurking beneath the surface of this conversation could rise up and bite her at any moment.

She glanced around the room, desperately looking for something to comment on, to shift the focus of the conversation. They were in a drawing room, just as sumptuously decorated as everything else they'd seen. Cathy had the feeling something was missing about the house but couldn't identify what. She scanned the walls, hoping to find a picture to say something about, but they were all landscapes and dull as dinner conversations at her father's table.

Then her gaze fell upon the mantelpiece, upon a little pebble lost amongst the gilded statuettes and candlesticks. It was painted lavender blue and she knew it had a flower painted on the top. She'd decorated it herself when she was six years old, and given it to her uncle when he had fallen ill. He'd been so touched he'd kissed her on the forehead and said she had a good heart. She'd forgotten all about it.

That was the proof she needed. This house belonged to the Master of Ceremonies, the link the Sorcerer wanted to his disappearance. She had to tell him right away.

"Are you feeling unwell?" Amelia asked, brushing her arm with a gloved hand.

"Yes," Cathy said, seeing an opportunity. "I'm feeling a little faint. I'll go and find somewhere quiet to sit for a moment."

"I'll come with you."

"No. I... I mean, I would much rather you find William and tell him that I'll come and greet him when I'm recovered. Would you do that for me?"

"Of course," Amelia replied, actually looking concerned.

They left the room together. Amelia headed for the ballroom and Cathy went in the opposite direction down the empty hallway. The nosey guests were still in the drawing room and everyone else seemed to be at the ball. It was the perfect time.

She hurried to the end of the corridor and chose the last door on the right, knocking first before entering. She had to pull the hammer cord to wake the sprite, revealing another lavishly decorated sitting room that smelt slightly musty. The room was on the other side of the house from the entrance, reducing the chances of curious visitors arriving late, seeing the light and wondering if there was a secret meeting at the other end of the house.

There was no way to lock the door. She considered jamming it shut with a chair but there were only plump Regency sofas in the room. She resolved to send the message as quickly as she could.

In a tangle of unravelled bandages, she finally freed the equipment and opened the capsule to pull out the piece of paper and pencil inside.

I have proof this house belongs to the MoC, absolutely positive. Most people in ballroom, come to rear window of room on left wing of house (as you look at it) – I'll hang a white bandage from it so you know which one.
C x

She had no idea why she'd put a kiss at the end, a habit from texting perhaps, but she couldn't rub it out. She rolled it around the pencil and dropped both back into the capsule, then, after resting it on one of the sofas, unwrapped the pipe part of the device from its stocking.

When the Arbiter had shown her how it worked, using a spare capsule, it had reminded her of the tube system she'd seen in a supermarket, used to send cash from the tills to some secret vault elsewhere in the store. They'd always made her think of the administrative system in the film *Brazil*, an observation that Josh had loved. She shut her eyes for a moment, wishing she could forget about him.

When she opened them again and looked at the runes engraved on the tube, she wasn't sure she could remember exactly what the Arbiter did. It was something about placing it on a solid surface, non-metallic, she could recall that much, and then twisting it.

She shrugged, opting for a corner of the room the large rug didn't reach. It wasn't like she could ask anyone for a refresher lesson; she'd just have to do her best. What could possibly go wrong?

28

Will stood at the edge of the ballroom, watching the dancers sweep past, wondering where Catherine was hiding. Nathaniel was lurking with him, bored, and Imogen was in a sulk because Horatio Gallica-Rosa was dancing with Elizabeth Papaver.

"Why don't you dance with Cornelius?"

"Don't be such an idiot, William, you know Horatio hates him."

Will sighed. "That's the point."

A smile burst across her face. "Oh!" she giggled and tapped him with her fan.

"Shouldn't you be dancing with that fiancée of yours?" Nathaniel asked, tapping his foot out of time with the music.

"I have no idea where she is."

"Lost her again? Careless."

Will was about to reply when he saw Amelia enter the room. Unfortunately Nathaniel saw her too.

"Ah, the lovely white rose returns," he said, straightening his dinner jacket.

"Don't get excited, Nathaniel, it's Will she wants," Imogen said.

"Ah, but dear Will is marrying the poppy." Nathaniel puffed out his chest. "A lovely thing like Amelia is definitely eldest-son material. Her parents wouldn't waste her on a middle child. Just as well you're already promised, eh, Will? Saves you the embarrassment of being rejected."

Nathaniel stepped in front of him as Amelia approached. Will tried to not let his brother's jibes affect him. It was difficult, partly because he was right and partly because when Amelia was nearby he found it hard to keep his head.

"Good evening, Miss Alba-Rosa," Nathaniel said, bowing deeply with a click of his heels. He bent to kiss her hand and she saw Will standing behind him. Her expression transformed from one of patience to delight.

"Good evening," she said to Will, but Nathaniel thought otherwise.

"Would you do me the honour of partnering me for the next dance?" he asked.

"I'm sorry, Nathaniel, I need to speak to Will for a moment. Perhaps later?"

Will smiled at his elder brother as he stepped aside, bristling. Amelia guided Will away a few paces with the lightest touch on his arm.

"You look beautiful, Amelia."

"Thank you," she said, and smiled at him. "I have a message from your fiancée. She's feeling a little unwell, but has promised to find you once she's recovered."

"What ails her?"

"She was fine one moment, we were having a delightful conversation about the house and then she went as white as our rose. She looked... shocked, but for no reason I could ascertain."

"Was it something said about the house?"

"No. I think I commented on believing her to be an interesting person. That's hardly shocking, is it? I offered to go with her but she refused and sent me to you."

"Does she need me?"

Amelia considered it. "I couldn't imagine how having you close could fail to make her feel better."

She held eye contact with him long enough for the music to fade to a whisper and the crowd around them to pale into theatre scenery. Her lips were a deep dusky pink, slightly parted, and it took every last bit of his self-control not to kiss them.

"I should go to find her," he said, stepping away reluctantly, disconcerted by the effect she had on him.

"She was in a room in the other wing of the house, quite far down the corridor," Amelia added.

"I shall find you later?"

"You can always find me, Will. It's one of your many talents."

Will used the walk from the ballroom to cool down. He'd seen Amelia every day for the last week and the gaps in between each time seemed less easy to bear as the week went on. He would even call Cornelius a friend too, which surprised him, considering he'd started out with the intention of giving only the appearance of friendship to win Amelia over.

He had to be disciplined. Amelia was never going to be anything more than a friend. She was too beautiful, and her family too wealthy and powerful in Londinium, for her ever to be a mistress, and he was fated to marry Catherine. The two ladies couldn't be more different. He felt like he was being spoilt by the finest champagne when he should be preparing to survive on bad wine.

There was no getting out of the engagement. His father had made it clear, so he just had to accept it and move on. He was still hopeful that once she was away from her abusive father Catherine might develop the confidence to make more of the little she had, but it was the optimism of a desperate man.

He passed a group of guests emerging from one of the rooms, chattering about the house, but Catherine wasn't amongst them. He peeped into the room they'd left but it was empty of people. They all seemed to be heading towards the ballroom, a few of them glancing at him with embarrassment at having been caught nosing about the place. He considered asking them if they'd seen her but decided against it. Catherine rarely caught anyone's eye.

He walked a little further. All of the doors off the hallway were closed. Then he heard a slight squeak from one at the far end, sounding like a window sash being forced, and then a thud as it was shut. He wondered if Catherine had climbed out, then dismissed the idea.

As he approached, he could hear her shoes on the wooden floor. She seemed mobile enough. When he reached the door itself, he could hear something distinctly odd, like a large jar being screwed shut.

He opened the door slowly, not wanting to interrupt the activity causing such a noise. Catherine was in the nearest corner, the perfect position to spy on from the door, wearing an uncharacteristically dramatic dress and holding a large wooden capsule. She was lining it up with the top of a tube, the opening of which was glowing with an ethereal light, the same light shining out from strange markings engraved into it. She dropped the capsule and it seemed to be sucked into the tube with a gentle "thunk", which caused her considerable relief.

"Catherine Rhoeas-Papaver, what in the worlds are you doing?" he asked, closing the door behind him without taking his eyes off her and the device.

She jumped and her hand flew to her chest as if she were trying to keep her heart within it. She darted in front of the tube, obscuring it with the voluminous skirts, her white face now regaining some of its colour. "William! I was... just about to come and find you."

"What is that you have there?"

"Nothing."

He glanced at the window, recalling the earlier sound, and saw a length of white bandage trapped between the sill and window frame, the other half seemingly dangling out of the other side.

"What's going on here?"

"None of your business."

"It is my business." His voice was getting louder as her behaviour angered him. "You're my fiancée and your conduct reflects upon me as well as your family. What did you just do with that wooden capsule? Where did it go?"

"Get lost, William, this hasn't got anything to do with you."

"You're clearly involved in something most irregular. Are you trying to sabotage the Gallicas' event?"

"No!"

"Did you hear about the rumour Horatio's been threatening to spread?"

"What rumour?" she asked, that brief flush of colour fading. She was frightened.

"That you've been living in Mundanus and that you've had an inappropriate relationship with a mundane man."

She was shaking again. "This hasn't got anything to do with that," she said. "And anyway, he's just saying that because he's angry with me."

"Why is he angry with you?" He noted, even as he asked the question, that she hadn't denied it.

"It doesn't matter!" she said, flicking a strand of hair away from her eyes. "It really doesn't have anything to do with this, OK? Just... can you just please leave me alone?"

He took a step towards her. "Let me see that pipe."

"No. It's none of–"

He pushed her aside, revealing the tube, but its glow was fading rapidly. He peered into the top; it looked like the pipe reached a long way down. Inspecting where it joined the floor, it seemed bizarre that such a thing would be placed there, in a corner of an obscure room in a patch of parquet flooring. He'd never heard of such a thing, had never seen anything like it at the Emporium, and had never come across any talk of it on the Grand Tour. Whilst he was prepared to assume he didn't know about every artefact in existence, he was certain he'd at least have heard about something like this.

"William, really, just leave it alone."

He checked the outside of the tube, ignoring her attempts to draw him away. When she tried to approach he held her back with a firm grip on her shoulder. There were no symbols he recognised, not one sigil of the Great Families. It looked utterly alien.

"Is this a sorcerous artefact?" he asked her and her throat blazed red.

"No," she said. At least she was an appalling liar; it would make married life so much easier.

"What does it do?"

"Bugger off, for God's sake, this is nothing to do with you."

"If you don't tell me what's happening here, I will go to Horatio myself and tell him you're using illegal sorcerous artefacts in his house."

"You wouldn't do that," she said confidently. "You're too scared of a scandal."

"Perhaps you would prefer me to go to your father? Perhaps this is just the occasion you've been wishing for. A disgrace such as this would free you of our engagement most conveniently."

It was a gamble: she would be tempted, and he was under strict instructions to maintain the engagement no matter what. But he suspected her fear of her father was the greater force. She sagged and he knew he'd won, but he didn't let her go. Instead, he relaxed his grip and chose to follow up the threat with a different approach. She was stubborn but he suspected that having been frightened by the threat of her father's wrath she'd be more pliable for a moment at least.

"If that is a Sorcerer's artefact, it's clear you're involved in something very serious. I don't have to be the enemy, Catherine. If this is a burden, I could help."

Her face softened, the defensiveness eroded away by his words. "If I tell you, do you promise not to tell anyone else?"

"Will I be able to keep that promise and not jeopardise my family's interests?"

She looked surprised by his question, as if the need to ask hadn't occurred to her. "Yes."

"Then I promise. Why don't we sit down? It seems to me that you've been under a great deal of pressure lately. Does it have something to do with a Sorcerer?"

She nodded, letting out a long sigh. "I don't have anyone I can talk to. And this is big stuff, William, I mean it."

He let go of her shoulder, planning to steer her towards one of the sofas, but she hurried to the tube instead. "I have to do this first," she explained, appearing to unscrew it from the floor, making the last of the glow disappear. When it detached there was no hole; the parquet was pristine. In moments, the tube started to collapse. She put it on the floor and it crumbled to dust.

She brushed her hands and allowed him to guide her to one of the sofas. She took a moment to arrange the dress as she sat down, irritated. "I hate this stupid dress, I only wore it so I could smuggle the messaging tube in."

"I beg your pardon?"

"I had it strapped to my legs," she said, and then started to laugh. "Oh, God, you look so shocked."

"Well, it is rather strange. Start at the beginning."

"The Censor came to pick me up for tea, but instead she delivered me to an Arbiter. I was blindfolded, dumped in a car boot and held prisoner in the Sorcerer's house until I agreed to help get a Fool's Charm lifted off a mundane. I had to take him into Exilium and it was absolutely awful."

Will made no effort to disguise his shock. "When did this happen?"

"A week ago. It turns out this guy witnessed Lady Rose's people carrying my uncle out of the house wrapped in one of his rugs. They charmed him to forget, but the Arbiter tracked him down."

"Why didn't they just kill him?"

She shrugged. "Something to do with his wife, I think. Their wedding ring or something. Anyway, once we knew it was the Rosas, I told the Sorcerer about this new house and he suspected it was connected. He gave me that tube thing to send him a message if I found proof that it is."

"So I assume you did?"

"Yeah. I saw something the Rosas missed. It only means something to me and my uncle. This is his house. He must have kept it a secret, that's why there was no road connecting it to the rest of Aquae Sulis until Lady Rose made one for this party."

Will caught hold of her hands. "You realise how serious this is, don't you?"

"Of course I do," she said, frowning at his contact. "I'm not stupid. I didn't want to get involved but the Censor made me, and the Sorcerer seems just as motivated to find out what happened. They want to get more evidence before they bust the Rosas. The Arbiter will be on his way. He'll be coming in through that window." She pointed to the one with the bandage hanging out.

"But the servants go past there to get to the kitchens from the ballroom," he said, standing up.

"I thought we were at the end of the house," she said, chewing a thumbnail in a most unladylike manner.

"We're at the end of the *Nether* house," he said. "The kitchen block is in Mundanus; the entrance is about ten metres that way. I only know because my mother remarked upon it earlier. She liked the fact that the servants didn't have to come through the house to serve the champagne."

She watched him point and stood up too. "Bugger. I've really ballsed this up."

He blinked. She sounded like a mundane. The more he spoke to her, the more he suspected Horatio was telling the truth. But there wasn't time to tackle that now. He needed to use this information in the best way possible. Helping the Arbiter would result in the social destruction of Horatio Gallica-Rosa, a definite bonus. He had the suspicion that Horatio had been biding his time, waiting for the best stage upon which he could perform and do the most damage with the information about Catherine. Tonight would be ideal, and Will knew it would force him to call Horatio out to protect her honour, exactly as Cornelius had warned.

But there were other factors involved. He had to act quickly to minimise the damage to the others who could be dragged down with the Gallica-Rosas.

"I'll do my best to cause a distraction," he said, formulating the plan as he strode to the door. "Give me five minutes, then go round the back, grab the nearest servant you find and pretend to be distressed. Tell them something is happening in the ballroom and to get help. That should bring the Head

Butler and the rest will want to watch. Then make sure the Arbiter gets in and isn't disturbed."

"What are you going to do?"

He sported his most wicked grin. "I'm going to get myself in the most appalling trouble. I'm counting on you to help the Arbiter destroy Horatio, Catherine, otherwise this may end up being my last ball."

29

Max approached the mundane anchor property, reviewing the information he'd received from the Sorcerer. It seemed the mundane could be useful now the Fool's Charm had been lifted; over the past week he'd managed to analyse all of the data and pinpoint the house he now stood in front of as the likeliest candidate for the secret Nether property. Its reflection was just within the city boundary, but far enough from the centre of Aquae Sulis to have gone unnoticed by the rest of the residents.

The data had revealed activity every Wednesday evening up until the night of Lavandula's disappearance. Two hours after Sam's encounter in the garden, someone had opened a Way into the secret property and spent three days there, then it had been silent until a frenzy of activity for the last two days. The movements in and out of the Nether suggested the house was being prepared for a grand event, one that was happening in the reflection of the property he was looking at.

The Sorcerer had passed on the puppet's note. Max hoped she was right as he walked the outer perimeter of the mundane grounds considering the best way to approach the house. He decided upon entering the Nether through the garden wall and then sneaking to the window she mentioned. He'd only ever snuck into a Nether property a handful of times before; the direct approach was much easier.

He found a spot sheltered by large bushes and rummaged in his pockets for the Peeper. His remit was to find the Master of Ceremonies and bring him back, preferably alive. There was no way to predict what he'd have to deal with to achieve that, but at least he was off the crutches and on to a walking stick, which was much easier to manage. His leg still ached like hell though.

His fingers closed around the Peeper and he pulled it out. The lens took up most of the circular device, consisting of two soapstone circles that fitted around the lens, each with its own formulae engraved onto them. A quick polish with the end of his coat belt cleared away the pocket lint.

He pressed the Peeper against the brick closest to his eye level and twisted the two circles in opposite directions. It clicked gently until the formulae were aligned and then the silver grey light of the Nether shone through the wall, through the lens. He leaned in close, peering through, catching sight of several servants hurrying across the back garden, chattering and looking excited. None of them had noticed the little flap of white hanging from the window at the end of the wing. So the puppet had been telling the truth, about the bandage and the window at least. He couldn't see if anyone was in the room as the curtains had been shut.

He whistled softly and the gargoyle came out from its hiding place nearby. "I'm not a bloody dog, you know," it grumbled as it squeezed through the shrubs to sit on its haunches next to him.

"Something's going on," Max said, looking back into the Nether. "Looks like it's distracting the staff. Could be an advantage. I can see the bandage. The window is about ten metres away on the other side of this wall. I'll go across first, then you follow."

"No, I'll go across first, open the window and then help you in, stupid," the gargoyle replied. "No point you faffing about with that stick when I can go faster and help you climb through."

"Agreed," Max said. "Why are you so bad-tempered?"

"*We* are bad-tempered because we have to tit about here when we need to go to the Cloister. There's something about what happened there that doesn't add up."

Max twisted the circles in the opposite direction until mundane brick showed through the lens again and the Peeper detached. "We'll go there soon. It has to be made safe." He dropped it back in the bag and retrieved the Opener.

"That's what comes of being dislocated from your soul," the gargoyle said, looking at the small doorknob and its bolt. "None of our tools have interesting names. No imagination."

"I have imagination," Max said, inserting the bolt into the mortar, the formulae inscribed upon it changing its consistency to that of butter. "I can imagine just how wrong this will go if that puppet has lied to us."

"What motivation would she have for doing that?"

"They don't need to be motivated," Max said, adjusting the brim of his hat and picking up his cane from where it rested against the wall. "They can't help it. Lying is like going to the bathroom for them, regular and necessary."

"Only someone with a dislocated soul would think that's a good analogy. Are you going to open a Way or not?"

Max twisted the doorknob and the outline of a doorway formed, looking like a line of burnt brick for a moment, then like a door frame. In seconds a door had formed in the brickwork. He opened it a crack, checked for any straggling staff and then waved the gargoyle through. He watched it bound across the grass in seconds, open the window and climb in before Max had a chance to detach the Opener. When it beckoned to him he stepped through and let the temporary brick door shut behind him, then dropped the warm doorknob back into his pocket. He hobbled across to the window as quickly as he could and accepted the gargoyle's help. He pulled up the bit of bandage and shut the window.

"Holy crap! I never knew Sorcerers could make walking gargoyles."

He twisted around, seeing the puppet he'd packed into the boot a week ago.

"That doesn't go further than this room," Max said, tidying himself after the scrabble over the windowsill.

"Does it feel like stone? Can I touch it?"

The gargoyle grinned at Max. "I reckon I've scored here."

She yelped and knocked an ornament off a table that smashed on the floor. "It can talk? Oh, my God, that's amazing!"

The gargoyle moved towards her slowly, like a panther hunting its prey. "Your dress might look like a lampshade but you got better taste in gargoyles."

"I had to wear this stupid thing to smuggle in the messaging tube."

The gargoyle stopped when its paws brushed the hem of her dress. She reached out and touched the top of its head with her fingertips as something like a purr rumbled deep in its gullet. "You can do that all day if you like," it said and she laughed, reaching behind its ear to tickle it. Stone eyebrows twitched with pleasure.

"When you've finished, we have work to do," Max said.

The gargoyle rolled its eyes. "Sorry, babe, he's a slave driver."

Max put on the knuckle-duster and the puppet's eyes flashed terror. "I did everything you asked!"

"This isn't for you," Max said. "This is to look for openings between the worlds or between residencies. The Rosas connect all their provincial properties with a London residence as standard, and my bet is that they've done that here too."

"But I thought they took the Master of Ceremonies into Mundanus."

"Only to transport him is our guess," the gargoyle said. "It would have been easier to hide. But they'll be hiding him in Londinium if he's still alive."

"You think he might be?"

It shrugged its stone shoulders. "Depends on how they want to use him. If all they wanted was this house, then no. If they wanted more, maybe. You worried about him?"

"He's my uncle."

"Don't worry, sweetheart." The gargoyle stroked her arm with a claw. "We'll find him." It noticed Max. "What?"

"You talk too much."

"I like her," the gargoyle said, tilting the top of its head back towards the puppet, hopeful for another stroke. "She has a face I can trust. Not too pretty."

"Thanks."

The gargoyle responded to the sarcasm with another of its scary grins. "That's a compliment from me, babe."

Max knew the way through to the Londinium house was likely to be in one of the rooms furthest from the ballroom, and would be disguised. It would also be the first place a visitor from Londinium would see, so it would be decorated to impress.

"Have you seen many of the rooms in this wing of the house?" he asked the puppet, who was looking, too closely for his liking, at the formulae inscribed on the gargoyle.

"A few."

"Any stand out?"

"In what way?"

"Was one more elaborately decorated than the others?"

"All of this place is like that," she said. "Something's missing but I can't put my finger on it."

"Do you think the same about this room?"

She looked around. "Yeah," she said finally.

The gargoyle did the same. "She's right. This is supposed to be a Rosa house, right?"

Max nodded. "It's the lack of roses."

The puppet snapped her fingers. "That's it! There are a few vases of them, but in my house there are poppies in all kinds of obscure places, and really subtle things too, you know, like in the cornice designs, or at the corners of framed paintings. There's nothing like that in this room."

"They've stripped out the lavender motif, in fact..." He studied the cornice in the corner nearest to him, noticing the lavender sigil embedded in the design. "What does that look like to you?"

She examined where he was pointing. "Oh, I was wrong, there is a rose. Damn."

"It's actually a lavender sigil glamoured to look like a rose, but they haven't had time to do a thorough job. They've covered the things they couldn't replace quickly enough, or would have to remodel in a major way, and they're still replacing the rest."

"Oh!" The puppet jumped in the air, making the dress bounce. "It's not just that! All of the paintings are landscapes. There aren't any portraits!"

Max nodded. "Temporary generic pictures... to glamour every single one in this house would cost a fortune, much cheaper to simply ship out the Lavandulas and replace them with harmless landscapes. Good. Now, think carefully, have you seen a room with something very obviously Rosa-themed in it?"

She shook her head. "But I haven't seen all of them."

"Go and check them, quick."

"I'll help," the gargoyle offered.

"No, if she's caught going in and out of rooms, she could talk her way out of it. You couldn't."

The gargoyle looked back at her. "Wanna see if you could smuggle me under your dress?"

"No," she said firmly and opened the door to peep down the hallway. "I'll be as quick as I can," she said and hurried out.

"You should be more careful around her." Max flexed his fingers to ease the knuckle-duster into a more comfortable position.

"She's OK, for one of them."

"Just because she scratched behind your ears doesn't mean she's trustworthy."

"She didn't run away screaming or faint, she thought I was 'amazing'. Doesn't that prove she's not like the rest of them?"

"It proves she's easily impressed, nothing more."

The door opened again and she beckoned them frantically. "I've found something!"

The puppet led them across the hallway and into the room opposite. As soon as he saw it, Max knew this would contain the Way to Londinium. Every detail of the décor featured a variety of rose motifs; the wallpaper and its rose design looked new and there were vases of dramatic floral arrangements featuring the red rose of the Gallicas. On the right hand wall there was a huge painting of Lady Rose, giving him the first place to focus: on the wall opposite.

"That will be the first thing they want people to see when they come through," the gargoyle said, pointing at the painting.

"I know," Max said, lifting up the rug and examining the wooden floorboards. He found the tell-tale scrapes in the varnish he was looking for. "This looks perfect to you, I assume?" he said to the puppet.

"What am I supposed to be looking for?"

"Glamoured again," he muttered. "This is it."

He knocked gently on the nearest bit of wood panelling with the knuckle-duster, listening closely for a tell-tale echo. It would be fainter than one caused by knocking on an anchor property's door, but it would still be there.

"Keep watch," he told the puppet. "Make sure no one comes in here." A metre to the left of the scrape marks the echo came back. "I've found it," he said and the gargoyle rubbed its paws together, making the sound of a pestle and mortar.

"Let's go break some stems," he said, grinning.

Once his father had been covertly warned that something ugly was likely to happen, and that he would have it under control, Will sought out Horatio Gallica-Rosa. He was in one of the rooms adjacent to the ballroom where refreshments were being served. As soon as he saw the Wisteria twins flanking him near the punchbowl, Will knew it was the perfect time and place, but he still had to take care to emerge from the evening socially unscathed. He hoped Horatio would leap at the chance to accuse Catherine publicly without any need for baiting.

"Glass of punch, old boy?" he said to Oliver, believing that if Horatio saw a friend with him he'd be all the more eager to cause a scene.

"Rather," Oliver said. "I say, Amelia Alba-Rosa is quite delicious, isn't she?"

"Mmm." Will was more focused on the challenge ahead.

"Any chance you could put in a good word for me?"

Will looked at his friend. "Are you hoping to catch Amelia's eye?"

"Is there a man in this room who wouldn't want to?"

"We'll talk about it another time," Will said, and fixed a smile on his face as he approached the table.

"Ah, the very man himself!" Horatio cheered, handing the ladle to Will. "Good evening."

"Good evening, Mr Gallica-Rosa," Will said, accepting the ladle as he unhooked a dainty crystal cup from the edge of the punchbowl. "May I congratulate you on your property, sir. It's a magnificent house."

"Isn't it? My parents have always said you can tell the worth of the man by the property he owns. Now I most definitely agree."

The Wisteria twins chortled on cue. Will poured the punch into the cup.

"And I don't think that's restricted to one's house," Horatio continued, in a voice loud enough for the entire room to hear, as well as those around the punchbowl. "One's cufflinks can speak a thousand words… a well-tied cravat speaks volumes… of course all of these pale in comparison to the worth one can infer from a man's wife. Or fiancée."

"I couldn't agree more," Will said. "Although I do beg to differ on one point. A well-tied cravat says more about a man's valet than about his personal worth."

Horatio smirked. "A good point. I find it fascinating that your cravat is so expertly tied when your fiancée is such a poor choice. What a shame your family has the ability to find good staff, and yet not find a good wife for you, sir."

"I beg your pardon?" Will said, setting the cup down.

"I was simply commenting on the curious situation you find yourself in. An excellent valet, a wayward, rebellious woman of dubious moral character as a fiancée. Seems rather backwards to me."

"How dare you speak of my fiancée in such a way," Will said. Even though he'd been expecting it, having heard the words he was amazed by how furious he felt. "I demand you apologise immediately."

The guests within earshot had fallen silent. Out of the corner of his eye, Will could see Thomas Papaver paling, and Nathaniel's eyes wide with shock.

"I never apologise for speaking the truth sir," Horatio said. "If you are foolish enough to stand by a girl who simply isn't fit for Society, I fear the problem lies with your poor judgement, not with my plain speaking."

"For the sake of good manners, sir," Will spoke in a calm, steady voice, projecting it as far as he could, "I ask you again to apologise for the insult you speak against my fiancée and my family, otherwise I will be forced to seek satisfaction."

"And I say again, sir, that I will not. Even my patron supports my views of Catherine Papaver as a loose woman with far too much affection for Mundanus. And its menfolk."

Surrounded by gasps and murmurs, Will straightened up. "Not only do you insult the honour of my fiancée and my family, you disgust me, sir. If you will not apologise, I am left with no choice but to defend their honour in the only language I suspect you will understand."

"A conversation with our swords, perchance?" Horatio sneered.

"Indeed, sir. Name your second and I will name mine."

Horatio cast his eye about the room, drawing out the moment, leaning casually against the table as he did so. "I name… Oliver Peonia as mine."

"I beg your pardon!" Oliver spluttered.

Horatio abandoned his theatrical ease, giving the Peonia a hard stare. "That isn't going to be a problem, is it, Oliver?"

He tugged at his cravat, gave a frantic, fearful look at Will. "I'm dreadfully sorry, old bean. It seems I must."

"And I will be seconded by my brother, Nathaniel Iris," Will said, eliciting a firm nod from his brother who came to his side.

"Afraid to pick a fight with me, Rosa?" Nathaniel said. "I find it laughable you choose to insult my younger brother. It seems you haven't the stomach to face me after all."

"If you had been betrothed to a whore, I would have been delighted to speak the truth to you and answer for it," Horatio replied and Nathaniel took a step towards him in fury.

"May I suggest we withdraw to discuss terms," said Oliver, stepping between them, "before this gets any worse?"

"An excellent suggestion," Nathaniel said through clenched teeth.

He steered Will out of the room, through the ballroom and into a corner of the lobby. "You did the right thing," he said.

"I did the only thing I could," Will replied, irritated by the way Nathaniel patronised him even when he was trying to be supportive.

"Now, I want you to agree that I should fight in your stead."

"Absolutely not."

"Will, I'm the superior swordsman and I've been told the Gallica always fights to the death. He's never lost a duel."

"Then I'm surprised at your eagerness, brother," Will lied.

"There's no doubt I would beat him. His reputation was forged in Londinium, and everyone knows there isn't a decent swordsman within a fifty mile radius of Buckingham Palace. He thinks he's a big fish; he just doesn't realise it's by virtue of growing up in a tiny pond."

Thomas Papaver signalled his approach with a clearing of the throat. "I beg your pardons," he said, bowing slightly to them both. "I wanted to thank you for your response to the

Rosa's insults. If there is anything I can do to assist, please, do not hesitate to ask."

"Thank you," Will said, seeing Thomas' wife hurrying down the corridor, presumably sent to find Catherine. He hoped that whatever the Arbiter needed to do had been completed. "Actually, I'd be very grateful if you could ask Oliver to come and speak to me as soon as he can."

"As your second I should negotiate the time and place, not you," Nathaniel said.

"I don't want to talk to him about that," Will replied and looked back at Thomas. "If it's not too much trouble? I'd like things to settle down in there before I go back."

"Of course," Thomas said, and took his leave.

"I'll push for it to be the day after tomorrow," Nathaniel said. "Then you can sleep in and I'll give you a refresher in the rapier and sabre. I hear he favours the rapier, but he may try to catch you out as everyone knows his preference. He'll suspect you're a poor enough swordsman for him to risk fighting with the weapon he uses less."

Will nodded, not really paying attention to the details. If all went to plan, Horatio wouldn't be around to see the duel, his reputation so thoroughly destroyed that the things he'd said about Catherine would be discredited by association.

"Are you listening to me?"

He blinked at Nathaniel. "I do apologise, I was thinking about what he said."

Nathaniel nodded, rested a hand on his shoulder. "It's best to put that to the back of your mind and focus on how to put him down."

Will smiled at that, heartened by Nathaniel's support. Then Oliver arrived, red-faced and sweaty. "I'm dreadfully sorry," he said, unable to look at Nathaniel and barely able to make eye contact with Will.

"Nathaniel, could you leave us for a moment?" Will gave him as reassuring a smile as he could and watched him go. "Would you believe he's actually being quite decent about this?"

"More than could be said for me," Oliver mumbled.

"Now, Oli, I suspect we don't have a great deal of time, and I need you to be frank with me. What does Horatio and his family hold over you and yours?"

Oliver winced. "Please don't ask me that, old chum."

"I wouldn't unless it was absolutely imperative I know. It's been clear from the moment we got back home that something is awry and, from the way you caved into his demand to be his second, I can only assume it's something very serious indeed."

"It is," he said, lowering his voice even though they were alone. "So much so that I can't tell you without breaking a solemn promise to my family."

"It's for the very sake of your family that I ask."

Oliver studied his face, then shook his head. "I hope I don't regret this. I wouldn't tell another soul, Will, but you and I, we've been through some scrapes, I know I can trust you. It seems my parents didn't have all of the funds necessary to finance my Grand Tour. They borrowed. Heavily. I'm sure you can guess who offered them the loan?"

"The Gallicas."

"They really are as bad as the rumours suggest. My father agreed terms and shook on it, as a gentleman. But Horatio's father demanded repayment before the agreed time, knowing full well my family couldn't afford it. Then he offered Father the opportunity to repay the debt in an alternative manner: Horatio being sponsored in for the season."

"And holding you over a barrel in the process." Will rested a hand on his friend's shoulder. "I'm dreadfully sorry, old chap. Must be miserable at home."

"It is rather," Oliver admitted. "I was so furious with them for borrowing above their means. I have no idea how the Gallicas got involved in the first place, but my parents certainly regret it now."

"They wanted to give you the best experience they could."

"They wanted me to have a chance to break into higher Society, Will, let's be honest. I'm sure they saw my friendship with you as a ticket to improving the family's profile. I just had no idea the lengths they were prepared to go to." His brow creased. "I hasten to add that's not the reason I'm your friend, Will. In fact, one of the reasons I find it so easy to be a chum of yours is that we can forget these things and simply get into scrapes and laugh about it later. I often forget how important your family is."

"Don't you fear, I know you're not a climber, Oli. Now, I need to speak to the Censor. And don't worry, old chum, I think this sorry state of affairs is going to improve sooner than you might think."

"Is this when I should express my doubt and you tell me to trust you?"

Will grinned.

"I see," Oliver nodded. "Well, then, I'll just leave you to it."

30

Cathy watched the wood panelling slide into place and any hint of there having been a door disappear. Moments later she heard someone knocking gently, nearby.

"Cathy? Are you in there?"

It was Lucy. Tom had probably sent her to avert parental wrath.

She went to the door, wondering what was happening to the Arbiter and the gargoyle, whether her uncle was still alive. Then she took a deep breath and opened it.

"I'm in here." She did her best to smile as she waved Lucy to join her.

"Are you OK?"

"Just felt a bit faint. What's happened?"

"William just challenged Horatio Gallica-Rosa to a duel."

"Whoa. I mean, goodness!" She listened to Lucy's account, trying to decide whether she was impressed by William's diversionary tactic or not. Was that really what he'd planned? "And William didn't bait him?"

"Not at all, in fact, he did all he could to defuse it. But the Rosa said some terrible things about you, Cathy. Thomas is really very upset."

"I'm sure it'll be all right," Cathy said, satisfied that Will had successfully done as he'd promised.

Lucy was aghast. "Don't you understand? Horatio accused you of sleeping with men in Mundanus, I'm certain everyone in that ballroom is talking about it right now. Your parents are going to be beside themselves."

"My father knows it's a lie," Cathy said, sobered, but still confident that if the Arbiter succeeded, whatever the Rosa had said would soon be forgotten.

"Even so, it's going to be tough in there when–"

A bang from the room above interrupted her. "A window being shut?" Cathy asked her and Lucy shrugged. Then there was another, this time from the opposite side of the corridor, an accompanying squeak of wood confirming her suspicion. The window of the room they were in opened by itself, just a few inches, then slammed shut. The clasp at the top of the lower sash flipped over and locked itself. There was the sound of others slamming shut, getting progressively quieter as the closing of windows seemed to run down the length of the house.

Speechless, the two of them rushed into the hallway to see servants and guests screaming as they ran down the stairs and out of various rooms, a few of the guests looking rather dishevelled, with several cravats being hurriedly tied.

Lucy caught hold of her hand and seemed genuinely frightened. Cathy suspected it was something to do with the Arbiter, which was just enough to keep her calmer than most of the people around them. They gravitated towards the lobby, the same direction everyone else was heading, the instinct to herd together strong. The large front doors, which had been still open for any late arrivals, slammed shut with a terrific bang. Everyone, Cathy and Lucy included, screamed and ran into the ballroom.

The music stopped as the windows running along the room all opened, shut again and locked in sequence. Last, the double doors into the ballroom itself slammed shut, eliciting

screams from those nearest to them. The head of the Gallica-
Rosas appealed for calm, but his voice was drowned out. His
son Horatio was silent and white-lipped.

Tom rushed over and put his arms around both of them
as a loud booming knock made the ballroom shake and the
chandeliers tinkle as they quivered. A second knock followed
as women whimpered and servants cowered in corners.
Tom's arm crushed Cathy to his side and he kissed the top of
Lucy's head.

"It'll be all right," he whispered.

Cathy searched the crowd and her eyes locked with
William's. He gave her a smile and raised crossed fingers. She
smiled back, noticing Amelia on his right and the Censor on
his left, looking remarkably composed.

The third knock was the loudest, echoing throughout the
house. A glass shattered on the other side of the room and
a woman fainted as a haze formed in the air at the centre of
the ballroom, like the shimmering above a road in the heat
of a Mundanus summer. Everyone pressed back to the edges
of the room, then, with a terrifying thunder-like crack, the
very air itself seemed to tear open, rapidly forming a doorway
through which stepped the Arbiter. Then Sam came through,
carrying her uncle's body, and following him a tall, thin man
dressed in a dark suit and cape. He was just how she imagined
a Sorcerer to look, even down to the top hat and white gloves.
He turned slowly, staring at the assembled crowd, but when
he looked in her direction she could see his face was obscured
by a thin scarf that looked more like mist than fabric. His
eyes were nothing more than two bright white dots shining
through it, making her shudder as his gaze fell across her and
lingered a moment. He held a black cane with inscriptions
twisting around it, its striking silver top clasped by his gloved
hand and glowing slightly.

More screams when the Way closed and the light from the chandeliers flickered as the sprites inside panicked. The Censor pushed her way through the crowd, desperate to reach her brother as Sam gently laid him on the floor.

"Is he alive?" she asked, and a hush descended as everyone listened for the answer.

"Yes," Sam said. "But he's not been treated well."

Cathy glanced at the Gallica-Rosas. Horatio looked like he was about to pass out, while his mother and father were doing their best to look as shocked as anyone else.

The Sorcerer completed his sweep of the room, leaving cowering guests in the wake of his alien stare. Then he turned to face the Gallica-Rosas and pointed the silver tip of his cane towards them.

"I, Sorcerer Guardian of the Kingdom of Wessex, condemn you, bearers of the Gallica-Rosa blood, for the kidnapping of Richard Angustifolia Lavandula, Master of Ceremonies of Aquae Sulis, within the boundary and jurisdiction of the Kingdom of Wessex, for the theft of his property, for the fraudulent declaration of ownership of his property and for seeking citizenship of Aquae Sulis under false pretences."

Every head in the room turned to watch the Gallica-Rosas react to the judgement. Horatio's eyes shut and he swayed slightly as his father clutched his weeping wife tightly.

"Know this!" the Sorcerer boomed, turning slowly, pointing the cane at the stunned crowd as he did so. "This crime originated with Lady Rose herself."

The crowd's collective gasp was almost comic. Cathy watched William shoot a look at Amelia as she closed her eyes, as pale as Horatio. Her brother pushed past the people next to her to wrap his arms around her, as if he could protect her from the repercussions of the Sorcerer's words.

The Sorcerer struck the wooden floor with his cane, sending splinters of wood into the air and starting a crack that snaked across the floor and then darted upwards, another tear in the air appearing, this time several feet away from him.

The crowd surged away from that side of the room, crushing people against walls, and Cathy almost lost her footing as the press of people forced her and Tom and Lucy back.

She could see sunshine through the rent in the air. The scent of roses filled the ballroom as the tear widened and revealed a part of Exilium familiar to her. She recognised the wooden table, though there was less food than when she and Sam had stumbled upon it. The statues were now dancing, their faces wearing masks of false frozen happiness as they twirled and spun. All were either oblivious of, or incapable of reacting to, the slow turn of the Fae lords and ladies towards the Way into the Nether house and the Sorcerer's glare. Cathy saw Lord Poppy and one she assumed was Lord Iris standing next to him, his long hair as white as Poppy's was black, both calm whilst the other lords and ladies shrieked in horror at the sight of the Sorcerer.

"Rose!" he roared, pointing the cane at her now. "Your crimes have been uncovered, your puppets identified as kidnappers and common thieves."

"What is this?" Lady Rose gasped as the other Fae lords and ladies drew back, reacting to her as if she were emitting an awful smell. The faerie Cathy had hit with the platter dived behind Lady Rose's back with a squeal. "How dare you accuse me, Sorcerer! What evidence do you have?" She looked just as she had in the painting: auburn-haired, youthful and impossibly beautiful.

"The Master of Ceremonies of Aquae Sulis, an eyewitness to his kidnapping and the very room I stand in, O foul creature of lies and manipulation. And do not think that your brothers will escape punishment; they are just as guilty and will meet with justice too." Cathy felt the Sorcerer's booming voice in her stomach, every word accompanied by the chandelier crystals tinkling above him.

Lady Rose saw the Master of Ceremonies lying on the floor, starting to regain consciousness, and lost her desire to protest innocence. "You dare to judge me, Sorcerer?"

"I am simply setting things to rights in the worlds I am bound to protect, Rose. I will leave it to your King and Queen to punish you as they see fit." Another gasp rushed around the room. "They have been informed of you and your brothers' actions, and will be with you very soon. Until then," he nodded to the Arbiter, "this Arbiter will see to it that you stay and face your monarchs."

"That's not necessary," Lady Rose's voice trembled.

At the Sorcerer's nod, the Arbiter pulled out a pair of gloves from his coat pocket and, tucking his walking stick under an arm, pulled them on. They looked bulky, like heavy-duty leather gloves used for gardening, but with small copper plates riveted to the palms and inner fingers.

"He doesn't need to come through." Lady Rose was shaking her head at the sight of him walking slowly towards the tear, the tap of his walking stick the only sound in the ballroom. She twisted round to address her peers, now in a tight semi-circle a few metres back as the dancers spun on. "Won't one of you stand with me? Won't one of you support my efforts to redress the balance in Aquae Sulis?"

They remained silent as the Arbiter stepped through, all of them flinching – except Lord Iris – as he drew closer to Lady Rose. He hooked the curved handle of the walking stick over his forearm and gripped her at the elbows. She winced as the gloves made contact and the healthy glow faded from her face. The Arbiter gave a brief nod to the Sorcerer, who turned his back on the tear to look at the Censor. The view into Exilium faded and the Way closed rapidly.

"Lady Censor, do you require any assistance in administering justice here in the Nether?"

She was still crouched next to her brother, who was now forming a few croaky words that Cathy couldn't make out. She stood and smoothed down her dress. "I most certainly do not, Mr Sorcerer. Whilst I thank you most deeply for your assistance in recovering my brother, I can deal with the Rosas myself."

"Then I will leave you to your business," he said, giving the assembled one last glare.

It had the desired effect: the vast majority looked either grave or terrified. Sam sought her out amongst the drained faces and mouthed, "You OK?" to her but she didn't dare respond in front of so many witnesses.

The Sorcerer opened a Way, less dramatically than before, simply scoring a line into the floor with his cane that rippled the air above it, revealing the dark room and single lantern that she'd caught a glimpse of before. Even though the Sorcerer terrified her, she desperately wanted to go through and talk to Sam. Just the chance of a normal conversation with a normal person was more than enough incentive to bear the awful presence of the Sorcerer. Though why he'd blindfolded her before, when he could evidently disguise his face, was a mystery. Then she realised it was all part of frightening her into submission and forcing her to take Sam into Exilium. Bloody Sorcerer, she thought. You'd better help me escape the Nether after all this.

Once Sam and the Sorcerer had left and the Way closed behind them, the room erupted into a furious din of shouting and speculation. The Gallica-Rosas were forced forwards, pushed into the centre of the room mere metres away from the Censor. The Alba-Rosas were also pulled from the crowd. Cathy watched Amelia's distress at being wrenched from William's side with an awful sickness in her stomach. Even if they weren't involved, it was clear that Lady Rose's high social status in Exilium was about to tumble and they would suffer for it.

"What will happen to the Albas?" she asked Tom.

"Well, even though they don't seem to be involved with hurting our uncle, I think this is the end of Lady Rose," Tom whispered back. "If the King and Queen are involved, nothing good is going to come of it, and likely she'll be punished harshly for embarrassing the Court so terribly. So the best outcome for the Albas is to be taken in by the Agency."

"What's the Agency?" Lucy asked.

"They supply indentured servants. They give people who've fallen from grace a means to survive, and a future for their children. I imagine the Albas will end up as servants to one of the Great Families."

"What if they don't want that?" Lucy asked.

"The only other option is slavery in Exilium," Tom replied.

"Or death," Cathy added.

"But no one has ever chosen to die instead of enter the Agency," Tom said. "That would be absurd."

"Would it?" Cathy muttered to herself. It sounded too close to slavery for her liking. She'd rather die than serve these vultures.

"Surely the Agency has problems keeping them in check?" Lucy seemed to have a grim fascination with the institution.

"They have many powerful Charms," Tom whispered back. "They're very wealthy, and rather ruthless people run it, my dear. Best you don't think of them."

"Do our staff come from this Agency?" she asked, but Tom didn't seem to hear that question.

Cathy's mother had wrestled her way through the crowd to tend to her brother and had taken over his care from the Censor, who held up her hands and called for silence. Eventually, she got what she wanted.

"Ladies and gentlemen. As this sorry affair has been exposed so publicly, it seems only right that it be dealt with publicly. Before I pronounce my judgement, the condemned will be given the opportunity to speak, and what they say may affect the severity of their punishment. I'm aware that this may be unorthodox, but there is nothing commonplace about these events, and no precedent, therefore this will be dealt with as *I* see fit. Before the condemned speak, I need to be certain that every nook of this filthy enterprise has been exposed. Are there any amongst you who have information to offer?"

People looked at each other. Their terror at being funnelled into a room and then locked in by a Sorcerer was now replaced by open *Schadenfreude*.

"Actually," a man called from the crowd, "I have a great deal of information that may well aid you, Lady Censor." The people around him stood aside, giving the rest of the room a greater view, but Cathy knew his voice too well. It was William Iris, and he was looking particularly pleased with himself.

31

Will enjoyed the attention as he strolled forward to the edge of the parted crowd. He'd found the spectacle quite enjoyable in the main, aside from the unpleasantness for Amelia and Cornelius, but he was confident he could protect them. The distress on Horatio's face was an extraordinarily pleasurable thing to witness; now it was time to get the best out of this that he could, for himself and his family.

"Lady Censor, I've suspected the Gallica-Rosas had a secret agenda in Aquae Sulis since I returned from my Grand Tour; however, without evidence I could not speak of such. My concerns were first piqued by Horatio's sponsorship into the city for the season, and, as I have explained to you privately, this was obtained via unsavoury means that would not be considered gentlemanly nor decent in any way."

"This is slander!" Horatio shouted but the Censor held up a hand in his direction.

"No more interruptions, Gallica, or I will have you removed." She turned back to Will. "You have explained that to me most eloquently, Mr Iris, and I would like all present to know that I consider the Mascula-Peonia family to be victims of the Gallicas' manipulations as much as I have been, and as such free of blame."

Oliver smiled at Will gratefully, an arm around his sister Cecilia, who looked like she was building up to a dramatic swoon. Nearby, Oliver's mother dabbed at her eyes as Mr Mascula-Peonia closed his with relief.

Will smiled back at his friend. The first objective had been achieved. "May I continue, Lady Censor?" At her nod, he straightened his waistcoat, giving everyone a chance to focus their attention back onto him. "As you've no doubt heard, Horatio Gallica-Rosa made some appalling accusations against my fiancée this evening. It may interest you to know, Lady Censor, that soon after the start of the season he threatened me with these accusations, urging me to break my engagement and making it clear that if I chose to ignore him, he would make them public." He paused as whispers rippled around the room. "When I heard his family had most conveniently awarded him ownership of a mysterious new property in Aquae Sulis, enabling him to press for citizenship, his motives became clear. It is my belief, Lady Censor, that Horatio has been planning to destroy my engagement to the innocent Catherine Papaver with the aim of causing a terrible rift between our families. Doing so would allow them to exploit the resulting instability in the Council of Aquae Sulis and thereby get voted in much more easily. In light of this, I'm sure the good people of Aquae Sulis can see why he would be so motivated to besmirch my fiancée's good name, and they will therefore treat his accusations with the contempt they deserve."

He glanced across at Catherine, expecting at least a smile or nod in acknowledgement. Instead she was looking at her father, trying to determine how he was reacting, and most probably how bad things would be once this evening was over. The sooner he extricated her from that household, Will thought, the better.

The Censor waited for the flurry of private commentary to pass. "I understand you and Horatio are to duel over this matter?" she said and he nodded. "Is there anything else?"

"I only wish to apologise for the distress caused this evening by the arrival of the Sorcerer. When someone, who I believe should remain anonymous, confirmed that this house in fact belongs to the Master of Ceremonies, I set things in motion to have him rescued by the Arbiter as swiftly as possible. I had no idea a Sorcerer would come in person and cause such a disturbance. All I can say in my defence, Lady Censor, is that I warned you as best as I could at the time, and to beg your forgiveness for being ignorant of his plans."

The Censor smiled as if enjoying the social dance. "You are of course forgiven. More than that, Mr Iris, you are held in the highest regard for acting so swiftly. In fact, I think everyone in this city should demonstrate their gratitude to Mr Iris for his bravery, quick thinking and excellent handling of the situation, for without him we might have lost the Master of Ceremonies and forever had the lowest of criminals in our midst."

She started to clap and in seconds the ballroom resounded with applause. He bowed and then straightened to see Horatio, who appeared to be on the brink of self-combustion. Apart from the Gallica-Rosas, the only other person in the room who seemed eminently unimpressed with him was his fiancée. Surely she hadn't expected her part in the affair to be brought into the open? Perhaps she thought the applause should have been for her. What an odd creature she was.

Once it had subsided he bowed to the Censor again and took a step back. He'd saved the Peonias from being taken down with the Gallicas and he hoped he'd cast enough doubt on the accusations against Catherine for it all to blow over.

He knew the Gallicas were doomed, but was less certain about how Amelia and Cornelius would fare in the wake of Lady Rose's certain punishment. Surely their family had allies in Londinium who would accept the majority of their wealth in return for keeping them safe in a Nether house in the country and out of the clutches of the Agency? They'd never enjoy the status they had now, and they'd never be invited to Society events, but it was unthinkable that such a wealthy and powerful family should collapse and be given over to the Agency wholesale. He'd heard of all kinds of deals done to avoid such a fate, but then again he'd never known one of the patrons themselves to be so horrifically disgraced. One thing was for certain: if the Albas had been involved, there would be no way to save them from the Censor's wrath and they would be collected by the Agency by the end of the evening.

"And what say you, Horatio Gallica-Rosa?" the Censor asked.

Horatio took a moment to compose himself. "I find it most interesting, Lady Censor, that William Iris always suspected me, without realising he was being played for a fool by the Albas. For they have been just as involved in this as the rest of my family, and are just as culpable."

"Horatio!" Cornelius said sharply as Amelia leant against him, clutching her brother's arm.

"What?" Horatio sneered. "You thought I'd let you stand there whilst I and my family were destroyed for playing our part in the same game as you? Just because you and your sister were lucky enough to be chosen to play the charmers and I was cast as the villain, it doesn't mean my family should be the only ones to suffer for it. And let's face it, we're all damned now. This is over. Why not lay it all out for them all to see? I'd like him to know the truth." He sneered at Will.

"Explain yourself," the Censor commanded.

Will hid the fact that Horatio's words were sending him into freefall. If this were true, Amelia and Cornelius would face the same fate as the Gallicas, regardless of whether the rest of their family could be saved somehow.

"Our families are not feuding and we planned the entirety of this season's events together in Londinium. There's no point in denying what the Lords Thorn did to the Master of Ceremonies, and how I was set to benefit, but it may interest you to know that the Albas were sent here to sabotage the engagement too, but in a more subtle and pleasant way."

"Will, it's not true!" Amelia gasped at him, but he kept his expression as impassive as he could. He didn't want anyone to see the effect she had on him.

"I was set up to be the one everyone hated, the hot-headed swordsman to be kept out of Aquae Sulis at all costs, while we played Cornelius and Amelia as the more palatable alternatives. I knew I'd never live here, and frankly I never wanted to. William Iris thought he was so clever, doing all he could to have the Albas accepted in Society, when he was playing into our hands all along." He laughed. "Not applauding him now, are you?"

Will knew Amelia was weeping, so he didn't look at her. It was time to make a decision. He believed Horatio; it made perfect sense. He'd watched the way Cornelius had been looking at him throughout the awful speech, and it was clear he was terrified and guilty. But, even knowing that he'd been played like a fiddle, Will couldn't bear the thought of them being turned over to the Agency. Not Amelia. Not a jewel like her. She wouldn't be put to work as a house servant, she'd be sent to a high-class brothel abroad, like the one he and Oliver had stumbled into by accident early in their tour. Her creamy skin and green eyes would make her profitable to the lowest forms of humanity and he simply couldn't bear the thought of it. He wouldn't be able to live with himself if he'd had the opportunity to save her and had never taken it.

"Lady Censor," he said, stepping forward, "Amelia and Cornelius confessed their remit to me earlier this evening."

"That's a lie!" Horatio roared.

"And," Will shouted above his objections, "they begged me to keep it secret so they wouldn't be punished by their family for their indiscretion until it was certain how this was to play out. I give you my word, Lady Censor, that their allegiance aligned to Aquae Sulis once they discovered how low the Gallicas had stooped in order to achieve Lady Rose's goals. Horatio is a bitter, cruel man who can't stand the thought that his bloodline gambled and lost. I see no reason for two innocent people to be dragged down with him."

The crowd's speculation was starting to drown out Horatio's curses. Will permitted himself to look at Amelia, who was gazing at him wide-eyed as she clung to Cornelius. He wondered why Horatio's parents hadn't spoken up, then realised they must be terrified of angering the Censor further. They knew they were lost. Their son was too young to accept it quietly.

"Ladies, gentlemen!" The Censor called the room back to silence. She levelled her gaze at Will, studying him. "Are you willing to vouch for these people, even though, as we speak, their patron is receiving judgement from the King and Queen of Exilium?"

Will felt his father's glare as he nodded. "Yes, Lady Censor."

Before the Censor could reply the crowd was showered in splinters of crystal as the chandeliers shattered above them. The sprites, now free, fluttered in circles for a moment as women screamed and people were swept into a crush for the doors. The light in the room became diffuse now it was no longer focused and reflected, and sprites battered the windows in desperate attempts to flee before being trapped once more.

Will brushed tiny slivers of crystal from his hair, feeling a splinter spike his thumb. As one of the sprites zipped over the Gallicas' heads, he saw Mrs Gallica's hair tumble out of its arrangement and the jewellery about her neck tarnish and crumble to dust. He cast an eye about the room, seeing plaster powdering into mist up in the corners where sprites were clustering, the previously hidden stylised sprigs of lavender revealed in the cornices once more.

When the initial panic was over, the crowd calmed once they realised that all the active Rosa Charms had failed and they were not in fact being attacked by a wrathful Sorcerer. "The Rose is dead!" someone called out. Will could hear Amelia sobbing into Cornelius's chest. He looked over to see her brother staring at him, absolutely petrified. Horatio's mother fainted with no one to catch her, as her husband was swaying himself.

"Silence!" the Censor called out. "It's clear that Lady Rose has fallen. The collectors from the Agency will be here very soon."

Catherine's father, who'd gone to his wife's side when the chandeliers failed, picked up the Master of Ceremonies and carried him out of the room at the Censor's nod. Will could see some were tempted to leave, but everyone stayed to see the horror play out. People moved away from the Gallicas; one man even stepped over Horatio's mother before her husband realised what had happened and tended to her. Horatio was clutching the sides of his head, shaking, muttering to himself.

Everyone knew what was coming. "The Gallicas are condemned for their crime and I forbid anyone within the boundary of the city, be they resident or guest, to take them into their care," the Censor commanded.

"We were only doing what we were told," Horatio croaked. "We were only obeying our Patroon. How can this be happening?"

"Mr William Iris is held in high regard and has vouched for the Albas. I will give them the benefit of the doubt," the Censor said after looking at him again. He suspected she'd been weighing up whether to let him have what he wanted since he spoke out for them. "Is there anyone in this room prepared to take them in?"

It seemed that no one even considered it. They all looked away as Amelia and Cornelius turned slowly, seeing nothing but the backs of people's heads. Will noticed Catherine bite her lip and stare at them but she was physically turned around by her brother. Will's parents, after a pointed stare at him, also turned their backs, as did the Censor herself.

Will looked into Amelia's eyes. They were reddened but still exquisite, and even though the tip of her nose was pink and her cheeks blotchy she was still breathtaking. He remembered the dull eyes of the whore in the Egyptian brothel, nothing left of whoever she had been, the Madame proudly introducing her as a maiden from one of the great European families who were disgraced by a scandal in the French Court. "Young and fresh," she kept saying as those eyes just stared past his shoulder. "Young and fresh."

"I'll take them in," he said, striding over and putting a hand on Cornelius's shoulder as Amelia snatched his other hand and kissed his palm fiercely.

"We are in your debt," Cornelius whispered, as the sound of carriages arriving set off murmurs about the arrival of the Agency's collection wagons.

"We'll address that another time," Will replied softly, and whilst everyone else was turned away and Horatio was crumpling into a howling mess he stroked Amelia's cheek, just once. "Don't worry. I won't let a soul harm you."

32

Cathy woke early and lay in bed, staring up at the ceiling and thinking about the Rosas. Like everyone else, she'd watched as the collectors had marched in and dragged the Gallicas out. Horatio tried to fight but they Dolled him before he could even draw his sword and was carried out, stiff as a lamp-post on their shoulders. She could still hear his mother's wailing and didn't think she would ever forget that sound.

The Censor sent everyone home soon after and she'd stayed silent in the carriage as her parents discussed the events. Her uncle looked as if he'd been tortured, her father had said. She wondered how he would know.

Elizabeth delighted in the fact that William had saved the Albas and speculated that his feelings for Amelia in particular must have motivated his chivalry. Cathy did her best to ignore her sister. She didn't care whether Amelia was set up in a distant country house to be his mistress. William could do what he liked. After the success he'd so readily claimed the credit for, the Sorcerer would have to make good on his word and she would find a way to earn a boon from him to cash in as an escape from the Nether. She planned to be away and protected from anything remotely Fae long before their wedding. Whilst she had no idea how she was going to do it, at least there was hope again. Not even Lord Poppy could work around sorcerous magic.

The gentle knock at the door and the key turning in the lock made her sit up in bed. The maid came in with fresh water for the washbowl, locking the door behind her. "Time to dress, I'm afraid, miss. Sorry it's so early, but the dressmaker is here to do a fitting."

"Now?"

"The mistress said I was to ready you right away. I'm sorry. I brought warm water."

"Clare, how did you come to be in the Agency?"

"I was born into it, miss," she replied as she pulled Cathy's nightgown over her head.

"Do you ever want to… leave?"

"Leave, miss? Where would I go?"

"Into Mundanus."

"You say the strangest things, miss. Why would I ever want to live there?"

"Never mind." Cathy allowed her to work uninterrupted.

She was escorted to her mother's dressing room, dressed in her undergarments and a long dressing gown, just like all the other fittings she'd had. Her mother was waiting, and the dressmaker was unwrapping the dress on the other side of the room. She slipped off the robe and waited until she was asked to raise her hands for the dress to be dropped over her.

It wasn't until it was being settled about her waist that she realised it was white.

"This isn't my wedding dress, is it?" she asked, feeling an awful bubble of nausea rise up from her gullet.

The dressmaker laughed and glanced at Cathy's mother whose stern face sobered her. "Yes, miss," she said.

Cathy resorted to deep breaths to keep the contents of her stomach, which thankfully were only a glass of water.

She watched the dressmaker pin the hem and edges of the sleeves. It was beautiful, although too full in the skirt for her liking, reminding her of a princess in one of the books she'd been given as a child. The bodice was delicately beaded and it was very flattering, but it didn't change the fact it was for her wedding.

She stayed silent, sensing a tension from her mother that made it more likely that anything she said would be wrong. The dressmaker worked fast and soon it was being unlaced and lifted off again.

"I'll be sure to have it ready on time, Ma'am," she said and bobbed a swift curtsy to her mother before hastily wrapping the dress.

Cathy put her dressing gown back on and her mother escorted her to the bedroom where a breakfast tray had been left. "Isn't it too soon to do the final fitting?" she asked.

"Sit down, Catherine," Mother said, pouring her a cup of tea. "And drink this, you're rather pale."

Cathy gulped down the tea to relieve her parched mouth. "What if I lose more weight before the wedding?"

"That won't be a problem, Catherine. The wedding is tomorrow."

"What!" Cathy dumped the cup and was on her feet in a moment.

"William Iris pressed for it to be sooner and, after what was said about you at the ball, we all felt it better to marry you quickly before the Rosa storm is old news. Then when people remember what was said about you, you'll be safely married and it will blow over."

"But... tomorrow?" Cathy's chest felt like it was being crushed. "You can't mean that!"

"I can and I do. Which you had better practise saying, Catherine, and you'll have plenty of time to prepare. You're not leaving this room until the carriage arrives tomorrow morning to collect you."

Cathy's ears started to ring, her toes and fingers became numb and her mother grasped her arms to ease her back down onto the bed. "You didn't put something in the…"

"Tea?" her mother completed the sentence for her. "Just a little something to keep you relaxed. I suggest you use your last day as a single woman and the bane of our lives wisely, and think about how you will best please your husband."

His duties discharged regarding Lady Rose, and the all-clear given by Ekstrand, Max and the gargoyle stood in the Nether, outside the cloister. The fortified exterior looked the same as it had through the scrying glass. Max looked at the gargoyle. "Are you sure you want to come inside?"

"I need to see it."

"But you know what's in there, you must do."

"I know they're all dead, I know some of the injuries, I know about the thorns. But… that's up here." It tapped its forehead with a stone claw. "It's… detached. I need to experience it."

Max shrugged. "All right. Whatever you think you need."

"It's what *we* need."

Max didn't reply, but instead set off with the walking stick on the approach to the doors.

The two bodies were still in the entrance; in the Nether their bodies wouldn't decay as they would in Mundanus. Once he was finished with the investigation they would have the task of clearing and disposing of the corpses. He decided the gargoyle shouldn't be involved in that. It would only get more upset.

"That's Jackson," said the gargoyle, pointing at the closest body. It'd stopped in the doorway, its frown so intense Max could barely see the stone eyes beneath the brow.

Max went closer to the body, taking care not to step in the pooled blood. He could see a set of red dots leading out of it from where the artefact's legs had been coated and left tracks. He lifted the clothing, saw the knife wound. "Looks like he was stabbed in the back," he said and peered over him to the other body, the knife still in the dead man's hand.

"If Lewis killed Jackson," said the gargoyle, taking a couple of steps closer to the bodies, "who killed Lewis?"

Max went to the second body, saw that his throat had been slit. "Whoever it was must have killed him after Jackson was stabbed, then went back into the cloister. Come on."

There was a pause but the gargoyle eventually came through the arch and into the cloister. It looked at the bodies and the blood. The rasping came from deep in its throat again, the same sound it made when Ekstrand first told it about the deaths.

"How could anyone do this?" it asked. "They weren't even Arbiters, they were just researchers... just staff."

"We need to find the Arbiters," Max said, making his way carefully, taking in as many details as he could as he progressed further along the passageway. "There are two unaccounted for."

Pieces of paper, pencils and smashed glass littered the floor. The staff seemed to have literally dropped what they were doing and started to kill each other. Most appeared to be victims of strangulation or creative uses of whatever had been near to hand. One body had a pencil sticking out of an eye. There were more knife wounds than visible weapons could account for, so Max kept an eye out for any members of kitchen staff with knives who'd probably rampaged through the cloister more effectively than those unarmed.

Here and there the stems of roses could be seen, but no blooms, only thorns. Most were growing out of mouths, some reaching across to others and piercing their skin, without any discernible pattern. Keeping the quad on his left, Max went to the door of the tower in the right hand corner, the one that contained his room. He didn't have any personal effects to retrieve; he'd lost any sentimentality when his soul was dislocated. He just wanted to see if it had been searched and whether the other Arbiters had been killed in their rooms or elsewhere in the cloister.

The stone steps of the tower were free of bodies. Max climbed slowly, relying heavily on the walking stick and hand rope as the gargoyle whimpered behind him. His room was the first off the stairwell and it appeared undisturbed. He climbed to the room above. It was empty. He expected the room at the top to be empty too; even if an Arbiter had been asleep the noise of everyone suddenly going mad would have been enough to wake him. The bodies were probably elsewhere.

He'd been wrong. The Arbiter, a man called Winston, was in his bed and the sheets were soaked in his blood. There were punctures in the cotton above his stomach – Max counted four stabs – and the knife was missing.

"Bloody hell," the gargoyle muttered.

"Almost literally," Max replied.

"That's not funny." The gargoyle left the room and clunked down the stairs.

"I wasn't trying to be funny." Max followed it down. "We need to keep looking for the other Arbiters. You can wait outside if you want."

"You think if I wait outside it will make this any easier?" The gargoyle rounded on him at the bottom of the steps. "I'm not being overly emotional – *we're* upset by this, you just don't feel it."

"That's the point." Max moved forwards to descend the last step, but the gargoyle wouldn't budge. He put a hand on its shoulder to try and push it out of the way and felt a surge of discomfort rise up from his stomach into his chest. He moved back and broke contact. "I don't understand what you want."

The gargoyle looked like it was about to say something but didn't manage to put it into words. It stepped aside.

Max searched room after room throughout the building, the gargoyle following silently. Everyone was dead, either strangled or stabbed. When they came across Max's former mentor slumped against a wall in a pool of his own blood the gargoyle rushed out into the centre of the quad and wailed up at the silver sky. Max watched it through the open doorway, deciding to wait for the worst to be over before moving on.

The gargoyle regained its composure and made its way back. Max met it at one of the openings onto the quad. "There's something not right about this," it said.

"What do you mean?"

"Something... I don't know. Something isn't right."

Max scanned the bodies. He knew the gargoyle meant more than just being surrounded by all the death. "I know what you mean. Let's find where they kept the soul vessels. The Chapter Master is probably there."

"He'll be dead," the gargoyle replied.

Max nodded and went to the doorway that led to the second quad. He hadn't been in there for years; everything he needed, such as the briefing room and dining room, was in the quad they'd already searched.

The other Arbiter was the first they found, lying face-down on the other side of the door. Max stepped over him and looked through each room in turn, not knowing where the soul vessels were kept. Eventually he came to a doorway leading down into a cellar space. There was a heavily fortified door that was open, a body lying across the threshold and the now familiar sticky blood around it. All but two of the oil lanterns had run dry but there was still enough light to see a desk and chair, the body slumped in it, and another member of staff lying nearby. The Chapter Master was near the door, his neck broken.

The far wall was dominated by a thick shelf the width of the room, upon which sat several large clay jars, all smashed. On the larger pieces Max could still make out sorcerous runes and noted the thick chunks of wax seal clinging to chunks of broken rims.

"These must be the soul vessels," he said, and the gargoyle went inside to look.

"A jar? I lived in a bloody jar all that time?"

"Not like you are now," Max said. "You never complained before, when I made a connection."

"No… I suppose not. It just seems… demeaning." It sniffed around the chunks of earthenware as Max went to the desk, intrigued by a length of chain left dangling from a corner. The man slumped in the chair had a pen in his lap, and the ink had soaked into his trousers.

"He must have taken notes," Max said. "The Roses must have taken the book he was writing in. Makes sense, I suppose."

"Something's not right," the gargoyle said.

"How did they get the messages I sent?" Max asked, looking at the broken jars.

"I don't know," the gargoyle replied. "Something to do with him, probably, why else would he be in here?" It pointed a claw at the one lying on the floor near where the jars were. "I don't like it down here. Let's go."

They went back up the stairs, looked through the last rooms and found more of the same. The gargoyle wandered off, muttering to itself. Max shared its sense of missing something. He thought back to when he saw the first body on the scrying glass. The sense of something being wrong began as early as then. "Let's go back to near the entrance," he said.

He found the woman with the thorn through her lower lip. She was called Carrie and she was one of the best liaison officers there. He remembered her thorough briefings before going into the field. It looked like she too had been strangled. He struggled to bend over to look at the marks on her neck more carefully.

The skin was only slightly discoloured. Now he was seeing it with his own eyes and not enlarged on a huge scrying glass he appreciated how light the bruising was. He inspected her fingernails, hands and wrists, then went back to the abrasion on her throat. The skin was damaged, like something rough had been pressed against it.

"She wasn't strangled," he said. "She would have struggled but there's no sign of it, and not enough bruising either."

"Maybe the bloody great big stalk growing out of her mouth had something to do with her death," the gargoyle said. "Maybe the marks are from her own hands as she was choking."

"Maybe..." Max muttered. He straightened up, saw the gargoyle heading back to the entrance and followed it.

It was staring at Lewis, at the cut across his throat, Jackson's body and the knife in Lewis's hand. "Something's not–"

"Lewis was left-handed," Max said and pointed at the knife held in the wrong hand. "And if he killed Jackson and then someone else slit Lewis's throat, there would be more blood, in an arc across Jackson's body. In fact, there should be more blood altogether."

He went back into the cloister, walked between the bodies. "I don't think any of these people killed each other, I think someone wants us to think they did. These wounds haven't bled as much as they should because they were made after the person had died. And there are no other injuries, no other signs of struggle on most of the people supposedly strangled. This has all been staged."

"Then how did they all die?"

"Quickly," Max said. "And all at the same time, otherwise someone would have raised the alarm. That's why Winston was in bed, because he didn't have a chance to get up."

"That doesn't sound like Fae magic to me," the gargoyle said. "And I can't see Lady Rose or the Thorns taking the time to do this."

"No," Max replied. "We need to tell Ekstrand. Even though there was Rose magic here, it wasn't a Fae who killed these people. We were meant to think that. There's no way an innocent could have found this place, and the Camden Chapter wouldn't have been able to kill everyone instantly... which means only one thing."

"It must be a Sorcerer," the gargoyle said. "And I bet it's that one in charge of London."

ACKNOWLEDGMENTS

Every book has its own story. This book was brought to you by a series of such unlikely events and good luck that it would better fit within the pages of the novel rather than this little bit at the end. The only difference is that these are true. And there were no fairies involved, thank goodness.

Firstly, there's the person this book is dedicated to. You know who you are, you know I could never have thrown everything into this book and those that come after it without your generosity, sense of adventure and just plain craziness. Thank you.

Next is Paul Cornell who told me to tell Lee Harris about the insane thing the person above enabled me to do. If you hadn't given me that advice Paul, I wouldn't be writing this now. Thank you.

Thanks, in turn, to Lee Harris who looked at me like I was crazy, discovered I actually was but still liked my book enough to give me the contract I never thought could be mine. Thank you for believing in the Split Worlds and for all your support and encouragement.

Thanks to Adam Christopher for listening to me freak out about one of the most difficult decisions I've had to make in my writing career to date and being so totally calm, truthful and sage at me over coffee. And for introducing me to DMLA and ultimately leading me to...

Jennifer Udden, my agent. Thank you for listening to me hyperventilate and try to explain a really big imaginary world when I was still very much in it. You've made me a better writer and you totally understand all my creative craziness. Thank you.

Thanks to my beta readers Conall, Tracy, Heike, Kate, Mum (hello Mum!) and my grandmother. Your feedback made the book better, I hope you like what it turned into!

Lastly, and by no means least, a great big fat thank you to my husband, Peter. You listened to the first drafts and told me the truth, you reassured me when the Fear got loud and helped me untangle plot and brain knots. But above everything else you have believed in me, even when I haven't believed in myself. Thank you, my love.

ABOUT THE AUTHOR

Emma Newman was born in a tiny coastal village in Cornwall during one of the hottest summers on record. Four years later she started to write stories and never stopped until she penned a short story that secured her a place at Oxford University to read Experimental Psychology.

In 2011 Emma embarked on an ambitious project to write and distribute one short story per week – all of them set in her Split Worlds milieu – completely free to her mailing list subscribers.

A debut short-story collection, From Dark Places, was published in 2011 and her debut post-apocalyptic novel for young adults, 20 Years Later, was published just one year later – presumably Emma didn't want to wait another nineteen... Emma is also a professional audiobook narrator.

She now lives in Somerset with her husband, son and far too many books.

enewman.co.uk
twitter.com/EmApocalyptic

Read over fifty short stories by Emma based in the Split Worlds at

SplitWorlds.com

Your new favourite books.

Twitter @angryrobotbooks

BUY STUFF, LOOK COOL, BE HAPPY

Never miss an Angry Robot or Strange Chemistry title again. Simply go to our website, and sign up for an **Ebook Subscription**. Every month we'll beam our latest books directly into your cerebral cortex* for you to enjoy. Hell, yeah!

READER'S VOICE: *Gee, that sure is swell. I wish other publishers were that cool.*

SHADOWY ANGRY ROBOT SPOKESTHING: *So do we, my friend, so do we.*

Go here: robottradingcompany.com

* or your Inbox, if that is more convenient for your puny human needs.